He Looked for a City

Books by A. S. M. Hutchinson

HAPPY WARRIOR

CLEAN HEART

THIS FREEDOM

IF WINTER COMES

ONCE ABOARD THE LUGGER

EIGHTH WONDER AND OTHER STORIES

ONE INCREASING PURPOSE

UNCERTAIN TRUMPET

BOOK OF SIMON

BIG BUSINESS

SOFT SPOT

AS ONCE YOU WERE

HE LOOKED FOR A CITY

He Looked for a City

A. S. M. HUTCHINSON

For he looked for a city which hath foundations,
whose builder and maker is God

DUELL, SLOAN AND PEARCE

NEW YORK

422719- 0

Author's Note

Lest the novelist should be supposed to subscribe to the views of all his characters I would have disassociated myself entirely from those of John Brecque, elder son of this story's central figure. Not the first son in fiction, much less in real life, to place his father in invidious position, he does so through his actuation by the principles he holds. To me personally these are misguided to the point of outrage of that very appeal to reason on which the John Brecques base them.

A. S. M. H.

Contents

Morning

One

It was just like the vicar, one couldn't help feeling, to have chosen to die five days before Christmas. The funeral could not be held over till after the holiday. It had to be arranged for, of all days in the year, Christmas Eve. It really was, one couldn't help feeling, just like him.

No one in the congregation attending the service wanted to entertain so unkind a feeling. The vicar had had his shortcomings, goodness knows. But, after all, one's vicar is one's vicar, and death is death; and on any other day of the year one would have attended his obsequies in entirely suitable frame of mind. As it was, one had to rush off to the service with one's mind full of the hundred things to be done on the hectic day that the day before Christmas always is, the last-moment presents yet to be bought, the larder omissions yet to be filled, the guest-room arrangements yet to be finished. You felt ashamed of yourself at such thoughts on so solemn and melancholy an occasion. Worse than that, you found yourself putting the blame for your shame where the blame nevertheless quite rightly belonged, in the coffin up there on the trestles between the choir stalls. You realized how hateful of you it was to do that; and there you are—wasn't that the vicar all over, making you, by his fault, not by yours, feel uncomfortable?

Look at the gay decorations all about, the holly, the Christmas-tree; everything set for brightness and carols and the happiest service of the year. You could not but have the feeling that it was all out of place and unkind and should have been stripped away; but whose fault was it, yours or his?

3

Obviously his. He had died, and ordinarily one would have forgotten and forgiven all his annoying little failings; but he had chosen to die when his church was wreathed and garlanded in brightness and the thoughts of his parishioners gay with generous festivity. Typical, you couldn't help feeling, of one who time and again had seemed deliberately to do the upsetting thing.

Yes, granting, mind you, his many good points, his unquestionable piety and all that (though piety and all that was, after all, as much a natural part of his calling as bedside manner that of a doctor's), granting all that, it really was extraordinary how to the very last he managed to annoy one. It really was, one could not help saying it, a good thing for St. Luke's that at last there would be a change. Thirty years of one vicar was definitely too long.

2

In all those thirty years, right up to this week in which they had ended, himself he ever could recall that glorious swelling of his heart with which on the afternoon of arrival, eagerly stepping from the cab, he had put his hand on the vicarage gate and turned to Laura and the children and Minna excitedly crowding out to follow him. Even as he lay in his brief last illness his eyes, dim to his surroundings, clear to this distant past, could see the beloved faces laughing and glowing as then, while opening the gate, he had seen them. He had settled with the cabby, cordially beaming on the jolly scene, and up the path they had streamed, each carrying a parcel or bundle, Mrs. Tufnell, the verger's wife, at the door to greet them. "Welcome, vicar. Welcome, madam. Oh, what dear children! Welcome, miss. I'm bringing up the tea this minute. You'll be wanting it, I'm sure."

Into the hall they had trooped, radiant, agog. On the table had been letters already arrived for him:

THE REV. GORDON BRECQUE,
ST. LUKE'S VICARAGE,
UPTON SPRINGS.

He could not resist immediately opening one. Sure enough, it greeted him by the title which, addressed to him in these surroundings, meant so much more than it had meant at St. Mary's, Knipstone, that hard-bitten, tram-riddled, industrial scene of his former incumbency.

"Dear Vicar."

"Look, Laura, 'Dear Vicar.' " Laura, her eyes shining, had squeezed his arm, then had kissed him. "Look, Minna: 'Dear Vicar.' " Nominally the children's nurse, virtually his and Laura's adopted daughter, Minna when excited was apt to blemish her English with the accents of her native German. "Oh, cholly splendit," she had cried and they had laughed at her enthusiastic loyalty.

Yes, Minna, in the plane of her devotion to them, knew the significance of "Vicar" in this vicarage, as Laura and himself knew it in the plane of fond association. As a small boy he had spent a year at Upton Springs. In after effects of scarlet fever he had been severely ill. Upton's tonic air had been prescribed for him. His parents in India, he had put in his fourteenth year here, living with an uncle who, a retired schoolmaster, had carried on his lessons. In that year he not only had attended St. Luke's but had been confirmed there. Here, therefore, linking up that point in his life with his life's career, he had first known the laying of hands on his head which subsequently was to ordain him deacon, then priest.

Here in this parish, some years later, he had first met Laura. A young curate then in his first title in another quarter of the diocese, he had been brought over by his vicar, an

Old Boy of Upton College, to attend the consecration of the college's new chapel. Laura's father, Colonel Harding, was then a churchwarden of St. Luke's. St. Luke's had been attended by the college during the rebuilding of the chapel, destroyed by fire. Its officers had an interest in the consecration ceremony. Colonel Harding had invited Gordon Brecque's vicar, and Gordon Brecque, with others to tea.

Four years later the young curate had re-met the Hardings during a holiday in Devonshire. "Imagine the years we have missed," Laura not long afterwards was saying to him. "Imagine the years before us," he was replying. And after one of those years had seen the period of their betrothal it was here to Upton Springs that he had come for his bride, here at St. Luke's that they had been married.

Laura's parents had since died. But here had been her home; here his first receiving of a laying on of hands; here their marriage. And now they were come back to Upton Springs. Now at St. Luke's his letters greeted him "Dear Vicar."

3

Not stopping to read the letter the implication of whose beginning could not, for these reasons, be foregone, he had laid it down and had marshaled his little flock into the study. This he had arranged with Laura should be their immediate action on first crossing the threshold of this their wonderful new home. It was gratitude to God which had caused that glorious swelling of his heart with which he had opened the vicarage gate. Now he knelt, all knelt, and heartfully, one arm lovingly about the shoulders of the eight-years-old boy who was his eldest, he expressed it. "And grant us," he concluded, "the blessing of Thy presence in these delightful surroundings to which it has pleased Thee thus to bring us. Bless with Thy continuous presence our dear elder

two, John and Mary, their little brother Philip, their baby
sister Ruth, their fondly loved mother, our dear Minna, and
me their head, Thy servant. Bless them and bless me with
realization of Thy active presence in all our thoughts, in all
our duties, in all our joys and in all difficulties which Thou
mayst call upon us to face. Amen."

Going then to each in turn, with the single word "Blessing" he had kissed each happy face upturned to his. A kiss
on Minna's brow had been the last. From her he had turned
to say "And Ruth?" and to look about him for the baby's
turn; and at once, discordantly breaking the happy solemnity of the occasion, had developed the absurd situation permanently memorable thenceforward in the family annals.

Where was the baby?

Minna, aghast, stared upon Laura, Laura upon Minna.
Each upon the other stared John and Mary. Suspecting some
sort of a game in the dumb and frozen attitudes into which
all were struck, four-year-old Philip stared raptly upon all.

"You were carrying her," cried Laura.

"Yah, yes, I haf her," blurted Minna, "on my arms!"

She held out her arms, gazing upon them as though in
one flash baby Ruth were there and were spirited away.

"You had her all the journey," Laura affirmed. "As I
stepped out of the cab you were behind me with her in your
arms."

"Minna," cried the vicar, "you've never left her in the
cab?"

He had dashed for the door, the pack following him. Wild
glances about the hall showed it bare of the missing one.
He had dashed from the house and down the path, all tum-
bling in his wake. The cab of course was gone these many
minutes.

"He couldn't have taken her," the vicar declared. "He'd
be bound to have seen her on the seat."

"Where is she then?" from Laura.

"Father," helpfully pronounced Mary, "I saw a very rough-looking man watching us from the other side as we got out."

"So did I," eagerly agreed John. "Selling something from a basket. A gypsy, I bet he was."

"She is stolen," wailed Minna. *"Mein Gott,* she is stolen."

"Absurd," said the vicar, "absurd." Passing through the gate he looked nevertheless up and down the road. All, crowding behind him, looked up and down the road. With or without basket no man was to be seen. No soul was to be seen. Loud with speculations and agitations the party returned to the house. Reaching it first, "She's stolen, she's stolen," cried John to Mrs. Tufnell.

The verger's wife, who was looking for them to announce tea, changed her summons to exclamation. "Stolen? Good gracious, who, sir?"

The vicar, that sinister basket disturbing his judgment, strove to be easy voiced. "Why, Mrs. Tufnell, we don't seem able to find the baby. We—"

"I haf her," interrupted Minna, "in my arms. I hold her in my two arms, so; wrapped in a shawl of black and red."

"In a tartan shawl, Mrs. Tufnell," Laura elaborated. "Did you notice when we came in—?"

"Tartan shawl!" cried Mrs. Tufnell on a faint scream. "Why, miss," she addressed Minna, "while you looked at that letter the vicar opened I took from you what I thought was just a bundle of wraps, tartan I well remember, and I put it, bless my soul now, in the confusion and all, where did I put it?"

She gazed wildly about. All gazed wildly about.

"Back of the stairs here," cried Mrs. Tufnell, suddenly remembering.

She headed a tumultuous rush to the darksome recess beneath the stairway. Here, awaiting disposal, had been placed the family advance luggage. Hence with delighted cries was snatched the tartan bundle and hugged to Minna's arms. The vicar turned back a fold of the shawl and beamed upon the cherubic face thereby disclosed. All crowded about the recovered infant. All beamed. Adorably, baby Ruth, wide awake, accepting incarceration in shawls beneath a stairway as part of life's ecstasy, beamed response.

In the high thrills of moving into a new residence there are no writings on the walls to forewarn what their new ownership shall see. They are traced, as diaries are written, after the events. In this hall in a day to come the vicar was to have a poignant flash back of mind to this raising of a covering from the face of his youngest child. It was the first writing. Destiny of thirty years here to be lived was to be inscribed beneath it. Prescient of its course no more than of its ending in the impatient feelings with which on a distant Christmas Eve his parishioners would take leave of him, jovially he sent off his family to their tea. He would join them presently. Smiling, his fingers, because of his thoughts, instinctively at the cross on his breast, he returned to his study.

4

His happiness in this hour was from his Lord and therefore he brought it to his Lord. That he had done so a few minutes before in the company of his household had given him one order of participation with the Spirit in which he lived. He sought now that order which lies in the human soul's aloneness with its Maker. Though kneeling, he did not pray in the accepted sense of prayer. He made no supplication nor, in set form, offered thanks. He thought things over.

Thinking things over is the commonest occupation of the

mind. On his feet, in his study chair, awaiting sleep in bed, Gordon Brecque pursued the practice as do we all. But he let pass no day on which on his knees he did not think things over in the presence of God.

The year was in the eighteen-nineties and in that day and in all his priesthood before it this new vicar of St. Luke's was something before his time. The worshipers who sat before him in his pews visualized the Deity in their own image; supernally and awe-fully different but nevertheless recognizably of their mold. They came to divine service in their tall silk hats, in their bustles or in their flowing skirts. This was not the attire for gymnastic exercise. The minds of its wearers, similarly, were not disposed to exercise in the supernatural. They thought of God as a person.

So to think, the new vicar was to teach his confirmation candidates, is apt to make prayer an appeal to human feelings, an asking of an all-powerful giver. It should be, he was to tell them, a communion with divine sympathies, a thinking in the mind of an all-creating beneficence. "Of a God, then," he was to say, "Whom we may identify by the word which conveys our highest expression of living force, the word 'personality,' the quality which we have in mind when we speak of a man's personality stamping his work.

"So I suggest to you," he was to continue, "to think of God not as a person of supreme intelligence but as a Supreme Intelligence acting without visible form as, for instance, a great wind acts. When you pray try to imagine yourself in the presence of that Supreme Intelligence, that Supreme Personality, and then, don't ask for things, just think over things—over your troubles, your joys; your work, your play; your friends, your enemies; your successes, your failures; your encouragements, your temptations. You will find, believe me, increasingly as you practice it, that your thoughts will be drawn away from your mind into God's mind. There in God's mind they will take to themselves other thoughts which will shape them for you as they should be shaped. There in God's mind all your difficulties will be resolved, all your happinesses intensified. You will be guided by God; and the life that is lived in God's guidance is a life, whatsoever its station and whatsoever its apparent drawbacks and handicaps, with which no other situation can begin to compare."

It was simple teaching. To see arising out of it, nevertheless, the origin of a small current of opinion against the new vicar requires momentarily to glance ahead as little as two weeks from this day of his arrival in the vicarage with his family.

5

The date of the annual confirmation service in the parishes of Upton Springs by the bishop of the diocese necessitated the immediate starting of classes for candidates of St. Luke's. The new vicar took his opening class within the first fortnight of his ministry. He spoke to the twenty or so boys and girls on not thinking of God as a person. Three days later there bounced up the vicarage path the mother of one of the boys, Mrs. Bagge.

The vicar saw her from his study window. She was a full-sized woman, impressively busted. Her own pony-chaise, which when she was in it looked too small for her and too big for the pony, set her down at the gate, and she discharged herself from it and propelled herself up the path with the suggestion of going straight through the front door without either knocking at it or opening it. The vicar in person saved her this crash. She was not one of those of his parishioners on whom he had already paid his duty call but he thought he had seen her face from his pulpit. He was readiness itself to meet all whom he should know. Here clearly by her mien came one charged with import. He was happy to have time to step quickly from his study to his front door and to greet her smilingly, "Good morning."

"I am Mrs. Bagge," she pronounced. From the top of her bonnet arose what appeared to be four or five boot-buttons on stalks. They shook agitatedly as she spoke. "With my family I have been a worshiper in St. Luke's for eleven years."

"How glad I am to know you. Do please come in."

A less charitable man, not to say a quicker-minded, would have sensed that a storm was here. Gordon Brecque invariably saw the feelings of others through the spectacles of his own feelings which were invariably kind. He was, too, undoubtedly a little slow in taking any meaning for which he was not prepared. He could appreciate a joke when he understood it, but usually he required a few moments, sometimes indeed a piecemeal explanation, before understanding came. That hostility was in the storming up his path, in the quivering of the boot-buttons and in the uncompromising announcement of her name and church status by his visitor did not occur to him until after her reception of the cordial hand which, with his invitation to enter, he extended to her.

Her black kid glove gave it a bite; no shake, a sharp nip only; and the vicar, slightly perturbed, showed the way into his study.

"Do sit down."

"I prefer to stand. Mr. Brecque, a child of mine has just said to me a most terrible thing. He has uttered a blasphemy."

The vicar never had required more the nimbleness of mind and the quick sense of humor which unfortunately he did not possess. Astonished, "A blasphemy?" he echoed.

"A blasphemy. And he attributes it, Mr. Brecque, to you."

"To me?" Dumbfounded the vicar went back a step. "Incredible. Impossible. Do I know your boy?"

"Certainly you know him." The boot-buttons, profoundly agitated, quivered with little clicks. "My boy Alfred, Alfred Bagge. He attended your confirmation class on Tuesday."

The vicar's mental eye ranged the young faces of that occasion. It had happened that one had stood out in a certain dissimilarity from the generality of the others. It had been a swart, heavy face, lumped on a neck which, conspicuously too short, caused its owner to have a slightly hunchbacked appearance. The name "Alfred Bagge" came at once with the face. Its resemblance to the large swart face beneath the quivering boot-buttons also came to mind. The vicar felt somehow reassured.

"Alfred Bagge? Of course, of course; how stupid of me not to connect you with him when I heard your name. As to what you say, I need not tell you, Mrs. Bagge— Do please sit down."

"I prefer to stand. Allow *me* to tell *you,* if you please. At the end of breakfast this morning I was mentioning to my husband something said to me by my cook about her brother-in-law. For very good reasons which I need not go into my husband said, 'A Mrs. Harris, if you ask me. I believe there's no such person.' I think that is a quotation of some kind from some book or other. My husband said it as if it was. He said very clearly and with a kind of accent, 'There's no such person'; and to my unutterable amazement and horror my boy Alfred said in a solemn voice, 'That's what the new vicar says about God.' I was struck dumb. We were all struck dumb."

Mrs. Bagge illustrated the dumbness into which she had been struck by pressing her lips into a tight line. The boot-buttons illustrated it by reducing their agitation to an almost imperceptible quiver. The vicar by the one and by the other found himself transfixed into a similar muteness.

" 'What?' I cried," now cried Mrs. Bagge, crying it so

explosively out of her pressed lips as to make the boot-buttons leap and the vicar start. " 'What is that you say?' 'The vicar said at the confirmation class,' replied my un-happy boy, 'what father said just now about Mrs. Harris. He said there was no such person as God.' "

Mrs. Bagge drew in a long breath, swelling upwards upon it to perceptibly more than her normal height. At the burst-ing point of her capacity she as it were flung the breath from her and at the vicar's head. "Now, Mr. Brecque!" she flung.

6

"My darling," declared Laura when, Mrs. Bagge having departed, the vicar reached this point in his recital of the affair, "my darling, you should have laughed at the ridicu-lous woman."

Five years younger than her husband, Laura at thirty-six was in appearance and in characteristics as much in advance in the 'nineties of her situation as a vicar's wife as was the vicar of the general religious ideas of his congregation. She was quick both of mind and of movement. She was merry of heart and of eye. In any sort of emergency she was at its exit, and laughing, while Gordon, grave and troubled, was still perplexedly in its jaws. She was of good height and was lissom; dark in coloring, sparklingly black of eye, and show-ing conspicuously good teeth.

Her face was laughing now; the vicar's very far from laughter.

"My dearest, how could I possibly have laughed? It was not only that I had to explain my meaning to Mrs. Bagge. There was the terrible thought that, if her son Alfred had so entirely misunderstood my teaching, all the class may have similarly misunderstood it."

"Not a likelihood of it," declared Laura. "This Alfred

didn't either, I don't suppose for one moment. He just took up in the comicalest way what his father had said about Mrs. Harris, and if his mother had had the humor of an owl she'd have been delighted. Really you should have laughed at her."

But the vicar stood staring before him, fingers to lips. "What about the class?"

"Laugh at them. If you find, which I'm quite positive you won't, that any of them have got this ridiculous Mrs. Bagge's idea of what you told them, laugh at them, 'Why, you funny little idiots you, you've got it all wrong.'"

"My dear, you can't speak like that to a confirmation class."

"*I* could!"

But then Laura, stepping to him, took his hand from his lips and, kissing his fingers, held them. "My darling, you made Mrs. Bagge understand what you had meant, didn't you?"

"She didn't like it."

"Because she saw what a fool she'd made of herself. And you'll explain it again to these children, if by any chance they have mistaken you. You're worrying quite wrongly, dear. You're forgetting, don't you see, that by what you have told them you are giving them the constant presence of God in the same way that you and I have it? You are forgetting that, aren't you?"

He brightened delightfully. "I was; indeed I was."

He threw up his head and braced his poise. "What should I do without you, Laura? How stupid I have been to let this upset me; yes, how wrong. Dear me, how I shall dwell on this when I think things over in my prayers tonight."

7

In that "thinking things over" in God to which he betook himself while the others began their tea on the afternoon of arrival, the culmination of the blessings of his priesthood in this preferment to St. Luke's was the subject of his meditation. Reviewing in ten minutes the vital incidents of as many years, he saw himself first deacon then a priest of St. Jude's, Brodham Common. That had been a London suburban parish. Drawing its worshipers from its well-to-do residential quarter, it drew them but insignificantly from the wide shabby-genteel area, straggling out into an open country of "desirable building sites," of which also it was composed. St. Jude's was too far for the dwellers in this district. To take the Church to "The Fields," as the quarter was known, since The Fields would not come to his church, the Rev. Peter Severn had carried out the installation there of a corrugated iron Mission Hall. He had found then that if it ever was to do what he hoped it would do it must have more service than himself and his curate could give it. It was as the instrument of this service that a newly ordained deacon came to him in the person of Gordon Brecque.

It was spade work, heavy soil. Young Brecque found himself among needy clerks and their wives, shop assistants, struggling landladies. Their environment was drab and makeshift; their minds were drab and listless. An age to come was to present their like with the radio, with cinemas, with dance-halls, with lively newspapers, with cheap and all-covering transport. The day in which they lived had no such amenities.

There came to them a tin meeting-house right there in their midst, a young parson in operation of it living right there in their streets with them. Curiosity was aroused; in-

terest was awakened. Penny-readings had been bright spots
in the village life from which many of them had originally
come. Here at the Mission Hall were penny-readings but a
few minutes away. Concerts had the sound of luxuries of
another world. Here in their own world was a young gentleman in a parson's uniform organizing concerts provided
by unsuspected singers, reciters and instrumentalists from
their own streets. At first, sparsely attended church services
in the Mission Hall were no better than mere adjuncts to
the variety of social uses to which the Hall was put. Gradually the entertainments, the sewing afternoons, the children's
romps, the men's evenings became adjuncts to crowded
Sunday services.

Watching these developments on his knees, the new vicar
of St. Luke's saw the narrow path to the Mission Hall
trodden into a wide path, then asphalted (by his own and
his parishioners' hands) into a permanent footway. He saw
the Hall enlarged that its worshipers might be accommodated, and again enlarged; the cost enthusiastically raised
by his congregations. He saw the proud day when there was
erected a notice-board, shaped, painted and lettered by his
own people, announcing this to be St. John-in-the-Fields; a
full list of services ranged beneath the name. He saw the
inauguration of the Building Fund which, attracting to
itself diocesan and other help, had, after his time, erected
the church of brick and stone which now stood in the tin
hall's place.

He saw himself living during the whole period of these
activities in furnished lodgings in a cheapest street in his
district; at first in a bed-sitting-room, then in two tiny apartments; at first on a stipend of £120 a year, then on £140,
towards the end of the Brodham days on £160. This was the
scale of stipend devised with anxious thought by Mr. Severn
when the need of a second curate for his parish had to be

met. A vicar deciding on such a step is in the opposite case
to an employer of labor. The business house pays additional
assistance out of and because of increased revenues. A House
of God, because of increased demands, must fee assistance
out of an unchanged revenue, augmenting it if it can as best
it can.

But when the thoughts of the man on his knees reached
the altitude of his possession of £160 a year he manifested
his joy of what that income had brought into his life by an
involuntary closer clasping together of his hands. For it had
brought Laura into his life. They had married on this income in the year 1890, as on the some £220 which is now
its equivalent priests will be found married today. It is not
a spacious income for two persons of education and refinement, much less for parenthood by such. Nations are said to
have the governments they deserve. Content to permit such
livelihoods for their clergy, members of the Established
Church are fortunate that the same law does not operate in
regard to their priests.

8

This priest, recalling his days of that livelihood shared
with Laura, saw now the happy year together in those two
tiny rooms in that drab street. He was then in his thirty-
first year, Laura in her twenty-sixth. He saw in this incident and in that his realization of a helpmate come into his
life; in that and in this a happiness of life doubled because
now shared. He saw the particular joys that money can give
when, means humble but sufficing, each separate sixpence
spent is definitely a spending, an event. In the swiftness of
his thought's eye he saw himself with Laura at the window
of a Brodham milliner's, and simultaneously, leagues away
and months later, beside her in the parish church of St.
Mary's, Knipstone, his first incumbency. At the milliner's

with delicious recklessness they were adding fivepence three-
farthings of a sixpence to the eleven sixpences budgeted for
a new bonnet at the sales ("All in this window 5/11¾").
At St. Mary's was that same exciting bonnet newly be-
ribboned for the occasion of the christening of John, their
firstborn.

He saw the eight years lived at Knipstone as vicar of St.
Mary's, benefice of £320 a year, starkly industrial parish of
the Midlands. "A parish without a blade of grass" as that
one of his two churchwardens termed vicar's warden at
their first meeting sourly had designated it.

His vicar's warden (who had come from the Cumberland
dales and could not forget them) was a small grocer. His
people's warden was a factory foreman. The hours of his
parishioners were ruled by the sirens of the mills or fac-
tories in which they worked. All that may be inferred from
the veritable fact that not a blade of grass grew within its
boundaries could safely be accounted to the parish of St.
Mary's, Knipstone.

He, nevertheless, in swift thought scanning the years
there, saw verdant plots. The vicarage, tucked away behind
the church in a graveled surround, was a pleasant little
house. He saw the first delights of exchange of the two tiny
rooms at Brodham for a home of his and Laura's own. He
saw the first thrilled realizations of increase of stipend from
£160 to £320. He saw the early pride of preferment from
third of three to the dignity of vicar with curate of his own.
The first memories of amenities such as these stood as background to the blessings under which he saw himself led
to these amenities, incomparably superior, which in this
delightfully situated, spaciously gardened vicarage of St.
Luke's, Upton Springs, now were his. He saw the coming
of those richest blessings his children. In this fond memory
and in that he watched them in the loving care of Minna,

their second mother, Laura's prop and stay. He saw Laura's every domestic problem solved by that devoted German girl, never more happy than when caused by exigencies to be cook, housemaid, nurse in one, their grown-up daughter. He saw Minna's coming to them.

9

With Laura he had been to Brodham to attend the laying of the foundation stone of the church in The Fields into which his Mission Hall now actually was to grow. Mr. Severn would take no refusal of insistence that the man who was "responsible for the whole thing" must attend, his wife with him.

The ceremony was in the afternoon. Returning by night train, it was at about seven o'clock that they came into Victoria station from Brodham, bound thence to St. Pancras. Victoria, then two separated stations serving separate systems, was not the spacious terminus that it now is. By modern comparison it was darksome and uninviting. Of an evening undesirable characters frequented it.

As they made their way out, "Gordon, stop," Laura suddenly said, her voice low. "Stand still a minute. Look just over there at that girl and that woman."

A pale young slip of a girl and a large bedizened woman were the objects of this direction. The girl had a fragile prettiness which was thrown now into a patent distress. The woman had a horrible face. As she stooped herself towards the other all her aspect and her pose were of a threatening air. She was obviously hectoring. The girl as obviously was trembling before her.

Laura said, "I believe something dreadful is happening. That child's obviously a foreigner, look at her clothes and that funny sort of box-bag she's carrying. And that woman's

obviously vile. She's one of those horrible creatures who trap
over young girls from the continent, I'm sure."

The couple stood within the seclusion of a bay formed by
loaded luggage barrows left against an office wall. They
could have been heard where Gordon and Laura stood but
the woman was hissing her words close into the girl's face.

"I think you're right," Gordon said.

"Do something, Gordon. We must."

"Shall I speak to a policeman? Will you wait here while
I find one?"

"Yes, find one."

His movement from Laura turned him directly towards
the mouth of the bay. The girl while they watched had been
casting frightened eyes towards the open platform. To his
surprise she stretched now an eager hand towards him, recognizing him, as it appeared; unquestionably greeting him.

In broken English, "Ach, das ees zair Herr Pfarrer, der
clairgeeman," she cried. "You are kom for me. I um zee
Minna Strauss."

He stepped up to the pair, Laura with him.

"No, I haven't come for you," he addressed the girl. "But
can I do anything for you? Were you expecting a clergyman, a pastor?"

The tears standing in the girl's eyes flowed and ran down
her cheeks. She cried out a jumble of German and foreign
English. The woman, stepping before her, fronted up truculently to the arrivals.

"No, she's not expecting no one. She's stopping with me.
I'm her auntie, matter of fact. She's bin in 'ospital and got
a bit upset like an' I'm just taking her 'ome. She's all right."

"She doesn't look all right," Laura said. "She looks very
unhappy."

"Well, thanking you for your trouble," said the woman
dismissingly, and turned her back squarely upon them.

But the girl, who had been looking piteously from one to another during this exchange, caught now at a word she knew. Shut between the wall and the woman so that her face could scarcely be seen she thrust out an imploring hand from her prison. "Unhappee. *Ja,* yais, I am unhappee. *Ich habe Angst.* [I have fear, I am afraid.] Help me, *bitte, bitte* [please, please]."

In the narrow bay, the woman's large back squared across it, there was no getting round to the girl. Gordon put his hand on the woman's shoulder. "I think something's wrong here," he said firmly.

She turned a flaming face. "Ah, an' you'll find there is if you don't take yourself off. Take your hand off of me."

He was never of commanding air. His face was the kind sort, his manner the gentle manner. But he stiffened his lips and spoke resolutely, maintaining his hand.

"I want to speak to this girl."

The woman swung round on him, ablaze. "You keep your hands off me. How dare you touch me? How dare you interfere with a lady? You be off, the pair of you."

Laura pressed forward. "We're not going off, not till we've spoken to this girl."

The woman swelled herself up for an outburst but at the peak of her capacity thought better of it and came down. With a nod backwards in indication of the girl behind her she stooped her face and spoke confidingly. "You don't want a scene and I'm trying, matter of fact, to stop one. She's hysterical, see? Just out of 'ospital, as I've told yer, and goes off in a minute anything upset her, see? You just leave her with her auntie and she'll come quiet in a minute and thank you kindly, I'm sure."

"She's a foreigner," Laura said.

The woman dropped her placating attempt. "What if she is?"

"She's expecting someone," Gordon said, "a clergyman."

"She's not expecting you, nor I'm not neither."

Turning, the woman took the girl's arm. "You come with me, dearie." With her other hand she swept a way before herself. "You get off away with yourselves. Any more of you and I'll have the police to you; so now."

The girl held back. *"Nein, nein.* It iss not goot. I am unhappee. It iss a beeg mistake. I haf no like for zees lady. Her house iss not goot." She was essaying to rid herself of the grasp that held her. She stretched a hand to Laura. "Help me. Help me."

Laura took the hand in both hers. "Dear girl, we will help you."

Gordon stood up to the woman. "Come along then, we'll find a policeman, as you want to."

Releasing the girl the woman made motion of preceding him. "That suits me. Let's find a copper. Give you in charge jolly quick, the pair of you. Assaulted me, that's what you've done. Struck me with your 'and and interfered with a lady and the girl she's in rightful charge of. You come to a copper, the pair of you, if you dare."

Attracted by her furious tones, waiting passengers came about.

"Where can I find a policeman?" Gordon asked.

"Out there," someone said.

He put himself on the girl's other side between her and the woman. "Come on, Laura. We'll soon settle this."

They moved forward and the woman's bluff showed itself called. Making no step to accompany them, "Go and sink yourselves," she screamed. Some foulest abuse followed them. As they came into the booking-hall Gordon looked back. "She's gone," he said.

If, as the three emerged into the station yard, a policeman had been in sight the upshot of this affair probably would have been different. Minna would have been succored by the law in the law's way. But it happened that no constable was to be seen. She was compassionated by her rescuers in her rescuers' way. Food and reassurance appeared her immediate needs. She had eaten nothing, as it came out, all day.

"Give me your bag," Gordon said. Each holding a hand that clutched theirs in piteous relief and gratitude they took her across the yard to the little A.B.C. teashop, original of the many-floored restaurant which now occupies the site. They found a secluded corner. Minna gulped eagerly of the coffee brought to her, then ate with increasing relish. She sat with Laura on a red plush bench against the wall, Gordon on a chair opposite them. All the time she used only her right hand. Her left hand clutched a hand of Laura's. All the time her eyes were alternately on Laura's face and on Gordon's. They spoke the devotion which thenceforward all her life was to show.

10

Not until she was obviously the better for her meal was she allowed to talk. Then in her broken English she told them in outline the story which later they came to know in full.

She was the only child of a one-time Heidelberg university professor. Her mother had died when she was ten. Her father after much trouble with his eyes had lost his sight. At fifteen she had gone with him to live in a little Bavarian town where subsequently she had become a junior governess in a girls' school. The school had incorporated with another. She had been dismissed and at the same time her father had died.

Thrown on the world, her only relatives unknown persons who had discreetly lost touch with her father when his self-support had ceased, she had responded to the advertised wiles of an employment agency in Berlin. It appeared, when she presented herself, and after she had paid her booking fee, that the scholastic posts of which they had glowingly written to her were all now filled.

She was at the end of her means when she found employment at last behind the counter of a cheap drapery store. In three months she was dismissed with four others on an indiscriminate theft charge. A fashionably dressed woman accosting her in the street, learning her plight and evincing pity for her, took her home to her flat and on the morrow to an agency specializing, she said, in posts for German governesses abroad. Here was a most friendly Jewish gentleman who, having heard her acquirements, professed himself as inexpressibly delighted to be able to say that he had just the very place ready and waiting for her in England. It was in the family of a *Pfarrer,* a pastor, a clergyman; two girls as pupils, salary £40 a year, a delightful house in a delightful suburb of London.

The golden prospect, enhanced by her desolating experiences since coming to Berlin, had caused Minna to dab her handkerchief at moist eyes. What about her clothes? In her exigencies she had sold virtually all but what she stood in. The kind pastor, she was told, was undertaking to provide her with all she should have. That was part of the arrangement. "Why, what a lucky girl, indeed," the lady who had brought her had cried. "And away almost at once, next week, in a fine steamer from Hamburg to Hull where the kind clergyman would meet her." The friendly Jewish gentleman had corrected this. In an undertone he had said something to the lady. Minna caught only, and understood not at all, something about Hull being unsafe, being watched. No, she was to travel, it appeared, by Paris (lucky girl!), Calais, Dover, and Victoria, London, where the kind pastor would be on the platform to meet her.

Very tired, very bewildered, very nervous now that the meeting with her employer was actually at hand, she had stepped from the train at Victoria, her white handkerchief bound, as she had been instructed, about her left arm, and agitatedly had looked about her for the kind pastor. Pushed this way and that by the crowd, increasingly forlorn on realizing the difficulty of finding and being found in such confusion, she suddenly, to her immense relief, was effusively greeted by the woman from whom she had now been rescued. The woman was, it appeared, the pastor's wife. Her husband had been unable to come.

II

Minna was taken in a four-wheeled cab to a street of tall, neglected-looking houses a short drive away. London was in fog. Unlit within, the cab was as dark as a cellar. The woman had an unpleasant smell about her; the cab also an unpleasant smell. Minna's rapturous expectations had never conceived of a woman, or of a fog, or of a pitch dark cab, or of evil smells. She had imagined a kindly faced pastor waving to her as the train came in; and then transport, no doubt in another train, through gay sunshine; and then arrival at a smiling white house on a lovely green lawn, two dear little English girls running out to greet and kiss her. She felt vaguely frightened.

Timid to ask questions, her dismay in this reversal of her preconceptions upset the little English she in any case possessed. She could not frame what she wished to say. Herr Smith was the name of her pastor, she had been told. Once she began, desperately chancing the rest of her sentence, "Mrs. Smeeth, *bitte*—Mrs. Smeeth, please you—"

Loquacious on the platform, silent once the cab was started, the woman interrupted her now, "Mrs. Smeeth? Oh, Smith you mean." She laughed. "Yes, I'm Mrs. Smith, that's right. Tiger, most calls me, though. Can you say Tiger? Try."

Minna tried. "Tiger" laughed shrilly at the sound she made of the name. In the new confusion of mind thus caused her, the English sentence she had planned slid out of her vocabulary. And now a further perplexity, too, was caused her by the instruction thus to call her pastor's wife. Tiger, its sound being so similar, could not but be the English for *Tigah,* the jungle beast. How should a lady be called *Tigah?* A nickname this must be. A not nice nickname; and should an employee, moreover, address her mistress by such a familiarity? To her children's governess the *Pfarrer's* wife surely should be Mrs. Smeeth, *Gnädige Frau,* Madame. "Tiger" was not right. All of this position in which she found herself—the pastor not at the station, the fog, this dark cab, this woman, her voice, her face, her smell—was not right.

The cab stopped; she was bade get out; and gazing at the place of her arrival she was seized of a conviction that indeed all was not right. Area railings stood on either side of the door. The fanlight above it showed an unpronounceable word followed by the word "Hotel." But it was a *Pfarrhaus,* a pastor's house, that she was to come to. This was not even a hotel with a portico and lights such as proper hotels have. This was of the evil boding sort she had seen in the cheap quarters of Berlin.

The better to read the lettering above the door she had gone forward to the railings. She turned to utter her misgivings to the woman. Tiger was paying the cab-driver. The cab-driver abused her. She shrilled return. He stood up from his seat shouting at her. She backed towards Minna shout-

ing reply. He made as if to get down. The woman grabbed
Minna's arm, pushed her to the door, opened it with a key,
cried back a last vituperation at the driver, and hustled the
girl within, slamming the door behind her.

12

Minna's account of it was that she was now in a narrow
hallway lit by a single gas jet in a wire cage and pervaded by
a newly unwholesome smell. A door stood on either hand;
at the end was another door and stairs ascending and descending. All these doors opened at the slam of the arrivals'
entry and people came out, stood on the thresholds and
stared and spoke and laughed; from one two women, from
another a man, from another a woman. The faces of all
were bad faces. Up the descending stairs appeared a grossly
fat man, all paunch and creases, wearing only a vest and
trousers. He called out authoritatively to Tiger, who called
reply, and he came forward commandingly.

As he did so there came down the ascending stairs a
further inmate of the house. This was a tall young girl,
raffishly dressed for the street, a gaudy hat perched on the
back of masses of red hair, her face heavily rouged. The
other women who had presented themselves were undecked.
Any sluttish occupation might have been theirs. In this new
arrival Minna recognized instantly membership of a profession she had seen in practice in Berlin. She knew herself
now decoyed and trapped, and knew to what. She had been
dragging back on Tiger's clutch, protesting in such English
as she could effect that a mistake had been made, that her
Herr pastor surely could not be here. Now at the sight of
this unquestionable street-walker she cried out to be released
and struggled in the grip that held her. The man in the vest
strode down to Tiger's assistance. As he did so words whose

tone was clearly that of remonstrance were cried from up the passage.

Oddly, the remonstrance, rising to a high expostulation, came from the very one whose garb had proclaimed to Minna the horror of her plight. Of all that passed in the house Minna's account was restricted by her inability to understand what was said. The utterances of the red-haired street-walker may however be guessed from her actions and were infinitely to her credit. As there is said to be honor among thieves so possibly there are scruples among women of the street. This one seemingly held by the principle of volunteers but not pressed men. The expostulation that she cried out from the stairs may be imagined as having been that that kid wasn't their sort, that Minna ought not to have been brought here and that she wasn't going to stand for it.

She ran down to Minna and by pulling and pushing at the vested man and at Tiger further demonstrated her views. She was bawled at and pushed away. Minna was hustled into a room. The street-walker followed, loud in continued expostulation. The man struck her back-handed across the mouth, an arm's length swing hit so that she staggered the width of the room till the wall stayed her. She wiped her lips with her hand, stared at blood upon it, and as if that and not the actual blow infuriated her, sprang across and at him, claw and tooth. He got her throat, pummeled her body with his other fist, then thrust her to the door and flung her out, following her ferociously.

Tiger pushed to the door behind them and turned to Minna with no more comment on the horrible affray than bland shrug of her shoulders. The room spun round with Minna. She fainted.

13

Her unconsciousness must have been of considerable duration. When she next knew herself she was on a bed in a carpetless room, a chair with a broken back, a dressing-table with a cracked mirror, and a washstand holding tin ware, the sole other furniture. Moonlight through the uncovered window disclosed these surroundings. The hour would have been eleven or twelve for a public clock was striking as she came to her senses and, automatically counting, she had counted ten. She realized the events which had befallen her and for some time lay stiff in their terror. Burning thirst overcame her dread to move. She got up, found water to be in the ewer, and drank deeply from it. There was no glass. The window's view into the moonlight showed her to be high up at the rear of the house, looking across backyards to what appeared to be the back of a factory. Tip-toeing to the door she turned its cheap brass handle but could not open it. It was not locked or exteriorly bolted for it came half an inch to her pull. She found afterwards that it was secured by a rope between its outer handle and the handle of a door opposite. Creeping about she saw now that her bag was on the floor near the table. It lay open, its contents ransacked. Her hat was on the table. The little satchel in which she had had a trifle of money was not to be seen.

Night's hours prowled their baleful way. Sitting on the bed, one of its blankets about her shoulders, another round her legs, she prayed, cried, fought the drowsiness which would deliver her to the perils of sleep. At any sound, from creak of furniture to a door's slam, from movements to noisy voices, she was stricken to a breath-holding, heart-pounding terror.

Exhaustion asserted itself. She gave it the capitulation of

two minutes' relaxation huddled prone. When she awoke broad daylight was in the room. She realized, terribly, that her abductress was standing over her, a tray in her hands.

Tiger, frowsily repulsive in a dressing-gown, was all elaborate smiles. Her greeting may be imagined. "Hullo. Had a good sleep? That's right. Nothing to worry about now. You're going to be a very happy, lucky girl and start with this jolly fine breakfast I've brought up to you. Look."

She displayed her bringings, her blotched and grimy face the counterfeiting ground of propitiations whose falseness her hard eyes menacingly betrayed.

Minna first was shrunk back against the headrails of the bed, then in a wild effort at self-assertion was out on her feet. "*Nein, nein.* Zair ees mistake. I belong not here. I belong to Herr Pfarrer who moos meet me. I go, please. Please I go now, *sofort,* at wons."

Tiger put the tray on the bed. All her face as she turned to Minna was set now in consonance with her cruel eyes' expression. She took Minna by the shoulder and with grimy finger of the other hand admonished her. "You listen."

Here her words, easy again of imagination, can be given in the snatches which Minna understood. "Be a good girl," "Have lovely clothes," these snatches were. "Lovely food, lovely jewels." "Or stop here and starve till you do." She took up the tray. "That's when you're good," she rasped, and bearing it with her went from the room.

If Minna had been the heroine of a film she would have done heroic things. She was, in fact, a gentle-minded, timid-natured German girl of eighteen. She was in a den of ferocious human beasts whose tongue she could not speak, in a country whose practices she did not know. She did nothing. It was with her every fiber petrified in terror that, as the day moved on, she heard feet stealthily approaching.

The ghost of a tapping came at the door. Loudly whispered accents said, "Hi, you. Come here."

It seemed to be a woman's voice. Suggesting secrecy, it appeared to be the voice of friendliness.

Minna went to the door. *"Bitte?* Please?"

"I—get—you—out." The phraseology, as also the deliberate spacing between the words, was that of one accommodating her speech to a foreigner. "I—get—you—out," the voice repeated. "You understand, eh?"

"Yais, yais. You get me aus. Yais."

"Five o'clock. You understand five o'clock, eh?"

"Yais, yais. Five o'clock. *Gott sei Dank. Vielen herzlichen Dank.*"

"Five o'clock you be ready? Eh? You understand 'ready'?"

"Yais, yais. At five o'clock ready. Yais."

"Right-o, kid. Keep smiling."

And stealthily as they had come the footsteps drew away.

Minna had long since found that her little gold watch, it had been her mother's, was gone together with its gold chain worn, in the fashion of those days, about her neck. She had heard the public clock strike midday but had missed the briefer notes which she felt sure it must have sounded since. "Be ready," the voice had said. She had ample time for readying herself, she was sure. Her urgency was to know how long. Face pressed to window that the next hour might not slip her ears she waited, and presently *dong* came the note, and twice again *dong, dong.* Three o'clock. She filled the basin from the ewer. There was no soap nor towel, but in the continental habit she had brought soap with her. She took off her blouse, gave herself the badly needed wash which her distress had put from her mind, made her toilette generally, put on her hat, repacked her tumbled bag, and waited then the longest two hours she was ever likely to know.

Four struck. The clock did not sound the hourly divisions. She started to count sixties, scratching each completed minute with a hairpin on a dusty floor-board; but when the marks were but twelve she found the necessary concentration to be impossible, and desisted, and waited . . . and waited. . . . Her fingernails, pressed into her hands in the intolerable strain she was undergoing, cut into her flash. Her teeth, similarly expressing her endurance, drew blood on the inside of her lower lip. . . .

Dong.

She sprang to her bag and went to the door. The strokes finished their toll. She stood there consumed by a trembling such as might be given to a figure vibrating on wires.

Footsteps came.

They were not stealthy now; but they were the steps, she knew, for which she waited, for a swift purposefulness was in their sound. Thus coming, pat to the hour of her warning, they spoke deliverance; and she waited, her heart pounding, but assured, while the arrival sounded to be fumbling with the handle of a door opposite.

Then her own door was pushed towards her. She stepped clear of it and saw the red-haired street-walker, in one hand a length of clothes-line and a brass door-handle, in the other a pair of scissors.

"Ready? That's right. Quick. Queek. You understand 'queek,' eh?"

The street-walker indicated the things in her hands and pointed to the door opposite. "Tiger think you pull it out, see?" From the other door projected nakedly the pin of its handle. Flimsy screws, obviously turned with the scissors, were in the handle which Minna's rescuer held. The cord attached it to the handle of Minna's room.

"Queek. Coast clear, see, but slippy an' quiet, see?"

The street-walker pantomimed these instructions by rising

on her toes and by a finger to her lips. She took Minna's bag and led along the passage, then down the first of three flights of stairs.

They came into the hallway of dreadful recollection. At the front door Minna's conductress handed her her bag, unlatched the door, then shut it again. " 'Ere, arf a mo'." She drew up her skirt, put her hand to a pocket beneath it, and produced a shabby little purse. "Ten, twelve-an'-six, fourteen an' a tanner," she counted, fingering among its coins. She extended three silver coins, replaced them and held out a gold piece, replaced that and snapped the purse's catch. " 'Ere, take the blooming lot." She thrust the purse into Minna's hands. Feet sounded up the basement stairs. The street-walker snatched open the door. Minna was pushed forth, the door soundlessly closed behind her.

Almost at a run she went in the direction from which she remembered the cab to have come. At the first corner—anywhere to escape this street—she turned and, when free of the quarter, for miles and hours wandered. Victoria was her blind objective. It was the only place name in London that she knew. More than that, it was clearly the railway station of continental arrival. Officials would be there who were accustomed to foreigners. Much more, her Herr Pfarrer, missing her yesterday evening, if not there again tonight would have left word of her, she hoped, with the station-master. For it never had occurred to her, as Laura and Gordon found, that the lady who had compassioned her in Berlin, the friendly Jewish agent and the woman Tiger were in league. Bitterly during her incarceration she had blamed herself for having allowed the woman to walk her away. With frantic longing she sought now the place of her ab-duction.

For three hours she sought it. Jostled in crowded thoroughfares, forlorn in unfrequented endless by-streets, she

got, seemingly, so far adrift that when at last she summoned
courage to put "Victoria, eh?" to passers-by she was met
with the blank look of one asked a problem in direction. A
gabble of incomprehension would follow. With "Tank you,
tank you" she would drift hopelessly away. Round a corner
she came suddenly upon a yellow omnibus drawn by two
horses. Halted to set down a passenger, it showed on a narrow board attached to its side the word of her longing,
"Victoria." Even as she realized it, the omnibus restarted.
With a cry she stumbled forward. The conductor reached
for her bag, and she fell in somehow and on to a seat, faint-
ing almost in the physical revulsion of sitting down after so
long upon her feet. When fares were demanded she ten-
dered a silver coin from the purse. "Victoria, eh?" With no
word the conductor handed her some change. She closed
her eyes, sick with relief.

Stoppings and startings, passengers out, passengers in;
consciousness then of a halt at which, all alighting, she was
left alone. The conductor called something to her. She got
to her feet. "Victoria, eh?" He jerked his thumb across what
she saw now to be a station yard and walked away. Yes,
there was the station, people hurrying in. Joining them, she
was borne in their press through the booking-hall to its
emergence on the platform square and some yards forward.
Dissipating this way and that to its trains the throng fell
from about her. She was left as if suddenly stepped out of
a thicket into a clearing. She was face to face with Tiger.

14

Of all this story the vicar's thoughts touched only those
scenes of its sequel in which himself and Laura had participated. Fondly numbering Minna among the blessings
which had fallen to him in days antecedent to the blessing

of this day of arrival at St. Luke's, it was finding her in the
rescue episode at Victoria that now he recalled, the teashop
meal and talk, the decision to extend the succoring of her
by taking her home to Knipstone and giving her rest and
friendship before committing her to the channels which
took charge of such cases.

He saw the train journey through the night, Minna dozing between himself and Laura, one hand in his, one in
Laura's, at intervals pressing her adoring gratitude. He saw
her a few days later crying to them, "Only let me always
live with you and I do anything for you. I work for you
till I drop. I do anything, everything, because I love you
like I loved my mother and my father." He saw through the
years the daily earnest of her love.

He saw her worship of the children, theirs of her; and
his survey winged from her devoted nursing when whooping cough was in the house, when John almost died, to the
haggard period of his and Laura's realization that life in
the parish without a blade of grass was robbing the children's needs. It was undermining their health. "I'll be
frank," the doctor said one day, long after the whooping
cough, called in to see John. "You'll lose that boy if you
don't get him away from here."

It had been a thing to think over in God. With earthly
friends you did what you were humanly entitled to do. You
told your rural dean, who cordially undertook to tell your
bishop, what your case was. You wrote also to your old
vicar, to Mr. Severn, lest haply in your old diocese, where
your work was known, an incumbency suited to your needs
might fall vacant. But with your Heavenly Friend you did
what you were divinely enabled to do. You asked nothing.
Abandoning yourself to the Supreme Intelligence in which
you had your being, you just thought out how things were
with you, with your loved ones but also with your work and

all else besides. Gradually you realized your thoughts to be lifted out of the trouble which had cankered them when you knelt down and into a communion with the Cause and Purpose of Life. Received into those transcendent realms of the spirit, compassionated and inspired in the mystery of the Great Understanding, you arose presently from your knees suffused with the sublime assurance that, come this come that, whatsoever betided you was God betided, therefore well.

He saw himself thus presenting his concern of mind for the welfare of his children. He saw the hour in which he had knelt before his altar at St. Mary's, Knipstone, his head upon his arms, in one hand the letter, amazingly arrived, offering him the living of St. Luke's, Upton Springs.

15

He had brought his survey of his blessings to this moment and to this place of their culmination. He stood up, his face irradiated, and swung apart his arms. His hands had been joined in spiritual satisfaction. He extended them now in human satisfaction. This splendid new study of his went the depth of the house, having windows back and front. He looked out a moment from the back across the wide lawn. It dropped over a bank on to a narrow lawn which fell again, beyond a hedge, into a kitchen garden. That narrower strip, he had already determined, should be the children's own particular preserve. The Children's Piece, it should be called. Against the wall at the end there he'd build them a summer-house, a settlers' cabin, for their very own.

Ecstatic he turned and went with eager strides to join the tea.

"Father; come on, father," shouts greeted him.

"Father, there's toasted buns, absolute rippers. We've kept one for you."

"And boiled eggs, father; brown ones."

"And, father, Philip refuses to eat his. Just look at his egg, father, not touched."

In front of all but Philip was an emptied egg-shell. In front of Philip an egg apparently untouched.

This game had been played with almost every boiled egg eaten by John and by Mary in their babyhood. Nowadays it was four-year-old Philip's game, and with expression suitably stern the vicar started to play it.

"Philip, I insist on your eating that delicious egg."

"No, father."

"Philip, I *will* not allow you to say No to me. Eat that egg."

Face shining with glee, Philip gathers all eyes around the table, inviting everybody to enjoy father's impending humiliation. "No, father, I will not."

The vicar makes a superb pantomime of controlling his fury. "Very well, then," he says, gulping his rage; "*I* will eat it. *I* will show you how delicious it is."

And he stalks upon Philip, seizes a spoon, plunges it into the egg—and as it crashes through the cunningly inverted empty shell superbly pantomimes his chagrin at the fool he has been tricked into making of himself.

Ecstasies of delight from Philip. Chorus of delight from all at Philip's delight.

The vicar has played this game at least a thousand times. Never, he feels, has it gone with such a roar as this. Never has the family looked so radiantly healthy and happy as this. Never has the company sat at such a table, in such a room, in such a house, in such a garden, in such a place, in such a world as this.

He seats himself, and jovially rubs his hands together. "Where's that toasted bun? And tea, Laura, tea, tea!"

Two

By what means precisely a new vicar comes into their church is known probably to fewer parishioners than those few who know precisely by what processes water comes out of a tap or illumination into an electric-light globe. You turn the tap or depress the switch and the desired element arrives. All you want is something to wash in or to see by. Who bothers about how it comes? In the generality of opinion, similarly, somebody, presumably a bishop, performs some equally simple action somewhere, and the pulpit of your church which you had heard was empty becomes automatically filled. All you want, and that indifferently, is that there should be matins on the rare occasions when you think to attend them. Who bothers about how was effected the change of face since last you were here?

As with the tap and the switch so with the pulpit there is a good deal more to it than the visible process of delivery. There are some 13,000 Church livings in England. Each of them is in the gift of a private person or trust, of a corporate body or of an office holder.

In unversed speech, a clergyman is presented with, or rather given, a living by the person or authority who owns it. In the conventional talk of those parishioners whose knowledge went further than the tap and switch process Gordon Brecque was given the living of St. Luke's by Lord Culverstock.

He had never seen and only remotely had heard of his patron. His patron had never seen or, until he nominated him, heard of him. Of matters pertaining to the Church he knew indeed so little, and cared so much less, that if he had been told off-handedly that an advowson (for so the right of presentation of a benefice is called) was bound up in the considerable area of land he owned in the Upton Springs district he would have replied off-handedly that he had not the faintest idea what an advowson was, and that anyway his solicitors handled all that part of his possessions for him; he wouldn't be seen dead in the place.

He was customarily to be seen alive, very much alive, on race-courses and in his own racing-stables, in the hunting-field and amongst his own string of hunters. One other deep attachment in life he had and that was to his only child, a boy aged eight in the year when the benefice of St. Luke's for the first time since his succession to the title fell vacant. The mother had died shortly after and as a result of the birth. The child had a seemingly incurable affection of the spine. If Lord Culverstock when in public was customarily to be seen on a horse or watching a horse, in any of his several residences his time was customarily spent with his small cripple.

He was wheeling the child in the grounds of his Berkshire racing stables when he read the letter from his solicitors apprising him, in respect of his advowson of St. Luke's, Upton Springs, of the impending resignation of the incumbent, the Rev. Lionel Phipps-Tracy, and of his duty to present a successor to the living. On a fine morning it was his frequent practice to toss his morning letters on to Tony's spinal carriage and, while airing the child abroad, enjoy the specially-invented fun which the two had in reading them together.

It happened that Tony had taken this particular letter to open it and, while his father talked to him, had fallen asleep, the envelope in his hands. His health had been causing anxiety apart from his permanent affliction. His face as

he lay there had a pallor which struck desperately at his
watcher's heart. Haply to find relief of occupation for his
thoughts, Lord Culverstock drew the envelope from the
thin, almost transparent fingers and glanced across the letter's contents. "From the usual sources," concluded the solicitors, "we shall no doubt receive many suggestions for the
presentation to the incumbency and these we will submit to
your Lordship in due course. We enclose herewith copy of
one letter already received in this connection."

To the enclosure he was disposed to give even less attention than to its cover. Docketed at its head by the solicitors,
it appeared to be from a clergyman called Severn who, having heard from his friend, the Rev. L. Phipps-Tracy, of his
impending retirement, desired to present for consideration
in the nomination of a successor a former curate of his,
now Vicar of St. Mary's, Knipstone, Staffs, the Rev. Gordon
Brecque.

Lord Culverstock was about to allow the letter itself to
go unread when his eye chanced upon a phrase at its end.
His interest sharply aroused, he turned to the beginning,
skimmed through the testimony paid to the candidate's
qualifications, and concentrated then upon the final para-
graph.

"Mr. Brecque," it ran, "is most anxious for the sake of his
children's health to secure a change of incumbency into
more rural surroundings. The fear is entertained that the
eldest child, a boy of eight, may be lost to the parents unless
given the benefits of country air."

It was this last sentence which had touched Lord Culverstock's desultory reading into sharp attention. He looked
down from it upon this other boy of eight stretched before
him, blue-veined upon the eyelids, twitching in the fragile
fingers, who also, God help him, was in danger of being
lost. He beckoned to his secretary, standing about across the

lawn awaiting possible orders, and handed him the letter. "Tell them that that chap referred to in the enclosure— Brecque, isn't the name?—is to have the incumbency. Tell 'em not to bother me with other names. It's his."

2

The living to which its new vicar was thus presented— divine outcome, as he would have seen it, of fellow feeling towards his child—was worth £530 a year.

" 'The laborer is worthy of his hire.' What Church people ought to inquire of themselves is whether the hire is worthy of the laborer."

Said to the Brecques by their first caller, this was one of an unfailing flow of pungent comments on Church people, and on Church discipline, made by one who, in his own fashion, himself was a servant of the Church. In troubled days to come the Rev. Hope Hubbard was to prove himself a stout friend of St. Luke's vicarage. From the first moment of his appearance there they greatly took to him.

It was as early as but shortly after the conclusion of that first tea of eggs and toasted buns that this prompt caller presented himself. The vicar and Laura were in the hall, sorting packages. The caller espied them through the glass panel of the front door and, as though he were an old friend, turned the handle and walked in. Of about Gordon's age, tall and dark, immediately noticeable in his face was a mobile quality. You could imagine him being suited by any uniform, official or fancy; typically suggesting the part; enhancing the role and himself enhanced by it. The uniform which in fact and with high distinction he wore was cassock and biretta.

Extending his hand to Laura, "My name's Hope Hubbard," he announced.

Much friendliness but also a certain quizzing was in the smile which accompanied his words.

"Oh, dear, we've heard of you," exclaimed Laura, and her own smile also had mischief.

The implication of her artless cry was known to all three of them. The Rev. Hope Hubbard was what in those days was still called a ritualist. His church of St. Monica's on the outskirts of Upton Springs was incense-pervaded, picture-hung, image-adorned. His altar-table showed coverings of colors differing with the ecclesiastical seasons. His celebration of the Eucharist, which he called Mass, showed him in alb and variety of stoles. His aisles staged processions, ornate with banners, crosses and vested attendants. He had thrice with his own hands, assisted by those of his churchwardens, thrown out disciples of Mr. Kensit. He had openly flouted his bishop. His name, notorious far beyond the confines of the diocese as "That man Hope Hubbard," was looked at askance in the other churches of Upton Springs.

And while he shook hands with the vicar he laughed delightedly at Laura's, "Oh, dear, we've heard of you," and replied to it, "Why, then, you'll want to throw me out, with a pitchfork."

The vicar had looked politely embarrassed at Laura's frank naivety. "Oh, my dear fellow, no. I've never met your persuasion before but I shall remember it as having come up here in friendliness, first of everybody."

It was with change to graveness that the other looked at him. "Very charmingly spoken," he said.

"Oh, but, yes, jolly nice of *you*," Laura declared; and when he turned his eyes to her his expression was laughing again. In these brief exchanges some sort of a kindred spirit had been felt by these two. After he had left, "You're rather a pair of you, you two," Gordon said to Laura. "I saw it as you stood together in the hall when he arrived. You'd that challenging sort of way of yours about you and it seemed to complement something in him."

"Yes, well, I liked him."

"So did I, very much."

"And didn't the children just!"

3

They had taken him into the drawing-room, and he had spoken amusingly of himself. "I really came at this preposterously too-soon hour," he said, "because I was the only local not at your institution service and that rather vexed me. But, of course, with the bishop there it was no place for me. He'd either have had to come at me with bell, book and candle or to simmer with abhorrence of me all through the service, which would have been unseemly to say the least. But I'll wager my absence was explained to you." He pantomimed a pompous fussy voice. " 'All your fellow vicars of the neighborhood are here in welcoming participation, my dear fellow, except St. Monica's, that, that misguided fellow Hope Hubbard. He would not have dared, I need scarcely tell you he would not have dared, to face our beloved bishop.' "

It was a recognizable caricature of the manner of the rural dean, the Rev. Carlton Willings, a recognizable version also of words he had actually spoken. Laura laughed. Gordon looked uncomfortable, Hope Hubbard leant towards him from his chair and touched his knee. "Bad form," he said. "Forgive me."

His charm of manner was undeniable. (His execrators, admitting it, would point out that so, by legend, was the devil's.) Gordon smiled acceptance of the apology. Unfamiliar, as he had said, with Hope Hubbard's persuasion, he was curious about the man's position.

"What puzzles me," he began diffidently. He hesitated, and Laura impulsively jumped his ditch.

"Yes, what beats me, too," she affirmed, "is how you ever got licensed in the diocese."

"Why, by the former bishop. He was of the Lincoln school. I was, as a matter of fact, the very last man he licensed before his sudden death."

"You're unendowed," Gordon said, "and yet you've abolished pew-rents, I've heard. Have you?"

"I have *and* we're unendowed." Their visitor's quizzing eyes and smile challenged inquiry as to how then his stipend came. "I wring my hire," he smiled at them, "out of the loins of my faithful. Pew-rents scourged them with whips and they supplied a beggarly £300 a year. All seats free and unappropriated scourges 'em with scorpions, that's to say I do since I established it, and they hand me out now a Vicar's Stipend Fund, Easter offering included, of £700 a year. Does that seem a lot to you?"

"Princely," declared Laura, so roundly that they all laughed.

"But amazing to me," said Gordon, "that such a sum should come to you purely by voluntary gift. How—?"

"The amazing thing," Hope Hubbard interrupted him, "is that every parish in the land doesn't have the self-respect to make some such figure the minimum. If every parishioner did his duty towards his priests as his priests do their duty towards him it would be so. Your worthy parishioner pays his doctor and his dentist, not to say his rates; he pays his son's schoolmaster and he pays, fatly, to be entertained of a night at a theater or to be otherwise amused."

He laughed, then proceeded. "But as to vicars the ideas are very different. Vicars, Mrs. Brecque, if you don't know it or if your husband has hidden it from you, are regarded by the majority of their parishioners as, on the whole, uncommonly lucky beggars. They live rent free in roomy houses with delightful gardens; and on top of what they are paid they get every year what must be a remarkably handsome bonus in the form of the Easter offering. When your worthy parishioner lays up for himself or herself quite a big piece of treasure in heaven by hunking out of bed at an unearthly hour on Easter Day (in order to have the morning clear for pleasure with an easy, nay, with an up-lifted conscience) he or she realizes—"

With his gift for pantomime Hope Hubbard assumed the voice and air of an empty-headed chatterer, dual-sexed. " 'You realize, bai jove, you realize, my dear, how hand-some that Easter bonus indeed must be. I was there at the eight o'clock service. Yes, positively at eight, my boy, posi-tively at eight o'clock, my dear. And the church was crammed, and the collection bag stuffed, absolutely stuffed. And there'd been two services, mind you, before that, and were to be at least two after it. Well, I mean to say, *imagine* what the man must get!' "

The vicar could not but laugh. Laura's ring of mirth made no bones about her appreciation of the truth within the fun.

" 'And that, mind you,' " said Hope Hubbard, with relish continuing his pantomime, " 'is only part of the pickings these vicars get. They get, if you realize it, free holidays every summer. We poor beggars of laymen, we poor wives of ordinary men, have to pay extortionate prices for August accommodation. These fatted vicars just swop off with a de-lightful vicarage in Devonshire or in the Lakes or wherever they like to pick and get a top-hole vacation, family and all, get the most comfortable homes in the most heavenly sur-roundings, my dear, just for the price of their return tickets. Imagine it!' "

He laughed and changed his manner. "What they don't even begin to imagine of course—"

He described pungently the plain facts of vicarage "pick-ings." In a reasonably well-to-do parish of some 3,000 souls the Easter offering will produce perhaps £100, possibly slightly less, improbably greatly more. The sum, whatever it may be, will vary indifferently from year to year. It is counted in as a component part of the "worth" of the living. The vicar pays income-tax on it. When with his wife and family he takes his summer holiday "free" in some other vicarage he does so of necessity, not of choice. Where to his parishioners the whole meaning of holiday is release from work, to him, thus accommodated, it is but change of situa-tion of work. He takes his fellow vicar's house but he takes on also his duties. "When anyone calls that a free holiday," said Hope Hubbard, "ask 'em whether they suppose that a doctor or a solicitor, exchanging his own practice for another for six weeks, would regard it as the most delightful form of vacation."

His listeners laughed. They knew, nevertheless, as all clergy know, the truth of his assertion, and they were to know it better yet. "If only this holidays," Laura more than once had said, "you could get a Sunday or two without duty, dear—"

That was at Knipstone. She was to say it again, looking at her husband a shade anxiously, at Upton Springs.

But the vicar of St. Luke's never did; he never had.

4

The annual worth of the living of St. Luke's was made up as to £120 by endowment of Lord Culverstock's grand-father; as to some £300 by pew-rents; as to an averaged £110 by Easter offering. To this £530, thus assembled, were to be added the fees paid by those who might elect to be married in or to be buried by St. Luke's.

To Gordon Brecque, accustomed over eight years to make both ends meet on an income of £320, this new worth appeared, when it was in prospect, to be worth indeed. Something short of £600 a year was not, in fact, an indifferent income in the years before the Great War. Newspapers sold at a ha'penny. Coal went at sixteen shillings the ton, summer prices. Domestic servants sought situations at £16 a year. Income tax ranged between 10*d*. and 1*s*. 2*d*. Cost of living throughout all its items was on scale according.

Those were comfortable days.

Comfort, however, bears definition in the term nonessentials. In ninety-nine of every hundred vicarages these are to seek. The vicar of St. Luke's lived rent free but he had rates and taxes to pay, dilapidations to provision. Those who spoke of his Easter offering in some such terms as pantomimed by Hope Hubbard spoke similarly of his garden produce ("No greengrocer's bill!"); but it required the payment of a gardener. Those who, spending annually on their pleasures twice times the sum of his total resources, were irritated by his appeals for this or that charitable purpose, assumed that himself he was "of course" free of such obligations. Any one day of his life, it was true, showed in its normal routine more good offices to the needy than could be shown by many of them in a year. Yet he set apart a twentieth of his income for "charities" and commonly exceeded that proportion. He had four children and the instinct to do the utmost that can be afforded for one's children, the longing to be able to do more, is not peculiar to the laity. Vicars also have it.

"Devotion to his duties," Hope Hubbard said, "in no degree materially profits the cleric."

"But he doesn't expect that it should," Gordon answered. "No one takes Orders with any idea of making money out of it."

"It's not a material profession," Laura supported him, "it's a spiritual profession."

"That's no reason," rejoined Hope Hubbard, "why the man's material life should be, as in most cases it is, a continuous struggle."

It was then that he launched his aphorism as to the hire being worthy of the laborer and he went on, "You're round about £550 here, aren't you? That's well enough today no doubt and especially when coming from decidedly less; I looked you up in Crockford. But you've four children, they tell me—I must see them before I go. You won't find £550 affluence as they start growing up. Your parishioners ought to realize it and to give you affluence, anyway competency. You're going to give your life to this parish. I can see that; you're that sort. Well, your people ought to give to you in measure as you give to them, and as mine, as I've told you, give to me. I got together my churchwardens and some of my more interested and influential people soon after I came here and I told 'em that, if I was going to be a pariah of the diocese through giving them the ritual that appealed to them, it was up to them to support me materially as—I made and I make no modesty about it—I deserved to be supported. Hence their vicar's stipend fund. Hence my £700 a year—"

As if the figure had been mentioned for the first time, Gordon Brecque opened his eyes. "Dear me, and you're unmarried?"

"I'm celibate by conviction. But, as I was saying, hence my £700 a year. Hence my library, which is my hobby, and my decidedly comfortable quarters in my vicarage; hence also my holiday abroad every year, sharpening my intellect, keying my health. Hence my congregation's wholesome respect for me; respect, mark you, not only for my parts, but for my station, my dignity."

"No, you're not, as you were also saying, plagued by modesty," Laura put in, and they all laughed again.

"Not one solitary qualm," declared Hope Hubbard. "One more 'hence,' though, to top the list; the pinnacle, remember, which all the others go to rear—hence the torch which I've lighted down there at St. Monica's. It attracts—we of my persuasion as you've called it attract—the very rich and the very poor. We attract people who come out of curiosity and remain out of revelation. We give them, as you give them, the Gospel of Jesus Christ. But we keep them in mind also of the Splendor of God."

His lambent eyes gleamed. His actor's face, as he pronounced the last words, took on the zealot's fire. But he masked it immediately. "But that's no subject," he addressed Gordon, "between us."

He jumped up. "There's such a heap for the Church to do that I'll be stopping the night if I complete the list. I'm off. But I must just have two minutes, may I, with the children?"

They took him to the garden.

"There's one of them," pointed the vicar, for there was baby Ruth sitting up in her pram, banging a rattle.

"I must have her out," said Hope Hubbard.

"She'll never let you," said Laura.

"You watch," said Hope Hubbard.

Deftly he unstrapped Ruth and in his long arms swung her, crowing with delight, to and fro to heights which, as he told them, she had never before reached.

"They've never, any of them, so much as imagined the heights of happiness they're going to have here," declared the vicar. "Listen to them."

Laughter and shrilling voices came from the remoteness of the kitchen garden.

"Children, children," called Laura; "John-o, Mary-o,"

trumpeted the vicar. "That strip down there we're going to call the Children's Piece. And, look, Laura, against the wall there I vote a summer-house that they can use as a wigwam and all that."

"Oh, jolly fine," cried Laura.

"Glorious idea," agreed Hope Hubbard. "Here they come."

5

"Father, mother," John and Mary came shouting. "It's marvelous, it's marvelous."

"This is Mr. Hope Hubbard," Laura announced to them. "Another Upton vicar. Oh, dear, you can't possibly give him hands like that to shake, what *have* you been doing?"

"Can't they," declared Hope Hubbard. "Here, hold this crowing machine." Relinquishing Ruth, he took the new arrivals' hands, one in each of his own.

"Do you always wear that funny hat?" inquired Mary.

"Always except in my bath, and these skirts too. Old Mother Hubbard, don't you see? That's what you must call me."

They laughed delightedly. "How many children have you *got?*"

"None of my own. I go about stealing other people's. Look, I'll tell you a lark. You go and hide down the garden and I'll be Old Mother Hubbard coming to steal you."

"Oh, fine, fine!"

He turned to Gordon and Laura. "You've heaps to do which I interrupted. Do go off and just leave me with 'em to rag about a bit."

"Yes, *do* go, mother," from John.

"Yes, *do,* father," from Mary.

"Well, we will, you loving offspring," Laura laughed. "But, where's Philip?"

"He's up a tree."

"Up a tree! Heavens!"

"He's perfectly safe," Mary reassured. "He's wedged himself and as a matter of fact *can't* move."

"He would go," announced John, speaking as of one who brooked no forbidding. "We put him up a little way to *appease* him—"

"And he clung and roared," chimed in Mary, "till we simply had to let go of him and up he climbed—"

"And kicks at us when we go after him. He *is* an awful chap, mother."

"Tell him," directed Hope Hubbard, "that Mother Hubbard's coming after him." The pair raced away. Making to follow them, "I like that 'he *is* an awful chap,' " he laughed to the parents.

"Well, Philip certainly is a handful," said the vicar. "He's only four and a bit but what he can't do with his hands and feet, and the way he hectors everybody—"

"I call him the bo's'n," laughed Laura.

"Delicious! I'll love to know him. And that other boy, what a brow and eyes! You've got a brain there, Brecque, a dreamer of dreams."

"That's what I believe," Gordon said soberly.

"And Mary a picture, and that scrap an angel, and up the tree, refusing to come down, a four-year-old bo's'n. You've a quiver of treasures, you two. Good-by."

He hurried off. "Mother Hubbard coming! Look out for Mother Hubbard coming!"

"Quiver of treasures," Laura smiled to Gordon. "And, oh, listen to their happiness."

"And imagine them growing up in these surroundings."

"Imagine it!"

The vicar pointed towards the walled end of the Children's Piece. "Above all and before all I must get that wigwam for them."

Three

A VICAR newly coming to a parish is comparable with a commanding officer newly posted to a battalion or a captain to a ship. As a battalion is the unit of an army, a warship of a fleet, so is a parish the unit of the Church. Its vicar has officers under him ranging from his assistant priests and his churchwardens to his verger and the distributors of his parish magazine. He is responsible for the well-being, which here is to say the spiritual well-being, of his personnel. He is responsible also for the efficiency of his unit that it may fight its share in the endless campaign against darkness.

Of these two responsibilities the maintenance of the unit's militant efficiency is commonly the more thankless. St. Luke's previous incumbent had neglected it. To Gordon Brecque his parish's duty towards the needs of the mission field and of the diocese was a vital concern. "We must not want," he said in an early sermon, "to keep ourselves to ourselves; we must want to be an active part of the great whole to which we belong. We do not want, if I may use this illustration, our Bible at St. Luke's to be as one of the old-time chained Bibles. We want all outside these walls to share it with us."

His congregations, he found, were not so sure that they did want this. Laura, who had a lively aptitude for sensing the reaction to her husband's sermons of those among whom she sat, and always faithfully reported it, said that the pricking in her thumbs on this occasion set up the idea of a flock of sheep suddenly uneasy. "You remember that summer when you took duty at King's Malford and we were constantly meeting droves of sheep in the lanes. They'd come around a corner perfectly docile and contented and then see us by the roadside with the pram and the children and stop stiff and stare out of their ridiculous heads and be ready for two pins to bolt. That's the feeling I got during your sermon this morning. You gave them something they weren't in the least expecting and they stopped dead."

She laughed.

The vicar did not laugh. First, as she spoke, he looked doubtful. Then, as she finished, he said, "Ah, sheep in the Gospel's sense, and his doubtful look cleared. He sat bemused a moment. Then his eyes kindled. "But that's a better illustration," he said thoughtfully, "than you know. That happened when we met sheep which were being driven. But we noticed, don't you remember, how collectedly they went past anything when they were being led. Isn't that just what I've been sent here for, to lead?"

She touched his hand. "Dear you." But then she laughed again. "All the same, you'll have a job leading them down the Banks. They didn't like the Banks bit. That was where I could feel them going baa-a."

2

The "Banks bit," as she called it, was in fact the specific application of the sermon. First the vicar had generalized on apathy towards the extension of God's Kingdom, then he had instanced a field of extension "for our loving interest here at our own doors. A field which, though I have been talking to you of needs outside our parish, is in fact a part of our parish. I mean the Banks."

The Banks was to Upton Springs much what the Fields had been to Brodham Common. Upton Springs, with its surrounding area of pine and heather shown on the ord-

nance maps as "Upton Forest," occupied a part of the considerable plateau of a considerable hill. It had no railway-
station either on its level or of its name. The railway when
first it came to those parts preferred to go round the hill
instead of up and over it. Upton Springs of those days was
a mildly fashionable spa. Both actually and figuratively it
looked down upon the agricultural denizens of the railway's
valley. Both actually and figuratively also it considered itself,
with its barouches, phaetons, stanhopes, and what-not of
equipage, above the noisy, smelly and disfiguring steam
transport. Its hillside falling picturesquely down to this
abomination was known as the Banks. The railway, as it
were dropping a station with high respect and secrecy and
then scuttling away for its life, called the station Upton
Bank. As "the Banks" all its district came to be known, as
Bank Hill the long road connecting it with (in Banks
phraseology) "the Springs." The Banks was, in fact, the
working-class quarter of what, from once being a resort of
the fashionable for the purpose of taking the waters, now
was in main a resort of the retired for the purpose of taking
their ease. Of these a goodly proportion were comfortably
retired, rich widows not a few. They lived in very large,
very ornate houses with many servants and considerable
grounds. A proportion, not so comfortably retired and more
modestly housed, were pensioned military and naval officers,
civil servants and the like. They attracted their kind and
their kind were attracted also, on their children's behalf, by
the admirable educational facilities offered by Upton College and, for girls, Upton Academy.

Such was in general the composition of the parish of St.
Luke's as its new vicar found it. Mr. Phipps-Tracy had bequeathed to him, along with other personal memoranda for
his guidance, a map of the parish boundaries. Across the
Banks portion of this he had written in red pencil the word

"Wesleyan." Other notes on the map were inscribed neatly in ink. "Wesleyan" was done in a bold flowing script followed by a heavy full-stop and scored under with a sweeping line. The suggestion was of a red pencil snatched up, a demarcation dashed down, and a "That's that" put into the underscore.

". . . A field for our loving interest here at our own doors. . . . I mean the Banks." And he had gone on to speak of the desirability of establishing a mission-hall down there.

3

"And how many of the Church of England belonging to us do you think I found down there among the Wesleyans?"

It was to his churchwardens that he was posing the question. A first specific duty which he had set himself was to get to know, by personally calling upon, each and all of his parishioners. Debating from what point he should start, by force of habit when making a decision in his work he had asked himself, "What would Jesus do?" It was down the Banks that, next day, he started, and the district had taken him all of three weeks of evenings to complete. Its householders, he had found, were not at home till knocked off from their varied jobs after tea. Evening after evening he had footed it down Bank Hill at five o'clock, trudging up it again well after ten, very tired but very happy. Now he had completed his round in the district written off as "Wesleyan." Now, the Anglicans there enumerated, he had got his churchwardens round to the vicarage. Now, excited triumph rosy-tinging his face, "How many?" he was asking them.

"I'd say not a dozen."

This was his vicar's warden, Colonel Gilling. Colonel

Gilling was an Anglo-Indian with a yellow face, an impressive gray mustache and a parade-ground manner. He did everything as it were by numbers. When he unfurled his umbrella in the rain it was done, unmistakably, one! two! three! In church when about to pray, one! two! he went smartly on his knees. When counting the collections in the vestry, left, right, halt! he stabbed out the coins in their different denominations. His speech, too, had the sharp jerkiness of drill-book utterance. Thus he spoke his guess now, "I'd say not a: dozen," and he looked stiffly upon the people's warden, Mr. Burgess, as though about to give him a sharp "As you were!" if he should venture to think differently.

The vicar's triumph went rosier yet. "How many, Mr. Burgess?"

Mr. Burgess, a retired bank-manager, had a conspicuously white face, cropped whiskers and a fringe of beard, and steel-rimmed spectacles. With a timid manner he combined a pertinacious habit. Laura said that the impression he always gave you, whether in regard to a lump of seed-cake which he had taken by mistake at her tea table and obviously detested, or at a parochial meeting championing a case which was in clear disfavor, was that he had somehow got himself into this horrible position and, though trembling, would at all costs to himself maintain it. He greatly disliked Colonel Gilling, who highly despised him. Whatever the colonel said he instinctively opposed. Aware now that the vicar's warden scouted the notion that so few as a dozen professing members of the Church of England belonging to St. Luke's were to be found in the Banks, on principle he contradicted him. "I'd say twenty," he defied.

"Nearer," beamed the vicar, "but still miles away." He swelled himself with portentous geniality. "Fifty-seven."

"Never; nev: er," commanded the colonel.

"You really mean that?" fluttered Mr. Burgess.

The vicar nodded proudly. "Fifty-seven. And that's, mind you, the men. Add the wives, add the children, and there's a community down there belonging to us that's not short, I'd say, of two hundred, and growing. Let me tell you."

He told that he had called first on the Wesleyan minister, Mr. Apps.

The colonel started. "Called on: him?"

"Yes, indeed. It's a Wesleyan camp down there, you know—"

"A hot-bed."

"So I thought I'd better as it were call at headquarters before I began to spy out the land. I found him a delightful person."

Addressing himself to the colonel, "I've always heard that," said Mr. Burgess.

"Where?"

"Oh, round about."

The colonel expressed the value of this by a sharp rap with a paper-weight on the table at which they sat. "Yes, vicar?"

"He told me that certainly there were church people in the quarter, hard though he'd worked to convert them."

"He told you: that?"

"In the most genial way, of course."

"Of course, of course," agreed Mr. Burgess, clearly implying that anyone but Colonel Gilling would have understood that.

"They must have come," declared the colonel, with flash of reprimand at Mr. Burgess, "in the dark. Phipps-Tracy never: saw them."

As Mr. Phipps-Tracy had not in ten years, since inscribing that comprehensive "Wesleyan" on the map, visited the Banks except for the purpose of taking the train, it was clear that its Anglican inhabitants, if indeed they had stolen in, unseen by him, in the dark, had had a tolerable convenience of nights in which to do so. The vicar had heard something of the kind from Mr. Apps. He had characteristically discounted it and characteristically averted any suggestion of it now.

"Several that I visited had only come there quite recently," he said. "There's been a drifting in of employees from the railway works at Thurstead. The point is—"

"Point is why don't they attend: St. Luke's?"

"Well, it's a long way."

"Decidedly a long way," emphasized Mr. Burgess.

"Quarter of an hour, twenty minutes. Why, I've marched men, goodness gracious me, to divine service good half-hour in: blazing sun."

"Ah, marched them," the vicar smiled. "But to come voluntarily, up that hill, the men on their only day off, the wives with the Sunday dinner to cook. No, you can't, I think, expect them to come to the church. What I'm leading up to is that, now we have found them, we must take St. Luke's to them." He looked at his wardens with shining eyes. "We must build a mission-hall down there."

4

Such support as he got from his churchwardens at this first intimation of his project was obtained, not out of their sympathies, but out of their antipathies, Mr. Burgess's to Colonel Gilling, Colonel Gilling's to the Rev. Hope Hubbard. Mr. Burgess had been the first to speak. Not noticing that the colonel at the idea of building a mission-hall had been struck into a species of fit, himself greatly startled by the probabality of overdraft debt which his banking mind immediately envisaged, "But that is a very serious undertaking," he delivered himself; "a matter, vicar, which calls for the closest examination on every side. I—"

"Mission hall!" burst in the colonel, recovering speech and, as it were, causing the orderly-room to rock. "You must let me tell you, vicar, that wouldn't go down with St. Luke's: at all. I know these: mission-halls. I've had experience of them. They're a constant: drain. They're a drain moreover to a class which up here is regarded as having too much done for it as it is: far too much."

"I oppose that view," instantly declared Mr. Burgess, trembling. "I oppose it *in toto*. I do not agree that a mission-hall need be a drain. I have known them to be self-supporting. I do not agree that our worshipers regard the Banks class in the light submitted. I think that they have a considerable concern for the million. I reject Colonel Gilling's view *in toto*. I support the project."

He breathed hard up and down his nose. The colonel's nose, also in high agitation, appeared likely at any moment to emit fire. The vicar, struck perhaps by the sight, touched his own nose with his handkerchief and spoke conciliatorily.

"You may both be perfectly certain, need I say it, that I know well that this is not a thing to be entered upon without much circumspection. That is why I am so glad to have such experienced men as you to discuss it with. What I've found down there, you know, is not a general indifference to religious influence but definitely, in quite a number of cases, an inclination towards it. Some, if they have not actually gone over to Wesleyanism, attend services under Mr. Apps to hear his sermons. His addresses have a great reputation apparently. Others, an increasing number so I gather, go to St. Monica's—"

The colonel staged an officer who has had the misfortune to sit on one of his spurs. "St. Monica's!"

"There's a cut across the slope apparently which makes St.

Monica's definitely much nearer than St. Luke's. Mr. Hope Hubbard—"

"Hope Hubbard!" The staging was now that of a commanding officer springing out of bed—"The enemy!"—and buckling on his sword.

"Hope Hubbard's practices," continued the vicar amiably, "his free seats, his, his decorative ritual, his, so I am told, denunciations of the sins of the rich and personal welcoming of the very poor—a habit, as I was told, of standing in his porch while his congregation is assembling—appear to appeal very much to our Banks people. He visits them."

"How dare he?"

"Dare?" trembled Mr. Burgess. "Why shouldn't he?"

"Because he's taking them," rapped the colonel, "to Rome. What you tell me, vicar, is the most alarming thing I have heard for: years. This Hope Hubbard; this scandal up and down the country of all good churchmen; this, this idolater whose association with Upton Springs has caused Upton Springs to be looked at: askance—that he should dare to, to suborn our parishioners; that his, his cloven hoof should imprint itself across our Banks! He must be fought, vicar. He must be counteracted. We must go down there. I will tell you what we must do. We must have: an outpost there. We must establish: a mission-hall there."

5

If in the persons of his churchwardens Mr. Phipps-Tracy had devised to his successor two supporters of the mission-hall project whose support was of equivocal foundation, in the person of his curate he had handed on to Gordon Brecque one who accorded it a wholehearted enthusiasm.

The Rev. Richard Oadbee—"Dick Oadbee" at Cambridge where he had just missed a cricket Blue, and almost immediately at the vicarage table—was a boyish-faced young man whose greatest difficulty in the Church was to comport himself during a service with the solemn carriage appropriate to his part. When called upon to take the lectern or the pulpit he would, if he forgot himself, spring from his place with the suggestion of a boxer from his corner, then remember himself, stop abruptly and proceed with, by comparison, exaggerated decorum. Similarly forgetful, he would begin his reading or his discourse on a startlingly high, quick note, recollect himself, blush, and as startlingly drop to a husky whisper. Laura loved him for it. The vicar, himself an ardent soul but of an inherently gentle disposition, found a tonic effect in his irrepressible virility.

His ultimate intention in his calling was to enter the foreign mission service, specifically, as he told the vicar and Laura when at tea early after their arrival, to go out to Patagonia.

"Why Patagonia in particular?" Laura questioned.

"Because my father was done to death by the natives out there."

"Done to death—murdered?"

The boyish face smiled boyishly. "Well, 'done to death,' I prefer to call it. He was a missionary. He went upcountry where no missionary, no white man, I believe, had been before. He thought he was doing well. I've got marvelous letters he wrote to my mother. I'd like to show them to you one day. And then there was a sudden turn against him and they killed him."

John was at the meal. "Are you going out to kill them back?" he asked gravely.

Dick Oadbee laughed. "No, I'm going out to cure them. That's better than killing, John; always you remember it. Isn't it, vicar?

"I know the tribe," he went on. "I know the name of the

chief who was responsible for the attack on my father. His son rules now and the tribe's as intractable, I've heard, as ever it was. Well, I'm going out as soon as ever I can to do for that son and his people what my father tried to do for his father."

"Jolly fine," breathed Laura.

"Splendid, Oadbee," said the vicar.

Philip the bo's'n was playing with soldiers on the floor, unnoticed but apparently noticing. "What did they kill your father with?" he called. "Guns or swords?"

"Hulloa, young man. No, with clubs and spears, I expect. They're savages."

"Well, I'd go with a gun and sword and shoot their heads off and then chop them up."

"Oh, shut up, Philip," commanded John, while the others laughed. "You're always killing."

"I was of Philip's idea," said Dick Oadbee, "when I was a kid, red-hot. I was eight when it happened, and right up to when I was about sixteen that was my private intention, to go out with a gun and seek out the chap and tell him who I was and let him have it, with the butt-end, I always hoped. But I had a dream, vivid as an actual happening. It was the first night of a holidays. I'd been looking, as I always did when I got back, at my father's things, and lay awake when I got to bed doing my ferocious butt-end act. Then I dreamt that I was out there and met my father and that he took away my gun and gave me a cross. And ever since then—" and Dick Oadbee laughed his boyish laugh and asked if he might have more tea.

He had not gone out yet, he told them, because he was not going to enroll for the mission-field while his mother lived. A permanent invalid and entirely supported by her son, Mrs. Oadbee lived with him in the shabby apartments which he rented. A familiar spectacle in Upton Springs was that of the curate of St. Luke's taking his mother about, at racing speed, in a wheeled chair.

When the vicar spoke to him of the Banks mission-hall idea, the offer of the bishopric of Patagonia could scarcely have outdone the excitement he showed. "If we can do it it will have to be almost entirely your show," the vicar said. Dick Oadbee swung his strong arms in the exuberance of his delight. Mr. Phipps-Tracy had severely repressed him, controlling his work as if he had been a newly ordained deacon. "Your show," a mission show at that, was to him as an open field to a colt after harness schooling. That very afternoon he whirled his mother down to the Banks. She was twice down and up Bank Hill the next day and the next, he nightly repeating the journey alone. A week had not passed when tumultuous he burst in upon the vicar.

"Vicar, could we rise to the hire of a little old workshop down there, to start in? I've found the very place. It's a wooden affair in a disused builder's yard. I say, vicar, do you think we could? If we're going to build, and to wait till we raise the money to do so, it'll lose us all of a year, p'r'aps more. If we started with this workshop we could start next week. I'd put up three quid myself, I'm that keen. I say, *could* we?"

This was poured out in a continuity offering no chance of interposition. The vicar had caught fire with the opening words. At the concluding he was as aglow almost as Dick Oadbee.

"Oadbee, it's done," he cried. "It won't begin and end with fifteen pounds, of course, but if I have to get it out of my own pocket we'll have it. What about my coming down right away to see it and clinch it?"

Dick Oadbee snatched for his hat. "Come on!"

6

On the evening of the Friday week following was held the first meeting in the cobbler's hut, on the yard gates of which Oadbee had painted from a pot of white enamel—

St. Luke's Mission Hall.

The meeting, recruited for by Oadbee by door-to-door invitation, drew five married couples, three courting couples, an old man who had thought it was something to do with the muzzling order, an old lady with a pair of shoes to mend, two youths who had understood there was to be a magic lantern show, "same as the Wesleyans" and, somewhat mysteriously, a small boy who had lost a top.

They were received by St. Luke's in full force, by the vicar, Oadbee and Laura. The small boy whose top, it appeared, had been lost in the yard, trotted off completely happy with tuppence to buy a new one. The old lady, informed of the cobbler's departure, was bidden to stop and warm the shoes she wore at the stove. The old man, likewise bidden to rest now that he was here, was promised a dog muzzle which the vicar knew to be in his gardener's shed. And presently, by chatty, unobtrusive means, the little assembly was divided into two groups. Oadbee, who had twice played against W. G. Grace, got the men deeply interested in cricket stories. Laura, somehow drawing the women about her, talked babies, cooking and dressmaking tips. The vicar moved from group to group until in some half an hour an opportunity occurred to draw the general attention and to begin cheerily with, "Well, what we've really come here to talk about—"

He sketched out "a little St. Luke's down here of our own." He announced a short service next Sunday morning at ten o'clock (giving the energetic Oadbee time to speed back to St. Luke's for matins at 11.15). He spoke of the use of the hall for men's meetings, for women's meetings, for a children's play hour, and "as we get on" for penny-readings and all manner of jolly socials. He suggested another gathering at this same hour on Monday. Those present were invited to bring their friends. There would be a general discussion of plans "and we'll elect ourselves into committees and officers and all sorts of interesting jobs." He suggested that they should close now with a prayer and a hymn and that then he and his wife and Mr. Oadbee would go off and leave them to have a bit of a talk about it all. Who would like to make himself responsible for turning out the lamp, locking up and holding the key?

With the motion of one about to start in a race and determined to win it, a brisk-looking matron on the front bench twisted herself about to look for rivals, then jumped to her feet. "Well, me an' my 'usbing, glad and willing, mister; an' I take the chance, speaking for all as well I knows I do, to say that this here's going to be a proper good 'appiness for us, an' you give us the services and what not an' we'll come to 'em an' welcome, as you might say."

" 'Ear, 'ears," murmurings of cordial assent and a strongly sympathetic shuffling by way of chorus, gave a resonant delight to the vicar's voice as now he made his prayer.

Lustily they were swinging along through the second verse of "Onward, Christian Soldiers," when the vicar, looking across their heads to the window behind them, espied the face of Hope Hubbard pressed against the pane. Hubbard's eyes, when he saw himself noticed, went wide in comically exaggerated amazement. With nods of genial significance the vicar sent the message, "What do you think of this?"

What Hope Hubbard thought, grinning broadly, he pantomimed by vigorously shaking one hand with the other. "Congratulating us, d'you see?" said the vicar, recounting this, as exuberant with their success, Oadbee, Laura and he trod homewards up Bank Hill together. "What I *didn't* understand, though, was what he did next. We were thundering 'Hell's foundations quiver,' and he pointed to himself, pulled down the corners of his mouth in the most comical fashion, turned up his coat collar, hunched his shoulders and sort of, but it couldn't of course have been that, sort of slunk away."

"Oh, delicious," laughed Laura; and "Oh, lovely," Oadbee.

"Delicious? Lovely?" The vicar turned questioning head from one to the other.

"Dearest, don't you see? The outrage he's held to be with his ritualism and Rome and all that; and then don't you remember what you told me that Colonel Gilling said—poaching. He was pantomiming himself as caught out in his little tricks and slinking away."

The vicar stopped dead. "Really? But, dear me, 'Hell's foundations,' and I was singing it most lustily and smiling at him as I sung. He surely couldn't have imagined that I was aiming it at him?"

"Yes, that's just what he was pretending," Oadbee laughed.

"The cream of the joke," declared Laura.

"Really? A joke; you're quite sure?" He gave a little laugh. "Yes, I think I understand it now. He thought, is that it, that, just in fun of course, I was sort of saying, 'Shoo! Go away with your tricks.' Really? Dear me, I'm afraid I'm very slow at seeing jokes."

Laura had his arm. She squeezed it. "Dearest, that's why the right people love you so much."

7

In a sense she was right. It was his simplicity that caused him gradually to earn the love of what were perhaps the "right" people. Jokes are subtleties of thought. He could not see them because he had no subtlety. He was not ingenious. He was ingenuous. When he delivered his text in his pulpit he would invariably, before he began to expound it, pause a moment smiling down upon his people. He had only one dogma, that God was love; that love, when all-embracing, was God.

At least in their simplicity of thought and diction all his sermons created among those to whom he ministered as it were a little heart of response within a husk of indifference. At St. Luke's he was seeking to serve God among a social class unrepresented in his previous experience in Orders. In the Fields at Brodham his people had been shabby, at Knipstone rough. Here he found himself among a people (above the Banks) of means; some of greater, some of less, but none without. They were leisured. Their chief preoccupation was to fill their time.

The emptiness of these people of Upton Springs was, in fact, a spiritual emptiness. Hope Hubbard, with those gleaming eyes of his observing it among his own following from his own pulpit of St. Monica's, with that pungent tongue of his scourged it. The vicar of St. Luke's, seeing good, and only good, in all, felt towards his sufferers from it as feels a fond parent towards the child whom illness keeps in bed. There was the sunshine outside. Here was the sufferer unable to enjoy it. Draw back the curtains, open wide the casements, wheel the cot to the window. Have love for all in your heart. Give entry thus to Christ. Realize then the surging within you of His strength.

The core of response which thus he created pulsed and gladdened him. The husk as it were drew the blankets over its head. A Bagge clique, a Phipps-Tracy clique and a Gilling clique joined forces in a general invidious contrast between him and his predecessor. It was epitomized in the fact that they spoke of the former vicar's "methods," of the present incumbent's "ways." Mr. Phipps-Tracy used to go about always in a tall silk hat. It suggested authority and he liked authority. He "ran the parish." The husk liked that. Colonel Gilling particularly liked it. It smacked of the orderly room. It enabled him to feel his office, and to conduct it as, that of adjutant.

In hat low, soft and of felt, the succeeding commanding officer, on the contrary, setting afoot many new activities, aimed to make St. Luke's parochial societies run themselves, himself urbanely, helpfully, in the background. He was for ever (as the husk said) bothering people to take an interest in them, "to undertake service in our parish" as he put it. Colonel Gilling, questioned by the husk as to his feeling about all this, gave his vicar that form of loyalty which is expressed by, "It is not for me to criticize."

Here were uphill stretches in this the first of the two periods, divided by the coming of the Great War of 1914-18, into which the vicar's ministry at St. Luke's was to fall. It knew also rich joys. In that period he brought to confirmation boys and girls on whose foreheads, as infants, he had inscribed with water the sign of his Saviour. He married those whom, earlier in his coming, he had prepared for the supreme rite of communion, lovingly administering it to them on their first general participation in it. He performed the last offices of the Church over the bodies of those whom he had known lusty in life, with whom he had had friendship, into whose hearts perhaps he had brought that quality, simply attained and wondrous in attainment, which was his preaching.

These are intimacies of human relationship such as only the priests of the Churches of God can reach. They are the rewards for a service which knows no material reward. To their recipients they bring a happiness no more realizable in material prosperity than the happiness given by love is realizable in material possessions.

Outstandingly this happiness was felt by the vicar of St. Luke's. If in this first period he had one not fully satisfied emotion it was that common regret of devoted priests who are also fathers of families that he could not devote himself as fully as he would to his children, that on his means he could not, further, do for them what he would. Nevertheless, it was in his children, in those two boys and in those two girls, that his heart beat.

Four

THOSE two boys, John and Philip, were as different from one another in character, in temperament and in tastes as if they were of different families. They did derive, indeed, from different strains. It had often been said of Laura that she ought to have been a boy. In her earlier years she had said it herself, sometimes had rather wished it. Philip took after his mother.

John was of his father's habit. Even in his nursery days he was gentle, quiet, tractable. He copied nothing of the vicar's limitations in sense of fun. Unusually quick at the uptake, as quite a little boy he would be laughing appreciatively at some family riposte or drollery, and laughing delightedly at his father's struggles with it, while still the vicar tried to see the connection. But, like his father, he never sought his own. In a crossing of wishes with Philip or with Mary, what game to play, what pudding to choose, he always gave way. He liked much to be alone, to sit and read, to get away down the garden and stand and gaze at things, at birds, at flowers, insects, clouds; but when Philip would come rushing, or Mary come calling, or Ruth come eagerly toddling, he always, with something of the vicar's smile, would detach himself from his preoccupation. "Oh, rather. Of course I will," he would say to their demands.

He was an insatiable reader; when being read to as a child a disturbingly perspicacious listener. When he was but four Laura read him one day bits of "The Water Babies." It became his favorite book. Before he could read it to himself he would watch her face while she read. Immediately she skipped because she thought a passage dull for him, or improvised her own words because she thought Kingsley's too difficult, unerringly he would detect her lapse. "You're missing, mother; you're missing." "Mother, you're making up. Read it, do read it." It was the same with Hans Andersen, the same with the "Pilgrim's Progress," two other volumes which fascinated him as did no others. "You're missing . . . you're making up . . . read it, do read it."

His acuteness in this observation of her face while she read used to make Laura laugh. "I come to an impossible dullness for him or to impossible language," she would tell the vicar, "some of the Hans Andersens are pretty well all descriptive, and you know how advanced for a child 'Pilgrim's Progress' can be. I can't help skipping or making up, and immediately I do I feel those eyes of his narrowing at me in that adorable way he has, and I begin to giggle, and in a flash he's at me. 'Read it, do read it.' But—"

"But how he understands!" filled in the vicar.

She would smile. "Matter of fact, 'but *what* he understands' was nearer to what I was going to say. What it is precisely that he gets out of it, I mean. He'll have some of the Hans Andersens over and over again. It's not for the actual story, I'm positive. It's for something, I believe, that he dreams into them. Same with—"

"Ah, he has a great head, that John," Minna from her pile of stockings to mend would join in, profoundly nodding her head. "I will not mean brains so much. Philip, he has pot of brains, that rascal. Oh, my mercy, has he not! I will mean for John a great mind, a great thinking. The questions he will ask me, the look of his eyes he will put upon me when I make try to answer him! 'There is more than that' his look will tell me. 'I am seeing,' it will say to me, 'what you cannot see. I see the pictures, I hear the music. They are behind it, and muffled up, but they are there. I see them, I listen to them. What they mean I do not know. But I know them that they are there. One day I will understand them.'"

And Minna would profoundly nod again. "He will be the great mind when he grows," she would nod. "Huge; you mark me what I have said."

Hope Hubbard, when he first saw him, had said much the same as these two women. "What a brow and eyes! You've got a brain there, Brecque, a dreamer of dreams" his words had been.

None would have said anything of the kind of Philip. In physical characteristics as in mental, the brothers were markedly different. John's hair lay smoothly on his head. Philip's was a curly mop. Both had gray eyes; but John's, rather deep set, a misty gray, were apt to be somber; Philip's were a steely gray, invariably shining. Across Philip's face "Mischief" was written in glowing pinks and browns. Across John's, in pale lettering, "Thought" was inscribed.

Four years stood between the pair. Philip was always at least half-way up the separating rungs. When he was four and John eight "He *is* an awful chap, mother," John had declared. That had been relative to his ferocious kicking when being dislodged from a tree. When he was eight and John twelve he was not easy for John to master, to race or to wrestle. When he was twelve and John sixteen most pickers-up of athletic sides would have picked the younger before the elder.

"The bo's'n" had been Laura's epithet for Philip, and that when he was only four. It was in the elder's fourteenth year that she came out with an epithet for John, frequently using it thereafter. He was in bed with one of the sick headaches to which he was then very subject. They were crashing affairs, never attributable to food. After excitement, after long reading, often with no apparent cause whatever, they would swoop upon him, utterly prostrating him. "Megrims," the doctor called them. "Just nervous attacks. He'll grow out of 'em." Bed, a darkened room, hot-bottle to his feet, were the only remedies.

On this particular occasion he had asked his mother, crept in before she went to a duty tea-party, to bring him up some sheets of paper she would find in his desk in the play-room, and a pencil, and leave them by his bed. He was forever scribbling now in his spare time, and as she carried out his wish she read two sheets on which he had written. At what she read she smiled, and, as she placed the papers by his bed, essayed some pleasantries to try to cheer him. "I say, I read those. You didn't mind, did you? I say, they're jolly good, old man, jolly good. Is that what it is you're always writing?"

"Oh, mum, I'm too frightfully bad to talk."

"We'll talk about them when I come back, darling. They really are jolly fine."

Verses were the "those," the "them" and the "they" of her reference; and it was when, two hours later, she returned, that she greeted him for the first time with her epithet for him.

"Well, how's the poet?"

Time was to prove her prophetic in both her appellations for her boys.

2

The vicar put them both, as their due times arrived, first to a local preparatory school, "Kilbracken," then to the College. Than that of his choice, there were better prep. schools in the town, one outstanding. Upton House, as this was called, ranked as high among preparatories as did the College among public-schools. It had impressive buildings and spacious playing-fields. A hundred and twenty boys were its quota, largely for Eton and Harrow. At half-term, when parents came down, its headmaster, Mr. Bartlett, a large, rather pompous man, moved about among the nobility and other bearers of famous names and in everyday life was somewhat given to familiar reference to them.

From his early knowledge of Upton Springs the vicar well remembered the spacious lay-out of Upton House and would immensely have liked to put John there. The fees, he found, were, however, far too high. When Mr. Bartlett told them to him, "I'd be sending my little chap as a day-boy, though," he said hopefully. "No doubt for day-boys—"

"Ah," said Mr. Bartlett, rising from his chair with the mingled kindliness and firmness of a familiar with the great who has given all the time he can afford to the lowly, "Ah, I'm afraid that we don't take day-boys. Our parents wouldn't like it. St. Cuthbert's does, I believe. So, I think—I say I think—does St. Hilary's. Quite pleasant little places both of them, I understand. *Good* morning, my dear Mr. er, Mr.—"

"Brecque," prompted the vicar, smiling.

"Treck," said the Headmaster who was composing in his mind a letter to a baronet. "*Good* morning."

Fees of St. Cuthbert's and St. Hilary's proved also higher than the vicar and Laura, anxiously debating, felt that they should spend. After all, the boys were going on to a really splendid place at the College. Grounding at "Kilbracken" (which derived its name from its gate, never had managed to shake off its inverted commas when referred to in the local Press, took only day-boys, and charged accordingly) was probably, said the vicar, just as good as at the others.

"Probably a jolly sight better," declared Laura. "Stuck-up little wretches at those other places, Upton House especially, what I've seen of them. And I took a great fancy to that little Mr. Needham."

"So did I," agreed the vicar. "All right, 'Kilbracken' it

shall be. All the same—" and he thought of the grounds, the chapel, the gym and the swimming-bath at Upton House, and of his dear boy John, and would have sighed had he been given to sighing.

So with Mr. Needham at "Kilbracken" first John, then Philip, started school life.

3

John did quite well at "Kilbracken." Its three masters and some forty boys comprised a simple, happy little school. It did not pay great attention to games. Its playing-field, a rough enclosure only recognizable from a grazing meadow by its goalposts or cricket pitch, was a mile from the school-house. Games there were in the nature of as-you-like exercise rather than strictly umpired contests. Sides were picked up. No matches were played. The school playing-ground was more popular as arena than the field. Here 'Prisoners' Base," "Cross-if-you-can," tip and run, and improvised football with a lawn-tennis ball were enthusiastically sported.

This suited John. He was immensely happy in go-as-you-please recreation like this, where no dexterity was required and blunders were part of the fun. When he came to go on to the College, games presented themselves to him as a very different matter. When it became necessary, as sharply it was necessary at Upton, to catch or to kick a ball adroitly, in the gym to swing on a bar or to vault a horse with grace and finish, he suffered poignantly in a total inability thus to perform. His hands when he tried to catch were all thumbs and holes. His feet when he made to kick were all shins and ankles. In the gymnasium his arms and legs appeared able to do nothing with his body. Games were a fetish at the College. In his performance of them he was mocked, he was cursed, he was despised. They were a haunting terror to him.

At the College, further, even his work, which at "Kilbracken" he rather enjoyed, became a trial to him. At "Kilbracken" his studies had shown decided aptitude, definite
promise. He was in the top form when a full year beneath
its average age. Mr. Needham, one of whose subjects was
English, told the vicar term after term that in English—in
history, in composition, in literature—the boy was much
above any he had previously taught. At Upton, however,
English took care of itself. At Upton you applied yourself
to the subjects that mattered, chiefly to the dead languages,
and John's application to Latin and Greek was, as the College masters said in his reports, indifferent, to mathematics
worse. "Dreams instead of applying his mind." "Too often
dreaming when he should be concentrating."

"Dreams," "Dreaming," were recurrent in his tutors' esti-
mates of his capabilities while he passed through what was
to him the ordeal of the College lower forms. Hope Hubbard had noticed the signs; Laura, when reading to him,
had observed them. Mr. Needham, enthusiastic to the vicar
over the boy's English work, had spoken of the predilection:
"He's eating up poetry now; you know that of course? Have
you noticed, though, how, in the sort of poetry he reads, it's
the descriptive stuff, not the action, that seems to get him,
and how he dreams over it?"

Yes, that *was* funny, Laura and the vicar had agreed, observing him, soon after his start at "Kilbracken," absorbed
in poetical narratives, and noticing the parts that appealed
to him. His school reading-primer had introduced him to
metrical form. It had excerpts from "Horatius" and from
"The Lady of the Lake." John had so thrilled to these that
Mr. Needham had lent him first Macaulay's Lays then a
selection of those of Scott. And the funny thing was, as his
parents said, that the passages which they remembered from

their youth, and now sought out for him to show him how stirring they were, attracted him not at all. In "Horatius":

> Then, like a wild cat mad with wounds,
>   Sprang right at Astur's face.

and all the rest of the superb fighting at the mouth of the bridge, moved him not at all. He appeared, if anything, not to like it. "Yes, but, father," he would cry, and take the book, "listen to this. Oh, listen:

> From lordly Volaterrae,
>   Where scowls the far-famed hold
> Piled by the hands of giants
>   For godlike kings of old;
> From sea-girt Populonia,
>   Whose sentinels descry
> Sardinia's snowy mountain-tops
>   Fringing the southern sky."

When he read passages such as this the book would be seen to be shaking in his hands. His voice would catch. The vicar and Laura would see the corners of his mouth strained downwards as they remembered him straining them when, as a very little chap, suffering some disappointment or hurt, he was "trying not to blub."

At the time of these particular readings he was but eleven. They were pictures of him which, all his life, the vicar never forgot.

He was wrapped up in John. As with the pictures of him reading from his first books of poetry, so ever remained with him the memory of the boy racing back from his first day at "Kilbracken," cheeks crimson, eyes glittering. "Father, father, I've got a desk of my own with a lid that opens. At lunch we had beef, and the boy next to me put mustard on his tongue and made *such* a funny face. We played a game called 'Cross-if-you-can' and once I had to start it in the middle by myself. We did sums called fractions and, do you know, father, the bigger it is under the line the smaller it is really. And, father, I've got home work to do, and do look at my books. And, father . . ."

It was mostly "father." His mother was entirely in the picture but it was to the vicar that his direct addresses were made. As he was, all his life, his father's dearest, and as in his quiet, yielding-to-others disposition he derived from his father, so, all his life, it was to his father that he instinctively turned.

4

It was to his father that, when the time came to leave "Kilbracken" and join the College, the boy confided—"You tell mother, will you?"—his wish not to go as a boarder. Day-boys were taken at Upton. The difference between the fees charged for them and for boarders was, as the vicarage counted money, immense. But the vicar had determined that, involve what screwing down in other expenditures it might, his eldest should have the fullest privileges of public-school life. "Dear old Philip," he had said to Laura, "I'm afraid we shan't be able to afford it for him when his time comes. We couldn't possibly afford the two, and I know we oughtn't really to do it for the one. But, Laura, I would like it for John, for our eldest child. Day-boys don't have *quite* the same time."

The chancellor of the vicarage exchequer wholeheartedly agreed. "Oh, rather, we must, for John." She laughed. "For your John. I'll manage it somehow. You leave it to me. We *must.*"

The time came and, very surprisingly to the vicar, the reluctance came. "Father, I really and truly would rather not be a boarder. I do like coming home every day to see you—and mother too and the others, of course," he added with childhood's naivety. "I do like sitting here in the evening doing my home-work with you at your table. I look forward to that. And I do like more than anything"—his youthful artlessness spoke again—"being alone in my own room at night. You know what a joy it was to me when mother said I might stop sharing with Philip and have the little dressing-room to myself. I lie awake there, father, as I've often told you, when I go to bed and in the morning, and it is such a *private* time to me. I couldn't possibly do that in a dormitory. *Do* let me not go as a boarder, father."

"But, my dear old boy," the vicar said, "you don't know, you really don't, what you'll be losing. I'll miss our jolly evenings in here together as much as you will. I'm hating the thought of it. But I would hate much more to think of your losing all the jolly companionship, and the topping rags, and the hour after evening prep. with your stamp-albums and your games, and the dormitory larks, that boarders have. Day-boys don't begin to get the real fun out of a public-school. They really don't. Old man, you haven't any idea—"

Unusually, it was this time his mother who understood him the more deeply. The vicar, as bidden, broke the news to Laura. "You know what I am about him," he said, "what he is to me. To let him go as day-boy would mean continuing to have him with me every day and I'm biased. You talk with him and decide, dearest."

Laura talked with him long and affectionately. They went a whole afternoon's walk together through the forest, sometimes she linking his arm, sometimes hand in hand. They had tea at "The Creamery," an enormous treat. But she had decided in the hall before they started. As they readied themselves, "Father has told me you think you'd rather be a day-boy when you start at the College, end of this hols," she said. "That's what I vote we talk about."

"Mother, I would; oh, much, much rather."

She gazed upon him the space of a long moment. Her eyes read his spirit on pages which previously she had never turned and which the vicar, for all his unity with the boy, with his slowness of mind perhaps was unable to read. She stooped and kissed him on the mouth. "Darling, you shall be a day-boy."

He threw his arms about her. "Oh, mother, mother."

5

There are those, no doubt, who would question the wisdom of the decision. In days to come the vicar's elder son presented himself as one of a class upon which popular opinion had no contumely too savage to pour. There were residents of Upton Springs, Colonel Gilling prominent among them, who declared then that if he had been put as a boarder at the College instead of being "milksopped up" at home "this would never have happened."

It was, nevertheless, to the full of his capacity, and something beyond it, that as day-boy he enjoyed those peculiar benefits of Upton which the colonel at least had particularly in mind. In the conventional use of the expression he was "half-killed" in his early terms.

Upton was no girls' school. Old Boys looking back on it were fond of saying that it was "a rough house." They said this while nodding their heads meaningly and they said it rather proudly. One likes other men, especially younger men, to think that one has been through the hoop in one's day.

Upton's specialty was "Toggers." Toggers was a horseplay ritual handed down generation by generation. When he had graduated out of it, which took your first three terms, every Lower School boy saw to it that those arriving behind him were similarly put through the course, in Upton speech were "togged."

One rite of Toggers was to be made to run the thirty-foot length of an ancient five-foot boundary wall. Chaps incommoded your legs with cricket stumps, essaying to bring you down, and more often than not succeeding. It was not permitted to catch at a gauntlet-runner's legs with your hands. To do that was "loutish." If caught doing it you might be made to run the wall yourself. Upton was frightfully down on "loutishness."

Another rite was to learn by heart and sing with aplomb three long and rather vulgar Lower School songs. There were some dozen of these rites. Some were brutish, some depended on ridicule for the entertainment they provided. All were sanctified by tradition. All were excused, if any practitioner ever thought to excuse them, by the principle of "same for one same for all."

There was no qualifying out of them except by time. At any moment, and however often he had previously performed, a first-yearer might be called upon to be put through a rite. Popular boys, which generally was to say spirited boys, were rarely victimized after having once been through the complete ritual. At the wall rite Philip, when his turn came to join Upton, created history, howls of delighted laughter, and immense popularity by grabbing a cricket-stump from one of the earliest of his dissuaders and gleefully lamming at knuckles and heads as he pursued his course. John to the last day of his third term was still being togged.

In his first term there was rarely a day, in his third never a week, in which he was not put through a rite, sometimes three or four on the string.

He never, while he was at Upton, told his parents of the togging. After he had left—when, with his back to the wall, he stood in the crisis of his life—he instanced Toggers to the vicar as an illustration of the principles he was combating, and told then for the first time what he had suffered under it. While at the College he sometimes would bring home marks of the ritual, bruises, torn clothes. But by "Oh, ragging, you know" he would explain them.

"Well, it's funny to me," pronounced Laura to Gordon, more than once discussing this, "what a lot of this ragging he seems to do. He definitely isn't the ragging type, as Philip is. And it's not only his clothes and that. It's what we've both noticed, and Minna too, in his manner since he's been at the College. Dearest, you don't think he's being bullied, do you?"

"It's crossed my mind," the vicar assented. "I've wondered several times. But he declares he isn't. I've asked him."

"So have I."

"I'll ask him again, this evening."

"Please do. He's more ready to confide in you, you know, than in me."

But when, as each worked in the study that night, the vicar made his inquiry, "Dear old boy, there's a thing I want to ask you, I've asked it before, I know—you're not being bullied up there, are you?"

"No, I'm not, father," was the reply he received. "Things are pretty rough, of course, sometimes. You told me I might find them so before I went. But there's nothing done to me that isn't done to everyone else. I promise you that, father."

While he was undergoing it it never, therefore, came out. And he passed presently into Upper School and, moving up it, drew away further and further from the diversions of the bear pit.

The early period set, however, its life mark upon him. The refuges to which, by its suffering, his mind was driven, acted as forcing ground for the qualities which already were in his instincts. On the lines on which he was to develop he developed early.

When he left the school gates of an evening he abandoned

himself into his "dreaming" with a completeness, with an almost physical embracing of it, such as probably his spirit never could have encompassed had it not been driven there as a hunted animal into its place of security. He was then but thirteen and fourteen. As he stepped from the gates into the country road on which they opened, he would gaze upon, he would ecstatically greet, the hedge before him, the trees, the ditch, the grasses, the very pebbles at the roadside, with feelings that drew forth for him tongues from trees, books from the running brooks, sermons from stones. With no conscious planning of his own, nature, thus embraced, made crude verse and sang to him. Its freedom was a song it tuned for him; also its haplessness. It was for man's delight, it rhymed to him, but also it was at man's caprice, frequently wanton.

The verses which Laura had found for him—"Well, how's the poet?"—were his transcribings of these songs.

6

When he got his remove into Upper School he had the run of the College library. This was a fine apartment, richly stocked. He now was able to sit in it and to browse. History had been his star subject at "Kilbracken." Conspicuously neglected in Lower School, it had comprised for him in both places English history in highly compressed text-books. In Upper School the subject recognized other developments of the course of human affairs than those only of the British Isles. In the library his innate predilection for the records of man's struggle through the ages transported him, fascinated, through histories not written that their readers might gain marks in examination-papers. They were contributions to knowledge but they were also, in the rarefied sense, literature. In both dimensions they enchanted him.

When he was sixteen he one day asked the vicar, "Father, shall I be able to go to Oxford or to Cambridge when I'm old enough?"

The vicar winced. Working out sums on pencil and paper with Laura, he often had thought about this. "My dear old boy, I'd love you to more than anything in the world. It's a question of means, you know."

"I know it is." Something was pumping a suppressed excitement into the boy. His face showed it. The vicar could almost feel its throbs. "I know it is. Father, would a hundred and twenty a year make a difference to it?"

"A hundred and twenty! My boy, a load of difference."

"Well, listen. An Old Boy who died the other day has left in his will a history scholarship to Wadham—"

The vicar leapt to the implications here. "A *history* scholarship!" he cried.

"History. My one subject, as you know. Every other schol. in the College is classics or maths. This is history, history! It's for three years, a hundred and twenty a year. It was announced in Big School by the Head today. That's why today I've asked you. Oh, father, if I could get that!"

The vicar took the news to his thinking things over on his knees that night: his boy's delight in working for this gift which the College had received, "inspired, as are all selfless gifts, by Thee . . . his happiness in thought of life at Oxford . . . his entry perhaps 'through Oxford into Thy service. . . .'"

He and Laura remained long awake in the darkness eagerly discussing.

7

John got the scholarship.

When he went to Oxford life changed for him as for one released from long imprisonment and greeted at the prison gate by friends. Here were sets, and immediately he found them, which though they played games made games no fetish. Here were men with dispositions kindred to his own.

He took up rowing. He delighted in it. His physique improved enormously. The vicar, Laura, Minna, Hope Hubbard, declared, vacation by vacation, that they would never have known him, so wonderfully had he developed in stature and in spirits. He proved himself an oarsman. He got into his College boat. Associations in this activity enlarged him among new, lively groups of friends. He was a changed man.

But in his principles and in his aspirations he was unchanged. In these his growth of intellect confirmed him.

This and that event in international affairs turned his set's discussions sometimes on war. He was always in a very small minority here, for with war he would have nothing to do. "I couldn't commit a murder," he would say. "In no conceivable circumstances would I take the life of a fellow-being. War is organized murder."

"Here, but wait a minute," a companion would cry. "That's rot. That's going too far. In no conceivable circumstances, you say. What about this liberty, this freedom from oppression you're always gassing about? You'd fight for that, man."

"I'd stand for it to death, to my own death. I'd never take a life for it."

"Well, what about invasion, man?" another would join in. "This absolutely terrific play 'An Englishman's Home' that you won't go to see. You'd fight then; if we were invaded; if your own home was attacked?"

"You're confusing the argument," he would reply. "You're confusing the policeman and the soldier. If there was no organized murder there'd be no organized invasion. Individual ruffianism I daresay there'll always be, and always,

naturally, the individual attacked will protect himself. I'd
help the police to restrain ruffianism. I'd help no army to
prosecute war. We're all fellow-creatures. At the back of
one side or the other in a war there'd be someone who was
using us for his own personal purposes. There'd be none
of us killing each other if it wasn't for him. Well, I'll kill
for no man. I *can't* kill."

His poems reflected his attitude. He was now composing
verse, if not freely in actual production, with a continuous
application of his mind, neglecting his studies in his absorption. He had it in purpose to write a great epic. This was
flying high, as youth will. Fragments, however, of this project of his were published after his fate befell him (and one
before). From them men said that the whole work, had he
completed it, must have been in truth an epic.

"Paradise Destroyed" was the name he had for it. "This
title," wrote a leading critic, reviewing his career, "obviously
challenging, was not taken by John Brecque in youth's pre-
sumption. He took it by genius's right."

It sought to tell of man's happiness destroyed by man's
ambitious savagery, of war as murder. The stanzas of it
which himself he saw published were entitled "Cain: A
Fragment." That was in the year in which he came down
from Oxford. He had achieved only a pass degree.

8

The vicar's cherished hope that he would take Orders was
never within even hesitancy's length of fulfillment. Father
mentioned it to son when John came home for his first
Christmas vacation. The undergraduate shook his head. "No,
father. I'd do anything in the world that would give you
pleasure, but that's a thing I know you wouldn't have me do
unless I felt called to it."

"Not on any account, dear boy. Perhaps later on you will be called."

"If I am I'll be doubly happy. But honestly I doubt it."

Not again till shortly before John was to sit for his degree did the vicar mention the subject. Influence towards priesthood should come, he felt, only from the Mind to which daily he took his thoughts about his son. The night before John went up for the last time he permitted himself inquiry. The terms of the answer he received were, he knew, final.

"No, father, I couldn't go into the Church. I never could."

"I'll not mention it again, my boy."

"Dear old father. I'll tell you what I am going to do. I'm going to be a poet."

"Wonderful, my dear boy!"

Not by its affection alone did the vicar's tone cover his disappointed hopes. Mingled in it was embarrassment similar to that felt by one unable to understand a French or Latin quotation but ashamed to say so. He found poetry, as he found jokes, difficult. John had had two poems in public print. Both were in the *Mid-Week Review*. Both were of fewer than thirty lines. Both had completely floored the poet's father. They did not appear to have anything whatever to do with the subjects with which, from their titles, they professed to deal. That was the vicar's chief difficulty with them. The first had been entitled "To the Grass." But grass as such the vicar nowhere could find mentioned. "On Finding a Dead Bird" was the caption above the second. But in all the fourteen lines there appeared no bird, dead or alive, that the vicar could see.

He was nevertheless, perhaps the more, almost absurdly proud of his boy's achievement. If he did not know what the poems meant, he knew well the literary standard of the *Mid-Week Review* which unquestionably did know or it would not have printed them. He walked about the parish with the paper under his arm, displaying it on each occasion to almost everyone he met. But as to comprehending either the one or, especially, the other, he was as far at loss as was Minna. Minna's difficulty, as she explained, was that she must put the verses into German in order to acquire their full meaning, and that to render poetry into German was particularly difficult. Triumphantly, though, she nodded her head over them. "What have I told you, then? The great mind, have I not said? Huge; you have heard me." She was clever with her fingers. She bought a copy of the *Review* on each occasion, affixed the poem to a card, illuminated it and hung it in her bedroom.

Laura's position was that she understood she poems but could not explain them in her own words. Fine poetry was often like that, Laura said. Look at Browning, for example. She came off best, too, in the vicarage's expressions of appreciation to the author. She learnt each poem by heart. This was that she might delight him, as enormously she did when he came home on vacation, by saying of each, "Why, I know it so well that I believe I could repeat it from memory. Let me try."

Confronted now with the declaration "I'm going to be a poet" the vicar's search for suitable addition to his "Wonderful, my dear boy" needed as great effort as had Laura's feat of memory. "It's a very fine, a very noble thing to be able to be," he presently effected. "And you've got the qualities for it, as you've shown. There's only one thing, and I do feel I must mention it, dear old boy. I doubt that one can live nowadays by writing poetry. I do indeed very seriously doubt it."

John said confidently, "I shall live by it all right—as well, anyhow, as I want to live—one day; and fairly soon. I'll take a bread-and-butter job, though, meanwhile. I'll take a schoolmaster's job."

9

His indifferent degree was unlikely to qualify him for a good public-school job. But he was not concerned to find a good job, particularly in a great public-school. Enough to keep him was all he sought; in a preparatory school for preference; and with surprising felicity the job offered itself, on the very day he came down, right at the vicarage door; at Mr. Bartlett's distinguished Upton House of all places.

Mr. Bartlett was a Wadham man. The Wadham boat, "our boat" as he spoke of it, had gone up two places in one year, three in the next, with John her bow. He had been greatly pleased and had expressed his pleasure and his congratulations to John when they met during the holidays. Twice he had had the Wadham bow over to dinner to talk Wadham.

Meeting him now in the street on the day of his return home he stopped him effusively for latest news. What sort of a boat would they have next Lents? And what was John going to do now? Ah, schoolmastering, eh? Got a post? No? Well, that was a funny thing, that was, meeting him like this just when, as a matter of extraordinary fact, he had learnt, that very morning, that himself he had a staff vacancy to fill. Carruthers was leaving him. Had John met Carruthers? Delightful fellow. Related to the family of Lord Winstock "Whom of course I know very well. Had his boy here." Never mind about that now; point was that Carruthers had unexpectedly come into money, lucky beggar, from his aunt, Lady Cressington ("I knew her well") and was leaving him. English was his subject. "Yours is English, isn't it? History, didn't you tell me? Yes, I thought so. What degree did you take?"

John admitted the lowly order of his degree.

Mr. Bartlett, perturbed, took the opportunity of looking away afforded by raising his hat to the occupant of a carriage-and-pair and by following the elegant turnout with his eyes. He was estimating whether certain of his more influential patrons really did know the difference between a pass and an honors degree, and was estimating also the saving he might effect by salarying the former, particularly in the person of the son of a father who had had to prep. school him, he remembered, at that unspeakable "Kilbracken." He hoped that on the social side Upton, Oxford and bow in the Wadham boat would counteract that stigma.

"You come up," he turned round with, "and have a talk about it. What about tomorrow, say, at three? Having you would suit me, I don't mind telling you, in another way, because we've got ourselves dreadfully cramped in the masters' quarters and if you could arrange to live at home, as I daresay you'd be glad to, it would be a convenient arrangement. Have a talk with your father, will you? Tell him, by the way, that I met the Bishop—of course I know him well —at a dinner-party at Lord Paddockwood's in London not long ago. All right then, tomorrow."

10

For John it was, satisfactorily completed, very much all right. Nothing could ever detract from the happiness of the Oxford days, yet the change to the conditions now enjoyed was as goodly by the new amenities it brought as had been the change to Wadham. He had his bread-and-butter, sufficiently congenial occupation in the earning of it, the evenings and all the week-ends to himself in his own home. Life was a song; and he was singing in it.

He did not mix very well with his fellow assistant-masters at Upton House. They were a clan, golf, bridge, and long association one with another its interests. He had his own. Mr. Bartlett, observing him to be apparently outside the fellowship of the masters' common-room and attributing it to the "Kilbracken" taint, allowed it to be seen that he sided himself with this entirely proper feeling.

It was in his second term at Upton House that he rose conspicuously in staff esteem. This was the Easter term of 1914 and the cause of his elevation was the publication in the *Mid-Week Review* of "Cain: A Fragment." From the space given to it the most superficial order of intelligence, knowing the *Review,* would have known that here must be something altogether out of the common. It occupied two and a half pages of a journal, published for the intelligent, which rarely gave as much as half a column to verse. An editorial footnote in the body of the paper said that "Owing to the privilege we have of presenting our readers this week with 'Cain: A Fragment,' several of our usual 'Middles' are held over."

The masters' common-room at Upton House numbered no dullards among its inmates. They were not all lovers of poetry but they knew the thing when they saw it and they were aware, too, that the *Mid-Week Review* knew it better than did they. The paper was passed from hand to hand. There was none of John's fellows but sought him out and sincerely congratulated him. Mr. Bartlett, a bit fogged by the poem but agreeably astounded, jocosely addressed him: "A pretty considerable 'fragment,' eh? But good, oh, uncommonly good. Bravo, Brecque. I'm very pleased." He made opportunity to write to a bunch of titles, working in in each case "Have you seen, by the way, the long poem which my new English master has thrown off in the current *Mid-Week Review?* Evidently the standard of my staff maintains its quality!"

As for the vicarage, its pride and its joy combined into a

thrill transcending adequate expression. John had said nothing of the poem's acceptance for publication. The *Mid-Week* containing it arrived for him by post. Not till just as he was leaving the house for the school did he show it to his father. Then, handing it to him opened at the poem's impressive spread, "Look at this, father," he said and hurriedly set out.

The vicar looked, open mouthed. Two pages! He turned the second. And a half! "Cain." He was bound to understand *this*. His lips moved in conscientious intake of the first three stanzas. His eye swept agitatedly over the remainder for comforting discovery of mention of the protagonist by name. It did not appear to be there, but unquestionably in so wide a spread it must be somewhere. What did it matter, anyway? Two and a half pages!

He bounded from his study, paper in hand. "Laura, Minna, where are you? John in the *Mid-Week Review* again. Enormous. Tremendous. Look, look, two and a half pages of it. Two and a half pages!"

The effects of the looking were sensational. Minna bounded from the house as though for the fire-brigade. Four copies were her purchase. Two for herself because the second page would gum down the concluding half-page on her illuminated cards, one for Laura, one for the vicar. Laura, elbows on table, hands to ears, applied herself to learning verses of which she could cry when her wonderful boy came home ". . . say them from memory. Hear me try." The vicar, virtually with a wet towel about his head, set himself to give the better part of the morning to getting meaning out of the thing.

In the right circles "Cain" caused indubitably a stir. John's post proclaimed the fact. Proudly he showed the vicarage letters, some from dignitaries whose official positions in the cultured world told the incidence of their congratulations, others from names belonging, he said, to poets of established reputation. One of these latter required no such introduction. It came from a poet whose name was as near to being a household word as in England any living poet's name can be expected to be. "In one step," said this letter, "you have come to the highest place among those of us now writing verse. You will go higher."

The vicar, when that was shown him, felt that his cup of happiness in John was full.

It remained full. It was overflowing on a morning of a succeeding month when John was telling him of preparations for the publication of a little volume. "Cain and Other Verses" it was to be called.

"A book; really, actually, a book of your own! Oh, my dear, dear boy, how proud, how happy I am!"

That was at breakfast. It was with indifference after so thrilling a communication that, when his boy had gone off to his work, the vicar picked up the morning paper.

However it had news in it of a very startling and shocking nature.

Some wretched persons, said to be Serbs, had assassinated the Archduke Francis Ferdinand of Austria and his morganatic wife, the Duchess of Hohenberg, at a place called Serajevo in Bulgaria.

II

That was on June 24th, more than half-way through the summer term of 1914. Six weeks later, early in the summer holidays (if anyone in those days could use the word holidays) John made a communication infinitely more moving to the vicar, and to the speaker, than had been that of "Cain and Other Verses."

He had gone away on breaking-up day, July 27th as it had been. He had taken a holiday tutor job with a small boy of Upton House and had conducted him up to his father, General Lethbridge, in Scotland. He had accepted the post in order that with the uncommonly good fee attaching to it he might give the vicar the duty-free holiday which he never had been able to afford. Now, after twelve days only, he had unexpectedly returned. He had but just arrived. Laura was out. He was talking to his father in the study.

"Everybody's 'joining up' as they call it," his words were. He named two of the Upton House masters. "Turner and Wright have, I hear. I've no doubt that the others who are of the right age and fit will too. Everybody is. I'm of the right age and fit. That's why General Lethbridge concluded my job with his boy and sent me back home. Perhaps you guessed that."

He paused. He was looking straight into his father's eyes as he spoke. Now an emotion more penetrative yet charged his own.

"Father, nothing will make me ever kill a man."

The vicar had feared that this was coming. He knew his son's feelings in this matter. Ever since, with Great Britain's declaration of war, her young manhood had flocked to her aid, ever since the newspapers and the hoardings had flamed her call to her sons, with profoundest anxiety John had been in his mind and in Laura's. He had guessed why thus unexpectedly the boy had returned. Hearing his step, recognizing his voice, for one instant he had hoped that he was come of his own accord, his principles vanished in the test which now had come to them. One look at his face had told him that the return was of his employer's part, not of John's. The test, he saw, had failed to shake the principles. And the test, he knew, had as yet scarcely begun development of the force which public opinion, already vociferous, soon would be giving it.

He had steeled himself to receive the words he now heard. Nevertheless his voice as he answered them shook.

"Oh, my dear boy, I was afraid of this. Your mother and I have feared it for you—feared what it may mean for you—ever since the posters went up, ever since the outbreak."

John's voice was very low but it was utterly steady. "Father, to me to kill a man as men are now being killed is the same as murder. You know that, father. I've told you a hundred times how I feel about war. There's no individual man out there that wants to kill his fellow man. It's mass ferocity, engineered. I saw the thing at Upton. I was badly bullied there. I never told you. Individual boys, one or two excepted as there will be exceptions out there, didn't want to bully me. It was the mass spirit, engineered by tradition. I'll never have part in that. Nothing will ever make me take a human life; nothing will ever make me part of a machine organized for the purpose of taking human life; nothing, father."

"My boy, we're all saying, God judge us, that here is a case where every fit man of our people must strike for truth, for righteousness."

"I'll never kill a man, father. I'll never be a party to the killing of men."

"My dear, dear boy, my best-loved boy, I realize your principles, I honor them in you. You are my son. Yet I know that in this hour it is being said that our country must have national principles, not individual."

"Father dearest, I can't, I can't."

"There's the non-combatant branch, my boy, the Army Medical Corps."

"It's a part of the army, a part of the war machine. If I could save life unenlisted, not under the military, not as part of the machine, gladly I'd do it. With the machine I'll have no part whatsoever."

There was a long pause. The vicar then put out his hands, which were trembling, and took his son's hands.

"God guide you, my boy."

His mind went to what already public opinion had said of those who might hang back.

"And support you," he added.

Himself he was to need support. In that hour the second period of his ministry at St. Luke's had begun.

Five

I<small>T WAS</small> in a very different pair of shoes that Philip presented himself at the threshold of this second period.

That boy, from days even earlier than when, declaring what he would have done to the murderers of Dick Oadbee's father, he had called down John's remonstrance "Oh, shut up; you're always killing"; from days earlier even than when with ferocious kicks he repulsed dislodgment of himself from a vicarage tree—that boy, from earliest occupancy of his first crawlers, had shown himself, as John at the tree incident had declared, "an awful chap."

He was born, in the nursery use of the term, a rogue. He was born, in the phrase of Minna, who in spirit kissed his footprints, "that rascal." He was born to stampede women's hearts and break men's heads. He was born to hold his own. "Such kicking, such roaring," the midwife declared when she assisted him into the world, "I never saw, not in the whole of my experience."

When he was six he contributed to Laura's cherished incidents of her children's lives a scene and an application of a biblical expression (the vicarage brood was well versed in the scriptures) at which she still laughed when she was sixty. Minna had stood him in the corner for some persistent misdemeanor. Laura met her emerging from the nursery door convulsed with suppressed mirth. "I cannot remain," Minna declared. "He growl, he argue; I split. I cannot remain."

"I'll superintend him," said Laura, much looking forward to the duty. "How long has he had?"

"Oh, poof, nothing; a minute. I hardly begin him there. I split."

Laura assumed a face of forbidding sternness and went in. Philip turned his head. "Hullo, mum. Can I come out now?"

"Certainly not. You've scarcely gone in. You've been disgraceful. I've heard all about it, and I'm simply shocked. Turn your face."

Philip turned his face. "How long have I had?" came his muffled tone.

"Don't talk. Two minutes."

"How much more have I got?"

"Did you hear me say 'Don't talk'?"

"Yes, but surely I can know how much more."

"You know that you're there for ten minutes. I've told you you've had two. If you don't know what two from ten leaves at your age you deserve to stop there till you find out."

"Well, I don't care what it leaves."

"Well, I'm perfectly sure I don't. *I've* got a nice comfortable chair and a very nice biscuit. Don't talk."

Silence for perhaps fifteen seconds.

"Can I have a cool drink of water?"

"Certainly not, till you come out."

"Well, I want to come out."

"Philip, will you kindlly not utter another word. You know perfectly well what I mean."

"Well, my tongue's as dry as desert sand."

"Why is it?"

"Because I'm licking over the flowers on the wallpaper."

"Then it deserves to be dry as desert sand, drier. If you don't stop doing such a disgusting thing you shall stay there longer still."

"Minna says that if I lick the paper poison will come out and I shall die."

"Very probably. Don't talk."

"Will you be sorry if I die?"

"We should all be very sorry but it wouldn't be our fault."

Prolonged silence, the prospective suicide presumably brooding over this.

"How long now?"

"You've had five minutes. Exactly half."

"Well, I call standing in the corner an abomination of the Lord."

Laura was taken with a severe coughing fit. She had to hurry out.

When he was read to and when he began to read to himself, his tastes, stage by stage, subject by subject, even author by author, were the exact opposite to John's tastes. He didn't care for Hans Andersen; he preferred Grimm. Where John had cried "Read, mother, read" in "Pilgrim's Progress" his exclamation was "Well, I don't think I like this part." But he was ravished by the fighting episodes. He couldn't bear "The Water Babies." When, later, he fell by chance upon the same pen's "Westward Ho!" it sometimes was by force alone that he could be separated from it. Before he could read he saw, when out to tea one day, a picture of the tossing in the blanket episode in "Tom Brown." Such was his rapture over the illustration that the book was lent him. The bits Laura read to him were, she always said, the thing that really started him, deplorably slow at any form of lessons, to try to read himself.

He was but seven when John brought home "Horatius" and "The Lady of the Lake." Listening to the parts unattractive to John he demanded that they should be read to him again and again and yet again. With a rapidity astonishing in one who Sunday by Sunday never could learn the Collect, he acquired strings of "Horatius" by heart. At once his favorite game was played between the backs of two chairs. That was the mouth of the bridge. He was Horatius. One of the red sandbags used in those days as window draught-protectors was his weapon. Devoted slave, unfortunate Minna was the unhappy representatives of the Tuscan army, turn by turn as he summoned them.

" '*But, hark, the cry is Astur.*' Come *on* will you, Minna."

"Well, but I am hurt. You hit me much hard with that sandbag. I rub myself."

"Well, you've hit me with yours, haven't you? I'm not rubbing myself. Do come *on,* will you. It's Astur, remember."

And immediately—

"Oh, Min-*na*. '*Forth with his ample stride*' . . . Didn't you hear me? You're just niggling your feet. Well, remember, '*Then like a wildcat mad with wounds.*' Oh, do *slog,* will you! Oh, as if *that* would make a chap feel like a wildcat! Well, anyway, look out for yourself. '*Sprang right at Astur's face.*' "

And at once—

"Oh! Oh, my mercy! You kill me like that! Oh! Oh! I will not be this Astur. I tell you I will not. I cannot. I am blue and black."

The greatest days in his literary life were that upon which a "Kilbracken" friend lent him his first Marryat, "Midshipman Easy," and that upon which, having tuppence a week pocket-money when he started at the prep. school, he found in the "2*d*. Box" of the local secondhand bookshop a tattered paper-covered copy of Dana's "Two Years before the Mast." The greatest day in the first decade of his physical life was that on which he tore off, forgetting his satchel, pursued by Minna with his overcoat, to begin at "Kilbracken."

There was nothing of the sufficiently excited but quietly affectionate scenes which had attended John's departure to first day at Mr. Needham's. Vicar, Laura and Minna, fondly moved, attended Philip to the gate; but he wriggled from embraces; to go was his only thought. On his return there was all, truly enough, of John's excited chatter of his novel doings; but Philip's subjects were different, his appearance highly different.

"Why, what *have* you been doing to your clothes?" Laura cried. "You've been rolling, surely, in mud. Oh, Philip, and that nice new suit, too!"

"And your forehead here," exclaimed the vicar, turning back a thatch of the tawny hair. "Why, my boy, you've a lump here like a—"

"He has had the fight," pronounced Minna solemnly. "On his first day he has had the fight, that boy."

He had promised his mother, earnestly entreating of him, that he would have no fight. With a defensive flash of his eyes at her, "Well, I couldn't help it," he now cried. "There was a mound of gravel there to cover the playground with, and chaps were getting on it and pushing chaps off it. So of course I got on, and a great bison of a chap called Bloxham said I wasn't to as I was a new chap and gave me a punch off it. So naturally I gave him a punch back, so he went for me. He weighs about two elephants so naturally he got me down, and I couldn't do a thing with him kneeling on me, so I bit his leg."

"Oh, but my dear boy," expostulated the vicar.

"Oh, but, Philip," cried Laura, "you can't go *biting* boys."

"Well, what could I *do,* mum? He was kneeling on my arms, don't you *understand?* Anyhow, I did bite him, and jolly hard, too, because I tasted his blood in my mouth, salt-ish. He gave a roar like four bulls, and jumped up hopping, and then stooped over his leg where the bite was; and I jumped up and gave him a running hoof on his bot— on the bent part of him."

The vicar's lower jaw was dropped, thunderstruck.

"Oh, Philip!" cried Laura, but her eyes were sparkling.

"He bunked," concluded Philip dispassionately. "I say, Minna, do for goodness' sake get me some tea instead of goggling there. I'm ravenous."

2

But the Marryats—his friend lent him also "Percival Keen," "Frank Mildmay" and "Peter Simple"—and the Dana, were the turning point. He got also at this time—still at "Kilbracken"—an illustrated magazine containing an account of naval cadet life at Dartmouth. That sent him crazy. He must go into the navy he implored his father and mother. Nothing ever would content him if he couldn't go into the navy. "Oh, do, do, *do* let me go into the navy."

It manifestly was the thing for him. On account of the cost involved it was, as manifestly, impossible. The vicar sought out one of his parishioners, Admiral Heneage, whose boy, then at Upton House, was being prepared for Dartmouth. The afternoon on which he returned with the admiral's information was the blackest he and Laura knew at the vicarage until the period of black days came. As compared with day-boy education at the College, the cost would be prohibitive, he told Laura. She heard the figures and could not but agree. There was not only the training cost, there was the fact that, once passed out to sea, a boy could not for some years live on his pay. The thing was impossible. It could not be.

"It will break his heart," Laura said. She wiped her eyes.

The vicar blew his nose. "It breaks mine—to have to tell him."

Philip had known that his father was going to make inquiries. He came tearing in from school. "Well, well, did you see him? Did you ask him? What did he say?"

The vicar told what the admiral had said. Laura told what it meant.

The corners of the boy's mouth went down. He stood tugging at his school cap in his hands, his eyes blinking.

"You must try, dearest boy," the vicar said, "to stand up to it like, like a Dartmouth cadet."

The corners of the mouth went lower yet. The lips strained together. The boy turned about and went from the room. "Oh, Gordon," Laura choked.

The vicar stood with face averted, his shoulders hunched.

Minna came in. Minna had been told and knew that Philip was to be told. The knuckles of one hand were pressed to her lips.

"Oh," she cried, "he is in his room. He is on his bed, flat. He sob, he sob."

Laura fled to him.

3

Another thing which just now was giving him immense satisfaction was his impending change over to the College. Delightedly his parents noted it. For terms back his interest in the doings "up there," dragged out of John, had been such as to give the impression that he, not his brother, was the Upton boy. Before Marryat and Dana came to dim "Tom Brown," public-school life had been above all things his desire. Such now was his excitement over the near prospect of attaining it that it was antidote, Laura and the vicar told one another, to the bitterness of forgoing the navy. It looked as if, denied Dartmouth, he was wholeheartedly accepting Upton as the next best thing.

His ideas about joining it were the exact opposite to John's ideas. "Mum, I simply must be a boarder"—"Dad, *do* let me go as a boarder"—"Mum, do entreat dad to let me be a boarder."

"Oh, Gordon," Laura, requiring no bidding, voiced her entreaty, "*can't* we somehow manage it for him? He is so set on it. He has been so good about giving up the navy. This would make up to him so much. *Can't* we?"

It had been herself who, as chancellor of the exchequer, had shown that the thing could not be. On that tragic day when the boy had sobbed his disappointment on his bed, it was the vicar who had wondered whether boarding at Upton, when the time came, could then at once be offered him in solace of his woe. They had gone into it and seen it not possible. "You won't find £550 affluence," Hope Hubbard had said, "when the children start growing up." Each succeeding year was proving that. Struggling to balance her budget, "You know, it's a mercy John didn't want to be a boarder," Laura more than once had said. Boarding fees for Philip at Upton were out of the question.

Nevertheless, now that the decision actually must touch the already once disappointed boy, "Gordon, *can't* we— somehow?"

"I'll go up and see Lambarde about it," said the vicar. "There's the reduction they make for brothers as day-boys or as boarders. I'll see what he's got to say about us having one boy one way and one the other. I get on rather well with Lambarde, as you know. I'll put the whole case before him, dearest, and make a tremendous effort for the boy."

Lambarde was the College bursar. He was a tall, thin, keen man, a great fisherman. Perhaps because the vicar was in every way so entirely his opposite, not knowing, among other differences, one end of a fly-rod from the other, the bursar appeared to like meeting him.

Interviewed now in his office at the College, replacing the *Fishing Gazette* from where, as he smilingly told, he had dropped it when the door opened, he was all sympathy with the case presented to him, but, at the outset, little helpful.

"We're tied hand and foot with the regulations," he explained. "Two day-boys may be brothers and two boarders may be brothers, fees reduced as per reg. twelve or whichever it was I showed you. But a day-boy and a boarder may not be brothers. The point's arisen and been turned down before now. I really am profoundly sorry, especially with the boy, as you tell me, so keen."

The vicar, watching a vision of Philip's mouth when the navy news had been broken to him, sighed heavily. "Well, that's that," he said.

"Or 'no man can lose what he never had,' as old Izaak puts it. Yes, that's the only way to look at it, I'm afraid."

But having affirmed this the bursar, nevertheless, sat regarding the other's troubled face with a look profoundly sympathetic. It quickened suddenly into a remarkable alertness.

"But wait a minute," he cried penetratingly. He knitted his brows in immense concentration. "Wait—a—minute." With a bang upon the table, "By Jove and by Jingo," he then cried, "it's suddenly come to me that there's a way of reduction which, if I could work it, not only would reduce boarding fees for your boy but would wipe 'em bang out. Bang out, Brecque. Ever heard of Lord Culverstock?"

Greatly more startled now by the bursar's astonishing demeanor than he had been by his blow upon the table, "Why, yes," ejaculated the vicar, "he's the patron of my living."

"By Jupiter and all the gods," cried Lambarde, "that makes the thing more possible than ever."

He drew a deep breath, pulled his chair towards the vicar's, and bending forward spoke intensely. "Listen, Brecque. That Culverstock family is mixed up with the foundation of this place. I'd occasion to dig into the matter the other day and I've got it all pat. Some Elizabethan

Culverstock was one of the three founders. And the three, in setting up the school, secured each to himself, issue of his body male and all that stuff, the nomination every four years of a boy who for the four years ensuing should be boarded and educated at the school—'lodged, victualed and instructed' is the phrase in the deed—free."

"Free," gasped the vicar, incredulous of what appeared to be coming.

"Free," affirmed the bursar, "not shot a bean—extras excepted; we look after that! Well, two of these nominations are now vested in benevolent societies. There's the Stapleton Foundation and the Hunter Foundation. Two boys here now are on 'em, eating their heads off at, so to speak, my expense."

He tapped the vicar's knee. "Now listen. The line of the third founder, the Culverstock crowd, do nothing with theirs. I never even knew there was a third gift foundation till I happened on the fact quite by chance once and then entirely forgot it again—till now."

He sat up and pointed a waggish finger at the vicar, "Till now, Brecque, till now. I'll write tonight, I'll write straight off, to this Lord Culverstock. He'll be in the reference books. I'll write him, by George, at his racing stables, he's an owner, you know, and perhaps he'll spring me a tip for the Leger. I'll acquaint him with the little cradle for a boy that he's got here and I'll tell him that the son of his own patronee—what would be the word to use?"

The vicar wiped his forehead. It was sweating. 'The incumbent of his own advowson of St. Luke's, I think would be the phrase," he managed to effect.

The bursar made a note—"That the son of all that is the infant who would most fittingly fill the cradle and—" He extended cordial hands. "And we'll see, Brecque, we'll see."

The bursar took his arm in a friendly hand and led him

to the door. "There's no counting on it, of course," he warned.

"There most certainly is not," the vicar agreed. In his agitation of mind he dropped first his hat and then, in stooping for it, his umbrella. The bursar restored them to him. "Thank you, thank you, my dear fellow, my dear Lambarde. Most certainly, as I was saying, there is no counting on it, if only for this reason that I do beg you will impress on Lord Culverstock that, should he know of more deserving cases, he must of course— I mean to say that with gratitude inexpressible I would receive the nomination for my dear boy but only if, if, *ceteris paribus*—"

The bursar smote him affectionately on the shoulder. "Saving your presence," smiled he, "as Palmerston once said to a bloke '*ceteris paribus* be damned: your man shall have it'—if I can work the office."

The vicar, as he told Laura, "walked home with God."

4

So Philip went as boarder. Mr. Lambarde burst in one morning, the letter granting the Culverstock Foundation in his hand. The boy was told. He stood on his head clapping his heels together for what the bursar opined to be the world's record length of time for the performance—and duly went.

The vicar on the last day of the holidays exchanged at the bank five of his own shillings, five of Laura's, for four newly minted half-crowns. Minna presented a writing-case, its surface marred by her attempts at erasion of a tear drop. Mary and Ruth were permitted to open their money-boxes, the one for a pocket pen and pencil, the other for a packet of butterscotch. John, despite he must occasionally glimpse his brother from Upper School precincts into which now he had been moved, gave a packet of foreign stamps. A tuck-box was stocked with a recklessness out of all keeping with normal practice of the vicarage commissariat. On the night on which the boy had gone, Minna, talking of him with Laura in the drawing-room, agreed a shade oddly that the tuck-box had indeed been splendid. Then she said portentously:

"And now I have the confession to confess. When all was packed I go, I cannot stay myself, to the store-room. There is a pot of strawberry jam. I have thought there were two but I see one only. I know he have strawberry jam in his tuck-box, but I know also how he like strawberry jam. I cannot stay myself. My heart split. I take the pot, I smuggle it in the box. I confess. I will buy other."

Laura looked rather funny. "Oh, Minna," she began, her voice on a curious note, "I think that was rather—"

The vicar came in. He was wiping his spectacles. He looked a shade foolish.

"Dearest," Laura said, "this really rather naughty Minna has just been telling me that although Philip's tuck-box was stuffed as you know how she—" She recited Minna's crime.

The vicar put on his spectacles. He looked more foolish yet. "My dear," he said, "it's the oddest thing, but I'd just come in to tell you, I didn't wish you to find out for yourself and then perhaps suspect Sarah, that just before the dear boy started I went into the store-room, and there was a jar of pickles there, and I— My dearest, whatever is the matter?"

For Laura with a kind of shriek had cast up her hands. "We're all thieves! Minna, I sneaked that other pot of jam into his box immediately I got out of bed this morning. We all three stole for him!"

5

Yet, ripping as it all was, Philip, at his own urgent plea, was but two terms at Upton. He came home for his first holidays, rosy indeed with all the doings of his new life, but, overriding these, crazy with a new aspect of his passion for the sea. He had heard now from someone whose brother was in the merchant service, and he had read too in an illustrated magazine article that the mercantile marine put you straight on to a ship, on to the training ships "Worcester" or "Conway." He had seen letters from the friend's brother who was second mate in a freighter trading in the Caribbean Sea. The combination of the cadet ships, of the rivalry between "Worcester" and "Conway," of the rank "mate," so prominent in Marryat, and of the romantically adventurous associations of the word "Caribbean," had swept him off his shore legs again as by a tidal wave.

He was somehow got back to school at the next term. He was promised—and no promise in the vicarage ever was broken—that immediately with next holidays the subject should be reviewed again. He was bidden to try "like a good boy" to realize—as it was the vicarage practice to encourage all the children to realize—that father and mother joined love with experience in what they decided. He was given for his reflection "like a brave, sensible little chap"—as it was the vicarage practice to give each child as occasion might arise—his parents' angle on the matter.

Laura set the angle to Gordon. Here on the one hand was free education on the Culverstock Foundation until the boy could earn his own living. There on the other, on the "Conway" or "Worcester," were immediate charges on the family budget. Not very considerable charges, but charges which at their least represented loss of the great difference which the unexpected free schooling had made to the slender purse. Here on the one hand were the dozen opportunities which time might open for the boy's career. There on the other was the casting him, at fourteen, into a service notoriously ill paid, of which they knew nothing, in which they could exercise not the smallest influence.

"And there's the adorable scrap himself!" Laura, sighing, almost invariably would conclude these anxious debates.

"Yes, there's the dear scrap himself," the vicar, sighing also, would agree.

And their eyes would hold each the other's; and neither would be seeing the other. Each would be seeing the sturdy scrap going off down the garden by himself in Bob Heneage's Dartmouth jacket; coiled in a chair spellbound by Marryat or Dana; stretched on his bed sobbing out his disappointment; pleading this last holidays, "Do, dad, do." "Mum, do let me, *do*."

Every letter of the term carried under its sprawled signature a P.S. in one or other variety of the same purport. "I am most truly thinking of all you said but, oh, if *only* I could go on the 'Worcester.' " The very first night of the ensuing holidays brought from him, the vicar absent at the church, "Mum, I do beg and implore of you to beg dad. Oh, Minna, do *not* sit there looking like a dying duck in a thunderstorm. If you don't jolly well implore dad too I'll put a frog in your bed every single night I'm home, like I did once last hols. I *swear* I will."

And it was Minna, in point of fact, who threw in the weight which appeared to tip the vicarage scales. Uncommonly dying duckish in appearance as, from time to time contributing her portion, she attended one of the almost nightly debates after Philip and the others had gone to bed, thus over her mending basket her nodding head presently delivered itself:

"That boy will go to the sea if he have to crawl there on his thumbs and toes. That boy will get himself on to a ship if he have to swim there tied up in a bag with a millstone on top of his neck. The sea is inside that boy, and if we do not let him go officer he one jolly fine day run himself away and go, how does he call it? Ah, yes, in front of the mast, the common sailor, eh? I say it; I tell you."

The vicar gazed upon her, then turned his eyes on Laura. "My dear," he said decisively, "Minna is right. My dear, we must do it."

Laura, arms upthrown, bounded from her chair with a bound worthy of Philip himself. She rushed upon the vicar. She threw herself upon him in his chair. Her arms embracing him, "Oh, Gordon!" she cried. "Oh, Gordon!"

6

When he came home from the "Worcester" on his first "leave," as he insisted his holidays must now be called, he brought some of his cadet uniforms with him. His brother and sisters crowded about him delightedly admiring. The vicar swelled and beamed with affectionate pride. Laura and Minna collided in their simultaneous rush to hug him in the hugs from which indignantly he wriggled.

"He looks in that uniform," Laura declared, "a cherub, an angel."

"Ah, and he looks also in those eyes of his," nodded Minna, "not a devil; how you call it? ah, the devilry. That boy will make the sea rough when he goes on it, and the fräuleins sad. You mark me. I say it."

The vicar, smiling when his thoughts with God came to the sailor figure, introduced them thenceforward with "They that go down to the sea in ships, that do business in great waters . . ."

Philip worked out his training-ship time. Rather surprisingly to the vicarage he failed, when passing out, to secure one of the two cadetships in the Royal Navy annually offered on the "Worcester" and "Conway," to obtain one of which he had expressed himself as determined when first going aboard the former.

"Never you mind about that," he declared with a glee and with a snap of his fingers which explained perhaps why he had not topped the passing-out list. "I'm going to sea, *next week,* that's all that matters. I've stuck myself down for the R.N.R. I'll get myself R.N. before I'm through, you bet I will. P'r'aps there'll be a war roll up; you never know. But I tell you I'm going to sea and that's all that matters now. To sea, Mary; to sea, Ruthie; to sea, mum, to sea!" And he struck an attitude and roared into a chanty:

> Farewell and adieu to you, fair Spanish laides,
> Farewell and adieu to you, ladies of Spain. . . .

He had got a berth as fourth officer in the "Devon County" freighter of the County Line, trading to the Malay archipelago. He remained in the County Line, trading here, trading there. He was R.N.R. and he was called up for his first spell of training in the navy. He arrived home on a short leave on a day rather more than four weeks after that on which the vicar had read with shocked surprise of the Archduke Francis's assassination at Serajevo. He just missed John, gone off as holiday tutor to General Lethbridge's boy. He was glad he had missed him. He well knew John's feelings about war. A great affection joined the brothers. He would have hated to exhibit before "good old John" the crazy excitement with which, arriving, he came bursting into the vicarage, and with which, as the hours of the pregnant days wore on, crazier and crazier he went.

Austria had presented her peremptory note to Serbia.

Serbia had issued her conciliatory reply. Austria had declared the reply to be unacceptable. Would they fight? Would Germany come in? If Germany, would we?

Canvassing these questions with every opening of his mouth, Philip hopped about the vicarage and down to the town for news and back again, unable to sit, unable to eat, unable to sleep. For him it was touch and go. As he had come ashore at Liverpool from the "Devon County" he had been handed his company's orders to report for duty with the "Sussex County," sailing five days hence. "Dad, suppose they cart me off in her, and after we're too far to set me ashore the Fleet mobilizes and the R.N.R.'s called up! Oh, I say, mum, imagine it! Oh, I say, I shall go mad if I don't get called up by tomorrow!"

He was, by telegram on the following morning. He was to report immediately at Portsmouth.

And he then, having secured that which he had declared alone could save him from madness, went quite mad. He had three hours before he need start for town for the train from Waterloo. He used them in such exhibition of his hopeless madness as could not but make the vicarage dab its wet eyes and laugh despite itself.

As he waved the telegram in the air he sang an adaptation of the old Jingo song of the music halls. Continuously then he would break into it, adding grotesque dialogue between himself and a commanding officer:

> I *do* want to fight
> And, by Jingo, when I do,
> I've got the guts, I've got the fists,
> I've got the weapons too!

"*Mr. Brecque!*"
"*Sir?*"
"*All our guns are out of action. All officers except our-*

selves are killed. Take away the third cutter, Mr. Brecque, and board that German battleship and capture her."

"Aye, aye, sir."

And then with hands to mouth, halloing so that the town might have heard him:

"Pass the word for the third cutter away, there!"

"Third cutter aw-a-ay!"

"Tumble in there. Tumble in. Stripped to the waist. Cutlasses in mouths. Cast off, coxs'n. Give way all. Hur-rah!"

> I *do* want to fight
> And, by Jingo, when I do,
> I've got the guts, I've got the fists . . .

They all went down to the station to see him off. With crazy abandon, kissing in public for the first time, he kissed them all from Ruth to the vicar, and then, leaning two-thirds out from the carriage window, all over again.

The train moved.

"God bless you, God guard you, my boy."

"Philip, oh, Philip!"

"Mine heart, mine boy of my life. Forgive I have scolded you. Forgive I . . ."

"Philip, Philip."

> I *do* want to fight
> And, by Jingo, . . .

"Put your head in. Put your head in."

"Oh, my mercy, he will crack his head off on the signals."

Laura took Gordon's arm. "Come, dearest, we'll go along."

"God guard him, God bless him," said the vicar. "Dear me, how very troublesome spectacles are when your eyes will keep—"

Six

THOSE two girls, Mary and Ruth, were as unlike one another in disposition as John and Philip were unlike. You could not say, though, in their case, that each derived from a different parent. Laura had a roguish eye, and Ruth's eyes, when she was of school age, were forever tailing about with a glint in them. But Laura's were a merrymaker's eyes; Ruth's a flirt's. The vicar was a tidy man and Mary was orderly. But while the vicar's neat little ways were amusing, Mary, even in her nursery days, displayed, Laura said, an almost alarming sense of method.

Each of these two girls had in fact a line of her own, inherent, not inherited. Laura was fond of calling Mary Little Mother Bunch. Hope Hubbard, inquiring after Ruth, would say, "And how's Miss Airs and Graces?"

With six years between them they were scarcely in the nursery together; but Mary was still playing with dolls when she was ten, and the difference between her dolls and her treatment of them and Ruth's and their management was as the difference between the inmates and the practices of a reformatory and the spoilt darlings of an indulgent home. Mary had as many as twenty dolls; Ruth never more than two or three. Mary never discarded a doll; Ruth would abandon one of hers in a month if its nose got broken or if in any other way its looks became marred. Mary's dolls were numerous because she made her own. Ruth's had to come, waxen-faced, completely dressed, from a shop. Mary practiced upon her dolls the rigors of stern discipline. Ruth's

were for the lavishment of an admiration similar to that
which she delighted to attract to her own person.

Mary made her dolls principally out of sticks of firewood.
One stick was one doll. One set of features drawn with a
pen was one face. One bit of rag was one complete outfit.
The faces were washed morning and night (eyes, nose and
mouth restored thereafter). Every Wednesday and Saturday
a complete bath, vigorous scrubbing with a toothbrush its
primary feature, was administered. The rag costumes,
though rags when obtained from Minna or Laura, were cut
garments, neatly hemmed, when bound about the dolls.
Each doll had as many such dresses as the supply of rags
allowed. Each such wardrobe was kept, regularly laundered
and neatly folded, in its own compartment of a cardboard
box. And the life led by this family was, as has been implied,
no doll's life. It was a life of unremitting discipline; not
harsh but unquestionably firm. They did lessons. They were
set home-work, awarded marks, issued with termly reports.

At any day between her ages of six and ten Mary might
have been heard in the nursery:

"Now it's geography, and I very much hope that this time
the lesson has been well learnt. Geography has been very
bad this term. Lucy, pay attention. Now then. County-towns
of England. Lily Brooks, what is the county-town of Devonshire?"

"*M-m-Maidstone.*"

"T'ch, t'ch. A *nice* beginning; a *very* nice beginning, I
must say. Next girl. Isabel Brown, as you evidently cannot
sit still but must wriggle in that most unladylike manner
you may stand. In the corner!"

The dolls, in point of fact, were all standing. A firewood
stick can assume the prone or the upright position but not
the flexed and they spent the greater part of their lives,
accordingly, in serried rank against the wall. Isabel Brown

would therefore be lifted from standing with her back to the wall to standing with her face to the wall and the lesson would proceed.

"Now, Dora."

"Exeter, Miss Smith."

"Good girl. I am very pleased with your work this term, Dora. I met your dear mother yesterday at tea at Mrs. Fisher's and told her how satisfied I was with your progress. Now, Sussex?"

And so on.

Marks were entered in a book made from sheets of the vicar's sermon paper folded and stitched together. Each doll had also a "Conduct Book." A great pleasure of Mary's was to engage Laura or Minna or the vicar to visit the table which was the dolls' seminary and hear read to them the conduct book of each inmate, the doll under review propped out for the purpose.

"Now, here," Mary would say gravely, "is Doris Wilberforce. Doris, I regret to say, is a willful girl. If we glance at her conduct book we see . . ."

She never spoke of them as her dolls. "My girls," "my children," "my young people," were the terms she used; and their portion though strict was by no means without the amelioration of kindliness and care. Tea-parties were frequently held; a sick girl was nursed with unremitting devotion.

Nevertheless, Mary's lips, during her engagement with her charges, were more often compressed than smiling; and often during the day, particularly when watching the others doing something, they would similarly set. She might be looking on at the boys doing their gardens. "Mary's got on her 'my young people's face,' " Laura would say aside to Gordon or to Minna.

"Most amusing, that censorious look of hers," the vicar would smile. "Only seven years old, mind you!"

"That girl you should have called Martha, not Mary," Minna would say.

"Mother Bunch!" Laura would exclaim and would run to kiss away the amusing solemnity.

Well knowing the intention of the kiss, Mary, even at six, did not greatly like it, much less at ten. She would wriggle away from it. "Well, but, mother, do look how badly the boys are planting those seeds," she would protest.

Often the censorious look would be assumed no doubt unconsciously. It was a habit. But expression of face has a direct influence on condition of mind. If when ruffled one deliberately causes one's lips to smile it is very hard to continue feeling ruffled. Deliberately to contort one's face into a frowning aspect is a certain means of inducing the gloomy view. Cast of countenance is thus apt to become mold of disposition. When, long years later in life, Mary was disapproving of something done by her ageing father or her mother, as frequently she was, their minds sometimes would go a little sadly to these happy early days in which the traits of censure on the childish face had been delightfully absurd. "Only seven years old, mind you!" the vicar would hear himself saying, and would see the little pinafored figure, lips compressed, and would sigh. "Mother Bunch!" Laura would remember herself laughing, and would recall her run to kiss away the sweet solemnity, and also would sigh.

2

Mary always seemed likely to be shorter than the others when full height was reached, and she was so. From their teens upwards, John, Philip and Ruth were on the tallish side, slim withal. Mary's stature and figure were of the dumpy model. This may have its own charm and Mary never lacked for attractiveness of her type. When she was a child it suited to perfection the solemn little air which she so frequently affected. Her hair was black, hung straight, and in the fashion of those days, was cut in a fringe along her forehead. As the right frame may be the last touch to a picture, so this dark fringe, Laura used to declare, gave the irresistible degree to the solemn little face. "Oh, I must hug you," she suddenly would cry, and would do it. "I could eat you, mother's own little daughter." She had never been gladder in her life, she told Gordon, "and never can be," than when they told her that the second baby was a girl. For the first to be a boy had been as should be. She had hoped then for a son as much as had its father. But as the time for her delivery of their second child drew on, more and more she had longed that it should show itself a daughter.

There would be, daydreaming, she would tell herself, the instruction of her in the domestic arts: the joy of watching her begin to do the housekeeping, of witnessing her self-important pride in running the vicarage ménage by herself in the holidays; the delight of teaching her sewing and cutting-out, of choosing her clothes for her. She would grow up and fall in love perhaps and there would be then the almost hallowed happiness of hearing her tell of her love. She would marry perhaps and there would be the almost sacred secrets to tell her. She perhaps would not marry and there would be the blessedness of her companionship and support as life's shadows lengthened. The roles would be reversed. The child would become the prop and stay. The devotion which had been given would be received.

"Oh, my little daughter of my own!" Laura would conclude her reverie, stretching out her arms to the girl-child who perhaps she soon would be holding in them.

3

It could not be said that Mary ever returned this devotion on quite the plane in which it was extended to her.

The daughter who was to have been the responsive treasure of her mother's heart loved her mother but, from the earliest days, loved her in her own way. Mary did everything in her own way. She was very determined; but so was Philip. She knew what she wanted; but so did Philip. But the difference between Philip's insistence on his own way and Mary's on hers was that, while Philip when in a nursery "scene" invariably was in the wrong, Mary, when thus involved always had justification.

"Well, goodness gracious me, what's up now?" Laura would exclaim, coming into the nursery to find Mary and Minna face to face, Minna all redness, volubility and gesticulation, Mother Bunch pale, calm, compressed.

"Mother, I appeal to you," Mary in her characteristic grown-up diction placidly would remark, "is it right that, although I mayn't borrow things from Minna's work-basket without asking her, she may come to mine and take what she wants without asking me?"

"Why, darling, I'm perfectly sure," Laura would begin, "that's Minna—"

"Why, poof, certainly not," anticipating the testimony to her scrupulousness in such a matter, Minna would break in. "I take up the scissors because they are near when I go to snip a string, and that Philip, because my back is turned two minutes, pile chairs as high as a house and fall off them, and I rush to him with the scissors in my hand—"

"Very dangerous," commented Mary dispassionately, "I told you that."

"Oh, yes, I know. You tell me everything. I cannot explain because you tell me so much."

"You have explained. It's you who won't listen to me. Mother, after she'd picked up Philip she put the scissors back in her own work-box without thinking and—"

"Well, darling, there you are. If dear Minna has explained everything, what is the use—"

"Why, that she won't let *me* explain to *her*. That's all I'm trying to do. It was yesterday that Philip fell off the chair, so it was yesterday that my scissors went into her basket. She must have seen them—"

"Yes, *ja,* I *tell* you I see them," cries Minna, fluttering her hands. "I see them often and I say, 'Ah, Mary's, bother me,' and then my mind slips—"

"Come, come," says Laura briskly, "for goodness' sake where's the india-rubber?"

This was her term for the kiss with which it was the vicarage rule that all differences of opinion must be erased. Minna with a glad laugh stoops to hug Mother Bunch. Mary gives a chilly salute.

"Next time I take the scissors," cries Minna, "I bring back my thumbs too and you cut them off, snip, snip."

Mary has already walked off towards her dolls. "I certainly don't want your thumbs, Minna. I only wanted you to admit that I've a right to be asked first when you want a thing of mine."

"I admit it, look, with my hands crossed on my bosom."

Mary's doesn't look. She has begun her game with her dolls. "That's all I wanted," she remarks.

Minna's upturned eyes and raised hands say to Laura "What a child!" Laura laughs back at her.

Philip happened to be the only child present when, at tea, the vicar was told of the incident. He also had a comment.

"It's more than mere neatness with Mary," Laura had said. "A place for everything and everything in its place and woe betide who moves it—lots of people are that without being what she is. It's not only her things, it's all the working of her dear little mind. She's definitely orderly."

"If that means giving orders," said Philip, "I agree. She's so *bossy,* that's what I complain about her."

"What I complain about you," affirmed Laura, after they had laughed, "is speaking with your mouth full."

4

The vicarage had not the same perplexities about accommodating the education of its daughters to its purse as it had in respect of its sons. Upton Academy was not so venerable a foundation as Upton College but the archaic flavor of "academy" as applied to a school, and especially to a girls' school, proclaimed that its roots went tolerably deep. At some period later than Miss Pinkerton's celebrated institution on Chiswick Mall, in the days when Upton Springs was something of a fashionable spa, it had been established as Upton Springs Academy for Young Ladies. Its title now had shed the particularization both of its locality and of its purpose. As Upton Academy it stood in the front rank of girls' schools and it specialized at both ends of its curriculum. Its Junior School ("Academy Junior") professed an admirable grounding for girls up to fourteen; "Academy Senior" refined even up to eighteen and nineteen those who, seeking such refinement, would normally pass on to a finishing school. And its fees for day-girls, of whom it had a large number, were remarkably moderate.

Mary started at Academy Junior when she was ten. Her going off for her first day had none of the emotionalisms of John's first setting out for "Kilbracken," much less of the sensationalisms of Philip's. When it was time to be off it was she, not her mother, who said in a business-like way, "Well, now I think we'd better go." In a business-like way she kissed her father and Minna. She would not indeed have kissed at all had not the embraces been pressed upon her. It was no occasion that she could see for fuss. John had already started for the College. Philip, of course, was not to be seen. To her sister she said, "Good-by, Ruth. Remember what I said about not touching my things," and business-like she stepped off with Laura.

Walking to school with her had been one of the many especial delights in the daughter of her own which Laura had fondly visualized while awaiting the child's arrival. She had imagined doing it, hand in hand, every day, calling for her, too, when work was over and hand in hand walking back home with her.

It was not a bit like that now it had come. Mary didn't like walking hand in hand. When at a crossing or other difficult point of ordinary walks Laura or the vicar sought to take her hand she always wriggled it loose as soon as might be. Laura's first words as now they left the vicarage gate were, "And I'll come to meet you, darling, punctually at four. *What* a heap you'll have to tell me. I'll come for you every day, I vote, except when I can't manage it."

Mary's reply was: "Yes, come today, mother, but once I've started regularly I think I'd rather you didn't. There'll be a lot of us coming out all together and I shall have my chosen friends and we'll walk together until each of us comes to where her road turns off. That's what it will be, you'll find I shall tell you."

She had the whole routine of school life neatly set out in her mind. It was a practical matter and she proposed to deal with it, as she dealt with everything, in a practical way.

They reached the Academy. Laura went in with her. "Yes,

I suppose you ought to," assented Mary, "being my first day." She was handed over to Miss Ollard, the junior school's head.

"We've got a worker here," said Miss Ollard. "I can see that."

"Yes, I like lessons," said Mary, assured, unsmiling. "Well, good-by, mother."

5

Workers at Academy Junior were called by idlers "smogs." "You're a smog, I can see that straight off," a freckled girl with a long thin nose addressed Mary in the first interval between studies. The new girls had been sitting in a bay of a large schoolroom engaged upon an examination paper which would allot them to forms. The conspicuously nosed girl presumably had been one of the class which had been at work in the body of the room. Mary had not noticed her. Her eyes and her mind had been entirely on the answering of her questions. She was resolved to be placed in as high a form as she could.

"What is a 'smog'?" she inquired.

"A mistress's own darling who swots her head off and appears to enjoy doing it. You do, don't you?"

"I like lessons, if that's what you mean."

"I knew you did. We've got one in our form, Barbara Pinfold. There she is, over there, looking as if she's going to be sick. She always does and most smogs do."

"Do I?" inquired Mary gravely. She rather liked the look of Barbara Pinfold, obviously a serious girl, and decided to make friends with her.

"Well, you've got that ghastly pious look that smogs have; the going-to-be-sick part will soon come. Our form's about as high as anyone's likely to get from the Entrance Paper and I rather hope you'll come into it."

"Thank you," said Mary.

"Don't thank me," said the long-nosed girl. "A form loathes having one smog in it. She rots up the whole standard of private study, which naturally we want to keep as low as possible, and she's so stuck on a pedestal that it's a wonder we don't all get sick ourselves having to gaze at her. If we had two of you I believe you'd form a sort of holy of holies of your own and we could stay outside and chase each other. What's your name?"

"Mary Brecque," said Mary, decidedly taken by this idea of entering a form in which the top places would be sought by only one other, friend and rival.

"Mine's Susan Absolam. Did you ever hear such a name in your life? Fortunately I'm always called Parker because of my nose. I say, Daisy," she broke off to a passing girl. "How do you think it would be if we had two smogs in—" She went along.

6

Mary was posted to Parker's form. The desk allotted to her was, to her great satisfaction, next to that of Barbara Pinfold. Barbara was also a day-girl. It was the combination of an extreme sallowness of complexion and a chin receded as if by the facial equivalent of a landslade that gave her, to the ribald, the appearance of suffering from the confirmed nausea of a first-class smog. To Mary lessons were an appreciated duty, with Barbara they were a passion. To Mary their mastery was a means of ascendancy and was therefore to be sought with all diligence, to Barbara their absorption and then, in the class-room, their faultless delivery, appeared, having regard to her unfortunate aspect, to give the relief of an emetic. Parker and those of Parker's kidney said that Barbara never looked so certain to be sick as when waiting her turn to speak, and never so nearly in heaven, with its awards of halo and surcease from all suffering, as during and immediately after the discharge of her office.

Mary, the Parkerites agreed, was not so utterly depraved a smog as that. She showed you, indeed, that a smog, though handicapped by her deplorable industry, can be quite a reasonably decent person. Barbara was loathed and appeared to relish being loathed much as the ascetic relishes his hair shirt; but Mary on the whole was liked. She was always ready to do things for you, always ready to lend you things. She helped Parkerites with their work in the only way in which a Parkerite wishes to be helped with work, namely, to have it done for her. It was the frequent practice of the mathematics mistress, Miss Stoop, to set a sum and then absent herself while it was being done. Immediately a Parkerite groan would go up, "Oh, Mary, how do you do this beastly thing?" Penciling swiftly and lightly on the other's paper, Mary would show. "And me, Mary," "And me," "And me." Of a morning, again, before the mistress's arrival in the class-room, haggard Parkerites would be seen attempting to crowd into five minutes the private study (as preparation was called) whose appointed hours had been used for more agreeable diversions. Mary, always early, would enter. "Oh, Mary, beloved, these ghastly irregulars, do tell us a few." "Oh, Mary, adored one, these repulsive decimals, do come and shove in a few dots."

With the same kindly smile which, when in indulgent mood, she had been wont to bestow on her dolls, invariably Mary would respond. With her classmates, unlike with her dolls, she was always indulgent. She liked the appeals to her superior intelligence. She liked the position of authority which the appeals gave her.

But she liked best of all the continuous struggle with Barbara Pinfold for top place. The two were on the best of terms. All the time that Mary was at the Academy Barbara was her greatest friend. But not by one particle of relaxation did either allow friendship to interfere with competition in class. "I think I've won the form-prize," business-like as ever, entirely without emotion, Mary at the first term's end told her parents. "I've kept Barbara's marks as well as my own, though not for the first fortnight when I hadn't realized things properly, and on those I make myself out to be twenty-seven ahead of her. In examinations I'm definitely better than she is; I write quicker and better. We compared our answers and she beat me, I know, in French and Geography, but my handwriting would count a bit. Free-hand drawing of course I can't tell; we couldn't compare that. But I've worked it all out very closely and I think I've got it. I really do."

They were to attend the prize-giving function.

"Oh, Mary," Laura cried, "I shall have to hold on to my chair to prevent myself leaping up and hugging you."

"My dear, you mustn't do anything like that," said the vicar. "Mary, I *shall* be proud and delighted," he beamed.

Their excited interest was repeated as Mary set off for school on the morning of the great day, for her own part only concerned now to rehearse them in their hour of arrival in the afternoon, where they were to go and what to do. "We'll remember," declared Laura, "and, darling, you remember, mind, what I've told you about not feeling disappointed should Barbara be the winner and not you. She's your great friend and you must feel just as delighted in her success, if it should be hers, as you would be in your own."

"It isn't the prize that really matters," endorsed the vicar, "it's the knowledge that you did your best to win it."

Mary received this as calmly as she had received the ardent expressions relative to the prospects of her winning. "All the same," her comment was, "I shall mind. I've set my heart on this. Now remember, please don't arrive before five minutes to three and not after five minutes past. Good-by."

"The way she laid it all down for us!" smiled the vicar as she closed the door behind her.

"I can see us having to behave very circumspectly," laughed Laura, "when she's of full age."

"That girl," nodded Minna from her end of the table, "will rule the perches in all her chicken houses. She will not be very sorry for Barbaras if they tumble off, that girl."

7

"Third form," announced Miss Arbuthnot, the Academy Principal, "Barbara Pinfold. Runner-up, Mary Brecque. A very close thing. Only twelve marks separated the two." She took up a handsomely-bound volume from the pile beside her and called forward the winner. "Barbara Pinfold."

Laura and the vicar had their eyes on Mary's face as her form's turn came. Mary showed herself sitting with lips compressed, hands tightly clasped. As the announcement was made the compression tightened. She joined in the clapping. Her lips remained pressed.

"Well done, our gallant little runner-up!" cried the vicar as, the distribution concluded, she joined them.

"I shall win it next term," said Mary composedly. "All the holidays I shall do geography and French, that's how she beat me. Now come this way to tea. I'll go in front with mother. We can't all walk together in this crowd."

That first form-prize was the only one she failed to win all the time she was at the Academy. The feat, term after term, as she went steadily up the school, had never before been accomplished, not, at least, in Miss Arbuthnot's time.

8

When Mary was within a few weeks of her seventeenth birthday she took her plan for the future to Miss Arbuthnot, then brought it cut and dried to her parents.

"Father, I'm going for a London University modern languages degree. You know how good my German is, thanks to Minna, and with hard work I can soon get my French not far behind. I've arranged it all with Miss Arbuthnot and it can all be very satisfactory. You haven't any objection, have you, or you, mother?"

The only objection possible to wholesome plans of any child at the vicarage was the vicarage's perpetual concern with costs. It was with anxious hope not to have to deny their daughter's aspirations that fondly parental feelings were spoken.

"Oh, darling," cried Laura, "how marvelous!"

"Why, Mary," beamed the vicar, "what a wonderful daughter I've got." He took off and polished his glasses, a characteristic habit in weighty moments.

They might have known that the plan, being Mary's, would have considered and surmounted financial difficulties. Mary, as Minna had long since affirmed, was Martha.

"It's all perfectly straightforward and simple," she said. "When I passed the London Matric in December with three honors I thought about it but I didn't say anything to anyone then. I knew that Miss Arbuthnot would have me in this term for the talk she always has with seniors who will be leaving after the term following their seventeenth birthday. That's next term for me, of course, so I thought I'd wait till then. Well, she's had me in, twice. Today was the second talk and this is what she's asked me to tell you. She's willing for me to stay on, if you're willing, past the ordi-

nary age as is done in the case of special girls, 'specials' as
we call them; you know, mother, Joan Lane is one. I'd stay
until I took my Intermediate which I'd do, she thinks, a year
from next October. That would be the only extra schooling
you'd have to pay for, father, and some of that I could pay
back to you, because then, while I'm working for the Final,
Miss Arbuthnot's willing to take me on as a junior assistant
teacher. Miss Concord and Mademoiselle Le Brun would
give me some coaching and I'd subscribe, Miss Arbuthnot
suggests, to the University Tutorial Correspondence course.
She'd pay me eight pounds a term for my teaching services.
It's not as much as a full-time junior assistant would get,
but I'd be allowed a lot of time for my studying and there'd
be the coaching thrown in, so to speak. I've thought it out,"
concluded Mary judicially, "and I think it's very good."

Laura had been controlling herself with difficulty. "My
darling," she now burst out, "I think it's perfectly marvelous. I know you don't like being kissed, but really—"

Mary submitted to the demonstration of affectionate delight, with placid detachment received also her father's
proud felicitations. The years of her prosecution of her
enterprise passed on.

With the same calmness as that with which she had stated
her intention to take a University degree she announced an
intention in disturbance of it.

9

As, returning home from the Academy to deliver this
announcement, she came into the vicarage hall, her orderly
eye noticed at once on the hat-pegs a hat that ought not to
be there. It ought not to be there because, recognizing it,
she knew that its owner should be in Scotland. Her heart
manifested a movement. The hat's owner had had place in

the thoughts on her decision which had occupied her as she came down to make it known.

She went quickly to the sitting-room. No one was there. She went to the study, opening the door upon the vicar seated at his table, not writing, deep in thought. She saw at a glance that it was anxious thought and she felt again that movement in her heart.

"Is John home?" she asked. "Has he come back?"

Unusually, the vicar did not smile. He nodded gravely. "Yes, dear."

"Father, is he going to join up?"

This time it was in negation that the vicar gravely moved his head. "He is standing by his principles."

She breathed, "Oh, poor John. Why has he come back?" she asked.

"General Lethbridge sent him."

She understood the implication of that. "Oh, poor John," she breathed again. Her hand still on the door, she drooped her chin to her breast and stood in thought of her brother.

Thus standing, thus engaged, she exposed herself a different character from that which normally she presented to the world, especially to her parents. These vicarage children, each so strongly his or her own type, were very devoted to one another. They had no mutuality of interests. This one was this sort, that one that sort. But they had a mutuality of affection. They were accustomed to one another. They were to one another rather as are the members of a litter of puppies. The puppies will range about, each absorbed in its own occasions, indifferent to its fellows. But it is as one that they will snuggle together when they are resting.

In the one-ness of the vicarage brood John had an especial place. He was the eldest. He had among his brothers and sisters the vested authority of that position. He had, more, an entire unselfishness which, never abusing that authority,

made it the greater. Three of these children lived actively
in worlds which were recognizable parts of the great world.
The fourth lived with a mysterious quiet in a world the like
of which they saw nowhere else about them. They did not
understand his gifts but they admired them enormously.
They did not understand his ideas about hating war and
all that made for war, but these were *his* ideas and therefore
they upheld them in him. He was John. Whatever John did
they supported him in doing.

Mary, for her own particular part in this affectionate attachment to the eldest born, was talented to appreciate the
quality of his verse. Emotionally it made no appeal to her
whatever, nothing did whose appeal was to the sensibilities,
not to the practicalities. When he had told her that he was
going to be a poet her reply had been: "Well, John, you *are*
a poet. I know enough about poetical form to know that.
But, you know, it doesn't lead to anything. It's not practical.
I hope you'll let it be only a second string." She was intel-
lectually equipped, similarly, to be able to follow his reason-
ing that to foster warlike interests was to foster war. "I
agree," she had said to him, "in theory; but to do away with
all that kind of thing is not practicable. You'll never get
everybody to refuse to let their children play with soldiers,
and you'll never get everybody to look the other way when
troops with a band are marching down the street. It's human
nature and to try to change human nature is merely silly."

Nevertheless the determination to set himself against war,
as the resolve to devote himself to poetry, was John and in
him was therefore to be approved. It was a familiar attribute
of your brother puppy snuggling against you in the litter
and therefore was not disturbing.

But Mary knew that to others, in this tremendous thing
in which the country now was involved, John's principles
were sharply disturbing. Already, up in the mistresses'

common-room at the Academy, she had heard what was going to be thought of men who might hang back from the call to arms.

Standing there, chin on breast, hand to door, she was profoundly concerned for her brother.

"Where is he?" she asked.

"He's down the garden, I think, poor boy," the vicar said.

"I'll go to him."

She turned to go. "By the way," she turned back—her head up, her pronouncement characteristically composed—"they're saying up in our common-room that there's bound to be a tremendous demand for women to take the places of all the men who are joining up. These Voluntary Aid Detachments that they're starting in connection with the Red Cross are only the beginning of it. Well, I'm going up to town tomorrow to arrange to join one. I've finished with my B.A. till this is over."

Without waiting for reply she closed the door.

Seven

WHEN it was Ruth's turn to go to the Academy her setting forth for her first day at school was a quite different affair from that of any of the others. Vicar, Laura, Minna, accompanied her to the gate; but it was under the chilly eye of Mary, who was accompanying her. In so far as her high spirits could be subjected to the process she was, as it were, marched off.

"We'll be late," voiced Mary. She parted for the warning the compressed lips with which she stood watching the final embraces at the gate. It was about the fifth time she had issued the caution. Half-way through breakfast it had been occasioned by Ruth's neglect of her plate consequent upon her excited chatter. At intervals it had been discharged at her ever since.

"Now are you ready? Oh, tchk!" For now Ruth, at last outside the gate, had flown within it again to fling her arms anew about her mother.

"Well, I must say good-by," cheerfully expostulated Ruth, started at last but still waving.

"If you were going," said Mary, "to Timbuctoo for life, as one well might imagine that you are, instead of a mile up the road for the day, I wonder how long that would take you?"

"Oh, golly," cried Ruth, fascinated by such tremendous speculation. "But that would be at the station, I suppose, or at the docks, and I should be moved off when the whistle blew. I say, Mary, where *is* Timbuctoo exactly? One's always hearing about it."

"It's about time you did go to school. It's in French West Africa. *Need* you walk backwards?"

"I'm only waving before we get to the corner."

"Well, if you must be so ridiculous, please stand while you do it, otherwise you'll fall. I'll go on."

"Oh, right you are."

And concluding presently an enthusiastic semaphoring and blowing of kisses, Ruth proceeded then after her sister in an airy manner of progression much her habit.

"That girl," pronounced Minna as the three watched the last glimpse, "has never walked of herself since she was born. That girl would skip to a funeral."

"She's gloriously light-hearted," said Laura as they turned about to go in.

"Isn't there some quotation," inquired the vicar, "about a star dancing when somebody was born? In her case though I'd say a sunbeam."

"It is more like," Minna agreed. "That girl there would shine herself through a—how do you call it?—an extinguish."

"An eclipse," the vicar said, and was taken as he laughed with a little tremor.

"Dearest," cried Laura, "what a shiver!"

"One of those funny shudders that one gets," he smiled. They stepped into the hall. "Dear me," he said, "how quiet the house seems without her."

She took his arm affectionately.

2

These were the happy years of the children's schooling. Laura knew that if her husband, as happily together they passed through them, gave, so to say, and as himself he admitted, his right hand to John, his other he gave to Ruth.

While he worked in his study John had the freedom of it for reading or for his lessons. Mutual in spirit, neither disturbed the other. Ruth also had a freedom of the room. It was not bestowed upon her. She assumed it as by right and her exercise of it was eminently disturbing. For ever, bursting in, she was disturbing the vicar at his work; but "No, she never really interrupts me," he would declare to Minna, wildly chasing her to prevent her, and he would lay down his pen and take her on his knee and draw pictures for her or show her a book she had brought with her.

She always on these occasions came to him with a kiss and left him with a kiss. If skipping was her gait and a sunbeam her presence, affection was her nature. Precisely Mary's opposite, she liked, when she was walking out with Laura, the vicar, or Minna, to hold hands. When being read to she liked to sit on the lap of the reader. In the midst of a story it was a common habit with her suddenly to twist about and give a hug.

"You don't want me to stop, do you?" she would be asked.

"No, I just love you, that's all."

"What else do you love?" it became a joke to ask her.

"Parties!"

Ruth no sooner knew what a party was, which was when she was but four, than to go to another became, and remained, the delight of her life.

Laura would come into the nursery, envelope and card in hand. "Ah, ha, I've got an invitation here. I wonder whom it can be for and what it is!"

Ruth would leap up from whatever she might be engaged with. "A party! A party!" she would cry, jumping up and down on her toes, face crimson, eyes sparkling, hands clapping above her head. She would count the days to it. When it came and, madly excited, she arrived at it, with utmost difficulty could Laura or Minna hold her while getting her out of her wraps and into her change of shoes. Away with a final wriggle she would escape, wildly into the midst of the assembly would fling herself. Devoted as she was to her mother and to her father, the smallest chance of getting away for some fun showed how elastic were the bonds that attached her to them. In the winter in which she was twelve the vicar was laid abed with a sharp attack of bronchitis. It had started during the last week of the Academy term. Going off to and returning from school Ruth had been all fondest solicitation. On the first morning of the holidays, having completed the open-air exercise with the others on which Laura had insisted, up she came bounding to the vicar's bedroom, rosy-cheeked, filled with affection.

"Now, my poor old darlingest dad, this is the moment I've been longing for ever since you got ill. I've had my walk and now I'm going to spend the whole of the rest of the morning with you, and all the afternoon too, after you've had your sleep. The whole, entire day; think of it! Now what shall we do? Shall we play something, halma or backgammon or draughts? Or shall I read to you? I don't care *how* dry it is. Or shall we just talk, or what?"

"Just talk first, I'd like best," said the vicar, his eyes adoring alike her loveliness and her affection.

"*Right.* Have you got everything you want? Sure? Well, now, I'll sit just here and while we talk I'll hold your hand and stroke it. That's jolly, isn't it?"

"Darling girl, it's delicious."

"*Right.* Now the talking. You'd like me, I know, to tell you things about the Acad., wouldn't you? Well, dad, I *may* get pushed up into the next form next term, but to be perfectly honest I'm not a bit *sure*. You see, dad, my worst subject *un*fortunately is—"

A tap at the door brings in Sarah, the maid.

"If you please, miss, there's a young lady at the door, Miss Joan Vyner—"

Up leaps the devoted nurse, suffering the invalid's hand to fall where it will, and rushes to the window. "Oh, golly to goodness," she cries, twisting herself to look down upon the porch, "she's brought that boy cousin of hers, it must be, that she was telling me about. Oh, larks! Oh, I say, half a sec., dad, while I just dash down."

Tumultuously she flies out of the room, leaving the door wide. Tumultuously in five minutes she is back again. "Oh, I say, dad, Joan and this cousin of hers, he does look such an ass but rather jolly I quite believe, want me to go in her pony-cart with them, her mother's driving, of course, over to Wildhurst where they're leaving a note and then back to lunch and stay the afternoon arranging some charades for their party. I know mother'll let me. Oh, I say, dad, will you mind most awfully if I stay with you tomorrow, oh, bother, I can't tomorrow, well, the next day instead of today? Oh, thanks awfully, most darling dad."

She throws herself upon the figure, opportunity for devotion to whose care she had been longing for all the week, grinds his spectacles painfully into an eye in the exuberance of her embrace, and with "I must fly" is flown, the door, as before, wide behind her.

3

Life, love and laughter were the essences indeed of this girl's disposition.

Mary marched up the Academy, duty her lodestar. Ruth danced up it, pleasure her aim. No idle Parker greeted her on her first morning. She entered a form of industrious and decorous young creatures, plain of features withal. From her first day she outstood among them alike in airiness of char-

acter and in prettiness of face. The "Character" which
she earned above Miss Ollard's signature on her first term's
report was comprised in two words: "Precocious. Lovable."
When she was fourteen and newly promoted into Academy
Senior, "Ruth," wrote Miss Arbuthnot, "has winning ways
both in achievement and in charm. It is to be suggested,
however, that, while 'Forward!' is a brave device for one's
banner, 'Forward but not too fast' is a wiser."

This might have been Miss Ollard's laconic estimate am-
plified. In a secondary application of its warning clause it
might, too, have been a presage of events little more than a
year ahead. Ruth was but shortly past her fifteenth birthday
when her precocity evidenced itself in the Victorian sense
of "fast" as applied to girls; as so much too fast, indeed, as
to come near to causing her career at the Academy to end,
as had poor Parker's, in her withdrawal.

Of all ill-chosen places in which to exhibit precocity of this
order a church was the scene. The Academy attended that
place of worship of Upton Springs which was nearest to it,
St. Saviour's, incumbent the Rev. Carlton Willings, rural
dean. Day-girls were required to go to Sunday matins with
the boarders unless home arrangements were preferred for
them. Naturally such had been preferred for Mary; but
Ruth, when came her first Saturday at Academy Junior, had
begged that she might take word to Miss Ollard that on the
morrow St. Saviour's with the school should be her portion.

Laura professed to be scandalized. "You, a vicar's little
girl, to attend another vicar's church! Whoever heard of
such a thing? My chick, of course you can't."

"Well, let me at least ask dad, mum," the chick demanded. "After all, it's for him to say as it's a church
matter."

This was a phrase much in use in responsible circles in
the vicarage. Its adoption by Ruth made Laura laugh.

"Well, ask him then; but do consider his feelings, you unnatural daughter, you."

The feelings stirred uppermost in the vicar when with
whirlwind rush up to his dressing-room the request was
taken to him were those of his fond affection for his
youngest born.

"But why do you want to go to another church?" gravely
surprised he at first remonstrated with her.

"Dad, it would be such fun."

He was brushing his hair, a brush in either hand. Ruth
had squeezed herself between him and the dressing-table,
her vivid face upturned to him. He suspended his toilet
operation to look down at her, slightly shocked. "For fun?
But, Ruth, one doesn't go to church for fun."

"Well, one ought to *like* going, oughtn't one?"

"Most certainly one should."

"Well, dad, to tell you the *utter* truth, sometimes I don't
very much like going; whereas, if I could go with all the
Academy girls, two by two in an enormous crocodile, I
really would look forward to going. *Do* let me, dad."

One impulse of the vicar's instincts bade him inquire into
this alarming utter truth. Another, drawing his heart towards the upturned face, presented the guileless confession
to him as a less matter-of-fact nature would amusedly have
taken it. He stooped to kiss her. "Well, try it tomorrow," he
said, and by the delighted arms flung round his head was
put to do his hair all over again.

The morrow's trial was the beginning of regular Sunday
incorporation in the enormous crocodile. Starting at its
head (Academy Junior pupils in front, Senior behind) Ruth
worked back along its length with her progress up the
school and correspondingly changed also her pew. The sittings occupied by the girls were the half-pews entered from
St. Saviour's left-hand lateral aisle. Occupants of the other

halves of their pews entered them from the central aisle. A partition effected the division between the halves and the girls to whom were allotted the partition corners (considerably sought after) sat therefore next to members of the general congregation.

To Ruth in the term of her fifteenth birthday fell one of these coveted partition corners and it happened that the central continuation of her pew was in this particular term occupied by new seat-holders. An army crammer had moved from wherever he had been previously located to Upton Springs. Ferguson's, as the establishment called itself in the list of army crammers in those days advertised on the front page of the *Morning Post,* brought some dozen aspirants for Sandhurst and Woolwich into the neighborhood. Mr. Ferguson, conventionally concerned for their souls as actively for their brains, took for them what sittings he could get in St. Saviour's. A pew allotted to him for six of his number was the pew against the partition of which sat Ruth.

The six were larky young gentlemen. On the first Sunday of their appearance, requiring to be shown the place engaged for their devotions, they rather sheepishly trailed behind the verger. On the following Sunday, knowing their place, they gave the impression of jostling one another up the aisle in their haste to be on their knees. Quite unmistakably there was a scuffling at the entrance to the pew. The young gentleman who had managed to head the jostling was about to step in when he was elbowed aside by an openly grinning companion who plunged in before him and stumbled over hassocks to the end seat. The grinner, sitting triumphant, had overlooked the wisdom of securing himself quite at the end. A fellow army candidate coming apparently to sit on his right, stepped across his legs, dropped himself half on the seat and half on his neighbor's knee, and after a grim silent struggle effected a squirming down of himself next the partition.

The Academy worshipers had not yet arrived. Had girls been in their pews during these indecorous proceedings it is probable that Ruth's imperilment of being withdrawn from the school as a result of her behavior in St. Saviour's would never have been precipitated. Any mistress witnessing the rivalry between the larky young gentlemen to sit next to the partition would have realized its object to be to sit in closest proximity to rows of young ladies, side by side indeed with one, and Miss Arbuthnot would have taken then and there the step which she did not in fact take until the deplorable outcome of this neighborship between Ferguson worshipers and Academy worshipers had befallen. Miss Arbuthnot wrote then, severally and sharply, to Mr. Ferguson, to the Rev. Carlton Willings, and to the churchwardens of St. Saviour's demanding immediate removal of Ferguson sittings from Academy sittings; her reason "the disgraceful incident witnessed at matins yesterday by a member of my staff."

Miss Sturgis was the name of this member. Diploma'd in the teaching of mathematics, she was certificated by the girls in the arts of creeping and pouncing, her soubriquet "Slippers" deriving from the stealthiness of movement whereby she effected her appearance during secret breaches of discipline. Uncannily penetrative movements of her eyes were also notoriously in this lady's gifts. Seated in church against the partition of a pew three rows behind that divided between pupils of the Academy and pupils of Mr. Ferguson she was ill placed, it might have been thought, for observation of it. She saw so much nevertheless in its Ferguson section, she suspected so much in the corner of the Academy section, that on the fourth Sunday of term she tapped on the shoulder at the church door the girl whose place in the sittings was immediately behind that occupied by Ruth.

"Go back to Agatha Hastings," she said, pointing down the queue. "You will sit next to her in my usual place today. I will sit in yours."

Ruth had already gone in. While the pew behind her filled she was on her knees in the devotions prescribed immediately on entry. If she thought anything at all about the place behind her she thought that it accommodated its usual occupant. But her interest in the seating arrangements of St. Saviour's was in point of fact agreeably confined, as it had been all the way to church, to the individual placing of six candidates for commissions in the army, particularly of one. They had not yet come in. She was speculating as to which of them, when they did, she would find beside her. She was diverting herself with the prospects of catching the eyes of the one in whom she was particularly interested.

On their return from service on the Sunday on which they had jostled to secure the partition seat, the six had drawn lots to determine the order of, in future, securing the privilege by turns. In the disclosures in Miss Arbuthnot's study following the event which now, during the singing of the third hymn, was to precipitate itself, it was revealed that Ruth knew all the larky young gentlemen by name, one by personal association. It was divulged that introduction of himself by the partition man of each Sunday was effected by his introduction of "Hulloa!" into an early verse of the first canticle. It was admitted that conversation was then hymned into all subsequent singing. It was confessed that one vocalist in the duets thus rendered had been met, as it were, off stage.

This vocalist was that resourceful member of the larky six who on Jostling Sunday had stepped over his victorious companion's legs and squirmed himself into the partition corner. Following his tuneful "Hulloa!" and encouraged by Ruth's

tuned-in return, he had skillfully adapted to the melodies of
canticles, psalms and hymns:

"My na-a-ame is Ja-a-ack Hartopp."
"I'm cra-a-aming fo-o-or the army."
"Wha-a-at's your name?"
"You're jo-o-olly pretty."
"Are you-ou-ou a boarder?"
"Cou-ou-ldn't we me-e-et somewhere?"

Much else besides Mr. Hartopp had melodiously rendered,
Ruth as melodiously replying. The two had met. So recently
as the evening before Miss Sturgis's posting of herself in the
seat behind Ruth assignation had been kept in the lane at
the bottom of the vicarage garden. It had been cut short by
the appearance of the vicar, bound homeward, at the end of
the lane. Mr. Hartopp had done his best to present the back
view of a young man pensively taking the air. Ruth had
scrambled through the hedge. Mr. Hartopp, this Sunday
situated, as it turned out, at the far end of the pew, be-
thought himself during the prayers before a hymn to indite
on the flyleaf of his prayer-book an inquiry as to how she
had fared.

Miss Sturgis saw Mr. Hartopp fiddling with a paper in
his hands. She saw his left fist then thump the right leg of
his neighbor. She saw movements of fists up the line of
army candidates. Miss Sturgis realized what was happening.
She waited, holding her breath under the strain, until a fist
hung nonchalantly over the partition before her. She made
then a spidery formation of the fingers of her own right
hand.

Drooping down to the partition, a delicate white Academy
fist had no sooner received the contents of the rugged brown
Ferguson fist there awaiting it than with steely grasp there
closed upon Ruth's hand the pounce of the Academy's cer-
tified pouncer.

4

"I nearly died," said Ruth.

This, some days later, was imparted to a fellow Academician, as raptly listening as raptly being told. Following that petrifying clutch upon her hand by the hand of Miss Sturgis, Ruth had in fact passed through several of those approximations to death to which trouble is rendered by the emotions of the young. The second was when Miss Arbuthnot concluded the interview in her study to which the culprit was brought from church. She was coming, she had announced, to see the vicar that afternoon. "And you may tell your father," she pronounced sentence of death as Ruth went to the door, "that you are no longer a pupil of the Academy."

Arriving home late for lunch Ruth excusably said nothing then of what had happened. Her woe-begone appearance, her neglect of her food, informed the family that much was amiss. When the meal was ended, "Dad, may I speak to you in your study?" she asked, her eyes blinking, her voice low. "And you too, mum."

The vicar put his arm about her. Laura took a hand. Mystified parents murmuring endearments, the melancholy procession found the study. "Please sit down," desired Ruth. The vicar went by habit to his chair, Laura took the sofa. Beneath her bowed head their daughter's bosom heaved convulsively as though an inward earthquake threatened. She rushed then to the vicar, threw herself upon him, with arms clasped about his neck cried out, "Oh, dad, I've been expelled," and in her sobbed recital of her story died her third death of the poignant series.

Her fourth was suffered when, a half-hour later, Laura took her up to her bedroom that she might lie down in recovery from the deaths already died. Laura knelt down by the bed. "Don't tell a bit more than you feel you'd like to tell, my darling. But telling does make you feel better, you'll find, my sweet." Reiterated murmurs of this description of understanding and sympathy, absence of least reproach, drew all the story, start to finish, even the kisses exchanged with Mr. Hartopp. This was a most agonizing death to die.

The fifth was died during the whole of the immensely long period which began with Laura's, "I think I hear Miss Arbuthnot arrived. I'll go down." The sixth was when the vicar came up. "Dear child, you're not expelled. You're going back tomorrow just as usual."

Yet more were died. One was during Miss Arbuthnot's forgiveness "for your parents' sake." Another was in her feelings during her mother's astounding revelation that she too in her schooldays had thought herself in love with boys. Laura indeed appeared to know the practices so well, and with such terms as owlish and goosish and calf-love laughed at herself so mockingly as to make Ruth squirm at having cut similar figures with the larky six. Then Laura swung round to how far from laughable was the foolish business when deceit was involved. That part made Ruth feel horrible. Her father's contribution to her funerals was made on the study sofa, his arm about her. "A sermon, darling. I'm going to tell you the text and then we'll make the body of it together. 'My house shall be called the house of prayer; but ye have made it a den of thieves.' Darling child, when you used the house of prayer, St. Saviour's, for talking to those young men and receiving letters from them . . ."

"I never realized, dad, I never realized."

This death, died in that realization, was the most agonizing of all.

5

Yet what, after all, is death when you are fifteen, when at as early as the age of five you were dubbed Miss Airs and Graces, and have airily and gracefully skipped through life ever since? What are ten deaths when, in the week following them, the only one you are impelled to describe to your schoolmate is the thrilling throes of the first when you were pounced upon with the note in your hand? Regarded by such volatile perceptions death is put where it belongs in Ruth's rendering of the most impressive passage of literature's most impressive threnody.

"O death, where is thy sting-a-ling-a-ling?" she would sometimes express her light-heartedness by singing. Her light-headedness, similarly, fluttered her always to the frivolous side of an event, however grave. Eighteen months after her exchanges with the larky six, candidates for commission in the army swarmed about the place not in pews of six but in battalions. Great Britain was at war. Philip was with the Fleet. Mary was with the V.A.D.'s. John had received a white feather through the post. People had been rude to father about Minna because she was a German. A letter—"I wonder if you remember me?"—written under a regimental crest had been received from Mr. Hartopp. The Academy was knitting socks, mufflers and Balaclava helmets for the troops. Life was thrilling beyond all previous imagination.

Ruth's knitting needles flew. In the Christmas holidays she transferred them from the Academy to the parish war-work party organized by her mother. It met every afternoon in what in earlier days had been the children's schoolroom. Ruth's seat was the desk she had used when she did lessons with her mother and Minna. She kept her knitting locked in it which rather amused the adult workers. So devoted was she to the work it held that not only was she often to be found at it of a morning but she would arise early and put in a spell before breakfast. Her habit in previous holidays having been to lie in bed till the last possible moment and scramble down late for breakfast her parents were uncommonly pleased. "You certainly are the most devoted little war-worker," declared the vicar, coming in from an early service and finding her taking the letters from the postman.

But her war-work was not in fact confined to knitting. There had begun to appear in the Press just then advertisements of the kind:

Lonely Subaltern would like cheery correspondence. Box ——, etc.

Ruth had contracted the admirable practice of early rising in order to intercept the vicarage mail.

Afternoon

One

THE whole parish will be buzzing with it presently."

This was said to vicar's warden Colonel Gilling in the third month of the war, in October, 1914. It was spoken by him who five years previously had been St. Luke's "new" curate, Dick Oadbee's successor, the Rev. Hilary Tweed.

Dick Oadbee's mother had died. He had asked at once to be released for his missionary resolve. It was due to the vicarage's combined profound regret, centered in the vicar, that Hilary Tweed had come to St. Luke's in his place. Mr. Phipps-Tracy, seeing the announcement of Mrs. Oadbee's death in his newspaper, had written sympathetically to his former curate. In grief we are peculiarly susceptible to compassion from unlikely quarters. Caught in an emotional mood, Oadbee had been greatly touched by this kindliness from one who in their relations as chief and subordinate had been the reverse of affable. His reply, expressing his feelings, had pointed them with references to his shortcomings of those days. Mr. Phipps-Tracy, mellowed apparently by his retirement, had written again, discountenancing the other's regrets, admitting his own austerity. Oadbee had mentioned that as soon as he could be released he was going into the mission field. His former vicar concluded kindly references to this by mentioning, in respect of the vacancy thus occurring, that his curate nephew, Hilary Tweed, was seeking a change and that he was anxious to help him in effecting it.

With characteristic impetuosity Dick Oadbee charged over to the vicarage with the letter, eager to be able to write back that the nephew would be considered for the post. That he might do so he presented to the vicar almost as a personal favor. The vicar, all the vicarage with him, was highly disposed to give pleasure to one who was affectionately esteemed and was now leaving them. The inquiries he made concerning Hilary Tweed were satisfactory. The young man was invited for a week-end. His qualities were approved.

It was by these impulses—Oadbee's of gratitude, the vicar's of affection—that the vicar came to succeed Oadbee with an assistant priest whom, later, he sometimes permitted himself to doubt was quite the man he would have liked. Tweed, five years on, was a big, fair young man inclining to be fat. He carried the back of his head bent over the back of his collar. This gave his face, which was large and shiny, the effect of a polished surface tilted to catch the light. It gave his voice, which was full and self-confident, the effect of being thrown with parabolic intention to go up and come down on top of you or behind you. When he read the lessons he stood well back from the lectern and delivered the scriptures as if discharging them from a mortar, spot-lit. It was like that, indeed, that he commonly poised and talked, catching the attention wherever he might be. Laura said that he liked catching attention.

He stood now shinily and self-confidently looking down upon the vicar's warden, who was sitting at a trestle table in the back room of shop premises now serving as Upton Springs' recruiting depot for Kitchener's Army. Predicting a buzzing throughout the parish, he had "just heard," he had previously been saying, that John Brecque had given up his post at Upton House School.

Colonel Gilling, receiving this news with the bulging eye-balls of one who would speak but for a lump of meat stuck in his throat, was in khaki. Restored to the active list, Dug-out branch, he was in charge of recruiting over the area of which Upton Springs was part. In his spurs and gaiters, Sam

Browne belt, South African and Indian Frontier medals, and insignia of crown and star, he now was all glitter and glare, moving and speaking by numbers as never before and nowhere so fiercely as when his leisure strutted him about Upton or his duties caused him to visit its recruiting station.

Overcoming the obstruction to his speech, " 'Given up: his post,' " he erupted. "He's been fired: sacked: discharged: with ignominy."

The tilted plane of the curate's face reflected interest rather than concern. "I'm afraid I rather guessed that. I used the phrase that was used to me by the Upton House matron when she told me as I was coming along just now. No doubt she felt that, to me, she had to put it kindly."

"The vicar hadn't told you?"

"No . . . he hadn't."

The inflection of voice invited comment on the omission and the colonel with a single sharp rap supplied it.

"Funny!"

Tweed registered a compliment to himself by a loyal, if possibly invidious, "Well, he naturally— It was dismissal, was it?" he then asked.

"Flung out. Bartlett told me so: himself. Put it to the fellow of course, that he'd better: resign; but with his term's notice check in his hand as he: did so."

"Really? When was it?"

"Yesterday."

Mr. Bartlett, in his recital of his action to Colonel Gilling, had not thought it necessary to state that his assistant master had refused to take the unearned check. The Rev. Hilary Tweed, forgetting, no doubt, the inflection of his voice when admitting the vicar's omission to tell him of the matter, was not reminded to say that he had not seen him yesterday nor as yet today. The Upton House headmaster had been concerned only with the honor of his school. The assistant priest of St. Luke's appeared to be concerned only with the repercussion of that vindicated honor on the parishioners. It was at this point of the interview that he made his prediction.

"The whole parish will be buzzing with it presently."

"It: will. And I say to you, Tweed," declaimed the colonel, saying it with sharp drum-taps of a paper-weight on the table, "that just as it was insufferable for Bartlett to allow his school to be made a: funk-hole, so it will scandalize the parish that the vicar should permit the vicarage to be a: funk-hole."

"What can he do, sir?" remonstrated Tweed, the loyalty of his protest that of one who, himself standing aside from striking a friend, makes room for another to have a go.

"Do? Force the fellow to: enlist."

"Force him? He's not a boy, colonel."

The tone was of the same order of invitation to his companion to have a whack, and the colonel, with reverberating drum-tap on the table, landed his punch with precision.

"He's a white-livered: shirker."

"According to the vicar, and to what John himself has told me, it's not shirking, it's a matter of moral principle."

"Balderdash."

"Well, it's what he says."

"It's what every coward up and down the country says. And will go on saying till we get compulsion and bring 'em into khaki clapped in: irons. Moral principle! Conscientious objection! Are you going to tell me that you believe that: rubbish?"

Tweed's own conscience was adapted by long practice to assisting him in his hobby of running with the hare and hunting with the hounds. It reminded him now that rubbish was not precisely the epithet with which he had received the vicar's explanations of his son's attitude to war. It warningly

figured for him a picture of the colonel declaiming in the
vicarage study, "Your own curate says it's: balderdash."
Tilting his face to catch the full light of nobility of character, "If a man pleads conscience to me, colonel," he threw
up from his mortar, "I am bound by my cloth to listen to
him. What I may think I may prefer not to say; but this I
can tell you, that I wish I had the chance that these objectors have."

"Good man, Tweed. Good man. If more of you fellows
spoke like that we'd shame out these skunks with hot:
pokers."

The curate, well-pleased at this approbation of his shelling,
ceased fire from his mortar and returned to normal speech,
now gravely concerned.

"What principally bothers me, attached as I naturally am
to my vicar, is what you said just now about the parish
being scandalized when this news gets around. I mean to
say, it's going to be a bit awkward for the vicar, isn't it?"

"It's going to be so awkward for the vicar," declared the
colonel, "that it's going to be awkward for everyone officially
connected with St. Luke's. When I'm addressing recruiting
meetings in other districts what am I, as churchwarden,
going to say if someone gets up and demands, 'What about
your own vicar's son?' When you're preaching one of your
fighting sermons down at the Banks, how are you going to
throw your full weight into it when you know that half
your congregation is thinking the same question. Eh? Have
you thought of: that?"

"Indeed I have," with simple earnestness returned the
curate, not adding that the duration of his thoughts upon
the subject was the few seconds since the vicar's warden had
brought it to his notice. For some moments the two gazed
on one another, as did stout Cortez' men, with a wild sur-
mise. The colonel saw himself on a platform knocking to-

gether the heads of an interrupter and of the vicar's son and hurling their bodies across the hall. The curate observed himself in the pulpit of St. Luke's (the vicar absent) winning favor from the Bagge and similar persuasions by references to those who hung back in this hour of our country's needs delivered in the form of caps which the congregation could place where they fitted.

The colonel was the first to draw himself from these engaging speculations.

"Have you heard anything said as yet?" he demanded. "Down at: the Banks?"

The Banks had greatly increased its population since the vicar's warden first had been seized of a species of fit at the suggestion of establishing a mission-hall there, then, suffering a secondary seizure on hearing of Hope Hubbard's poaching of souls, himself had proposed the idea. Thurstead, additional to expansion of its railway works, had been found conveniently placed for minor factory sites. Upton Bank had become its dormitory. Quickened by the needs thus brought about, the vicar, Oadbee eagerly supporting him, had increased by all means his efforts to take St. Luke's into the Banks. His ceaseless activities for the purpose, his "beggings day in day out" as it was termed, had not added to his popularity with the critical elements, with the husk, of his parishioners. Undaunted, unconscious indeed that offense could be given by pressing the furtherance of the Cross, he had been enabled to bring to his daily thinking on his knees a great happiness of success. From its beginnings in the cobbler's workshop, the missionary enterprise into the Banks had grown into the dignity of a daughter church. St. Mark's, as it was called, was housed temporarily in a structure of corrugated iron. Work had been started on its permanent home. Two retired priests who had come to reside in Upton Springs augmented the vicar's staff by giving voluntary service. Tweed, as latterly Oadbee before him, acted as curate-in-charge at St. Mark's.

Called upon now as to having heard Banks' opinion of his vicar's recreant son, "Well, not very much," he replied, "yet." As if in apology for the admission, "He's not known down there, of course," he added, "as well as he is up here. Even as it is though, more than one mother I've spoken to about persuading sons to join up has said, 'Well, there's other folks' sons, so I've heard, as might set the example as don't.' Things like that, you know; and I've known perfectly well who is being referred to. When it gets around down there that the vicar's son, so far from setting an example, has been sacked from his job because he won't, I shall hear it pretty straight. They don't mince words down at the Banks, you know. Which reminds me," he changed subject, his tone newly weighty, "there's another matter, by the way, that's being put about down there rather unpleasantly. Do you know, it's not liked that the vicar has a German in his house."

"Ha!" interjected his listener, stiffening as might one of the recruits for whom he was in search when first seeing an enemy between the sights of his rifle.

"That Miss Strauss, you know."

"Very well I know it," declared the colonel. "And let me tell you, Tweed, by no means only in the Banks is it being remarked upon. In the club here only yesterday the matter was put about pretty: seriously. Why hasn't the vicar, it was being asked, sent her: packing. Why: hasn't he?"

"Well, I've thought myself, sometimes—" began the curate.

"So have: I. She's been with them a long time and all that, I know. We all know her. I know that too. But we know also what these Germans are. Once a German always a German. Blood is thicker than: water. We're supposed to have rounded up every male Boche into internment camps but still they're catching spies, still there's spying going on; lights being shown at night, cypher messages in the newspapers, God knows what."

"Why, yes," took up Tweed, concerned to show, as it were, that others beside God were in the know, "it's for that reason they've actually had to stop chess problems being printed."

"I hadn't heard that. Really? It only shows you. Does she play chess this: Strauss?"

"I don't know, colonel. I'm not suggesting for a moment that—"

"If they've stopped the things it doesn't now matter. The situation, Tweed, is that every German woman was free to leave the country when war was declared and in the case of those who didn't the point is Why: didn't they? That's what people are asking up and down the country, as you can see in every paper you pick up, and that's what they are asking in the parish about this German at: the vicarage. You've heard it. I've heard it. It's unpleasant. The whole state of affairs at the vicarage is unpleasant. You're naturally attached to the vicar, as you said just now; so am I. But that doesn't blind me and it shouldn't blind you to facts as the whole parish sees them. You must know as well as I do that St. Luke's doesn't get from the vicar's sermons nor yet from the parish magazine the full-blooded war stuff that it expects to get. Taken by itself that might merely be: regrettable. But the parish looks across to his home and what does it see? It sees the vicarage sheltering: a shirker: and, er, harboring: a Hun. It's arousing: feeling. Does he realize it, Tweed?"

2

He was being made to realize it. On the day week of his curate's and his churchwarden's conference about him he was realizing it, drooped back in his seat at his study table. His left hand held an arm of his chair, his right, its fingers half closed, lay forward on the blotter; his head was bowed. It was the pose of dejection and there was upon his face that look of trouble which pronounces itself not as a shadowing but as an imprint.

Three months had set that mark. Those same prodigious months had altered, indeed, the customary expressions of the majority of civilians; in October, 1914, grave looks were the complexion of the day. But whereas the widely reflected concern of face, being of a common cause, was of a common cast, here, in the vicar's case, were lines of a private stress. His household was being assailed. His son was being openly avoided; people were openly hurting that dear Minna who stood to him as daughter. He could not understand it. For fifteen years in this parish seeing only good in his neighbor, he could not credit what now he saw in the attitude of his parishioners towards members of his family and, through them, towards himself. It bewildered him.

"But, father," in this week John had said gently. The two had been opposite one another at the study table. They were in the familiar positions in which one as a little chap had sat doing his home-work, the other serenely at his sermons. Now the fondness between them carried momentous things. "But, father, you knew that this sort of thing was going to happen to me." His dismissal from Upton House School was the thing that had happened. His distress at his father's moist eyes, at the tremulous plucking at his lips, was the cause of his gentle remonstrance. "From the first you knew

it. You told me so when I came back from General Lethbridge."

The vicar's voice had been in consonance with his expression. He made effort to control it. "I knew, dearest boy, what
public opinion was likely to say. I never imagined that
among friends, amongst those who knew you—"

He stopped. His son, reaching across to touch his hand,
sought to allay the tide of emotion. "Well, look now," John
said, "it's as public opinion that you must take Mr. Bartlett,
although he's a friend. In what he has done he's interpreting
the feelings of his boys' parents, of the General Lethbridges.
He has a responsibility towards them and he's bound to
exercise it. You mustn't think of what he's done as personally unfriendly."

A dawning showed behind the misty eyes. "That's true,
that's true; of course he's driven."

"Of course he is."

The dawning shone. "Of course, of course. God forgive
me, I was misjudging him."

The dismissed assistant master took a mental glimpse of
the misjudged man unctuously reveling in a circular letter
to the baronetage. "You will be interested to hear that, on
account of his pacifist ideas, I have parted with the services
of—" Preserving, however, the picture of the headmaster
which he had caused his father to see, that of a good friend
painfully pursuing an unpleasant duty, "You misjudge no
one, father," he smiled. "You couldn't if you tried. But what
I want to talk to you about is this, that just as Mr. Bartlett is
actuated by the feelings of his boys' parents so you must
expect to see many of your people in the parish here similarly actuated towards me by the national feeling. You've
seen something of it already. You've seen their looks and
their manner when we've been out together. You saw that
white feather which came by post. I opened that in front of

you, not suspecting what it was. All the other incidents, so as to make you think that perhaps you had only fancied them, I have pretended not to notice."

He paused. Lines were about his mouth which had not been three months before. His voice had an intense quality not formerly its note. In his pause the lines sharpened. When he resumed speech its depth was newly evident. It was as if, having readied his plow, now he gripped on the handles and drove his furrow.

"There's no use," he said, "in pretending any more. This dismissal from Upton House has finished that. You'll see things and you'll hear things more painful than any you've seen or heard as yet. Or you would, so far as seeing them is concerned, if I stayed here. I'm not staying. I'm going away."

"You're going away?"

The recovery in the vicar's face had died. While he listened to his son's references to the hostile mien of friends —never previously alluded to by either—the mistiness had reassembled in his eyes, the plucking at his lips had been resumed.

"I'm going tomorrow."

"But, but where?"

"To London for a start. I—"

A great sound without, gathering volume, broke upon the attention of speaker and listener. Two miles away along the forest a military training camp had recently been established. Singing and the tramp of feet composed the sound. A route march was approaching, now as they listened was passing, the vicarage gate.

It's a long way to Tipperary, it's a long way to go;
It's a long way to Tipperary, to the sweetest girl I know.
Good-by, Piccadilly; farewell, Leicester Square,

It's a long, long way to Tipperary,
But my heart's right there.

It died away. John Brecque had put his elbows on the table. His head was in his hands. The pressure of his fingers showed white beneath the nails. He raised eyes of pain. "If that could leave me unmoved," he said, "I might suspect that I am, as they tell me that I am, deficient in everything that goes to make a man." He put down his hands from his head and held them clenched upon the table. "It tears at my heart, father."

Slowly he sat back, slowly drawing back his fists till they rested before him on the table's edge. In this posture, "But because it tears at my heart," he said, "I know my strength. Do you remember a sermon you preached on our strength lying in our weaknesses? Something about glorying in our infirmities; do you remember your text?"

Yearning towards his son at what he had seen him suffer in this interlude, the vicar gratefully betook his mind to the treasury of his every need, unerringly to a particular casket in it.

"It would have been from Corinthians, my boy. It would have been St. Paul's 'Gladly therefore will I rather glory in my infirmities that the power of Christ may rest upon me. For when I am weak then am I strong.'"

"That was it. Father, contempt, revilings, white feathers, all that stuff, shake my principles not in the slightest degree. They are shaken when I hear the call of my country like that." He motioned towards the windows through which the singing had come. "I resist it, at what cost of effort sometimes God alone knows, and I feel then within me, as I have felt just now, the surge of strength which can only be the assurance of the highest within me that I am right, that I am acting by my highest."

He paused. A flicker crossed his look. "As such as you, father," he said, "if ever tempted, ever weak, feel the surge within you of the power of Christ."

The vicar knew well the bearing of the flicker on the words which followed it. It signaled the son's distress at his inability to share the father's beliefs. Long since belief had been spoken of between them only in, on the one side wistful allusions, on the other tactfully evasive rejoinders; and wistfulness now, at this tentative glimpse across this gulf between them, shadowed the father's eyes.

The son, responding, said, "I'm so sorry, father—

"It is because the bearing of all this on you is brought to a head by Bartlett's dismissal of me that I am going away from you. I shall be freshly called a coward for doing so. 'Daren't stay where he is known' will be said of me; but it will be better for you to hear that until it is forgotten than to be exposed to the results of your people being daily reminded what sort of a son you have. It's not only, remember, that your son is a pacifist, it is that his grounds are not even religious grounds. If to censure of me you could reply by telling people that my views were my interpretation of the spirit of Christ within me I would not feel that I was injuring you beyond your defense. As it is, you could not, honest as you are, allow people who spoke to you about me to believe that I had, so to say, the shelter of your church. I for my own part would be coward indeed if I did not at every opportunity disclaim that shelter. To the grief you would be caused through me as pacifist would be the added grief of acknowledging that what you are here to teach has left me untaught. That is why I am going away from you, father, tomorrow."

3

And then there was dear Minna. Sitting drooped there at his study table the vicar had followed the matter of his son to the point at which his mind's eye watched receding up the line the train which had taken him away. He found his thoughts engaged now with her who, standing with Laura beside him on the platform of Upton Bank station, then had been the first to speak.

"And I, too," Minna had said dolorously. "I should take myself away from you as that poor John has done."

Laura had given her a playful slap on the arm. "Why, you ridiculous person you, how can you talk such utter nonsense?"

"Did you see the station-master," Minna had replied, "talking to those soldiers and pointing to us? Too truly I know it what he was saying. Watch you his look at us when now we pass him."

"Good morning, Mr. Hewett," the vicar had said urbanely as now they came up with the man.

The station-master, notoriously a socialist, had always had a reputation for surliness. He had now a bitter sore which had exacerbated his nature beyond his control of his feelings.

" 'Morning," he returned shortly. He eyed his vicar meaningly. "Your son gone off to join up?"

He stood in the platform gateway. It was not to be passed through until he chose to move.

"No, Mr. Hewett," the vicar said quietly.

"Ah." The man's mouth worked. "My boy did, first day of the war." His mouth worked again. "Now I've lost him."

"We tried to tell you," Laura said, "how deeply sorry for you and your wife we felt. The vicar wrote to you."

The station-master glowered. "That don't put me with fathers whose sons have stayed at home."

He grudgingly gave room. The three went past him.

"There's one thing," he broke out, and the vicar had felt he could not but stop to hear him. "There's one thing. Better my lad should drop in his tracks, bullet in his head, charging on 'em like the brave boy he was, than fall into their hands prisoner like some. There's a bit I read in the *Mail* this morning"—he looked at Minna—"p'r'aps you read it, miss, about German women at a station where there was wounded boys of ours laid out on stretchers on the platform off the train. Spit in the mug of water by one dying boy's side, one of 'em did, and not the only neither." He stared savagely in Minna's face. "That's Germans for you. That's what German women are."

He turned violently away and himself obtrusively spat.

The vicar put his hand about Minna's arm. It was trembling.

"My dear, my dear," he sought to soothe her. "You must think nothing of that. Poor fellow he—"

"Oh, Minna darling," Laura cried. Her cheeks were flaming. "A boor, a brute."

"Laura dearest!" the vicar remonstrated. "Minna must pay no attention to that, nor we of what he said to me. Poor fellow, he has but just lost his boy. He is beside himself."

But as they moved towards the station exit his shoulders were bowed.

4

When first war had been declared the possibility of an awkwardness in Minna's position, a hundred times less the likelihood of such manifestations of feeling against her as that of the station-master, had never remotely occurred to the vicar. In the sense of ever calling it to mind he had forgotten even that she was German. The vicarage never thought of her as a foreigner. For twenty years she had been one of themselves. The parents had found a daughter in her when she was a girl of eighteen; the children a second mother. At thirty-eight she now was, as it were, the family aunt, lifelong resident. She was so completely a member of the family that it was with eyes widening with surprise that the vicar, staring upon her on an August morning, had realized that she was a German.

"Why, Minna—" he said wonderingly. "Why, my dear girl—"

It was at breakfast. Ruth had rushed out for the newspaper and declaiming its headlines had rushed it into her father's hands. With profoundest gravity the vicar had read out what his daughter had shouted: "War. Ultimatum to Germany Expires"; and then the supplementary captions; and then the black type summary beneath them; and then, lowering the paper, had gazed across it into the faces before him, into Laura's, into Mary's, into Minna's.

On Minna's his gaze, rounding into wonder, had remained. Laura's face and Mary's had returned him the profundity of concern which at first had been in his own. Minna's, as his eyes came to it, was red and deepening red. It was puckered up and puckering tighter. It was suppressing frightful pain or devastating burst of grief.

And realization dawned upon him.

"Why, Minna— Why, my dear girl— Why, you—"

His words and Minna's expression caused the others also to realize. There was a moment's silent tension. Then from behind the vicar's chair came Ruth's voice in astounded exclamation.

"Why, good golly, Minna, *you're* a German! Snakes alive, we're fighting *you!*"

Minna plunged her face downwards into her hands. Her

pent emotion burst. She shook with sobbing dreadful to hear.

Ruth rushed around to her. "Oh, Minna, you aren't, you aren't." She hugged her arms around the quivering shoulders, striving to press kisses through the hands that hid the face. "Forgive me, darling Minna. I only suddenly remembered you were born there. You're one of us, of us, you know you are."

Laura came round, Mary too. The vicar got up. His feeling that he, not Ruth, had precipitated this painful scene worked on his face in agitations of contrition and distress.

Laura disengaged Ruth's arms. Putting her own about the huddled figure, "Our own dearest Minna," she said. "You'd like to come outside with me, wouldn't you?"

She helped her to her feet, "There, there," and drew her, handkerchief to eyes, sobs choking her, from the table. At the door Minna snatched a recovery of herself. "I kiss them all first," she cried. She turned upon Ruth, the nearest. "My Ruth, my baby of all," she hugged her, pressing her face, running with tears, against the face lovingly given to her. "My Mary!" and the reserved elder daughter with sympathetically reproachful "Minna, what is this all about? It's too foolish," gave kiss in return. The vicar stood with wide inviting arms. Minna threw herself into them. He patted her back, murmuring endearments. She went then with Laura.

Later, by what she told when the girls had gone off to the Academy, was explained the astonishing violence of her emotion. Its seeds, as now she showed, were in the family's neglect till that morning to give mind to her nationality. Vicar, Laura, Mary, Ruth, each with his or her particular reaction, unitedly in the general atmosphere of suspense, had been too immersed in the distractions of the critical days now come to head to have thought for so forgotten a thing

as Minna's origin. There had been Philip's crazy antics in
the house. There had been preoccupation with what might
be John's position up with General Lethbridge. "My dear,"
exclaimed Laura when Minna now drew hers and the vicar's
attention to this oversight of theirs, "you might have had a
baby, any of us might, and none of the rest of us would
have noticed it."

But from the first mutterings of Germany's concern with
Austria's case Minna, as now she told, had been conscious of
her birth. "If any of you, immediate when the war talk
began, had reminded to me that I was German all had been
all right. We would have laughed at it. 'How funny this is
that you are of that country,' you would have laughed. 'Yes,
it is certainly droll, this,' I would have laughed; and we
would have fun in it, and everything had been all comfortable to me. But no one remembers, and the days go, and the
news is more black and more blacker, and I myself, who in
the first might have reminded you what you forget, now
feel 'How shall I suddenly say this to them?' and feel I
cannot know how I shall."

They comforted her, their own dear foolish Minna. What
possible bearing had the place of her birth on the love they
all had for her? German? British? East or West or North or
South, she was one of them, that was all that counted. To
which, yes, yes, she eagerly responded, of course she was
what they were. She never thought of Germany. It had gone
right out of her life. These disturbing days had made her
think of it and of course she was fond of it. It was her native
land. It was there that she had known her dear papa and
her dear mamma. But it was here in England that she knew
"the lives of my life." That did not make her English; but
it made her, she said, "so that no country is any country to
me as all of you are my country. I am fond there," she
gestured an arm, "in Germany. I am fond here," she ex-

tended the other, "in England. But I love, I live, I think, I dream, I have all of everything of me here," she pressed both her hands to her bosom, "in my heart's home"—as if handing them the casket of her breast she turned her hands outwards towards them—"with you."

They took her loving gift. Emotion ended. The air cleared. Then laughter had its turn. To be German had now a special significance, but to look at Minna sitting there and to credit her with any significance other than that of her familiar self was impossible; it was ludicrous. Laura made spectacles of her fingers and thumbs. Using the words which Minna had used and pronouncing them with her accent, "How funny this is that you are of that country," peering at her she declared.

"Yes, it is certainly droll, this," joined Minna. She put on so funny a face, shaking her head as it were in wonder at herself, that they all laughed amain. The vicar said it was one of the funniest bits of pantomime he had ever seen. They must repeat it for the girls when they came home, he said.

5

It was Violet, the maid, who first, and that within twenty-four hours, showed that agreement, however cordial within the family, was unlikely to be general. In three years Violet was the fourth different maid at the vicarage. As so often happens in domestic management, an enviably long period without servant trouble had been succeeded by the vexations of constant change. For twelve years had been Sarah, the coveted of all the housewives of the parish. "How she stays there goodness only knows," enviously the Mrs. Bagges, engaged in their popular pastime of criticizing the vicarage, would say to one another. Then Sarah, weeping, left to get married. Pronouncing on their vicar's wife one of gossip's most comprehensive strictures, "She can't keep a servant" at once became the critics' tune.

Minna was head-cook and maid-of-all-work. Laura, in her own description, was tweeny maid. Sarah had been under-cook and house-parlormaid. When Sarah left, Laura and Minna laughingly described themselves as "perms," Sarah's successors as "temps." Alike towards household economy and in respect of a mistress who helped to make the beds, the temps had in common, Violet in marked degree, the airs frequent among those whose own homes subsist largely on perquisites smuggled back from charing. They had also, towards Minna, the kitchen's ingrained dislike of govern-esses, companions, lady nurses and the like. "They're paid same as us." To wait on them is an indignity resented in accordance with the particular circumstances.

In Minna's case the circumstances were provocative; indif-ferently though sensibly even to the peerless Sarah, acutely to the temps and outstandingly to Violet. Minna not only was paid, so they believed, "same as me." The wages which thus put her on the kitchen's social level were largely earned, not in the aloofness of schoolroom, drawing-room or nurs-ery, but elbow to elbow at the cooking-range, over the sink, and with the broom, brush and duster. She not only, on a second count of the issue, took her meals with the family and must be called Miss. She acted with them as she pleased and where she pleased in a degree unknown (they told their friends) in any gentry's house in the land. "If you call parsons gentry," frequently said Violet on her afternoons off. "Live the way they do, they wouldn't know what they was eating, some of the gentlemen's tables I've served at. Why, they call sweets 'pudding' an' that's a fac'."

Violet had left the line of life in which puddings are called sweets because a gold coin left in a room she was dusting had disappeared when she had gone from it. This forced her into the line which would accept her indignant protestations of innocence in place of a character from her last situation. Always ready to help a hard case, the vicarage was prominent in that line. Violet, a large puffy-faced creature of twenty-eight, presented herself for interview with her mouth all butter and honey. When she came with her box these mellifluences, as is their frequent shortcoming, incontinently dried. They left her speech elaborately affected and used chiefly in evidences of her superiority to the conditions in which she found herself.

"She is the very high and mighty," said Minna, grimacing awe, after Violet's reception of the news that the table-napkins—"Oh, do you mean the serviettes?"—were changed only twice a week, not daily.

"Oh, we'll soon make her happy once she gets into our ways," declared Laura, laughing at Minna's pantomime.

"Oh, yah, yes, of course we will. I will show her how to cut out a nice dress. Although me, mind you," and Minna grimaced again, "I am just the mud, the no better in the house than she is and not so goot."

Definitely, and that on the lofty grounds of patriotism, Minna was pronounced not so "goot" on the evening following the day of the vicarage's realization that she was German. It was Violet's evening out. Due to come in at half-past nine, she appeared through the front door as Laura happened to be crossing the hall at considerably after ten.

"Hullo, Violet. You're late, aren't you?"

The pleasantly voiced question was not answered in the spirit of its delivery. Violet wiped her feet purposefully on the mat rather as a dog scratches with its hind legs before a fight. "Gone the half-hour, has it?" indifferently she rejoined.

"It'll go it again in a minute or two," said Laura, a shred

of laughter accompanying her return of the other's diction. "Half-past ten."

Violet gave a couple more backward thrusts of her soles. Had the mat fiber been loose it would have flown in clouds. "Oh?"

This time the indifference was not to be missed. She had been off-hand lately. Laura had given a deaf ear to it. "I feel snappy myself sometimes," she would say when the kitchen atmosphere was huffy. "It's only natural that servants should too." Now challenge was unmistakable. With the light weapons she used for such she accepted it.

Smiling, her head to one side as though bantering a naughty child, "Violet," she said, "I think that when you come in nearly an hour late and have the bad luck to run into me at the door, I *think* you ought to make some sort of explanation."

Violet assumed Pose Two of the dog-fighting code: trembling rigidity. "I've never bin before," truculently she delivered from it, "where I've not had till ten."

"It's the first you've said to me about it."

"Yes, well, there's plenty I might have said and haven't."

"Well, that's very silly of you. How can things be put right if one doesn't know when they're wrong?" Laura straightened her head, maintained her smile, but substituted a shade of seriousness for the banter in her tone. "Violet, I've noticed you've seemed a little dissatisfied lately. Let's come into the kitchen and have a talk together."

"Plenty I might have said," repeated Violet, visibly swelling, "and out here without going into no kitchens."

"All right. What is it?"

"Am I to go on takin' orders from Miss Minna?"

"Go on taking orders—?" Laura was mystified. "What *do* you mean?"

"From a German," declared Violet. "That's what I mean."

Normally Laura would have checked, quietly but immediately, the raised voice with which this was delivered. Here her attention was too engaged by the bearing of the words to give notice to their manner. The vicar had he heard them would have been stupefied. He was when they were reported to him. Laura's taking aback, though sharp, was but momentary. Then she saw Violet's point of view and she hastened to correct it.

"Oh, Violet," she cried, "that you needn't feel, I do assure you; not in the slightest. You're so at fault in that idea that, believe me, if you'd said this to me yesterday I shouldn't have known what you were talking about. Miss Minna has lived with us practically all her life. She's so little German that until yesterday, when somehow it came up that she had been born in Germany, we'd all of us completely forgotten it."

Violet's asseverations in the matter of the gold coin at her previous situation had been of her natural instinct for falsehood. The professional liar's inveterate suspicion of untruth in everybody else had been hers from childhood. It concentrated now in a beading of her eyes. It proclaimed itself in a triumphant cunning of her voice. "Ah, funny thing, if you'd forgotten it, that I should have known it, isn't it?"

Laura thought it less important to correct rudeness than to make her point. "Who told you?" she quietly asked.

"She did."

"Yes, and it was she who reminded us. That's what I'm telling you. She told you she was German soon after you came here, I sunppose. You see how open she is and you know how friendly she's always been with you and how kind. She's—"

"Hur!" Violet's puffy face, red with emotional heat, emitted a contemptuous snort. "That's what they all are."

"All who?"

"Spies."

"Oh, Violet." Laura could not but laugh. "How can you be so silly? Miss Minna's had no more to do with Germany since she was a young girl than you have. She hasn't a relative or a friend there."

"Likely!"

Laura changed her tone. "Don't talk to me in that way, please. Come, if you can't be talked to sensibly you must be spoken to sharply. Are you doubting my word?"

"I'm doubting German's words, that's what I'm doubting. We've bin talking about this down to my home tonight an' there's bits in the papers showing you what these Germans are. Thousands of 'em bin put here years back as governesses an' that, same as 'er. Spies, that's what they are. An' what I've come back for to ask—"

Laura stood aside. "You better go up to bed."

Vulgar tirade requires for its maintenance a spur in its own kind. Want of opposition defeats it. Violet thumped past her mistress. At the stairs she looked back. "I'll have me answer, though, all the same to that. Am I to go on takin' orders from a German born and bred?"

"If you mean from Miss Minna, certainly you are."

"Ah, well, I'll take me munf."

Laura administered to her the chagrin of having to ascend four steps unanswered. "But listen to this, will you?" she then spoke. "If you refuse to obey any proper orders or if you repeat tomorrow any of tonight's insolent manner, you'll take much less than your month. You'll be paid to the day and will go immediately."

Violet did her best at an insulting laugh. "Ha! That's vicarage way, that is, I suppose."

She thumped up.

6

She stayed her month. Her manner was sullen but she did her work. Not until the day of her departure did she again voice objection to living beneath the same roof as a German. By means even harder to endure she evinced it. Yet to send her off on that account would be, Laura saw at once and realized increasingly, most unwise.

Early morning of the day after the incident in the hall disclosed her plan, Minna had been told of the matter. Sparing her the hurt of the spy references, Laura had represented Violet merely as, in the first heat of the war fever, being stupid about taking orders from a German. "Just be tactful, dear, for a day or two. The silly creature will soon find herself doing without thinking what you put in her way to do and soon will forget all about it."

Minna was troubled. Her concern put an especially cheery warmth into the "Good morning, Violet" with which next morning she entered the kitchen.

Violet made no reply.

"Bother me if you're not down first again," painfully noticing but resolutely unheeding, Minna went on. "That's two running days you beat me."

Violet, who was making tea, one cup on the table instead of the usual two, turned her back.

With that silence and with that gesture she opened the attitude towards Minna which during the remainder of her stay she maintained. She would not speak to her. She would not look at her. Such instructions as Minna in the course of the vicarage domestic regime could not but bring before her she accepted with a silence more injurious than open refusal. Minna's distress at it was painful to Laura to witness. Already by the evening of the first day of it she expressed her wounded feelings in tears. By the same hour, nevertheless, Laura had decided that to dismiss Violet solely for such conduct far from benefiting Minna would do her disservice. Violet would go back to her home in the Banks with worse against the German than she had brought up with her on the previous evening. That would never do.

And if it would never have done at the end of the first day, much less would it do, Laura saw, by the end of the first week. What exercise of her tongue Violet now lost by refusing speech in one quarter was more than made up by its loquacity in others. Not a tradesman came to the vicarage but he was held in dark whisperings, infinitely prolonged. Back-door gossip is the civilized equivalent of the mouth-to-mouth postal service of bush and jungle, incredibly swift, omitting none. It wanted not a tithe of the reports which came back to vicarage ears to assure Laura that to dismiss Violet because of Minna would be in effect to hold up their loved and faithful friend for public stoning.

That feeling enough already was aroused. Minna's reception in the shops had offered the first evidence. Going out on her customary marketing for the vicarage table on the morning after her tears at Violet's manner, it was in tears that she returned, her provisioning incompleted. The shops had been crowded. Everybody was laying in stores fearing that supplies would fail. At the grocer's, her first call, Minna had had to wait her turn in a jostle. Everyone around her was saying things about Germans which made her self-consciously unhappy. In the crowd she saw first one face then another which she knew. Both, catching her eye, were immediately averted from her. Both whispered to neighbors. Unfriendly looks were bent upon her. When at last her turn came at the counter it was the grocer himself, Mr. Thompson, who should have served her. She gave him pleasant greeting. With no response he requested the order of a lady

standing beside her. When presently he turned to her it was
with a peremptory "Yes? What's for you?" and he threw
down her requirements in a manner and with an air that
had made people look at him and at her in surprise. As she
turned and pressed back through the throng, her cheeks
burning, "Well, I don't fancy serving Germans," she heard
him explain; and "What?" "Is she, though?" "You don't
say?" followed her to the door.

She came straight home.

7

So it begun. All that the vicarage could do to shield her,
lovingly it did. Laura took over the marketing. Always she
or the vicar, or Ruth when free from the Academy, accompanied her for a daily walk through the forest, chattering to
her with an especial cordiality while going through the residential streets leading to it. Minna's attempts to respond in
kind, to look unconcerned, unself-conscious, especially when
passing people, were piteous to witness.

Wretchedness of this sort was, nevertheless, but secondary
in her unhappiness. Chiefly she felt the trouble which her
presence brought upon the vicarage. Even the solicitude
which would not let her go out unaccompanied gave her
distress. Once when the vicar, she knew, had interrupted his
work in the study in order that her outing should not be
missed, "I am a dog," she cried bitterly, "that must be exer-
cised."

"Minna, Minna, how can you say such things?"

The comparison with her situation that she had drawn
seemed somehow to overwhelm her. She cast herself into a
chair. "Yes, it is a troublesome dog that I am," sobbing, she
reiterated. " 'Why you keep this horrible dog?' they all ask
you. They run from it in the street and tell the police of it.

It loves you all more than its life but it brings misery on you, misery, misery."

Laura and Ruth came in just then. Learning the trouble, "Why, they were dying for a walk," they declared. "And so am I, as I keep telling you," declared the vicar. All three took her but it was after this incident that she began to slip out by herself and walk up and down the lane at the back in which larky Mr. Hartopp had kissed Ruth. "There! I have walked by myself a whole hour and a half," she would come in and announce. "It is fine. I can do it." When they found out that perambulation of the lane was the extent of these walks she nerved herself to steal off and go afield through unfrequented parts of the forest, in triumph announcing one day that she had walked "miles and miles."

Ruddy with her tramp, excited by her proof that she need not be for ever dependent on their escort, she stood among them almost the Minna of old. "I haf been, where do you think, you will never guess in a million. I haf been to the Giant's Gyll, that most dear spot."

They acclaimed her. Giant's Gyll was a picturesque ravine in a wooded clump five miles away. When the children were small it had been a favorite spot for picnics, a donkey-cart hired for half-a-crown taking the packages and the smaller legs. Philip's birthday, which fell in June, always was celebrated at the Gyll. Chief among the jolly reminiscences now started by Minna's walk were those of the birthday when the established site was forbidden by the vicar because a suicide had been committed off the footbridge which spanned the ravine. "That's all the more reason to go there," Philip disgustedly had declared, later stalking in with the announcement, "I don't mind so much now not going to the Gyll tomorrow. They've found the body."

In the evening they were laughing again over this recollection, over John's "You horrible little ghoul, you," when a ring at the front door at once interrupted their mirth and marked the end of Minna's solitary excursions. The vicar answered the bell. Violet's place had not been filled. Not only were maids now very hard to get but "The fact is, Mrs. Brecque," the registry office had told Laura, "the girls have a feeling against that German lady you have with you." *"Far* better, not to say cheaper, without them," Laura, coming home with this, had pronounced; and Minna, all her time now on her hands and eager to give compensation for the trouble she was causing, delightedly agreed.

It was to her that the vicar addressed himself as, very troubled, he reappeared in the drawing-room. "Minna, my dear, it's some inquiry from the police station about your walk this afternoon. Just come a minute, will you? Ah, take my arm, my dear, it's nothing, it's nothing, only a formality."

Uncompromisingly formal the police sergeant who had been brought into the study made it. "Miss Strauss? It's with reference to an alleged breach of the alien regulations that I've called."

From information received it appeared, he said, in part to Minna, in part to the vicar, that she had been seen that afternoon "at the place known as Giant's Gyll situated on the Netherhurst border of the forest. By measurement on the approved ordnance map of the district Giant's Gyll was, he read from his notebook, "five miles one thousand four hundred and ten yards from the central point of Upton Springs." By the Consolidated Order in Council, he went on, dated (notebook again) September 9th, 1914, aliens were not allowed to travel more than five miles beyond their registered address. He was instructed by the Chief Constable to remind the alien here resident that this fact had been clearly brought to her notice when, in accordance with the same order in Council, she registered at the police station. The Chief Con-

stable was well prepared to hear that the clear infringement
of the regulation now committed was inadvertent. He admitted that in itself it was trifling. Nevertheless it had very
properly been reported to him by a resident of Upton
Springs and the police sergeant was to warn the alien that
any further infringement of the same must lead to the
taking of whatever steps might be deemed necessary.

He snapped to the band of his notebook. "Bound to do my
duty, sir," he said pleasantly as the vicar took him to the
door.

"Oh, of course, of course, sergeant. And you've heard, and
will tell the Chief Constable, I'm sure, how entirely uninten-
tional the, the offense was."

Painfully he recalled his return to the offender. He had
left her seated on the sofa. He found her twisted about on it,
her hands clinging to its back, her head between her arms,
her sobbing lamentable to hear. Poor Minna. . . .

8

There was his own case. His thoughts on John and on
Minna had put in his mind's review his position in his
parish's regard as father of a "shirker" and protector of a
German. Additional to his perplexity at that was his perplexity in his people's reception of his spiritual attitude towards
the war. His attitude was that however rightful our cause
by temporal standards, always must we beware against bending spiritual standards to meet them. While, therefore, responsive to "Gott strafe England," many pulpits up and
down the land preached, in effect, "God strafe Germany,"
he sought to present the attitude towards the war of God,
the All Loving, only as might be that of an earthly father
who watched his children carrying dispute among themselves to the taking of one another's lives.

"'Are not these evils come upon us because God is not among us?'" was the text of one sermon in which in particular he spoke these views. By "us" he meant equally, he said, the German and the Austrian nations. "For we are one, are we not," he asked, "in the fellowship of Jesus Christ? God so loved *the world,* not a particular section of the people of the world, that He sent His only beloved son into the world. Our Lord and Saviour Jesus Christ so loves the world, not the Allies and the neutrals alone, that He is as anguished at the broken hearts of the bereaved and at the pitiful carnage in German life as at those and at that in our own."

He paused. Rigidity faced him like a wall. Laura, sensing it, felt her heart twist. He leant forward confidingly to his people. "My friends, let us each one of us bear our part in this terrible war as best we are fitted and to the utmost of our endeavor, but let us refuse to allow our sensibilities to be numbed, our natures to be coarsened and brutalized by what is going on around us. We have entered this war with clean hands, let us seek God's help that in all our parts in it and in all our thoughts of it we may preserve clean hearts. The spirit of evil is abroad. It presses upon us, threatening to engulf us, in the mass. Let us pray for God's help to keep within us individually, and so nationally, the spirit of light.

"There are some," he went on, "who say that this evil, this war, is God's judgment, His sentence, upon an erring world. That cannot be. From God only goodness can proceed, not hurt, not punishment. Mankind's punishment comes from itself as its evil comes from itself. When mankind keeps God with it evil is kept away. When it neglects God evil gains the upper hand and wreaks its power in the world. If in the nations engaged in this war each individual soul from highest to humblest who professes God had lived in accordance with the spirit of God war could not possibly have come upon us. How could it? We speak of a body of public opinion doing this or that or preventing this or that. Here would have been a body of Godly opinion, internationally wide, such as no evil could withstand. We estimate in hours such as these the military strengths of the opposed peoples. Here would have been in every Christian nation an army mustered under Jesus Christ numbered not in millions of effectives but in the tens of millions of population. What evil could have penetrated such? War has come because God has been forgotten. My friends, let us bring God back among us now. Thus, his spirit among us, we will be able to endure what we have helped to bring upon ourselves. Thus, his spirit abiding among the nations, will war pass away from us, not in the termination of this conflict only, but for ever."

All this was far from well received by the parish of St. Luke's in general. Even the members of that heart which the vicar had formed within the husk of his people questioned among themselves what he told them. They did not nowadays feel individually, they felt nationally. Was he giving them, they questioned, quite what the nation's need demanded? Churches of every denomination drew crowded congregations in this hour of the nation's trial. The congregation of St. Luke's thinned. Down at the Banks St. Mark's represented in full the national increase in church attendance. Hilary Tweed was drawing crowded congregations there. Parishioners were going down from St. Luke's to hear him. Faces which the vicar's mild eyes missed in St. Luke's were cascaded with spirited war stuff ejected from the uptilted countenance of the curate-in-charge of St. Mark's.

In the old days it commonly would take him twenty minutes to get from one end of Upton's short High Street to the other. He was for ever being stopped and held in conversation. He now was infrequently stopped. For fifteen years he had enlarged to himself the good in all his people here about him. Now suddenly and increasingly they appeared to manifest ill towards him and his. Had it been told to him he would not have believed it. Compelled by his own eyes and ears to know that it was so, his resource was as the incomprehension of a child who, approaching customary affection, is roughly pushed away. He could not understand it. Daily he felt sure that on the morrow these signs of reprobation would have dissipated. Morrow on morrow he would greet those who had thrown stones at John, at Minna, at himself, at Laura as if unconscious that aspersions had been cast. Morrow by morrow his advances were rebuked, his parishioners' attitude newly evidenced.

He was grievously perplexed.

9

Laura came in. She had letters in her hand. Her face bore good tidings. He could not recover from the dejection of his pose before he knew by her change of look that she had seen it. He stretched out his hand and by her loving pressure of it she expressed her understanding and her sympathy.

"And look," she cried, "letters from the front, from both of them, from Philip and from Mary."

She came round to his side of the table, reiterated her understanding with an arm put about him and a kiss, and drew in a chair.

His oppression went from him at the sight of his children's handwriting on the envelopes. Both were addressed in indelible pencil. Mary had been in the first V.A.D. unit to go to France. Her envelope presented itself to the vicar in her precise calligraphy, neatly spaced; Philip's in his rushing sprawl. "Oh, fine, fine," he said, lovingly fingering them. "Which first?"

Laura shuffled them excitedly. "Shut eyes and choose."

Smilingly he obeyed.

"Mary's," Laura cried. "You open it."

They read it together. It was written from Boulogne, where the unit had established a rest camp. "My dear Parents," it began, "I hope that you are both in good health, John, Ruth and Minna too; also that you have good news of Philip. I am very well and immoderately hard worked, which I enjoy, though there is much here that could be eased by better individual method. I am remedying this in my own group, but it is astonishing to see how people will cling to the inefficient way of doing a thing even after the efficient has been patently demonstrated to them. Of the general organization I have little to say . . ."

Of the details of her life in the novel conditions now surrounding it she had, as the letter disclosed, still less. That it would not have been her had it been otherwise was the spirit in which delightedly they enjoyed it. In every line they saw her as they loved her, at this or that characteristic touch smiling at one another as over her head they had exchanged covert smiles when she was little Mother Bunch.

"The darling," Laura exclaimed, as they came to the letter's end. "Now Philip," she cried.

"Hulloa, mum and dad," Philip's letter jovially hailed. "I'm having a perfectly glorious time as per. No more compulsory bathing yet, you'll be surprised to hear, but absolutely on tip-toe for giving a dose of it where it's wanted because—"

Here for four lines a censor had intervened. Philip had twice experienced in the North Sea what he called compulsory bathing. The first occasion had been from a light cruiser when she was sunk with the loss of nearly all hands

by a U-boat early in September. The second had followed in
the same month in the disaster, also by U-boat, which befell
three old-type armored cruisers at cost of nearly fifteen
hundred officers and men. Philip had been three hours in
the water before being picked up. Previously to these two
escapes he had been in the battle of Heligoland.

This was probably as generous a share of hazard as had
come to any single member of the sea service in the first
three months of the war. It was Philip all over that he
should be where the doings were wildest. Three days' leave
at home after his second compulsory bathe had dissipated
the shadow which hung about the vicarage as sudden flood
of light and music into a shrouded room. The tonic of his
cheery presence, the rattle of his adventure-laden tongue,
were far from the only relief he brought to minds oppressed.
A service uniform in the house, one moreover still wet, as
it were, with participation in the fray, bestowed upon the
inmates that incorporation with the national spirit which
Upton Springs had chosen to feel was wanting in them.
Everybody wanted to see and speak with its wearer. He had
arrived on a Saturday afternoon. Everybody seemed to know
he had come. Everybody knew he would be in church next
morning. Everybody came to get the chance to see him. The
vicar had not had such a congregation for weeks. His heart
was filled with pride and happiness in his dear handsome
gallant boy sitting there with his mother and Ruth and
Minna. It seemed to him that all the faces upturned to him
were rejoicing with him in his boy. When he came out after
the service a throng stood about his family. Philip was holding Minna by the arm. Dear Minna positively was laughing.
He hurried to the group and people on the outskirts, two
who had given up attending St. Luke's, another couple
whose manner had long been constrained, effusively greeted

him with, "Oh, vicar, how delighted you must be to have your boy home."

Philip had been told about the feeling against Minna. He had been first incredulous, then in his own fashion furious. "Dad, you put your fingers in your ears, all of you put your fingers in your ears, and I'll tell you Navy-fashion what I think of the stinkers." Jumping on to a chair then and feigning to harangue a mob of Uptonians, "Why, you leprous pack of smallpox riddled tripe-hounds," he had declaimed, "You—" He opened and shut his mouth in wordless vituperation, its violence judgeable by the contortions of his face necessary to produce it. He hugged Minna to his breast. She should walk arm in arm with him whenever he went out, he declared. He gave finally a first performance of the demonstration he would make at every street corner in Upton. An arm round Minna's neck, "This old-fashioned sweetheart of mine," he lustily sung. "This old-fashioned sweetheart of mine."

Minna had mixed tears with her laughter. At some of the surges of happiness within him caused by the difference in things while his boy was at home the vicar, too, had found his nose in want of blowing. Fondly he laughed now with Laura over the characteristic letter. By the time it was finished the sense of Philip being again in the house was so strong upon him as to lift him out of the oppression in which the letters had arrived as if it had never been.

Laura rejoiced. "Now I can leave you ever so happy, can't I?"

"Yes, yes, indeed."

"I'll leave the letters so that you can keep having a peep at them."

"And I shall, you may be sure." He smiled his farewell, "Until lunch, my love."

When she had gone he sat a moment in reflective happiness. Then, briskly arousing himself, he took up one of the three local letters which also Laura had brought in. He was about to open it when something about the handwriting made him pause. The script was rounded but not with the roundness of an uneducated hand or of a child's. It suggested an unnatural penmanship. Two letters in disguised hands lay in a drawer beside him. He had a sick misgiving that this was a third. He opened it and knew that it was. Without address or signature, on a half-sheet of distinctive notepaper, matching the envelope, were four lines in block capitals:

"WHAT SORT OF A VICAR DO YOU CALL YOURSELF? YOU ARE HARBORING A GERMAN, YOUR SON IS A COWARDLY SHIRKER, AND YOUR SERMONS ARE ONLY FIT FOR GERMANS TO HEAR."

He drew out the drawer in which were the two previous anonymous letters and dropped this third upon them. He drooped back in his chair into the position in which his earlier thoughts had thrust him, one hand desolately upon the table, the other holding the chair's arm as if for support, his head bowed.

Two

FIFTEEN months later, towards the end of January, 1916, the vicar read in his newspaper of the passing of the Military Service Act. This enjoined upon all unmarried men from ages eighteen to forty-one to obey calling-up notice to join the army. They were required to present themselves for attestation on receipt of formal notice addressed to them personally. A man failing to report when due would be arrested as an absentee, taken before a magistrate's court, and handed over to the military. For any who might seek exemption on conscientious or other grounds local tribunals would be set up. There would be also appeal tribunals and a central tribunal, and exemption might be granted in one of three grades, absolute, conditional or temporary. The Act was to come into force not later than two weeks after it was passed. Calling-up notices would begin to be issued not longer than three weeks thereafter.

It was with the heavy breathing of concern that the vicar read all this. John, he saw, was now by law deemed to be a soldier. Within little more than a month he would, unless exempted, be compulsorily enlisted.

He had been home but once since leaving the vicarage after his Upton House dismissal. A mastership which he had found at an indifferent private school in Dorsetshire had been terminated (by pressure of local opinion) at the end of the summer term. Labor was hard to come by by the farmers. He had engaged himself for the harvesting season on a farm which he had happened upon while tramping after the school's break-up. It was from there that he came to the vicarage for the National Registration, returning two days later.

Laura thought the meeting between her elder son and his father very affecting. John had been unable to give an exact time of arrival. He stepped suddenly through the front door while she was arranging flowers in the hall.

"John."

"Mother."

They had no more than embraced, no other word yet spoken between them, when the vicar appeared from his study. It was perhaps because she had just noted the deep sunburning of John's face, just felt about her the strength of his arms and of his sinewy form, that she noticed how run down under the troubles of these months the other had become. He gave a little stagger against his door-post. Then he called out, stretching out his arms, "My boy, my boy!" John said, "Father, father!" They went into one another's arms. "And they just stood there," Laura afterwards told Minna, "holding one another, saying nothing, and I just slipped into the drawing-room and left them."

John, though well, was looking under strain, the vicarage thought. His manner was subdued. "You're very quiet," Laura smiled at him that evening. Parents and son were sitting together after supper. Minna had drawn Ruth temporarily away. "Well, it's rather dreadful knowing yourself a pariah," he replied. "People don't speak to me, or, if they would, don't like being seen at it. Apart from my work, the only speaking to I've had pretty well since I left here has been by looks." He gave a mirthless little laugh. "They've spoken volumes, as the saying is. It makes one quiet, naturally."

The vicar put out his hand to him. He smiled as he took it.

That night the National Registration form was filled in. Two questions related to helping with the war. John replied to them as one. "No. I am opposed to war. On principle I will do nothing that makes for its prosecution."

Upton Springs, by its attitude during his visit, might have been looking over his shoulder as he wrote. Public feeling now was in hue and cry against shirkers, conscription the angry demand. Had compulsory service been decreed with the declaration of war, there would have been a seemly calling up to the colors draft by draft, no cause for animadversions. The government temporized with the issue. There they were, the shirkers, strolling about at their ease, and there, unused, was the means of getting at them. Let them be got at, then, by what expressions of contempt and indignation the private individual and the public Press could devise. There was that vicar's son come home for a holiday. Let Upton Springs show him and show his father what they thought of him.

It did. Since that day on which the vicar had sat bowed beneath his perplexities their burden had increased. Two happenings in the constitution of St. Luke's had been approvingly seized upon by hostile opinion. His vicar's warden, impressively clicking to his feet by numbers in khaki at the Easter vestry, had announced that he was not seeking reelection. His curate, flashing about the parish with head more firmly than ever against the back of his collar, had cast aloft, mortar like, the news that he was seeking khaki. He was going out to the front as a Chaplain to the Forces as soon as ever he could be liberated for the purpose.

Regarded as release from the co-operation of a churchwarden who not invariably co-operated with him, from the services of a curate who not always had served him as he would have wished, in normal effect these events might have caused the vicar no profound regret. The effect they were given by the manner of their performance was that of withdrawals of support.

Colonel Gilling was closely occupied by his duties as chief recruiting officer of the district. It was natural that he should need to relinquish those of vicar's warden. Gossip somehow got hold of it that he had "resigned" because St. Luke's was not taking the attitude towards the war that it ought to take. The Rev. Hilary Tweed let it be known that it was with reluctance that the vicar had consented to his wish to apply for an army chaplaincy. The additional work entailed by the parish now having two churches to staff might have accounted for the reluctance. Gossip somehow attributed the reluctance to the vicar's feeling that his curate's longing to take the field showed up his son's shirking of it. "That shows you what *he* thinks," was gossip's comment on the colonel's action. Of the curate's patriotic dash for khaki, "Of *course* he would," said one and all. *"What* a contrast to that white feather son."

John, arriving into this newly inimical atmosphere, went out with the vicar only once during his stay. They had scarcely left the vicarage when two errand-boys, who had stared meaningly at him as they passed, cat-called behind their backs. As the top of the road council laborers excavating a drain also stared, then broke into loud comments, scraps of which could be overheard. Round the corner a Special Constable who was a parishioner, turning his back as they approached, pretended not to hear the vicar's friendly "Good morning, Mr. Hoskins." In the High Street similar signs of disapproval were manifested by persons of all social grades. John went out only by himself after that. He could and he did deliberately brave these things alone. He could not bear to see them shared by his father.

The only local acquaintance with whom he spoke during his stay was Hope Hubbard. From across the road at a much-frequented point of Upton's activities he was loudly hailed by the tall figure in cassock and biretta. The priest of St.

Monica's came swiftly over to him, taking both his hands and shaking them in warmest greeting. Then he slipped his arm through John's and walked with him back to the vicarage, where he was due, he said, for tea. As they went along a lady, known to both of them by sight, stared pointedly at Upton's recreant. Hope Hubbard broke off in an animated sentence as pointedly to stare at her, then resumed. For some months now he had made a habit of frequently taking tea at the vicarage. When he could persuade her he would take Minna for walks. These always were as public as his persuasions could effect. Stalking along with her in his distinctive dress he would elaborately give stare for stare directed at the enemy national within Upton's gates. Once he had stepped swiftly back and clouted a boy who had shouted *"Boche"* after her.

In keeping with all this deliberately manifested friendship was the jovial fashion of his entry when now the vicarage was reached and the two went in. All the household were in the drawing-room. Presenting himself before them Hubbard struck an attitude as of one making a surprise arrival, thrilling to both sides. He took the vicar by both hands much as he had taken John in the street. Then he kissed Laura and Minna and laughed at John an explanation of this newly developed intimacy.

"I'm a beggar," he announced, "for kissing the girls. It's a grand war, the license it's given old rips like me."

He turned to Ruth. "But this is the one," he declared, "that I really came to kiss. This is where the elopement and the scandal threaten. John, man, do you realize what a peach of a sister this has grown into while you've been away? Have you heard that they're thinking of moving the camp because of the drain among the officers by suicides and duels for love of her?"

Ruth was pushing him away, laughing at him. John had

been struck indeed by her development in the months of his absence. She now was just eighteen. She had left the Academy at the end of the Easter term. Adjoining the forest camp a commodious dilapidated and disused cottage had been taken over by the Upton Springs' Ladies' War Work Guild and established as a canteen and recreation-rooms for the troops. Here Ruth was working all day, enjoying herself enormously, pouting sometimes over the Guild Committee's refusal to arrange an officers' room, but by some means establishing sufficient acquaintance with youthful wearers of Sam Browne belts to offer grounds for Hubbard's exaggeration of the distress she was causing among them. She had come home early to be with John. The butcher-blue blouse and short tweed skirt which was the uniform of the canteen workers suited her delightfully. She was strikingly pretty.

"She's Philip on leave in petticoats, which she doesn't wear," Laura laughed. "When Hope's here as well it's like having two Philips in the house." She smiled at the vicar. "And does us a world of good, doesn't it, dear?"

It certainly appeared to. Tea was a rattle of fun. Its joviality was maintained throughout Hubbard's stay. Attitude towards war was a delicate topic as between his own views and those, each in its own kind, of the father and son whose guest he was. Even this he touched with a pungency of phrase at which even the vicar could not but smile. An address by the bishop of the diocese had been reported in that day's papers. Mention of it led to war sermons. Hope Hubbard paid tribute to what he called the vicar's "gentle teaching"; then he contrasted with it his own pulpit deliveries.

His mobile face quick with point and vigor, "For me, I can't," he declared, "cramp what I want to say with this need for national penitence, much less with admonition to love the enemy. Make confession of your own heart's contribution to the evil that now is loose upon the world. Do that by every means, I tell my people; but then gird up your loins, I tell 'em, and go forth and smite these Amalekites hip and thigh. If you can smite harder by burning with wrath against 'em, burn. I'm not believing that even Jesus Christ was loving the money-changers when he scourged them out of the Temple. Today it's out of Belgium that they've got to be scourged."

"Pass him the sugar," smiled the vicar. "He needs sweetening."

This was the first occasion in history in which the head of the Brecque family had deliberately produced effective humor. It was greeted with a moment's spellbound wonder, then with a shout of delighted laughter. The vicar went rosy with bashful pleasure. His rosiness was still happily coloring him when Hubbard left. John took the invigorating guest out to the gate and thanked him deeply for all that, by his visits, he was doing to bring his father cheer.

"Mere whiffs of smelling-salts," declared the tall priest, "to the tonic he's had of seeing you. I noticed the change in him at once."

There fell conspicuously from the younger man the briskness in which the two had come out together. His face assumed the preoccupied air now frequent in him. "The change I noticed in him," he said heavily, "seeing him again after these months away, was the effect all this has had upon him." His eyes looked somberly into his companion's. "You can imagine that my own contribution to it goes pretty hard with me."

The other's face had suited itself to the changed mood before him. He gave grave sympathy. "I know," he said.

"Yes, you know what we are to one another, he and I. Yet if I come to see him now it has the effect of reminding people what kind of son he has. I have to keep myself away from him."

They stood in a moment's silence. The younger man's eyes were directed up the road. The elder knew that they contemplated a path of the spirit, not of the feet. He put his fingers about the arm nearer him. "Hard road," he said. "When will you be letting him see you again?"

His eyes still upon that which his spirit saw, John Brecque slowly shook his head. "How can I say?"

"Hard road," Hope Hubbard repeated. "John, you have trod it now a year. I believe that you are but at the beginning of its tests of your convictions."

"No test," John answered him, "can equal the conflict between my purpose and my natural impulses."

"Aye." The resonant voice made the syllable as the sound of a deep bell. "Aye, and the measure of your courage in what you may have to face will be the measure, remember, of the distress of those who love you."

With note as deep, "That is the conflict," John made answer; "that and my conflict also with the natural instincts of my manhood."

His eyes mingled pain and purpose. Those of the priest as now he spoke were penetrative, profoundly charged.

"I have a new thing to say to you, John, in this matter of conscientious objection to war. It has come to me in these months since last I saw you. It is this. I believe that you and those like you, whether their objection to war is of Christ or of plain reason, are doing the right thing at the wrong time. You are showing the light that is in you at a time when men have eyes for no light but the flames of war and counter war. You are not influencing men; you are antagonizing them. Worse than that, you are not hallowing the name of peace, you are causing it to be debased. You are peacemakers. Peacemaker is a goodly word; but by your works, as men in this hour of battle see them, you are causing it to be rendered in a word now opprobrious, pacifist. Peace is a lovely word. Men are calling it, because of you, by a word now scurrilous, pacifism."

He had taken his hand while he spoke from his listener's arm. Now impressively he laid it upon his shoulder.

"'There is a season,'" he quoted, "'for everything, a time for every purpose under heaven.' This is the time of war. Preach peace, John, when peace is being enjoyed. Then you will be speaking to men happy in peace after storm, open to reason, open to God. Then moreover you will be speaking to men who also, because sore of the wounds they have suffered, will be prone vengefully and unreflectingly to sow as terms of peace the very seeds which would come to fruit in war again. Speak then, you men of peace, for then indeed will you be speaking in season."

He stopped. John said no word. He saw from the look upon the young man's face, serene yet resolute, mystic yet valiant, that no word was coming. He passed through the gate and drew it between them.

"Let this be my last," he said. "You are planning, all who think as you think, for a better order. After this war will come the peace in which that better order may be established. Do not let your plans have bitter associations in the minds of those who then will hear them—association with pacifists and pacifism as today those terms are used and as in that tomorrow they will be remembered. You especially with these high gifts of yours will be able supremely to influence the world towards that better order. Whether will you better exert that influence do you suppose—if your countrymen say of you, 'Yes, this fellow proved himself when we proved ourselves. Let us hearken to him.' Or if they say of you, 'He is of the pacifists, this preacher to us. They did their best to help the enemy in the war. It is of the enemy, not of their own country, that they are thinking now in the peace. Beware of them'?"

There was still no word in answer. He put out his hand, "Good-by, dear John."

John pressed response. "You speak," he said at last, "of my gifts, of my work. Whether will I be abler to write do you suppose—if I am true to myself, I who have said that I never will help the war machine to kill my fellow men, or if I am false?"

He pressed again. "Good-by."

2

A month after he had read of the passing of the Military Service Act the vicar forwarded his son a letter "On His Majesty's Service." Five days later John came home. The letter was the reply to his application to appear before his local tribunal to state his grounds for seeking exemption. The tribunal under whose jurisdiction he came sat at Thurstead. Rather avoidingly, Laura thought, of questioning on the point, he was to attend it, he seemed to say, two days hence.

Laura sat up late with him on the evening of his arrival. Unlike most wives she was a more intelligent reader of the newspaper than her husband. She knew as much as was to be known about the procedure of the tribunals. She asked him what preparation he had made for statement of his case.

"Nothing especial, mother. I'm just going to tell them."

"You're allowed, you know, to call witnesses to show that your objection to war has been life-long, that it isn't just a sudden excuse."

"Yes, I know that. The only witness I could call with any effect would be father. I wouldn't do that on any consideration."

They were crouching over the remains of what little fire the cost of coal, not to say the fuel restrictions, permitted the vicarage drawing-room of an evening. Laura put a hand on her son's, extended to the warmth.

"Darling, I know what you mean. You mustn't think, though, that devotion is the privilege only of the child. You are our boy. Father will insist on going with you."

He pressed the hand she had given him, smiling at her. "You must join with me in insisting that he shan't."

"If I succeed then I shall come with you instead."

He shook his head, smiling affectionately the more. "No good. Don't you see, mother, that in this business the natural one to speak of a conscientious objector's sincerity is his father. If he doesn't call his father as testimony to his case he blankets calling anyone else, you, for instance, or Hope Hubbard. These tribunals are only too anxious to be suspicious, I can promise you. 'Your mother!' they'd cry if you presented ourself. 'This gentleman!' if Hubbard came. 'Why hasn't your father come forward?'"

She puckered her forehead. "I daresay you're right. As you put it, though, it's the first question they'll ask you if you go without him."

"Highly probable."

She thought she saw a glint, a suggestion of quiz, in his eyes as, a shade dryly also, he spoke the words. But she was too concerned with her point to question it.

"Well, then," she said. "He must go with you. That settles it."

He patted her hand, leaning towards her.

"Mother, do you mind frightfully that I'm not like Philip and all the others who are fighting? If you were a man you'd have been in khaki from the first, I know; and you think, I know, that every man that could be should be. Do you mind frightfully that I'm not, mother?"

The second time that night she put her hand on his. "Oh, my darling boy, have a son of your own one day and then you'll know that whatever he is or does he's always your boy. My country right or wrong; my boy *whatever.*"

He squeezed her fingers. He got up then. "Well, now we'll go to bed," he said. He gave her his hands, drawing her to her feet. "And I'll tell you something for good night."

The glint, the suggestion of quiz, which earlier she thought she had noticed in his eyes now clearly was there. "Yes? What?"

"The reason I've been telling you that on no account would I let father come to the tribunal to speak for me was so that, when it was over, you shouldn't be able to say, Why didn't I? Well, it is over. I've been before it."

"You've been before it?" She remembered now his avoidance of questioning about the date.

He nodded, smiling at her. "I was taking no chances with you people. It was this afternoon, on my way here."

"What happened?"

He was grave. "What I knew must."

"They refused you?"

He smiled gravely. "Like slamming a door."

"Oh, John."

3

But when John's case was called before the appeal tribunal sitting at Binsley, the county town, neither by artifice nor persuasion was the vicar to be prevented from speaking for his son. His insistence on appearing admitted the support also of Hope Hubbard, much upset at not having been called to the Thurstead occasion. The three went in company to Binsley and were given there a hearing whose consideration and courtesy served but, in the result, to emphasize the hopelessness of the case which John presented.

By the local tribunal it had been rejected with a contumely which, when the vicar read the local newspaper's report of the proceedings, had wounded him for his boy as deeply as it had highly pleasured other quarters of the parish. "What, you mean to stand there and tell us," one of the members, aghast, had shouted, "that you're one of these atheists, that you deliberately don't believe in God, and yet you dare to argue with us that your conscience prevents you from fighting for your country? How can you have a conscience if you don't believe in God?"

John had lost by then whatever hope he had had of secularistic idealism being understood by his judges. "How can you sit there to judge conscience," he asked, "if you don't even know what conscience means?"

"We want this man," rapped the military representative.

"I should say so indeed," ejaculated a third member, believing apparently that the armed forces of the Crown were some sort of a branch of the Salvation Army, hot after agnostics.

Binsley was very different. Here the chairman was a white-haired old Indian Civil Servant, kindly and wise, whose fellow-members followed his lead. He questioned John interestedly and sagaciously. He listened with sympathy to the vicar's witness, devotedly faltering, to his son's sincerity, and to Hope Hubbard's testimony, vigorous and assured. When all was heard he consulted with his colleagues.

"Our difficulty," he then addressed John, "is your insistence on absolute exemption. The tribunals have authority to grant that, but it is done only in the most exceptional cases and we do not feel that yours is such an instance. Let me read to you from a notice sent us by the Local Government Board for our guidance." He adjusted his spectacles to reading focus. " 'The exemption should be the minimum required to meet the conscientious scruples of the applicant.' " He laid down the paper and bent forward in the applicant's direction mildly smiling:

"Some of us here, anxious to do our best to meet the scruples you have put before us, feel that your views could perfectly well be reconciled with non-combatant work; all of us, including myself, agree that with conditional work, civil work of national importance that is to say, they unquestionably could be reconciled. May I say that I do hope you will consent to accept the conditional exemption which we are willing to grant you? How would it be"—he passed his eyes invitingly to those of the vicar and Hope Hubbard earnestly bent upon him—"if we adjourned your case for half an hour while you talked things over with your father and your friend?"

Those watching saw a grave smile touch John's face. Clear symbol of gentle negation of a gentle offer, it needed not the added firmness which the slow shake of his head then gave it. The vicar half rose to his feet, a hand towards his son. John said, "Please, father," motioning him down. All in the room had been seated throughout the proceedings. Getting up, the young man presented for the first time the focus of a standing figure.

"Sir," he said, "I profoundly appreciate the considerate hearing you have given me. I greatly hope that you may be able to understand my reason for declining, nevertheless, your offer of conditional exemption. You will find it hard to do so, I am afraid. None knows better than myself how, how paradoxical my reason must sound."

He spoke with marked quiet. The grave smile hovered still about his face. Hope Hubbard, telling Laura afterwards, said, "Laura, if ever I have seen a bearing and a countenance touched to fine issues it was there. Always I shall carry in my mind the figure he made. It was a study for Watts': 'Excelsior.'"

"Sir, from the first in this war," the quiet voice went on, "my natural instincts, the promptings of my manhood, have urged me to take my part in combatant service as other men. My acquired principles, my mind's reasoned motives, withhold me. I am termed a shirker. Sir, if I accepted any form of war service except that service in arms which nothing will make me accept, then I should feel myself a shirker indeed; in the world's view a shirker of danger, in my own view, much worse, a shirker of my conscience. I should be compromising with my conscience. That I will never do. I would like to be fighting at the front. But I will not fight. But I will take no back door out of fighting. I will take only the state's unqualified recognition of my principles by giving me that absolute and unqualified exemption which, as you now have told me, it will not give me."

He smiled now openly. "I said my reason would sound paradoxical. It sounds, I am afraid, grotesque now that I have put it in common words." He bowed to the chairman. "Thank you, sir, deeply." He stepped back, then moved away towards his father.

Hope Hubbard stood up. Addressing the chair, "There is a central tribunal—" he began.

As sympathetically as throughout, as gravely firm also, "Appeal," said the chairman, "can only be carried to the central tribunal by our leave. We pass on to it only issues as to which we have doubts or facts which we feel may be susceptible of other reading than our own. On this issue, carried as it has been by us to offer of conditional exemption, we feel no doubts, we consider its facts perfectly clear. I regret to assure you that no purpose would be served by

sending it on to the central tribunal. I regret that we do not
feel justified in granting appeal."

He turned to his usher. "The next case?"

4

Hubbard, seated in his own handsomely equipped study
with the rejected appellant, told John that he thought he
was conducting his refusal to serve maladroitly. "I think,
now, that you ought not to have gone before the tribunals,"
he said. "By doing so you have put yourself in the position
of admitting the validity of the Military Service Act."

"I do admit it. It's the law."

"Which you won't obey?"

"Only at the point where it seeks to force me to be a soldier. Up to there I've been, by going to the tribunals, law
abiding. How would it have served me if I hadn't been?"

"It would have saved you, I believe, from arrest as an
absentee. There's an implication in what I've read that in
cases of men who appear to allege that they are not within
the Act—that they don't recognize it, that's to say—proceedings would be taken by summons. That's at least more
seemly than police coming to the vicarage to arrest you."

John winced. "I didn't know of that." He was silent a
moment. It was of his father, Hubbard knew, that he was
thinking. "All the same," he then said, "I wouldn't have
taken that line. I do recognize the Act. I'd have been pretending that I didn't and I can't pretend in anything." He
lifted a troubled face to his mentor. "How can I save my
father from seeing me taken from the vicarage under
arrest?"

Of the treatment of conscientious objectors at some of the
military depots sufficient was known to make Hope Hubbard vision with profound concern what might be awaiting

him after arrest. "You could go down to the recruiting office," he said heavily, "and give yourself up."

The young man shook his head decisively. "I can't do that. That's voluntarily presenting myself at the one place where I refuse to go."

Hubbard could not restrain a laugh. "Your etiquette in all this is decidedly complicated. But come," with earnest sympathy he went on, "we'll think out a way, old man, of keeping the vicarage out of the actual business, never fear."

The way they devised took the form of a call by John at Upton Springs' police station. In charge here was a grizzled old retired superintendent, rheumatic and spectacled, who had rejoined the Force early in the war. As a young constable he had known the vicarage brood as children, thence upwards. An old friendship stood between the two now met. Nothing of John's notoriety as conscientious objector had impaired it. Explaining the procedure of arrest as absentee, a warrant, the superintendent said, would be applied for by the recruiting officer at Thurstead. It would be served from Upton Springs, coming up by hand from Thurstead, probably about mid-day. How avoid it being served at the vicarage by a police officer? He listened to John's plan. Repeating already expressed distress at such happenings, he agreed with it. Its effect was that shortly before one o'clock every day thereafter call was made at the police station through an unfrequented passageway by one whom on a day the superintendent, looking up from his desk, gravely addressed.

"Yes, there's something for you this morning, Mr. Brecque."

John read the warrant. It was issued on information laid by the chief recruiting officer at Thurstead. Laying it down he looked meaningly at the superintendent. "Supposing I wasn't here, when would you be sending it up to the vicarage to take me?" he asked.

The superintendent put an eye to the clock, then turned it, also charged with meaning, on his inquirer. "Why, the lads here," he said, "have got to take their lunch, same's all of us. The magistrates are sitting today, you know; and they've got to lunch." He permitted himself a wink. "I wouldn't be sending to serve that not before half after two, I don't suppose."

"You'll trust me to be back here by then?"

"If you should happen to be about here by then," affirmed the superintendent portentously, "why, it will save my lad a journey."

5

Ruth was away from home at lunch-time on her canteen work. Sitting at table between his parents, and with Minna, John waited to break his news until the vicar, always the slowest eater of the party, had laid down his spoon and fork after his rice pudding. Then with a manufactured smile, "Well, that's my last meal here," he said, "for a time."

They stared upon him. Maintaining the smile, he nodded. Misgiving mounted in their eyes. His plan to avoid arrest at the vicarage was shared with them. Generally either he would come in from his morning walk with a cheery "No, not yet," or one of them anxiously would inquire of him. Once or twice this observance would be lost in some other matter which, pursued and leading on to fresh, would establish by default that he was yet free. Now each remembered that today had been such an occasion. He laid an affectionate hand, palm upwards, on the cloth before each of the two beside him. "Yes, it's come," he smiled.

Minna caught her hands to her bosom with stifled cry.

Laura took her boy's palm to her lips. The vicar with trembling fingers drew his eldest son's hand to his breast.

They would go with him, of course, to the police-court proceedings, his parents insisted. Dear Minna, it was agreed, had better not. When the time came to be starting, "You'd like me to kneel down with you, father, wouldn't you?" he said. He always remembered the flushed pleasure in his father's face. They all four knelt together. "Bless our dear boy's wish," the vicar prayed, "to do what his conscience tells him is right. Bless his love for us and our love for him. In separation from him our love cannot avail him. Avail him, loving Father, with Thy love."

This was in the same room as that in which all the family had knelt when the vicar, his arm around his eight-year-old eldest, had led happy prayer on the day of their arrival in the vicarage.

6

The proceedings in court were very brief. Three magistrates were on the bench. All were acquainted with the vicar, though only through formal meetings. The chairman's manner made it very clear that they found their duty highly embarrassing. Sir Douglas Fernshaw had an extensive property in the district and, very noticeably, two chins. At the lower of these he plucked unhappily while the prescribed ritual was gone through. He appeared to find nothing amiss in the superintendent's not very clear account of how the warrant had been served on the prisoner. He plucked more uncomfortably than before over the statement by the young captain sent up from the recruiting office to take charge of the case.

All being finished, it was painful to the Bench, he said, to have to perform an unpleasant duty in respect of the son of a prominently placed and highly respected member of their community. The prisoner's bearing, and what had been spoken to by the police witness of his behavior on arrest, were entirely commendable. The Bench could not enter into the views which he had told them were his reason for absenting himself after being called up. They trusted that he would now accept the inevitable without demur and enter cheerfully into his duties as a soldier. It was clear that the case was one for summary jurisdiction. The prisoner would be fined two pounds and ordered to await a military escort. He looked inquiringly at the recruiting representative. "Yes, this afternoon, sir," said the young captain. "In an hour or so's time." The court adjourned.

John's adjournment was to the charge room, the vicar and Laura accompanying him. The superintendent presently brought them heavily stewed tea in a huge pot of chipped white enamel and thick slices of bread and butter. He did what he could to keep the room secluded for them but there was constant going and coming. They whispered fitfully over the fire. As often when there is much to say, little was said.

At half-past four a smart young corporal preceded a heavily built private into the room. John stood up, the others likewise.

"Come for me?" asked John.

The corporal had entered the room very slick and assured. At sight of a clergyman and a lady with the prisoner for whom he had arrived he went suddenly sheepish.

"Er, that's right," he assented.

He fingered a button. There was an embarrassment. It was grotesque in the circumstances, and grotesque, Laura afterwards felt and told Minna, was the accustomed social conventionality which came involuntarily to her lips. "Well, you needn't go at once, need you?" she palely smiled. She lifted the huge teapot and poured a drop from it. "I don't know if this tea is still fit to drink."

"Looks all right to me, thanking you," affirmed the corporal, red.

"Clean cups—" nervously murmured Laura.

The corporal took off his cap. "All one to us," he said and grinned.

"Oh, really, I don't like—"

But she filled two cups, then lifted the bread and butter.

Three slices, for the vicarage party had not eaten, were on the plate. The corporal, exercising the privilege of rank, took two, the private the other. They ate at astonishing speed, with the suggestion however of habit, not of haste.

"Will we be able," Laura asked, "to see our son to-morrow?"

"I reckon," champed the corporal, nodding. "You'll be sent to the depot, Binsley," he champed at John, " 'morrow morning."

"Twelve o'clock that train goes," affirmed the private, articulating more clearly for his lesser rations were consumed.

The corporal swallowed largely and convulsively. Crimson by the effort, "No, it don't then," he sharply reprimanded, "twelve two."

The private, crushed, removed crumbs from his tunic with heavy blows of his hand. The corporal took up his cap. John gave both his hands to his mother, then to his father. The vicar clung to them. John whispered, "I'll be perfectly all right," and gently drew them away. He turned to the corporal. "Yes, how?"

"With him." The corporal nodded towards the private, now at the door.

They moved out, John beside the private, corporal behind,

vicar and Laura following. "Good luck, Mr. Brecque," said the superintendent, passed as they went to the exit.

News of the sensational event toward had got about the town. A gathering of people was in the street. When prisoner and private were down the four steps leading to it the corporal passed his cane smartly under his arm and saluted the prisoner's parents. "Thanking you again," he said. Then he took cane in fist and briskly ran down.

"March!"

The vicar and Laura, hand clutched in hand, saw their eldest son go from them under escort through the little crowd.

They were never again to see him out of custody.

Three

KEEP step there, can't you?" snapped the slick young corporal.

"He keeps changing of it," aggrievedly retorted the burly private.

"Sorry," said John pleasantly and abandoned the intention which had caused the trouble.

At "March!" he had moved off mechanically. "Left, left!" smartly from behind him shortly after the police station was quitted, had come to him as military authority's first voice since receiving him into its custody. He intended to obey no order of that authority directed towards making him part of its machine. Because he was wrung at recollection of his father's face in that final good-by it gave him impish relief, whimsical satisfaction, to start now with refusal on this trivial point of keeping his left foot in unison with his companion's left foot. At the man's complaint against him he realized the absurdity of his behavior. Cynosure of the long descent of Bank Hill and of the Banks he kept in step until, the recruiting office reached, sharper ordeal began.

A private house had been taken over for the accommodation of Colonel Gilling and his staff. In the lobby were several men in civilian dress. They were queued towards a room in which attestation papers were being filled in and signed. A sergeant marshaling them addressed the corporal: "This that absentee from Upton?"

"Yes, sergeant."

"Special case, he is. Take him straight up to the colonel."

"With escort party?"

"Don't want two of you to take him up a flight of stairs, do it?"

The private was left behind. Conducted by the corporal, John was taken to a large apartment on the first floor. Here were Colonel Gilling warming his back before a generous fire, a sergeant seated between two privates at a trestle table displaying buff and blue papers stacked and aligned with military precision, at a smaller table the captain who had attended the police court proceedings.

The corporal saluted and clicked heels. "Absentee from Upton police station, sir." A nod was jerked at him, he smartly repeated his performance, smartly withdrew.

Colonel Gilling put out a friendly hand. "Hullo, Brecque, glad to: see you."

"He was thoroughly decent to me," John next morning told his parents. "Until I refused to attest no one could have been pleasanter. I think he had laid himself out to forget all he had against me and to start afresh."

The colonel obviously had. Executing a brisk smile by numbers, "Been a little trouble about getting you: here," he amiably went on, "but here you are, as good as the next man and bygones: bygones. You've had ideas of your own, I know. Now you're going to feel, I know, that you've made your protest, done what you could, and now find yourself in the army and are going to: forget it all. You'll know that you're doing your: duty: and you'll find that it's a thoroughly: happy duty. The army's very different in this war from what it was in: my day. The nearer you get to the front line the more you'll find that we're all of us, officers, N.C.O.'s and men: all one. In all ranks there's a spirit of: fellowship, of: camaraderie—"

Here he broke off to introduce a side of this camaraderie to the notice of a young private now entered into the room, docket of papers in hand.

"Private Smithers, how the dick many times have you heard me say that I will not have men entering this room, never mind how engaged downstairs, without belt and cap? Sergeant-major, run this man for being improperly dressed while on duty while on active service."

He glared a moment, red, pop-eyed, at the repellent Smithers. As quickly returned to amiability as he had sprung into heat, he turned again then to John and with a single syllable, done with the click of final poise in a rifle movement, invited response to the lead he had given him.

"Eh?"

A nervousness in John's voice accentuated rather than detracted from the firmness of his tone. "I'm ever so grateful to you, Colonel Gilling, for your friendliness. I hate to seem obstinate, ungenerous, in return, but I've got to tell you that though I'm here it's, it's by compulsion and under protest. I've got to tell you that I will do nothing that conflicts with my conscientious refusal to be a soldier."

Red a moment before in his indignation at a man improperly dressed, Colonel Gilling had then been but a delicate pink to the crimson with which his features now became suffused. Swollen to his tunic buttons' limit, he appeared, nevertheless, to be crimsoning, swelling yet.

"You said," John concluded, "that I had made my protest. I'm sorry to say, I'm sorry, I mean, to have to tell you after your friendliness, that my protest has only now really begun."

"*Wat?*"

The question exploded from the colonel's face without, however, relieving its congestion or that of the swollen chest beneath it. It exploded again, "*Wat?*"

John said steadily, "As I've told you."

With a noisy rush Colonel Gilling released now the pressure with which he was charged. The flame of his deflation could almost be felt. His voice now like an iron bar tugged with difficulty through a grating, "Let me tell you," he rasped, "that the only part of your insubordinate statement of which I have taken: cognizance: is your use of my name. Let me tell you, Private Brecque, that you will in future address me, as all other officers, not by name but as 'sir.' Let me tell you—"

He had borne as much of the extraction of the rasp from his throat as apparently he could endure. With drill book correctness, sharply-turning-head-and-eyes-to-the-left-without-moving-the-body, "Sergeant-major," he commanded, "attest this man."

"Yessir," said the sergeant-major, springing to attention with one movement, back into his seat with a second, drawing a blue paper from a stack before him with a third, and stabbing an inkpot with a pen with a fourth. "Full name?" he called.

"Is that for me to sign?" John inquired of the colonel.

"Certainly it is."

"I'm sorry, I refuse to attest."

Colonel Gilling repeated the crimsoning and swelling process, held it a moment at its apex and repeated then the explosion from it. "Take him away."

The sergeant-major repeated his own first movement, brought himself by clicks to John's side, threw his chest further forward and his head further back than even during these processes they had been, and inquired, snip-snap, "Where to, sir?"

"Medical examination room."

"Before he's attested, sir?"

"Haven't you heard him refuse to: attest?"

"Yessir."

"Then don't ask ridiculous questions. Remember it in: evidence."

"Yessir."

"Put him through the doctor. Take him then to the attesting room. If he refuses again put him in the cells. Tomorrow morning, depot by depot train. Captain Harvey, you hear that?"

The captain sat smartly upright. "Yessir."

The colonel flicked violently in John's direction, rather as if a wasp had stung his hand. "Take him away."

Gloweringly he swelled back to bursting point.

As John was about to pass through the door opened for him by numbers by the sergeant-major, "And let me tell you, Private: Brecque," he erupted, "that whether you attest or don't attest makes not the slightest difference except in the punishment you will be awarded for refusal to obey: an order."

Another wasp stung his hand.

2

The door well closed and his ram-rod deportment relaxed with the action, "Well, you've made a tidy good start an' all, not 'arf you haven't," pronounced the sergeant, to John's surprise entirely genial. " 'Ot as ever I've known him, you made him, an' I've known him warm." He gave John a friendly poke. "You won't see him again. Take my advice and do what you've got to do, army fashion and no silliness. When the army's got hold of you you've no more chance sillying than a baby with a kicking mule."

As if in excuse of non-commissioned affability to contumacious recruit, "I don't 'old nothing against a man while he's in civvies, see?" he explained. "When they get you in uniform tomorrow, why, that's different, see?"

"They'll never get me in uniform," John said, palely smiling.

"Aw, don't be silly."

He was the last case for medical examination. The younger of two doctors hesitated a while over his lungs and stepped over then to the elder. "Bit of a—" John caught. The elder stethoscoped him. "Oh, nothing; right itself."

Led then by the affable sergeant to the attestation room, business in which appeared to have finished for the day, John refused again to attest, this time to an elderly civilian manipulator of the blue forms, wearing a badge and looking tired. The sergeant detailed the upstairs refusal. The civilian glanced wanly at the clock. "Well, if he won't attest what's the sense," he asked lugubriously, "of bringing him to me?"

"Colonel's sense," cheerfully affirmed the sergeant.

The civilian shrugged.

"Come on, then, Brecque," said the sergeant, serenely moving off.

"Cells now, isn't it?" asked John as they returned to the lobby.

"Yes, except that there aren't no blinkin' cells."

Cell accommodation thus wanting, John passed the night in what affected to be the guardroom of an adjacent requisitioned residence. Used partly as a rest house for recruits, partly as billets for men employed about the recruiting station, the place was a noisily light-hearted barracks, echoing with door slammings, heavy boots on boarded floors, whistling and snatches of song. Part of the stair banisters and strips of skirting-board had been scrounged for firewood. Beds were represented by the mattress sections known as army biscuits. A horsehair couch, sociably given up to him in the guardroom, gave John as good accommodation as that enjoyed by any in the building. At ten next morning the orderly-room captain, looking in on rounds—he walked with a stick and a limp, John now saw—pleasantly remonstrated with him and advised him for his good. Yesterday's refusals would be overlooked if he would attest now. He would find the depot a roughhouse. "Chuck this silly nonsense, man, and put your back into what you can't help and will soon enjoy."

"It's not silly nonsense to me."

"You're public school, aren't you?"

"Yes, Upton."

"Upton! Good God, I'd have thought Upton would have knocked out any germs of your sort of stuff."

"It knocked them in," John said.

The young captain stared at him. For the first time in their intercourse, stretching now from the police court to the guardroom, a certain cogitation veiled his eyes. He frowned it away. "Well, your people'll be here in a shake," he said. "They telephoned the office and I told 'em eleven. You'll parade for the depot train eleven thirty. Good luck." He gave his hand and limped off.

Eleven brought the parents. Debiting Colonel Gilling only with an amusing ramrodishness after his opening geniality, John enlarged upon the general friendliness which had been shown him, the comfortable night by the guardroom fire, the jolly good supper and breakfast. Things weren't going to be half bad, he assured them. He'd always told them so, and look at this outset of it in proof. Alleviated of the anxiety in which they had arrived, the vicar and Laura went to the station when he was fallen in for the depot party. To the platform they saw him come with nine other called-up men, yesterday's corporal and private in conduct. The corporal recognized his police-court tea hosts. He had placed John to march immediately in front of him. Now standing the others easy under the private he brought over the son to the parents. Laura slipped to the buffet and bought him a packet of twenty cigarettes. She hoped he would go back to his party but he did not. She tried to hold him in talk while John might move aside with his father but he somehow effected to keep the conversation general. The train came in. A carriage had been reserved. The private and the nine filled it.

"Us'll go in here," the corporal said, indicating the next compartment and standing aside while John entered.

Both the vicar and Laura took this as a friendliness in keeping with what John had told them and with what themselves they had seen. "You're being given special attention," Laura smiled to her son through the window; she felt tears coming.

"Well, he's a prisoner, see?" said the corporal simply.

The tears came.

The vicar stood bareheaded till the train was out of sight.

3

Four weeks thereafter John was brought before court-martial. His face was of a marked pallor. It had a drawn look. Charged with disobedience of the command of his lawful officer to put on his uniform, he was still in his civilian clothes. They yet bore signs of the handling to which he had been subjected in the brief but sufficient period between his reception at the guardroom and his committal to cells to await the trial at which he now stood.

It was in the brand of togging at Upton that these signs disfigured his appearance. With a wry smile he had recalled the similarity.

Alone unchanged by his experiences was the expression of his eyes. Unflinching before the staring-down of the tortoise-shell mustached sergeant, it had remained unquelled before more practical manifestations of the depot's rough-house reputation. At Upton the twig left outside the school gates had been his mind's anchor during his dismays. He had become a man; the twig had become a tree. Its roots were his ideals and his faith in them, its topmost reachings his visions and his powers of expressing them. In rough testings here it had stood him as a tower. In the long solitudes in the depot cells, not the first visionary to profit by imprisonment, he had climbed its heights and watched the stars. His aspect was the more serene.

Physically he was something debilitated. He had been well treated while in cells. Want of exercise and of fresh air had run him down.

These were the qualities, a mental heightening, a physical lowering, that he took with him to the new stage of ordeal to which by judgment of the court-martial he was now committed. Sentence when promulgated, read out on full parade at which his was the sole civilian dress, declared itself in twelve months' hard labor, commuted to 112 days' detention at a military detention barracks. Here he was taken on the following day under escort. A four hours' journey by slow train, its greater part long waits on wind-searched junction platforms, terminated in a long tramp uphill to an impressively walled and gated building, forbidding in aspect in degree such as to suggest that it had won a prize in architectural competition for state institutions of repellent design. Its portal opened and closed for his admittance with a prodigious manipulation of locks and bolts. The march from the station had been in gale and rain. He had carried a heavy kit bag containing the clothing issue made to him at the depot. When he let it fall from his shoulder in the courtyard, lift it down with numbed arms up which the rain had run he could not, he reeled and almost fell on it. He felt sick and faint.

"Do you intend to make any resistance?"

In the gatehouse where was performed the routine of reception this was the first question put to him by the

sergeant-major to whom he had been handed over. It was
addressed to him, as by rote, in his capacity of conscientious
objector from whom trouble might be expected. It was in
his capacity as, according to his lights, law-abiding citizen,
that he answered it.

"No, none at all." Lest a spasmodic chattering of his teeth,
due to his wet and chilled condition, should be thought
fear's signal of his reason for this disavowal he took a hold
on himself. "I'm here for punishment which I've lawfully
earned and I mean to take it."

"Better get into that for a start then," said the sergeant-
major pointing to the kit bag.

Envisaging this prospect while in the train he had reasoned out his response to it. At the depot he had refused to
wear uniform as being the token of military status. Here,
if ordered, it would be the dress of the punishment to which
rightly he had been committed.

"Is that," he asked, "the p-prison dress?"

"That's the detention dress."

"Very w-well then." He was desperately chilled.

"Good for you," commented the sergeant-major. "We've
had some of your sort here," he added dryly, "not so wise."

Had he interrogated the range of the newcomer's wisdom
in similar regards he could have predicted his outlook as
not so good. To all that met him here John directed that
"decidedly complicated etiquette" of Hope Hubbard's remark. Thus the uniform was prison dress but the regimental
badges with which the tunic shoulders and the cap were
provided were solely, he decided, military insignia. Released
to the cell which was to be his home for four months, he
was fit only to collapse upon his planks and there lie. In
the morning, ill but something recovered, it was without his
badges that he took his place in the general parade for inspection by the commandant.

The commandant was a short, bony-featured man with the jib and the air rather of the navy than of the army. He spoke to men here and there. He had young eyes in an old face. When he came to John he took a slightly whimsical stare at him, then questioned him, and was answered, much on the lines of the interrogation by the sergeant-major.

"Good, then," he agreed; "and, if you're going to be sensible enough to take your punishment and obey orders, where are your regimental badges?"

"I want to say as respectfully as I can, sir, that they're part of the very thing I am here for refusing to accept. While I am undergoing the consequences of what I've done, I feel I ought not to have the causes forced on me."

The commandant gave the twist of a smile. "I'll say, then, as respectfully as I can, that you'll start with some P.D. to think it over." Out of the corner of his mouth, delivered in the manner of a humorous aside in which the prisoner was invited to share, "Two days," he told the sergeant-major at his elbow and with a not unfriendly glint at the offender passed on.

Days, one hundred and twelve of them, at the detention barracks, even when unharshened by punishment diet, were greatly more arduous than, once he had been relegated for court-martial, John had found them in the depot cells. Punishment, when adjudged necessary by the commandant, was in terms of that P.D. of which John had had early experience. This was continuous confinement in cell, dry bread and water the sole sustenance.

It proved to be the frequent portion of the vicar's eldest son. Never once was it given him in spirit other than the quasi-humorous manner of its first infliction.

"You were given this order. You refused to obey it. You give me no option but to punish you, do you?" the commandant, twinkling behind sternness, would ask.

"No, sir, I perfectly well see that. I hope you see equally that with my convictions I just can't do this thing."

The whimsical stare, the twitched corners of the long mouth, would precede the invariable reply, "I'm shut-eye to all that, stone blind. But I do wish to goodness you'd offer me something else to look at. Two days."

It was inescapable. All would be going sufficiently well with him. He would be within reach of the amenities earned by good conduct. Then would come up some order which, because it appeared to him an accessory of military training, he would refuse to obey. Now it was instruction in saluting, now drill with rifles, now skirmishing with an armed party. Not complying and stating his objection he would be fallen out and marched to his cell. P.D. would follow. Earned conduct marks would be lost. The amenities of three slabs of adamant mattress, twice weekly change of library book, writing of one letter and receiving of one visit a fortnight, rarely reached were quickly lost.

This told very heavily, the enfeebling punishment diet especially, on a constitution already debilitated at the depot, sharply touched by the chill on arrival at the detention barracks and lowered by the two days' P.D. then immediately awarded. The periods of solitary confinement were not in themselves greatly felt. In greater measure even than at Binsley they afforded him those unbroken solitudes in which the tree into which the Upton twig had spread was his mind's resort, in which Bunyans have drawn their meditations and given of their fruits. Doing nothing to make himself feel hungry, he had no desire for food. The bread and water sufficed him. But he would come out ill able to cope with the "at the doubles" and the "as you weres." Frequently on the first day of return to normal work the taxing of the drills or the schedule of the tasks would be beyond him. Renewed punishment would follow.

Much impaired from the man he had been when first delivered to the tortoise-shell mustache at Binsley, he was returned there on the expiration of his sentence at the detention barracks. Again bringing himself before court-martial he again, in the same place as before, served commutation sentence, this time of 140 days. Again was return, again arraignment, now for "willful defiance of military authority."

This was early in 1917. Long upon the road, there had now reached his court an Army Order of some months previous directing that an offense against discipline as result of conscientious objection must be punished by committal to a civil prison, not to a military detention barracks.

He was sentenced to two years' hard labor.

Philip at this time was in Q-ship service, decoying U-boats to destruction. Mary was writing home of qualifying herself in her off-duty hours in car driving and running repairs through friendship with a captain of an Army Service Corps unit stationed at the place of her base hospital. Ruth, wildly excited at thought of uniform and closer association with Sam Browne belts, was insisting on joining the Women's Army Auxiliary Corps, organization of which was just then announced.

An occasion of these activities found their actors dressing their parts. Philip was admiring himself in a newly purchased slop-shop outfit suitable to the mate of a tramp steamer. Mary, transferred to W.A.A.C., was drawing on the gloves of a woman staff car driver in France. Ruth was hugging herself before a mirror on first attire in Waac uniform. On the same day their elder brother sat in a garb hideous in pattern and texture before its broad arrows had added their repellent effect to the design. He sat on a stool in the cell of a convict prison. He was midway through that first month of his sentence of which the convict of that period spent twenty-three hours and ten minutes of each twenty-four in solitary confinement. He sat with his left shoulder and his head inclined against the wall, the head so lamentably dropped as to suggest that the neck was dislocated. At his feet was a mailbag, partially sewn.

The corridor without sounded to a footstep, the spyhole in the door showed an eye.

"Get on with it there, you," a voice called.

John Brecque fumbled his hands down to the mailbag and drawing it on to his knees got on with it.

Four

DOMESTIC trouble and professional work consort never so
injuriously as in the case of a vicar of a parish. The layman
at least has his office and his home in separated worlds.
Those who observe his one hand in his business need know
nothing of the conditions of his other in his house. The
parish priest not only has his work and his family affairs in
the same compass; his home, alone among the homes of
his fellow men, is not his castle. Vicarages are built of glass.
All that goes on in them is discerned by the parish eye.
Easiest of cock-shies for the stones of the gossip and of the
censorious, they are also the safest. It is of their nature not
to hit back.

In 1917 the floors of the vicarage of St. Luke's were strewn
with stones. Laura with her cheery smile and her devoted
love was for ever sweeping them into corners and pretending
they were not there; but the vicar, do what she could, was
constantly treading on them. His gait, too, she noticed, had
become that of a man older than his years. It pained her to
see the droop in his shoulders. It pained her more to watch
him wince at this hurt and at that as he trod about the
apartments into which he had stepped so eagerly on that
afternoon when, his brood about him, he had taken up that
letter from the hall table. "Look, Laura, 'Dear Vicar.' Minna,
look."

Of all that chattering, ecstatic throng then with them only
Minna now was left. Ruth had been posted to a Waac detachment at Aldershot. Had Mary, had even John, been the
last to be withdrawn from the circle, the void, the silence

left had not been so profound as that occasioned by the going from the vicarage of the vivid creature who was second Philip. Now at table, at prayers, at every occasion of the day they were but three.

It was very quiet.

And the vicar, Laura saw, not only had distresses, not only had lost now the tonic of Ruth's cheer, he was overworking. Hilary Tweed's absence had thrown virtually all the duties of St. Mark's on his hands. Ceaselessly in his mind was the picture of his eldest in prison; always before his eyes was Minna imprisoned in the house; continuously were the painful stabs of the littered stones, thrown in at his son, at his adopted daughter, at himself for shielding them, at his wanting in the militancy of the day. His doubled work nevertheless must go on, his face always must show his Master's smile, never his private griefs. It always did show that smile. It was only, Laura knew, when alone in his own room, sometimes alone in his church, that he would suffer himself to enter his Gethsemane.

Tweed, with every credit to his zeal, had left a full duty at St. Mark's.

Not for anything would the vicar allow the rota of services to be cut down. To and from St. Mark's daily he went. The stubbly chin and the yellow frequently were dubiously handled in his presence. He was not the first vicar who, having created a daughter church in his parish and allowed its conduct to fall almost entirely into the hands of his curate, has subsequently been made to find reflective reading in the third chapter of I Corinthians:

"There is among you envying and strife and divisions . . . one saith, I am of Paul; and another, I am of Apollos.

"I have planted, Apollos watered. I have laid the foundation and another buildeth thereon."

To conduct a service as it were under Tweed had been one thing; to administer it in his own custom by himself was quite another. Skirmishing in advance of the Revised Prayer Book, Apollos had both pruned and originated. The old-fashioned husbandry of Paul was taken as a reflection on the methods of his gardener-in-charge. "Mr. Tweed never did that," "That wasn't Mr. Tweed's way," "Our curate won't like to be told of this," were frequent hearings. Offertories declined. There appeared to be a feeling that money put in the bag was a direct expression of loyalty to him who raised it for acceptance before the altar. What was earned by Apollos was not, apparently, deemed payable to Paul. The thick hand and the white fingers, reckoning the totals, made no nicety over drawing attention to the diminutions. "Not altogether surprising" was the tone, if not the words, of their comment.

To a mind grievously occupied in its brief leisures these were new sources of perplexity. To the invidiousness of being regarded here at St. Mark's as a stranger within his own gates the vicar brought neither the qualities of humor nor of self-assertion; to that of being looked upon as in a sense a usurper he fronted the armory neither of thick-skinned indifference nor of waspish taking of offense. He brought to the finding of his way in these new difficulties the sole light of his character, which was the lamp of his Master, and it befell that gradually he began, first to be accepted, then to arouse interest.

St. Mark's people began rather to like the unassuming little old vicar with those simple talks of his. Knowing of him what they knew, seeing him as he bore it, they began to "feel a bit sorry for him, you know."

Trudging up Bank Hill after an early service one week-day morning he was overtaken by a farm cart carrying a load of garden soil. Mr. Bennett, one of his churchwardens, was sitting on the off shaft. Once or twice before he had similarly gone by. This time he stepped down.

"You take a ride, vicar. 'Tis a long climb for you, this."

Always a little furrow of perplexity had been carried up the hill by the vicar's forehead when, with no better than conventional greeting, the cart previously had overtaken him. Immensely gratified now, he thanked the nursery-gardener warmly but presented scruples at accepting the invitation. "It wouldn't be fair on the horse, two of us."

"Ah, but I'll walk."

"Oh, but I couldn't hear of that, really. Why ever should you?"

"Well, because I've just come off a fine big breakfast, which is more'n you have, for one thing. As to the horse, anyway, d'you know why I sit the shaft 'stead of walking as frequent I've a mind to?"

"If you'd as soon walk, no, I don't."

"Why, because if a carter sits the shaft uphill he brings the weight down to the collar, see? Horse lifted half off his legs otherwise, no purchase to his feet, see?"

"Dear me," exclaimed the vicar, profoundly interested in this principle of equipoise, "I never would have thought of that."

"You get right up," said Mr. Bennett, preparing now to assist him there. "More forward you sit more pleased the old mare'll be to have you there."

The vicar was no Philip either in attaining a perch or in accommodating himself thereon when he had gained it. His legs hung with the tense flexion at the knees of one who seeks to clutch them about the air. He clung with both hands to harness and wished that it was more yielding to his grip. Nevertheless not Philip when he first swarmed a rigging on the "Worcester" was more exhilarated than was he. This kindliness of this good man amiably chatting beside him was the banner of his Lord floating from a citadel which long weeks had denied him entry. Gaining confidence with his happiness, soon he allowed his legs to swing, his grip to relax. He laughed at imagination of the figure he, elderly vicar, must cut balanced on a shaft, leaning against a huge cart-horse, rumbled after by a load of loam.

"I must look a funny sight up here," he said.

"A more proper sight than you look walking, vicar," declared Mr. Bennett, "and that's a fact. 'Tis a long pull for you, this hill, specially without breakfast, as I've said. Tell you what, sir, I'm up this way two days a week working a contract I've got with Mr. Dukes over to the Manor. I could make it two of your Communion mornings easy as any other."

From the top of the hill the vicar made homewards as light of heart as of foot. Until the Manor contract ended twice weekly he made journey on the shaft. Frequently afterwards Mr. Bennett, having a load for Upton Springs, made a Communion morning the day of it. Few were about at that hour, but from windows many saw the unconventional sight and, smiling at it, were charitably warmed as by observation of a simple kindliness and its recipient's enjoyment of it the human heart frequently is. They spoke of it to one another. When next they met the vicar they smiled again at recollection of it and stopped and spoke of it to him. Charitableness towards him found exercise, too, in other little things. Mary and Ruth once were simultaneously on leave as Waacs. It was realized that, after all, three of his children out of four were in uniform. It was reflected, further, that the eldest at least was no longer hanging about shirking. If he was still in prison it was, come to think of it, it was felt, rather sad, you know, for his father. As to those sermons which in 1914 used to irritate one so much well, really, in this the third year of the war it really was rather a relief to get away for an hour from "blood, mud and khaki" as someone had aptly phrased the thing. And when you remembered the vicar's rather delightful little ways before all this began, and if you'd seen him perched on that shaft this morning, well, really, you know . . .

2

Thus befell it that by this and by that in mid-1917 there was generally a perceptible thawing in the ice which had frozen about the vicarage. Down at the Banks they found that they rather liked the unassuming little man, his services were restful, oddly helpful. Up at the Springs it began to be noticed, not without self-reproach here and there, how much older had grown the face that still, as always, carried everywhere that gentle smile. In general John became forgotten. In considerable degree bygones of the vicar's causes of offense were let be bygones. Sole public reminder of the vicarage's bad odor, and she was hardly ever seen, was its harborage still of a German.

In this wintry sunshine thus bestowed, Minna indeed became the vicar's and Laura's particular object of concern. John was never from their minds, but they could only picture him as the occasional letters he was permitted to write presented him and he was at pains always to omit from his accounts of himself all that might give his father distress. That he was ever in ill-health he never hinted. That his case, through P.D. and the like, was harder than it might have been he never told. Hope Hubbard was certain that visits to him were allowed. His parents inquired of him about this but by adroit evasions he always concealed from them on the one hand that the privilege again and again was lost to him by his forfeiture of good conduct marks, on the other that he was deliberately keeping them from seeing him in order to avoid the dismay he knew they would be given by his physical appearance.

They saw him twice during his first term at the military detention barracks, once during his second. The visits were in bad light. His right to them had been earned between bouts of malaise. Yearning beyond his control for sight of his father he had, as it were, gone into training that in appearance he might present himself as fit as his letters sedulously had declared him to be. Of purpose he came into his parents' presence with springing step. Of the animation of his spirit, aloft in the branches of that tree, there was no question. Distressed at his thinness, newly saddened by actual sight of him as prisoner, the vicar and Laura on each occasion left him, nevertheless, with what he had concealed as to his conditions and frequent condition yet concealed. They went to him, as one goes to a prison, as comforters. It was he from whom the comfort flowed. "Don't you worry one tiniest shred about me" always was his reiterated behest. "Imagine me whenever you think of me as living in a palace surrounded by everything I need. I'm living in my mind. If suddenly I were to be transported to the luxurious freedom of a palace but lost the feelings that fortify me here, *then* you could imagine me wretched, *then* I'd be hungry, then, although on swansdown, I should be tossing on planks. I tell you I'm *fine*."

They would go back to the vicarage encouraged despite themselves, and it was when they thus came home that, by contrast, they noticed particularly the desolation of the one there encaged. Minna knew neither bars nor jailers, neither duress nor punishment. But she was in Coventry, estranged from all in a degree that even John, smile-exchanging with fellow-prisoners, was not. She had not, as had he, the consolations of idealism, the resources of intellectualism. His conscience approved him; hers charged her, month in month out, with printing the stain of her presence upon her beloved protectors.

She would greet them on their return from the visits to their son with gladdest welcome; a meal cooked with her every art to their especial tastes would be ready for them; some startling piece of housework always awaited their inspection; on each occasion she had contrived to bring to head some personal gift for each, a knitted scarf for the vicar, an embroidered fancy for Laura, on which secretly her deft fingers had been employed. But always they knew, by signs clear to loving eyes, that their absence, however superficially filled, had been given to brooding alone upon that feature of her case which was her overwhelming oppression, the trouble which she felt that her presence brought upon them. The clutch of her embrace in greeting them told that. They had only been gone a few hours. She would throw arms about them as though the separation had been of years, straining each to her with a hug that told what was concealed alike in her face hidden over a shoulder, in her heart pressed to a heart in her emotion.

"Minna, Minna," the vicar would say, patting her back.

"Dear, dear Minna," from Laura, holding her away to kiss her.

It was a return from a fourth visit to John that brought a direful beginning to what was to be the outcome of these relations. This was when John had been two months in the civil prison to which his third court-martial had committed him.

3

From the depot he had written briefly and bravely of his sentence, telling where it was to be served. Unlike the military detention barracks of his former incarcerations the civil prison he named was familiar to the ear. It had a grim sound. The vicarage was greatly cast down that day. Long weeks went by with no further news. Increasing fears began to be felt. Hope Hubbard, distressed at the anxiety he saw, wrote on his own account to the prison governor, and came up one morning with the formal reply he presently received. For the first two months of sentence a prisoner undergoing hard labor might not, it appeared, write or receive a letter. That period ended he was permitted a letter in and out and a visit. The official statement named the date on which this prisoner might be seen by his parents. On that day the vicar and Laura, giving John no chance to deny them, made the considerable journey involved.

They were not prepared for the hideous broad-arrow dress. They were dismayed by the conditions in which the meeting took place. They were distressed by the manifest ill-health in which they found their son. They stood in one of a row of narrow stalls fronted with wire mesh. Opposite to them in a similar stall similarly fronted stood John. Up and down a passage between paraded a warder. Through the two thicknesses of mesh, across the passageway, and at intervals across the figure of the warder, the conversation took place. Its duration was twenty minutes. John coughed intermittently throughout it. With smiles too clearly manu-factured, he wished, he said, that they hadn't come so soon or so unexpectedly because he feared that they would go away with a quite wrong impression of his circumstances. He was jolly comfortable here as a matter of fact. He had a bit of a cough but otherwise he was frightfully fit. There was a jolly good library here and he believed he might get work in it. The first two months had been a little trying in some ways but when they came again they would find him in grand form.

A prisoner in an adjoining stall began suddenly to beat his hands against the mesh that caged him from a young woman meshed opposite him and to scream. A warder coming in behind him pulled him away. The young woman, tearing at her encaging, screamed "Charlie! Charlie!"

Laura, who always stifled her emotions when the vicar was with her, nearly broke down when they got outside. They sat on a bench while she battled to control herself. The vicar was very brave. He put his arms about her and drew her to him. "Oh, Gordon," she said chokingly, "I wanted to tear down that wire as that poor creature wanted to, and touch him, touch his hands, his face. Oh, Gordon, our John, our John!"

She controlled herself and never would forgive herself, she thought, for her betrayal of her care of her husband. "It's you," she said, "who are less fitted to stand this than I am. Forgive me, my dearest." He was still brave but he declined sadly on the long way back. The cross-country journey involved two changes and long delays. On the first and second stages the trains were very full. She had to sit apart from him. His woe-filled face kept twitching as she watched it. On the last stage they had a compartment to themselves and she sat beside him, holding his hand. "Try to doze, dearest. Close your eyes and try."

"I'd rather keep them open. I'm seeing the boy."

Just before they got to Upton Banks, "Do you know what I'm thinking of now?" he suddenly spoke.

"No, tell me, dearest."

"Of the first time Minna saw him. It's being in a carriage to ourselves at night like this, I suppose. I was thinking of when we sat like this with Minna between us, taking her up to little John at Knipstone."

She pressed his hand. "Now it's to Minna that we're going," she said, essaying brightness. "I wonder what little presents she'll have for us this time? And what supper? How you will want it!"

He shook his head. "I'm not hungry a bit."

"Oh, but you mustn't disappoint Minna.

"Kind Minna," he smiled.

4

The London train was due in on the other side of the platform when, at nine o'clock, they alighted at Upton Bank. As they went up the steps of the footbridge they had to stand aside to give passage to three men who came down abreast, a police-constable following them. The flankers of the three were big built men wearing blue overcoats and bowler hats. The man between them was in a fawn mackintosh, mud-stained, and a soft felt. He was in handcuffs. Laura's hand tightened involuntarily upon the vicar's; the vicar made a sharp indrawing of his breath. Poignant throwback as the incident was to the associations from which they had come, neither remarked upon it while they ascended the hill in the fly which, after the long and taxing day, Laura felt was necessitated. The bleak coincidence newly chilled their minds, already numbed. When they reached home they found that indirectly the vicarage was touched by it.

Startlingly four or five people were standing about the gate, a police-constable bearing down on them as the two stepped out.

The man knew them by sight. Laura was nearer to him. "Good evening, madam," he saluted her. She peered inquiringly at him in the faint gleam of a street-lamp, its rays dimmed by the war lighting regulations. "Nothing, nothing the matter, is there?" apprehensively she inquired.

"Nothing at all, ma'am," he assured her. He glowered upon the group of idlers. "These 'ere just stickin' about curious, nothing better to do, I suppose. Good evening, sir.

Detectives down from London there's been today after a
wanted man thought to ha' bin campin' in the forest. They
took him in the lane back of your house there." He opened
the gate. "Stand aside there, can't you," he addressed the
loiterers, "and move along off of it. I've spoken to you
once."

The idlers had pressed about while he was speaking.
Clearly they were agog for details of what appeared to have
been an Upton Springs man-hunt sensation. Laura recognized a woman's face. It was Violet of the stoutly Germano-
phobe feelings.

She took the vicar's arm. "Come along in, dearest." She
thanked the gate opener. "In our lane, really? I do hope
our friend in here wasn't alarmed?"

"Well, she was a bit upset, ma'am. With her permission
they had a look round the house, the detectives; knew the
man was round about, see, and found the back door un-
locked. Good night, ma'am. Good night, sir."

"There you are then," came Violet's voice. "What did I
tell you? Searching the house! What's that if he wasn't a
spy come to 'er, eh?"

"Ain't you got no homes, then?" from the policeman,
heavily sarcastic.

5

They opened the front door. Always Minna would come
rushing at their entry. This time the hall stood empty, no
sound in the house.

"Minna!"

No answer.

"Oh, my dear—" began the vicar. He was white, agitated.

"Minna!" Laura called again.

She was moving towards the drawing-room door when
that of the kitchen premises down the passage cautiously

opened and Minna's face appeared, fear twisted. "Ah, thank to God it is you, thank to God. I heard wheels and voices. I was frightened, frightened." She came forward. In tragic whisper as though still, tip-toe, she crept about in quaking dread, "Oh, I have been terrified," she told. "Police have searched the house; a crowd has been outside; they have shouted things; they have broken a window; a stone has come in, crash. . . ."

The story within these bated utterances was, when told, of the appearance at the front door of the two plain-clothes men seen with the handcuffed prisoner at the station. "We are police officers." Minna thought they had come for her. "My heart bang and stop. I tumble and they catch me. They were kind, but, oh, there were people at the gate staring horribly."

The detectives believed that the man they were after had come into the garden but, not being found there, had perhaps slipped into the house. They searched the house, then left, but the people outside remained "long and long." Minna had showed herself at a window, drawing the blinds, and there had been pointing at her and rude cries. Then there was shouting in the lane at the back. Afterwards there was more disturbance outside the house and then a stone was thrown. "I was here in the hall in the dark, listening, terrified, and the awful crash came and there was laughing and running away."

"Which window, my poor darling?"

"The study, the study." She was crying.

They went there with a candle to see the damage. It was the window immediately before the vicar's table which had been broken. Falling glass had overturned the ink container, red and blue. A flower vase had added water to the streams. Wind had disturbed the papers since Minna had done what she could with the mess; the floor was strewn with them.

The vicar looked rueful but he said at once, he was holding Minna's arm, "Well, that's nothing much; and they've chosen luckily the pane that was cracked."

"It is I who have made this done to you," Minna cried. "It is because of me, of me."

That the demonstration certainly had been against her, and why, already had been advertised by Violet's overheard declamation. The morrow brought the reasons full. Upton Springs had gone to bed agog with its sensational man hunt. In the morning it seethed, mouth to mouth, with details, each mouth contributing addition. The man the Scotland Yard detectives took was, the sensation said, a German spy. By one version they got him after a desperate fight in the vicarage garden; by another he was held up with revolvers actually in the house itself; by a third he was trapped in the lane at the back while eating provisions with which that German woman there had supplied him. She had been provisioning him for days past; that, anyway, was an absolute fact for Violet Cross had seen her lurking about in the lane at all hours and had seen a strange man, hosts of people had for that matter, going and coming in that direction. The man was the head of the whole spy organization in this country. He was shot at dawn in the Tower that very morning after the Scotland Yard chaps got him back. As good as certain it was that that German woman of the vicar's was going to be shot at dawn, too; any moment the detectives might come for her.

That they did not, as it turned out, choose for their descent any moment either of that particular day or of any following took no jot of veracity from the story. Much the contrary indeed for, as the story now was told, they had changed their plan. They were using her now as a bait for another notorious spy they were after. Any day now he might come to her for supplies or for passing information—

she was, as a matter of fact, one of their chief agents, had been ever since the war began—and then they were going to take the two together, shooting at sight if necessary.

All Upton, Springs and Banks, believed all this as, three years previously, all England had believed the story of the Russians in Euston Road. The arrested man was in fact a common embezzler. Hope Hubbard, furious at the mischief being done to his friends, ascertained this from the police and by all means in his power put the facts in circulation. In wartime, however, an effect of the restriction of news is that rumor takes official denial as being made for reasons of state. In vulgar quarters, "Naturally they tell that yarn," was said. "How can they trap this other spy if it gets to him that the chap before him was caught and that now they're waiting for him?" In places more refined, "Well, some of the story," was the voice, "may be exaggerated, I never supposed it wasn't; but invariably there's some truth in a thing as widely spread as this is. The woman is a German, you can't get over that, and the vicarage *was* searched. Say what they please, it's a funny thing that out of all Upton they should go *there* to find him, *and* catch him, remember."

It was from the former body of opinion, probably, that anonymous letters again began to fall into the vicarage box, opprobrious chalkings to appear on the gate and walls; from the latter that kind friends came forward to do neighborly duty in terms of "Mrs. Brecque, I scarcely like to mention it, but I do feel that you ought to know what's being said about the town. . . ." "I say, vicar, this is rather an unpleasant story that's getting about. . . . I'm sure there's nothing in it; nevertheless . . ." To what lengths indeed, grotesque or deplorable according to the point of view, obsession by the story was carried was evidenced by Minna's reason for giving up her daily promenade in the back lane.

A week after the distressing night, "Minna, my dear," the

vicar said, "it's a lovely day; do go for an airing in the lane for half an hour."

She shook her head. "No, it is good here by the open window."

"But much better to be walking. Come, I'll go with you."

She shook again. "No, there is always now someone in the lane."

"My dear, absurd; it's hardly ever used."

"Look from my room. You will see if I am right."

Minna's bedroom window commanded the lane. Much mystified, the vicar went upstairs, more mystified returned. "There does happen to be someone there. It's that girl Violet, up at the Church Road end with another woman; but surely—"

"There is always someone. I have told you."

"But whatever for?"

Her head was bent above her sewing. "They are watching for me and if anyone comes to meet me."

That such a watch was being kept had been told the vicar by one of those who made it a neighborly duty to do so. He had thought it hearsay of a part with all the rest of the sensation. Even at this seeming confirmation of it he blinked incredulity. "Oh, I cannot believe that people can be so silly, really I cannot."

She looked up. "It is true. Because of me the house is watched."

Her eyes were heavy with grief. They had so been ever since, on the night of the affair, she had bent them upon him and Laura surveying the broken window, the marred table, the paper-littered floor. Even at hearing of the distressing case in which John had been found at the civil prison her look had signaled no new emotion suited to pain at what she was told. The pools of woe that her eyes were had deepened, that was all. She had brought calamities upon this house. Here, the deepening said, was desolation from another source for her to witness. Fondly she had rejoiced in the recent manifestations of the parish's relegation into bygones of offenses charged against the vicar. At his beaming announcement of that first ride on Mr. Bennett's shaft, at every other little sign of kindlier public heart towards him, delightedly she had clapped her hands. "They are loving you," she had cried, "like old days they are loving you again." Now, through her, her eyes said, all this glad headway that had been made was lost. All the old feeling was afoot again, and was worse.

"It is true. Because of me the house is watched."

He went to her. "Dearest Minna, you simply must not take this stupid business like this, you must not."

She bowed her head again over her work. "Because of me your window broken, because of me your table spoilt, because of me"—her voice was breaking—"your house watched and all that was getting better for you now all begun again."

He put a hand on her hands. "Minna, Minna. Because for a few days people are so stupid, are you to forget that for all the days of twenty years and more it is to our dear Minna that half our happiness is owed?"

She dropped her sewing. She clutched his hand to her lips. "Oh, I go to cry," she then said and she went quickly from the room to her own.

She was a little late with the tea that afternoon. She had been writing to Philip she said. Up in her room she was at the letter again in the evening, as she told when she came down to prayers.

"Goodness, it's a thick one," Laura smiled when given it to post next morning.

"Well, it says a thousand times 'When are you coming home again?' " she replied.

"Ah, won't that do us all good when he does, you especially? Now I tell you what, Minna, hear me now vow and declare it. I declare that when he comes he shall take that old-fashioned sweetheart of his for a wild orgie in town, theaters and dinners and goodness knows what. Perhaps he was starting on leave the very moment this thousand times appeal to come home was being written. You never know with Philip. Coincidences do happen!"

Five

COINCIDENCE of a sort between the letter and the lawful occasions of him to whom it was addressed was in fact in process of junction. In the moment when the urgent appeal to come home was being dropped into the posting-box a torpedo launched by a German U-boat struck a tramp steamer in the Bay of Biscay with certification of shipwreck leave for possible survivors of her crew. Already she was in flames, her engine-room holed, settling fast, her bridge shot away. By loosing that torpedo into the mess the U-boat commander confirmed himself as being one who took no chances. That, indeed, had been the trouble with him throughout the action. Obviously someone had been telling him things.

"Brecque, that blue-eyed boy has promised mother he won't be rash."

This was spoken by the tramp's youthful skipper to his junior surviving officer aboard. It was said when his second "abandon ship" ruse had been played and still the U-boat, now awash, now submerged, coyly kept her distance. The armament of her kind was greatly inferior to that of its modern development. Where today's U-boat need strike but once she must hit many times.

The tramp was flying the White Ensign. Her initial abandon ship card had been played when, then plugging along under the mercantile flag, she had first, to her commander's great content, espied a torpedo coming at her on her starboard quarter, then had taken it amidships. That was what she was there for. Her officers of the watch had the standing order that on a torpedo being seen approaching speed was to be increased or decreased as might be necessary to ensure being hit.

"Panic party, away!" The order was unnecessary. Well trained and twice previously experienced, the portion of the ship's company detailed for the purpose had made a masterly unseamanlike rush for the boats. One was jammed in her falls and left hanging end up. Three were scrambled into with every attribute of frantic haste. One hero rushed back to reappear with the ship's cat, another bundled himself over with a stuffed parrot in a cage. Distinctive in a gold-braided cap, an impressive-looking party made himself, as captains should, the last to leave the ship.

"There she spouts," said the captain who was left behind. He was prone on the bridge, focusing glasses through a slit in the wooden screen which went round it. Twelve hundred yards away where had been only a periscope now was an agitation of the surface; immediately then, throwing off water and surfacing as a monster of the deep emerging, the conning-tower and the upper line of the German submarine appeared. Her lid opened, men swarmed up. Her gun was manned. There began from her with direful effect a species of leisurely target practice.

It was taken lying down; of necessity because she was out of range of the tramp's armament; of guile because, to lure her on, all not in the steamer's engine-room were prone or crouching behind the devices which concealed also her guns. Fire broke out forward and could not be efficiently tackled owing to the necessity of showing no movement. Two guns went out of action, their crews out of muster. A shell burst in the boiler room, adding inferno of steam to death's ministers; another killed all on the bridge, the captain alone miraculously hurled free.

Still the U-boat commander, suggesting that he had heard

of panic parties before, kept his distance. Desisting fire awhile, he suddenly, as if with "Ah, thought I wouldn't see someone moving there, did you?" reopened it. Then he watched again. Then he partially submerged. Then very cautiously he approached.

It was a little later that he was to be credited by Philip's commanding officer with having given promise at home to take no foolish risks. If his you-don't-fool-me second bombardment, followed by his approach in trim in which he could emergency dive, was in the nature of execution of that pledge, it was, to his coming consternation, an insufficient demonstration of his undertaking.

He now was within four hundred yards on the tramp's port quarter, partially submerged, his lid shut, but offering a chance not to be missed, the more so that ability to seize one was fast diminishing.

A whistle blew. The White Ensign fluttered aloft. Dummy screens, hatches and cabin structures flattened out of sight. A broadside of four guns plunged its destruction to where within the holding of a breath the U-boat had been—but was not.

At that moment when the whistle went to the tramp commander's lips and before he could stop his blast upon it, some instinct, some qualm, twitched the submarine captain's nerves. He crash dived. Fifteen minutes later, again a torpedo showed its wake from his hand fired from a thousand yards.

Aboard the tramp the respite had been used, immobility no longer being imposed, in effecting what could be done to grapple with the fire and general damage and in reckoning the sorry bill of casualty. The U-boat surfaced again, prepared again for leisurely target practice, and vented its spite for the shock it had received by opening with a machine-gun towards the occupants of the panic-party boats. They pulled towards the tramp. Her commander had determined that the second torpedo must surely have been regarded by the U-boat as a settler. That would give every appearance of natural sequence to the step next in his mind. "We'll give him Number Two abandon now," he announced. "He wants a lot for his money, this bright young Tirpitz."

As "panic-party abandonment" was the ruse of a Q-ship while still apparently a harmless tramp, so "No. 2 abandonment" was the lure employed when, as now, identity as a fighting unit had been revealed to the enemy. With less sign of precipitance, yet with the ordered urgency of vacation of quarters too hot to stay in, the personnel detailed for the purpose went over the side. Elaboration of reality was given by a panic-party crew coming in to help their escape. There now were left alive on the tramp her commander, his next in rank, Philip, and ten ratings.

"And now we'll see if that'll make him come out for the milk," said the commander as the No. 2 abandon party drew away.

It seemingly would not. For some twenty minutes the U-boat, flitting aloofly, dropped bombardment about and in the havoc she had already wrought; those who caught it, now again lying concealed, dying where they lay.

It was then that, "Brecque, that blue-eyed boy," said the commander, "has promised mother he won't be rash."

Philip gave a lick at the blood which ran from a scalp wound to a corner of his mouth and grinned. Between two ratings he was lying flat on his stomach beside the now only remaining serviceable gun of the tramp's equipment, a twelve-pounder mounted amidships. "I'll kiss him for his mother if he'll come for it quick," he said.

"He'll be damned if he will though," returned the other. "How much longer can you stick it here?"

Philip twisted a look over his shoulder. The deck in that

quarter was rolled over on itself towards the gun crew like a half-turned mattress on a bed. Flames were wreathing it. "To hell, sir," he answered and glanced his eyes for confirmation to right and left of him.

"That's right, sir," from one of the ratings.

The other who, resting on his elbows, was passing the time by sucking blood from a wounded hand and dextrously squirting it at a jam of debris in front of him, nodded impassively.

"Good stuff," said the captain. "I've got an idea." He squirmed away, trailing his full length behind his forearms.

In three minutes he squirmed back. "She's getting a brave little girlie now," he announced. "She's creeping up"—he nodded his head in the direction towards which Philip's was pointing—"to starboard. Mac's out," he said. "Brecque, here's my idea. We're going to stage a third abandon, a caught in our own trap one; Nelson would swallow it. I'm going to drop a detonator into the firework box. Immediately she goes off, all hands left, except you three—"

"Two," said Philip and motioned leftwards.

Splinters of a shell burst had savaged the gun crew in the commander's brief absence. The man who had been squirting sucked blood lay now, forehead on hands, vital stream pooling beneath his face.

"Two's enough, him to up the gun and you to fire it. Immediately the magazine goes off, all except you two will jump overboard, to starboard here, loud as they can splash. Young Tirpitz will laugh and pretty soon will close, full surface trim, all puffed up to gloat on what he's done. One hit on her pressure hull and you've got her. You'll wait till she's bang opposite you, point-blank so you can't miss her. Then you'll sink her, wop. Oke?"

Philip might have remembered the wild nonsense he had performed at the vicarage when called up for service with the navy. *"Mr. Brecque, all our guns are out of action, all officers except ourselves killed."* He grinned joyously. "Absolutely, sir." His face went serious. "Look, though, half a minute, sir, let me blow the magazine. That should be my job. You ought to see it through here."

The other, already squirming off, shook his head decisively. "You've got your orders." He grinned. "If it's playing a golden harp you're anxious for it'll come at you all right, don't worry. So long." He shuffled a yard, then turned and now with expression set grim, "But, by God, Brecque, you're to sink her first, remember. That's an order."

"You bet your immortal."

2

From his position Philip now could just see the U-boat, sure enough very slowly approaching. How long before she'd think that she could safely close? The magazine was under the poop and there were the other hands for his commander to warn for their part in the act. How long? Five minutes perhaps, four, three? While he waited his heart pounded between the deck and his chest as if drumming with double stroke. He glanced at his companion, a cartoonist's matlow, fists on shoulder of mutton model, neck as a bull-calf's. The man grinned. Philip was about to speak when an appalling explosion shuddered the ship as though a Titan's hands had seized and shaken her. Abaft he caught a momentary glimpse of the figure of his commander apparently running backwards towards him at astonishing speed. Then he realized, as it went from sight, that the body was headless.

Debris showered about him. A wall reared up to his right. It was a wall of flame. Flame first or U-boat first? She was drawing level now, rapidly. Even if she should see the gun she yet would be deceived. Supported on a tilting mounting, it had been put back now right over on its side. Observed by one unfamiliar with the tilting device it had all the appearance of disablement. One push could up it. That was the matlow's job and Philip now gripped his arm holding him ready.

Now!

In one moment a rectangle of grey sea was their outboard view, in the next, gliding at point-blank range, the U-boat filled it. Her lid was open, her gun manned. She was there for the plucking as a ripe plum on a garden wall, and Philip plucked.

"*Up!*"

The gun clicked to alignment, Philip fired. The shell plunged through the submarine's pressure hull. Her conning tower flew away. Internal explosion sounded. She settled the briefest moment, men struggling upward from within, spark-shot fumes enveloping them. Then she threw up her head and plunged from view.

"Got her, by Jericho!" Philip screamed, waving, hopping. He put his hands into the crushing machines which served the seaman for fists, then with a yelp cast himself overboard. "Because," as he subsequently explained, "my blighted trousers were on fire."

3

Picked up with his fellow survivors by a destroyer, Philip three days later was in Plymouth. This was his port for orders. His scalp wound had been comfortably dressed; he had got to his kit, reassuming uniform in place of the slops appropriate to the tramp. He had heard chaffing speculation among his messmates relative to a V.C. adorning his manly chest. He was due for a shipwreck leave. On the morning after his arrival there belatedly came to him the letter of

Minna's reiterated "When are you coming home again?"

It was of great length. Philip was no critic of epistolary style. Minna's despatches to him always swung between effusive endearments of her most cherished of the vicarage brood and bewildering leapings to and fro in subject. Here, however, both in the one characteristic and the other, were extravagances which from the outset struck him as a little odd.

"Oh, my most beloved Philip, my boy of my life that has always lived in my especial heart," the letter began, "if only you could come home to your Minna who has nursed you from your cradle, and worshiped you in your baby suits, and then those first knickers and the first long trousers that you tore the first hour you put them on and then flung in my face when I insist you take them off while I mend them, and those Etons shortened down off John that you hated, and those angel uniforms of the "Worcester," and all you have ever worn. Yesterday I tidied the lumber-room because I must leave everything perfect in order before I do this, if I must do it, and I know I must do it because this can't go on with his face like that and hers too because of me."

"Do what the dickens?" was Philip's thought, here laying down the jumble to relight his pipe. "What *is* she talking about?"

"And everything I touched in that lumber-room was pieces of you, all that you had played with, and that I had scolded you for breaking, and my eyes gushed so I hardly could see to tidy them, and I found that red sandbag that you thumped me with when you played that awful Astur game, and my eyes streamed then and I thought my heart would burst. It was torn and half the sand gone out so I mended the tear, but it is rather flabby and wet too where the mend is with my tears dropping, but that will dry, and if you want it one day shake it down and tie up the end with string.

"Oh, my baby boy of my life, as I always call you in my heart, most terribly terrible things have been done here because of me, because I am German in the house. They have broken the study window; and his table that he has loved and that I have polished all my life and was the very first thing I polished when they brought me in the train to be their Minna and all of your Minna, is stained with ink, and they are watching the house and everything was getting all right but now all has begun again and is worse and will never stop until I do this, if only you could come home quickly, but every day is worse and worse for them with me."

"What the devil?" Philip ejaculated aloud. He put down his pipe. Into his bewilderment an apprehension was merging.

As if the incident had not been mentioned the letter announced anew the breaking of the study window, proceeding then with better coherency to set out the events of that night, of the conditions arising thereafter, and of the writer's feelings in regard to their effect upon the vicarage. Abruptly it took its reader on to ground towards whose end with shock he felt his heart, as feet suddenly upon a quicksand, begin to sink.

"Listen to this that I have copied from a letter that John wrote your dear, dear father from his second prison before he went to this terrible place with convict's arrows where now he is so ill. This is it. 'It is with unbounded pleasure that I read in dearest mother's letter that with my disappearance here I seem to have dropped out of public memory in Upton, that old scores have thus become forgotten and that faces are greeting you kindly as of yore. Bitter distress I have caused to fall upon you, my dearest father. How happy

I am to feel that, by my removal as it were from life, the slings and arrows of the parish's disapproval have ceased their woundings.'"

From "by my removal as it were from life" to the end of the sentence the quotation was doubly underscored.

"He is grave, that dear John," Minna then went on. "Well, why, my own little Philip that I love so, shall I not also be grave? . . ."

The heart that had faltered in the sudden quicksand stumbled deeper, a sickness seized it. Philip jumped his reading to the letter's end. He was in the anteroom of the naval barracks. Swiftly he snatched up a railway guide, an eye to the clock as he did so. Delaying for a celebration dinner that night, he had arranged to proceed on his leave on the morrow. Now with every speed he impelled himself from the building and by conveyance to North Road station. The Paddington train was drawing out as he reached the platform.

"Stand back, there, stand back."

A ticket inspector grabbed at him, then a porter. Eluding the one, rugby handing-off the other, he flung himself aboard.

There was a train, he knew, from Charing Cross to Upton Bank at four o'clock. If he was punctual at Paddington he should just catch it; have time, too, perhaps, to send a telegram.

He was not punctual. Again was the impulsion by every speed to make the train; again the rush and swerve and push to board it. At the Banks he took a cab up the hill. It was in the gathering dusk of close upon six o'clock that he threw open the vicarage front door and presented himself.

"Mum!" he called. "Dad!"

From the drawing-room, its door ajar, astounded *"Philip!"* came.

He was in to them before, amazed, they had moved to come to him. Standing up staring towards his entry, their pose had the suggestion of a starting forward at the sound of the hall door, a checking at the arrival not being the one expected. He leapt into and delivered hugs such as the bull-necked matlow might have thought a tidy squeezing. Then he gabbled a twelve-word explanation of his appearance, "You'll never believe it, another compulsory bathing. I've skits to tell you." Then he asked, "Where's Minna?"

"Oh, Philip, how wonderful, how too marvelous to see you. Minna? She's out. We're rather worried about her, as a matter of fact."

"We're very worried," the vicar affirmed. He was holding one of his boy's hands in both his own, but his face, behind its smiles, reflected the anxiety of his words.

"She went out," Laura began, "at two o'clock—"

"Went out?" Philip's tone was searching. "But she never does go out, does she, by herself?"

"No, that's what's been making us so worried, her being away so long, I mean."

There was briefest pause. The faces that held one the other were overridden of joy of meeting by concern of mutual cause. Philip with deft interweaving of another issue broke the tension. "Mum, dad, I tell you what I want to do. I've an absolutely crashing headache, been fugged up in the train since ten o'clock. I absolutely must just get a pipe-opener in the fresh. I vote I go for a bit of a look for her. She's bound to have gone up to the forest; may have ricked her ankle or something. Good idea, eh?"

"Oh, but, darling, if you've a headache, a cup of strong tea; the kettle's on."

"And an aspirin, dear boy."

"Honestly, it's air and a stride I really must have." He

took up his cap. "And if I pick her up as well that'll be two birds at one hoof."

They went with him to the gate. He kissed them both. "Imagine arriving with a head like this. But imagine Minna's amazement when she sees me!"

"Darling, it's wonderful having you, wonderful. And Minna's been simply longing—"

"Too marvelous. Now don't get anxious about *me* if I'm long, will you? I may have to hunk her on my back!"

With gay laugh he was gone.

4

While he was in their sight he walked briskly, head well back as though gulping in much-needed air. At the corner he waved cheerily. Then his brisk step went to a determined speed. When he reached the border of the forest he began to run. Minna's letter had muddled a familiar location among its incoherences. It was towards the birthday picnic haunt, Giant's Gyll, that he made.

When he came within sight of the little bridge that spanned the ravine he slowed to a walk, recovering his breath. The moon stood in a clear sky. Figures were on the bridge, two bicycles leant by its approach. Nearing, he saw that one figure was that of a policeman, the other a workman in a cloth cap. They were pointing downwards.

He came to them. "Anything up?"

The policeman took a stare at Philip's uniform and half touched his helmet. "Something down, sir," he said grimly. "Looks like someone's fell over." The bridge rail stood breast high. He put his hand to it significantly. "Or jumped," he added.

"I seed it," the workman joined, "half hour ago, clearer nor what you can now. Legs I saw or mighty like 'em. Look there, sir, that dark stuff atween they two rocks; white bit on it as it might be face; then white lower down, that's skirts I reckon; then black again, hanging. That's legs, sure of it."

Philip was peering. Patchily bushed and saplinged down its sides, its head showing the trickle of water which in heavy rains became a cascade, the ravine fell to a bottom massively bouldered; and there, between two rocks as the workman had said, showed something unnatural, something which, the more stared upon, the more assumed the semblances the man had pointed out.

"Went for the copper, I did," he now declared. "Suicide there was here tidy few years back. I remember it."

Philip from his bending over the rail swung up towards him. "So do I," he cried, rasping the words so harshly that the man stepped back astonished. He had been remembering a flaming row up here with Minna on the day before his tenth birthday because he had cunningly dragged her in the Gyll's direction and then had declared his intention of trying to see the suicide's body. He swung about, passed between the bicycles at the end of the bridge and then skirted along the paling fence which guarded the ravine.

"Here!" the policeman called. "You can't do that."

Philip was attempting the fence. Time and neglect had decayed it. It wobbled to his weight. The job was awkward. He was but just over when the other two came hurrying.

"You can't see no better from there," the policeman cried. "That's dangerous."

Philip plunged five steps among dense scrub. He sat down, turned on his face, and the policeman, aghast at the obvious intention, began to attempt the fence after him.

"You can't climb down there," he shouted commandingly.

Philip's legs were over the side. He was grasping a bush.

"The hell I can't," he called back. "Don't watch me, you fools. Go for ropes, and for help, hard as you can."

He swung to a lower hold.

That was not a descent that any would have essayed but one who recked nothing but to get to what lay below. Sometimes he found both feet and hands baffled at further movement. Groping at uttermost stretch for just that half inch beyond the grasp upon which always the unquenchable spirit will insist, he would grind finger-nails or toes into some crack which they thus reached and make new purchase. Sometimes he slithered, grabbing as he went to stay what seemed irrevocable crash. Once when a stone sprung from its bedding at his weight he was turned clean about to swing, his back to the cliff, his legs dangling, by a twist of tendrils whose roots he felt to be giving. When miraculously he reached the pit it was with hands torn as if raked by claws, in a uniform rent beyond possibility of repair.

The rocks here, sufficiently great when viewed from the bridge, were of man-high proportions, tumbled one upon the other as if avalanched from a tip. He scaled one, treacherously slimy, upjutting among others, and looked about him for the object of his search. He fell but he had glimpsed it, horridly substantiative of its suggestion from above. He clambered, hands and knees. He gained a boulder down which he looked into a cleft between two jagged jaws. There lay the thing. He slid down and stooped above the face. Astonishingly it was unmarred; impossibly in life twisted on its neck.

He cried aloud, "Oh, Minna, Minna!"

This boy had looked on death in shocking forms, on messmates barbarously wrenched from living semblance, and had set grim jaws. Himself he had felt death's breath upon his cheek, its fingers at his throat, and had mocked it. He nevertheless at twenty-three was but a boy, his emotions yet unbaked, his sensibilities not yet repressed; and he was kneeling here in the lifeless presence of one who had nursed his earliest years, who all his life had been his slave and his champion, who had blended her adoration of him into his blood, who had been sister and more than sister, mother and more than mother.

There is no other but a schoolboy's word to express his uncontrollable release of his distress.

He crouched there by her body, blubbing.

5

Burials in St. Luke's churchyard had been discontinued since the opening of the Upton Springs public cemetery ten years before. They still were permissible, however, and there was a little vacant corner beside the vicarage garden wall. This was that portion of the wall against whose inner face the vicar, on that famous day of arrival, had planned to build the children a wigwam summer-house. It never had been built. Year after year the £8 5s. of its irreducible estimate somehow had been swallowed up by a more practical necessity. In the schooldays' period its recurrent impossibility had constantly smitten the vicar's heart. Even now he sometimes would stand and look at the site, and would give a regretful little shake of his head.

It seemed most fitting that there, just on the other side of where, how many thousand times? she had given herself up to the children's games, their Minna should lie. Ruth, come from Aldershot, and Philip, Laura and the vicar and Hope Hubbard were the only mourners. When the coffin had been lowered, Ruth in her Waac dress and Philip in a new uniform stood hand in hand to look upon it. Laura held the vicar's arm tightly in hers, her other hand clutching his hand; he stumbled a lot on the out-thrown soil. Hope Hubbard stood alone at the head of the grave, chin dropped on breast.

Ruth went back on the next day, Philip at his brief leave's end. Now there were but two at the vicarage board where seven once had sat. That felt very strange. At the first few meals they talked, because of the strangeness, scarcely above a whisper. Then Laura realized that they were doing this and made point of brightening her voice; but they never somehow spoke more than very quietly. They sat side by side. The vicar would forget that he was supposed to be eating. That was why Laura put herself close beside him. She would slip bits on to his plate when he wasn't looking.

"Dearest," she then would exclaim, "your plate; look, you've scarcely begun."

The vicar would look. "Dear me, why, I thought I had eaten that."

"Well, have you? Come, you must eat something."

She said to Hope Hubbard at this time. "The tears are always behind my eyes." She closed her lids and pressed her knuckled fists upon them. "I must not shed them. A long time, long before this, it's been like that. Now—"

Hubbard took her hands and held them. "Brave lady."

But the repression of the tears for the vicar's sake was but approaching then the strain it shortly was to know, the hand that seemed so heavily closed down upon the vicarage not yet had fully closed. They had had one letter from John written a fortnight after their visit. It was rather badly written and very brief but very cheery. He was in hospital, he said, with a bit of a chill "and in luxury you wouldn't believe. Sheets! Soft pillows! Glass of milk by me and some grapes!! Think of me, beloved ones, as fairly wallowing—and doing fine!"

But five days later, however, was a buff-enveloped letter "On His Majesty's Service." It was from the prison governor.

It said in formal lines that convict John Brecque had been recovering from influenza but that congestion of the lungs had set in and was not taking satisfactory course. "Your early attendance is suggested."

The morning mail had brought the letter. Setting forth immediately they caught the same train that previously had taken them to the prison. From the first junction of change the service, as they found, had been accelerated. At their destination station, "Look," Laura cried brightly, those tears behind her eyes burning at their repression through the long journey. "Look, I told you everything would go famously. We've arrived a whole half-hour sooner."

But it was not, by an hour, soon enough to see their boy alive.

When they got to the prison it was to be told that he was dead.

Evening: Also Dawn

One

FIVE years after the war were changes in Upton Springs which, imagined five years before it, would have been regarded as sheerly fantastic. Road transport had conjured with the place. Its population had more than doubled. Where formerly had been a little nest perched high up on the forest, suitable only to those who, as the saying goes, were prepared to live and die there, now, to preserve ornithological metaphor, was a wide-spreading rookery, its inhabitants winging to and fro afar.

Cars were the wings. An eight-mile flip and you were at Milford Junction, whence was an admirable service of trains to town. That brought the residents in all the pleasant little houses standing in their own grounds in the new roads which led one from another into the forest borders. Up and down Bank Hill plied a fifteen-minute service of motor omnibuses penetrating away into Thurstead in the one direction and far over the forest in the other. That brought the dwellers in the several "garden estates," planned, not in streets or roads, but in Ways and Closes and Lanes. At Netherhurst in Giant's Gyll direction an admirable golf course had been laid out. That gave the last excuse for attractive little properties remotely situated, the impressive cars of whose owners brought them shopping into Upton Springs.

As to shops, indeed, and trade enterprise in general, the place was scarcely recognizable if not seen since before the war. Where had been only the old-fashioned rather poky little premises of the High Street, now, in thoroughfares leading off it, were establishments of garishly modern front-age, slick with every artifice of modish design. You remember Butler's Mews? old residents would ask. A long way you'd have to go before you saw the spacious equal of the car showrooms and garage which now occupy the site. Other garages commanded each entrance to the town; there had arrived also Regal Cinema and Ritz Picturedrome, tea-shops, "Guest Houses," a new hotel . . .

All this in its full tide was a progress covering more years than five beyond the war. Sufficient of it there was in 1923 to make the changes in Upton Springs—fantastic.

2

At and pertaining to the vicarage the changes, though as considerable, were perhaps but normal developments in the life of a family and of its friends. A dispassionate observer, speculating forward from 1909 to 1923, would have seen nothing particularly odd in them. The case of Hope Hub-bard would have been a daring shot, that of John, post-humously, also. Merely to foresee on the other hand, four-teen years hence, the then standing of Mary and of Philip would have been but pedestrian exercise of prophecy. So for that matter would have been justified prediction in regard to Ruth.

For vicarage changes let epithet be chosen, then, from point of view of the family circle sitting round the fire before the war and playing at futures. How the guessers would have laughed at such ideas! Droll would have been the epi-thet for the changes, not fantastic.

Mary was married and had two children. Philip (R.N.) was married. Ruth, living at home in intervals of bubble enterprises, was sometimes causing her parents anxiety. John's unfinished "Paradise Destroyed," written in prison, had been proclaimed undying. Hope Hubbard, called to a see of notably Anglo-Catholic persuasion, was a bishop. A bishop suffragan but nevertheless, too comically to speculation of before the war, a bishop.

New churchwardens stood in the room of Colonel Gilling and of Mr. Burgess. St. Mark's stood up complete in brick and stone. The Rev. Hilary Tweed, first having stood at the altar with an elderly widow of some means, now stood in his own elegant vicarage, which she had built for him, in a salubrious quarter of Upton Banks. St. Mark's, consequent upon the growth both of the Springs and the Banks, had been constituted a separate parish, Mr. Tweed its first incumbent.

Of the incumbent of St. Luke's, newcomers to the parish, guessing his age, guessed it at considerably more than in fact it was. They said that he looked, behind that singularly benign expression of his, as though he had seen a lot of trouble.

Two

Mary, when the war ended with the armistice, went into Germany with the Army of Occupation. Use was found for her fluency in the language. She remained thus employed till May, 1919, when she came home to be married. Philip, by the good opinions he had earned, had been gazetted into the Royal Navy. Ruth was demobilized from the W.A.A.C. five months before Mary's return to civil life.

Mary's marriage made her Mrs. Walter Norman, wife of that officer, temporary captain, R.A.S.C., who had instructed her in car driving. Philip's, three years later, was with the daughter of a retired naval paymaster resident at Southsea. The vicar received the announcement first of his daughter's betrothal, then of his son's with much less astonishment than did Laura. Principled to view the married state as mankind's appointed case, sequent in the processes of life as the summer upon the spring, that his children in due course should enter it seemed always to have been in his mind.

"Yes, but not Mary," and later, "but not Philip" was Laura's reaction to the news and to this reception of it. Not Mary, astonished she felt, because, unemotional, self-complete, self-centered, dearest Mary was impossible to imagine as being emotionally thralled, as sharing her self with another's self, as abandoning her singly purposed academic career, just as she might have returned to it, for a joint career, conventional not distinctive. Not Philip, laughingly incredulous when his turn came Laura felt, because to conceive of that irresponsible spirit, of "that Philip" in dear Minna's comprehensive phrase, as a married man was just wildly absurd, grotesque. Her first surprise at each announcement was, moreover, to spring again, in Mary's case at a comment made by the bride-to-be on her fiancé, in Philip's on her first meeting with the young woman of his choice.

Not then demobilized, Walter Norman had paid his devoirs at the vicarage in his uniform. Prior to the wedding Laura always thought of him in uniform; so apparently had Mary. Living at home while awaiting the great day, Mary had been to town for a setting-up-house shopping expedition with him on the day on which, in the current phrase, he had got into civvies. On her return Laura greeted her with a woman's excited interest in so momentous a choosing and buying. The Little Mother Bunch attitude towards exuberance, "Please don't make a fuss, mother," had evidenced itself in all the daughter's references to her approaching wifehood, from its announcement onwards. Laura, had she dared, could frequently have hugged her for the—to her—characteristically comic restraint of it. On this occasion she was not thus moved to secret amusement. Mary was as soberly reserved as ever in her account of her doings but she was this time also something more, something different. She was a shade distrait. She presented the look and the air of someone who is talking of one thing and thinking of another. Her brow showed frequently what appeared to be a puzzled little frown. A tiff? Laura transiently wondered but dismissed the suspicion. The signs were not, somehow, those of a tiff. "And how was Walter looking?" she inquired later in the evening. "I ought to have asked that before."

The frown had not at the moment been in evidence. Markedly it now reappeared. "He looks very different in mufti," was the reply, and that was all.

"What a funny thing to say," was Laura's remark when telling this later to the vicar.

"But, my dear, he naturally would look different," was the characteristic observation she received.

She smiled at him the affectionate smile always evoked by his profundities of this nature. More to herself than aloud, "It was the funny way she said it," she murmured. She went on with her knitting, puzzled little frown now her own brow's evidence of manner of thought.

No frown, amused mystification rather, was the order of her surprise in the case of her first contact with Philip's partner-to-be. She had expected a Philip's self, a gay creature of precisely his own wild-spirited mentality. "Frightfully pretty," was the sole description given in the letter announcing the engagement. Laura visualized at once a boyish figure of Philip's own fair coloring and, on slender lines, his own athletic build. She imagined the two as engaged always in rattling chaff interspersed with "rags," hand-to-hand wrestling, headlong rushes to some form of violent exercise. "She's called Prudence," Philip had written. "A corking name, isn't it?" It made Laura laugh. One of those singularly unfortunate choices, she guessed it to be, which on the one hand deserve parents the sympathy due to frustration of hopes and on the other support the wish of children to be allowed to choose their names themselves.

It proved, astoundingly, to suit exactly the appearance and the manner which the girl presented.

"Here she is. Isn't she marvelous?" was Philip's excited introduction of her.

Laura and the vicar had gone down to the station to meet her for the initiatory visit on which Philip brought her. He was leaning from the window to the waist, both arms frantically waving, as the train drew in. There was a glimpse on the corner seat beside him of a timidly pretty little brunette, somewhat discommoded, poor creature, by these exuberant gymnastics beside her. Laura made no doubt that Philip's fiancée-counterpart was hidden behind his vigorous frame, probably thumping him on the back to let her "have a squint." He hurled himself out, flung himself first into his mother's arms, then into his father's, then, as one turning for luggage, dived back, and with that "Here she is. Isn't she marvelous?" pulled forth (reluctantly issuing) the demure little creature of the momentary glimpse.

Laura was captivated immediately by her appearance but was surprised almost to loss of words. Had she, however, the vicar too, lost speech completely on the taxi drive home, Prudence, by the suggestion of her demeanor, would have had a greeting to her liking. She scarcely spoke. Her responses, when she made them, were nervous little utterances brought out with a little gasp as though by considerable effort of will. Warmly kissed anew in the hall by Laura and by the vicar—"Welcome again, dear Prudence"; "In our own home, welcome, my dear"—she found something of a tongue at tea; but it was the softest little tongue, the briefest little sentences. She sat there, sipping, nibbling, smiling, the demurest little thing in suitably demure brown, a little mouse of a personality, a little thrush; no, with those big lovely brown eyes of hers, swept by those long lashes, a little fawn, Laura decided, exactly was the suggestion that she gave. How at first sight of so robustious a hunter as Philip she could have done other than flee in panic to the nearest thicket; how Philip, for his part, could have conceived so gently shrinking a thing as companion for the wild enterprises of his predilection, was not to be imagined. But tea was not far advanced before some inkling of the mystery was disclosed. From the fawn to the sailor sidelong glances could be caught being shot. In the midst of his conversation with another privy glints of the eye were to be seen from the sailor to the fawn. Laura felt little squirms of delight within herself as she caught these interchanges. The squirms were spasms of excitation at proximity to life's most exquisite emotion. The two, she knew, had stumbled upon life's loveliest secret. Nature's affinity flowed between them. They call it love.

2

There, anywise, in 1923 they were, Mary and Philip, lost to the vicar's family circle with that odd sundering which marriage cuts. There is a sundering by the grave, a sundering by neglect, a sundering by quarrel. That of the grave is beyond earthly reunion, yet may be always bleeding. Those of neglect and of quarrel always are susceptible of junction where broken off, no wound remaining visible, union often the firmer. Sundering by marriage differs from them all. Between the offspring and the parents there is no rupture, no severance of ties. More subtly estranging, there is on the part of son or daughter a giving away of affection to a new object, likewise a receiving of it from a new source. There goes with the process a subconscious, a vaguely uncomfortable feeling as of having cut off a charity, as of having, also, enlisted under new colors, changed uniforms. When, married, the offspring revisits its home it does so, as it were, shyly, conscious that it no longer is centered here and seeking to hide the fact; conscious also that it now is invested with a new taint, no longer with the home smell, and seeking to disguise the alien quality. It feels something of a stranger, a shade awkward. It was wonderfully glad to come again but it is a little relieved when the day comes to go.

In every sundering the onus is upon the stayer behind; to the setter forth are the novelty and the thrill, the distraction and the adventure. At their child's marriage the parents remain constant. Both parties are aware of a change in the old relations; the offspring with transient discomfort, the parents wistfully.

Thus was it that the vicar cherished more dearly than ever before the last remaining in the nest.

John lay where the summerhouse would have cast its shadow. Mary's home was with her two babies and her husband at his place of business in the Midlands. Philip's came to be where he stabled his fawn in rooms now in this, now in that naval port from Mutley to Malta, according to his base of service. The vicar cast his all of fatherhood on Ruth who stayed to fill the place of all.

3

She did not stay often or long. When she had been able to announce the exact date of her release from the W.A.A.C. her letter had told that she was thenceforward going to live at home "for ever and ever." Nothing was going to induce her to go out even for a tea-party. Every moment of the rest of her life was going to be spent "with you, most darling daddo, and with you, beloved mummo." She was going to "leap out of this foul uniform" which she now "simply loathed" and leap into "that beloved tweed skirt" of hers and "into that cherry-red blouse, and live and die in the darlings." She voted that she would become dad's secretary "with one arm and leg" and mum's Minna with the other. She voted that they scrounged up all the money they could, she'd "bung in her savings' bank wad," and bought a little car by installments, which she would drive them about in. She voted finally that the three of them would tie themselves together with a rope like mountaineers and go about everywhere together, never separated. She'd be in the middle so as to look after them both. "Oh, whoops," her letter ended, "for this day month and then never out of the vicarage again except with you!"

Whooping into it, sure enough, on the due date at four o'clock of the afternoon, she whooped out of it again, however, off to town for the day, so briefly as at nine on the following morning. She had made an appointment to meet a demobilized pal just to have a celebration kick-up together. She knew they would perfectly understand. "You do, darlings, don't you?" she inquired when, in the very hour of her arrival, announcing the engagement.

Of course they did, they assured her. The vicar, indeed, for his part, had had a long course of private lessons in such understanding. It dated back at least as far as that remote first morning of a holiday when her intention to live beside his sick bed had been shattered by the exciting appearance of school friend Joan Vyner and her boy cousin, looking an ass but believed to be quite jolly. Well versed, it was with fondest happiness that he received her own happiness in her excursion. A five-pound note, presented to her just as she was starting, manifested the completeness of his and of Laura's accord.

Ruth was overwhelmed. In the vicarage the crackling white bond of the Bank of England's undertaking to stand for so munificent a sum had a significance even above its staggering face value. With appropriate ritual one was presented to each child on attainment of twenty-first birthday. When John's had been given him none of the brood had ever seen such a thing, much less handled one. The sensation had been tremendous. It ever afterwards had invested alike the ceremony and the token. "I could die," now declared Ruth, bringing the vicar within gasp of the same fate by the hug she gave him. "But you know," she then said doubtfully, "my twenty-firster isn't till April. I oughtn't to have it two months ahead, ought I?" she appealed to her mother.

The vicar and Laura wagged delighted, mysterious heads at one another.

"We'll see when the time comes," beamed the vicar, "whether it *has* been in advance."

"Your father insisted," beamed Laura, "that you must have this to celebrate your return. We went to the bank together to choose an absolutely new one."

"I could die," declared Ruth again, again imperiling the breathing first of one, then of the other. "Golly, look at the time!" and with fresh kisses for adieu, ecstatic, agog, radiantly lovely, she was off.

Thrilling purchases in the haberdashery line for herself, a magnificent pair of red morocco, wool-lined slippers for her father, a handbag such as the vicarage walls had never seen for her mother, together with a sixpenny-piece and three coppers in her purse by way of balance, were the material features of her return in the evening. "Which, considering," she said, a shade ruefully counting out the inconsiderable specie, "that I had jolly nearly two quid of my own as well as the fiver, does seem a bit thick, doesn't it?"

To her hearers it certainly, accepting her phraseology, did. Laura was startled. "Oh, but, Ruth, really—" The vicar, had he not been seated, clearly would have reeled. Openmouthed, he could not credit it as possible that in a single day's pleasuring six pounds nineteen and threepence had been spent. Ruth's infectious laughter abated their shock. Sinking then back in her chair, "Oh, but I have had," ecstatically she sighed, "a too glorious time."

4

The time she thenceforward lived shed rather rapidly the gloriousness with which, in her preparatory letter, she had invested it. Her immediate discountenancing of the beloved

tweed skirt and the cherry-red blouse was perhaps symboli-
cal of the dissolving of all the rainbow as soon as she came
to closer view of it. The darlings, tweed and linen, in which
she had proposed to live and die would have limited her life
to three days had she carried out her intention in regard to
them. On the fourth morning of her return the moldy
things, as she now termed them, together with most else of
her former wear, were cast ready for Laura's next jumble
sale. Her savings-bank deposit, raided for their substitutes,
was not, when she had finished, a loan to the State on which
the Postmaster General was likely to plume himself. She
found herself transported with excitement and joy when the
vicar, during her first week, dowered her with the thrill and
spaciousness of a dress and pocket-money allowance of £30
a year, paid quarterly. Nevertheless the Postmaster General,
again, could have put but a glum eye on what remained to
his use very briefly after the first quarter's amount had been
consigned to his care.

Gaily to the limit of her means she decked herself, gaily
flitted about Upton Springs renewing old friendships, con-
tracting new. Nothing was to have induced her from the
amenities of the vicarage, even a tea-party. Tea somewhere
proved itself, often enough, but third to midday coffee and a
lunch invitation in the overpowering seductions from home
society of a single day. Always she had an engaging compunction in the matter, "sweet" was her parents' fond term.
"Just at first," she would excuse herself, "it's bound to feel a
bit of a lark chasing about with pals again. You don't mind,
do you, if I hoof off till this evening?"

They were delighted that she should. All that they wished
of her was that she should be happy. This radiant and lovely
third at the space-haunted vicarage table and in the lonely
presence-haunted rooms lit up the vicar's face as, after John's
tragedy had followed Minna's, Laura, anxiously watching

him, had believed it never would light again. Never, now, lit it so happily as when his vivid daughter, compunction pricked, hugged him before a sallying forth; as when, "to make up," she devoted herself to him on her return. The more she found entertainment with her friends the brighter the entertainment she radiated when in the house.

It was, as days went on, when "chasing about with pals again" appeared to have lost the exhilaration of movement it had given her that symptoms of a desire to chase further afield began to show. In fewer than the eight weeks which stood between her return home and her twenty-first birth-day social distractions of Upton Springs palled. She turned then to the secretarial and household duties of her quondam enthusiastic planning.

"I'm going to start helping you tomorrow, dad," was her announcement, one evening, of her intention, "and you too, mum."

Both declared that it would be delightful. Each, at her request outlining routine, proposed items with which a beginning could be made. The vicar hazarded the fear that she might find his own suggestions a little dull.

"Well, it will be something to do, anyhow," she said.

Not precisely an ardent embrace of the proposed occupations was thereby evidenced. Their pursuit had not long indifferently engaged her before that evidence was reaffirmed.

"Mum"—she turned one day from the window at which she had stood gazing—"I do wish I had something to do."

"To do, dear? Why, I thought you were just going off to change your library book and bring back a tin of peaches for lunch."

"I mean to do always, some sort of a job."

Laura laughed apology for her trivial filling of a full-time requirement. "Oh, that. Why, darling, you're doing two—helping your father and helping me. It's I who am beginning to want a job, the way you're taking things out of my hands."

Ruth had seated herself on the window ledge. She was toying with the blind-cord tassel. "It's not very exciting."

Knitting on the sofa, Laura had had her eyes on her stitches. She raised them now. The picture they took of Ruth, head disconsolately drooped over the idle engagement of her fingers, increased the sudden concern in which she had lifted her gaze. "Oh, Ruth, darling, you're not finding it dull here, are you?"

Ruth flipped at the tassel. Her aim seemed to be to make it wind over a forefinger without springing back. Three or four attempts were necessary. Then, not looking up, she spoke. "To tell you the truth, mum, I am, a bit."

"Oh, my dear—"

The daughter tossed aside her plaything. She went quickly to the sofa. "Oh, mum, it's beastly, I know, to feel dull with you and dad—"

"It's not a bit. Yes, come and sit, darling. It's not beastly a bit in the way you mean, as if it were a willful crime. It's beastly to *be* dull. I am sorry to hear it. I'm really concerned."

Ruth patted her mother's hands. "Oh, forget it, mum."

"I certainly shan't. I shall lie awake," Laura smiled, "and worry over it. I do see, darling, that just sticking round the house with dad and me may well be dull. But there are things outside, you know, lots of them, that you might well fill your time with."

"Oh, fill my time!" Ruth echoed. Her note was not that on which the words had been given her. "What things?" she inquired doubtfully.

"Why, parish things, dear; the sewing guild, the missions' working society, the Sunday School, visiting, the girl guides, heaps of them. Dear Minna, as you know, used—"

Ruth had wrinkled her pretty nose before the list was through. She here smoothened it in order to state what had caused it to wrinkle.

"They're rather smelly," she said.

Laura laughed delightedly. "You could open the window. Well, no, one or two in the sewing guild are rather touchy on draughts. But, Ruth, tell me. If not that sort of work, and not your jobs here at home, what sort of job are you meaning? What have you in mind, dear?"

Ruth regarded the patent leather points at the toes of her outstretched legs, thoughtfully tapping them together. They advised her, perhaps, to keep secret between themselves and her what actually was in her mind. "I am finding things a bit dull, mum," was the reply she made.

"I do now see that you are. Ruth, I tell you what; why not go on a little visit to one of your friends to cheer you up, to this Freda Stuart in London you're so often corresponding with?"

Ruth drew in her legs with a jerk. She turned an excited face. "Oh, mum, would you mind, you and dad?"

"Mind! My dear, why should we?"

"Why, it seems so rotten bunking off when I've little more than arrived. I'd adore it, of course. I've thought of it often and Freda's begged me a dozen times. But, as I say, to buzz off so soon—"

"Darling, buzz off tomorrow; as soon, anyhow, as you can arrange it."

Ruth threw arms about her. "Oh, mum."

"Oh, Ruth. Oh, what a child not to have suggested it yourself. Look, if you went almost at once you could stay a fortnight and be back in time for your birthday. We would like you home for that."

"Oh, mum!"

5

Great in its celebration, the birthday was greater yet in its issues. On Ruth's breakfast plate were parcels; an impressive envelope disclosed that, as had been hinted, the tremendous custom of the coming-of-age five-pound note had not lapsed by the presentation of its fellow two months before. By custom started in the nursery years, lunch was normally the vicarage staple meal. Today lunch was made a scratch affair, lifted to festival significance by a noble bunch of grapes. Tea showed an iced birthday cake, "The first dear Minna hasn't made and not nearly as good, I'm afraid," Laura said; but "Oh, scrumptious," Ruth declared, and "My dear, delicious," the vicar. Dinner, the banquet, brought a pheasant, a trifle, and a bottle of ginger wine from which the established toast was drunk. "May God continue to bless you, my dear child," across the vicar's glass; "Amen" from Laura's.

This was the first coming of age in the flock, the vicar realized, on which one voice alone might utter the endorsement. John's voice? Minna's? His tone trembled a little. His invocation, called now in benison of his ewe lamb, was however therefore the more fervent; with the greater fondness he gave himself to the closing hours of the great occasions which thus had marked the day. Spent in jolly talk around the fire, it was during this that Ruth launched the momentous issues which were to flow. Breaking a happy silence into which conversation had lapsed, "Dad, mum," she suddenly broke out, "I am of age today, aren't I?"

"We've got your birth certificate," roundly declared the vicar, "in my study table drawers to prove it." He was in sparkling form.

The smile that she gave his esprit was but perfunctory. Her manner showed her to be highly charged. "Well, I do feel, dear dad and mum, that I ought to be, I do most fright-fully, frightfully want to be, on my own, earning my own living."

The vicar made round eyes. "On your own?"

She nodded vigorously. "Yes, dad."

Laura reached for her hand. "Oh, tell us, darling."

"Freda's starting a shop," Ruth, leaping straight into her desired aim, began her telling. "A little hat shop in Knights-bridge. I went up to her simply longing to have a job of my own of some sort, as I told you, mum; and there, just waiting for me, was the very most glorious thing, this hat shop. Oh, dad, if only I could go into it with her!"

Divorced from the ecstatic and imploring tones in which it was described, the enterprise presented itself as a matter of fifty pounds with which to buy a footing into paradise. Freda had done five years at a fashionable milliner's in Bond Street. She had a flair for trimming hats. Equally important she had a flair for selling them. Not less substantial in the art of transferring money from pockets to till, she had the gift of making friends with customers. It was with the promise of support from several of these, with the backing of one in the matter of security for rent, that she was about to open a knowing little hat shop in a knowing little street off the Brompton Road.

Ruth had become acquainted with her nearly two years before on a day-off visit to town with a mutual friend in the Waacs. A great friendship had struck up. Short leaves, spent with her at the business girls' Pimlico boarding-house of her residence, had consolidated it. She was putting a hundred pounds into the hat shop. Another girl, Ann Mudge, was coming in with fifty. A third was to be found with the like.

"Oh, dad, if you possibly could let me have fifty pounds and let me join them! I know it's a simply enormous sum, but just wait a minute, most darling dad and mum, and I'll show you that really you'd be the gainer, dad. You really would."

Ruth opened her showing of the profits which must accrue to the vicar with the smashing fact that, "to begin with," the birthday five-pound note reduced the required sum from fifty to forty-five. The three girls were to establish a chummery on a virtually self-contained floor in South Kensington. "One jolly little bedroom that two of us would share, a corking little crib for the other, a most glorious, positively huge, living-room which we're going to call the studio, a duck of a little kitchenette, and use of the bathroom on the floor below. Oh, a peach of a place; you just can't imagine what a peach."

Running expenses of the peach were to be paid out of the business. Ruth and Ann Mudge were each to have, additionally, ten shillings a week pocket money, and after the first year a percentage of the profits. "Well, what does that mean," dramatically inquired Ruth, "so far as this fifty, no, forty-five, pounds is concerned? It means, don't you see, dad, that my thirty pounds' allowance stops bang off at once. Thirty from forty-five's fifteen. A year from now all that you really will have given me will be fifteen pounds. Two years from now you'll be fifteen pounds in pocket, every year after that thirty pounds in pocket, and all that, mind you, is to say nothing of what you score on the saving of my eating my head off here at home. *Now* you see what I meant by your being a gainer. Oh, dad, *could* it be done?"

"Of course it shall be done."

The vicar had stretched forward a fond hand to lay upon the millinery aspirant's hands. His face, with his words, was lit with delight at giving her delight. Laura had been watching him. His rounded gaze with his "On your own?" had told her his misgiving at the accepted meaning of the phrase in application to his daughter, his Ruth. He had learnt that definite emancipation from the vicarage roof was indeed what Ruth meant, and Laura had seen the shadows of wistfulness pucker about his eyes. But they had shown only momentarily, no more than a wince. Immediately affection's sunlight had taken their place. "Of course, it shall be done," and the fond wrinkled hand had been laid upon the pretty fingers in testimony of the love with which the bond was pledged.

It was Laura's turn, thus seeing, to wince. Later, indeed, she took counsel with herself whether she should not lay before Ruth what her presence brought to the heart heretofore coupled with John's heart, now, because reft of that support, pulsing slower. Her own feelings similarly prompted her. She was alone with her life's comrade who now, older and more susceptible to taxing than herself, was her charge. Into the hauntings of their home from which, stifling her own breast, she strove to distract him, Ruth had come as veritably that daughter of her own towards whom long since she had yearned. She saw, however, a duty wider than that owed to her husband, one admitting, too, no thought of her own feelings. Wisdom instructed her that youth is not to be sacrificed to years. Always the parents have had their day; never the child's must be denied.

With a single "Your father will miss you," she contented herself.

It was spoken softly, with an earnest look.

"Yes, I'm going to come down ever so often for weekends," was Ruth's gay reply. "I've just been arranging it with him."

Handsomely also had been arranged all else. Cost of living had doubled since the war. The maidservant now kept involved a pound a week where the peerless Sarah had cost but sixteen pounds a year. In every direction money went less far. Nevertheless diminution of expenses consequent upon contraction of the circle to be supported had caused a little balance for the first time to be growing in the vicarage passbook; and gallantly for Ruth the vicarage now drew upon it. Her birthday five pounds were not deducted from the fifty required for her footing. That in full flight should be her winging into the knowing little hat shop and into the chummery, ten pounds indeed were added to her privy purse. On a day within twelve of her announcement of the tremendous project, ecstatic, "fairly rolling," she winged.

6

Mary, when she wrote from Cologne on hearing of the winging, did not approve it. That Ruth should earn her own living had her complete accord. "I was very much afraid," said her letter to Laura, "that you and father would want to keep her at home. That you have not done so I am well pleased to hear. On the other hand, her choice of work, and your support of it, appear to me most ill-advised. At her age and with her irresponsible character a post in which she would have been subjected to some sort of discipline surely should have been a first consideration when placing her out in life. Training for a secretarial post would have been a far wiser expenditure of the £50 which I am surprised, moreover, to hear that father was prepared to pay out in one sum. It sounds to me a great deal of money to put into what is obviously a speculation."

The note thus sounded, more that of a great-aunt than a daughter, was the quality indigenous in the writer. Her long absence, independent, from home had matured it. It still— as yet—caused her parents to smile.

When she came home for her wedding she made early opportunity to inspect alike the shop and the chummery. Returning from her visit, "Just what I expected to find," her report was. "Just what I told you was my feeling about it all when I wrote to you."

She looked severely at her parents, driven somehow by her eye to sit side by side on the sofa before her, herself fronting them from a straight-backed chair.

"They've got a divan in there," she continued, "and a grand piano."

"In the shop?" inquired the vicar, startled.

Mary compressed her lips. "In what they call their studio, in what they call their chummery."

"Those are new," said Laura brightly, "since we had tea there."

"There's a good deal new, I should say," coldly affirmed Mary, "judging by the difference between what you've told me and what I saw for myself. Was this Freda Stuart—I disliked her intensely—wearing an eyeglass when you saw her?"

"She held one up when she wanted to use her right eye," said the vicar. "Poor girl, she lost the use of it," he continued chattily, "by a most unfortunate—"

"She had it stuck in her eye," Mary cut him short, "nearly the whole time I was in the shop. Anything less likely to prepossess a customer I would find it hard to imagine. Not that there was reason to object to it on that score during the good hour at least that I was there. In the whole of that time the only people who came in were a lady who lives above, very angry indeed because a wireless set had again been left on after the shop was closed—imagine *having* a wireless set in a shop—a chauffeur returning a box of hats with which his mistress was unsatisfied, a decidedly unpleasant individual about an unpaid bill, and a policeman to warn them that their cellar trap in the pavement was still dangerous and that they would be prosecuted if it wasn't repaired. Did you meet any of their friends, father?" Mary concluded this tabulation of the knowing little shop's clientele by sharply demanding.

The vicar, who had been trying to visualize each member of the list in turn and was bewilderedly behindhand in the task, gave a small jump. "No, dear."

"I think you would scarcely have invited them to the vicarage if you had. I looked in with Walter both last night and the night before. Each time, two nights running, mind you, such a crowd in the space and such extraordinary types I have never seen—sprawling all over a divan and banging on a grand piano. It just about suits them. Walter said it reminded him of a night-club to which"—here Mary swallowed pointedly—"he was once taken by a friend. If they served in their shop half as many customers as they entertain friends in their 'studio' Ruth's prospects might be reasonably good. As it is," concluded Mary, rising with the suggestion of one dismissing a class, "I give her a year."

7

Ruth took, as it turned out, precisely eighteen months, at the end of which the vicar, instead of finding himself, as by her figuring, the gainer, was in fact the loser by two further checks of fifty pounds each into the shop and by sundry small checks into the chummery. The fifties steadied the hats round windy corners unexpectedly encountered, but failed to place them on the crowded heads there said to be waiting. The small checks were drawn into Ruth's purse by the draught which kept out of it the expected weekly pocket-money, not to say the percentage of profits after the first year. Came finally a devastating gale which blew first the divan and the grand piano back into the vans of the hire-purchase firms which had supplied them, second the hat shop into the books of the Official Receivers and third, Miss

Freda Stuart behind a store counter, Miss Ann Mudge to her friends, and Ruth back to the vicarage.

Squire Brown's reception of Tom after his first half at Rugby well might have stood for the vicar's welcome of Ruth's return. "The squire looks rather blue at having to pay two pounds ten shillings for the posting expenses from Oxford. But the boy's intense joy at getting home, and the wonderful health he is in, and the brave stories he tells of Rugby, its doings and delights, soon mollify him, and three happier people didn't sit down to dinner that day in England than the squire and his wife and Tom Brown."

The vicar, if he had been caused to feel a little blue at drawing on his balance checks so unprecedented an amount as fifty pounds, would have paid them, had he been able, twice over for the hug with which Ruth came into his arms; thrice for her gay chatter of all her experiences as the three sat up late together that night; four times for her declaration, made after a little silence, seated between them, with a sudden hand put out to each. "Oh, it is jolly to be home again," she declared. "I'm going to stay now forever."

8

She stayed three months.

She never really settled down. "Bound," at her previous home-coming, "to feel it a bit of a lark to be chasing about with pals again," she showed herself caught by the same obligation, excused with the same delightful compunction, now. The difference was that the pals were not this time of Upton Springs only and that their society did not pall. A Road House had been opened five miles down the London arterial way. Elaborately conducted, the "A.O." as it called itself (in full, "The Always Open"), drawing patrons from as far afield as cars might bring them, offered a species of club membership to dwellers in the neighborhood.

With its sports facilities, swimming pool, squash and lawn-tennis courts, together with its indoor comforts, its dance-floor, cocktail bar and other amenities, it offered a resort incomparably more attractive than the coffee shops in which last time the local pals were met. Casual friendships with dropped-in motorists were always to be made. The season was high summer. It was nothing of a whizz down, evenings and week-ends, for members of the wide circle of companions designated by Mary as just about suited by the divan and the grand piano.

Ruth, enormously enjoying it all, spent the greater part of her time there, sometimes her bicycle, more often friends' cars, her means of conveyance. Compunction at the absences from home thus caused found happy expression in the fact that on five days of the seven the A.O., before evening fell, wore a decorous air. Twice a week, a friend providing transport, Ruth took the vicar there to play croquet, Laura accompanying them. Laura's part in the treat is thus designated because for her the treat was to watch the delight her husband had in these games with his adored daughter. Never so carefree, never so lifted out of memories as when with Ruth, the happiness her company gave him seemed to tide never so high as on the airy, sunny freedom of the A.O. croquet lawn. A startlingly bad player, his delight in her peals of laughter at his more excruciating shots, his proud joy in her "Oh, *jolly* well done, dad!" when his aim fluked true, were almost misty work for loving eyes to watch. Afterwards would be a scrumptious tea, served at cheap rates to members. Then the same obliging friend would take the three home; and always then, her conscience handsomely cleared, "And now you don't mind, do you, if I go back for an hour or so?" Ruth would ask. "Don't wait supper if I *should* be late. There's dancing, you know, tonight and I *might* feel like staying."

The waiting car would return her to scenes which, as the evening advanced, showed continuously less of the A.O.'s simplicity of atmosphere during croquet hours. Now would come to the Road House the set, Ruth's friends, not the vicarage's, resident in the rookery extension of Upton Springs, not in the original nest. By them, as by car owners as far away as London, the A.O. in its evening guise often was jocularly referred to as the A.F., Always Full. They spoke of it also, and they were tolerably well qualified to judge, as a Hot Spot.

It kept late hours. Permitting herself participation in these on the croquet days, sometimes on other, Ruth was brought back to the vicarage at times of the morning which caused gently deprecatory remark on the occasions when her father or her mother, aroused by the shattering car accompaniment of modern leave-takings, chanced to know them. Other of her disportments with her friends, certain of the rookery friends themselves, also caused little twinges of disquiet to her parents. It was to be remembered, however, they reminded one another, that things had changed utterly in these regards since the war. Young people were not restricted as they used to be. If they were not given freedom, with effect much more disruptive of home influence they took it. They had it today at as young as seventeen. Ruth now was twenty-two.

And she was Ruth. Joy eager she might be. It was in little marks of her affectionate loyalty to her parents' principles that lay their reassurance at modern ways disquieting to old ideas. Scrupulously, in example, she observed unspoken wishes of the vicar to which, Laura knew, by no means all of her years and of her predilections would have subscribed. When she went to an A.O. dance on a Saturday unfailingly she was in by midnight, before the Sabbath's dawn. Sundays were the Road House's gayest days. She never went on Sunday.

These traits in her, as others of their like, belonged to what Laura saw as the home side of her nature. As clearly the mother perceived again, gradually evincing, the signs of her disposition's other face, the toying with the blind-cord tassel face, the call, once more, to be on her own. It came to head as suddenly as before. This time an interior decoration business offered, as had the hat shop, the chance of a lifetime. Its announcement was sprung, as had been that of the other, on an occasion of happiest association of the three together.

9

A particularly jolly game of croquet was culminating in a particularly scrumptious tea. It was being enjoyed in a secluded arbor of the A.O. lawns. The vicar was saying how famous it had all been. Ruth was projecting her familiar "Well, you won't mind frightfully, will you, if after I've seen you home I come back here for a bit? Some rather jolly friends of mine are coming down at sixish. You won't mind frightfully, will you?"

They assured her they would not.

"Darlings!" she said gratefully.

She looked away across the lawns. She returned her eyes to watch her stirring of her teacup. "I'm afraid I'm simply awful about being out of the house so often," she pensively stirred. "And, I say, dad, mum," decisively laying down the spoon she suddenly appealed, "will you think me *too* awful if I tell you that I do feel, after all, that I still want to be out on my own, earning my own living? There's a most—"

She stopped her flow in unison with the arrest of action by her audience, the vicar in regard to a pink-sugared cake almost at his lips, Laura as to her cup midway raised. The articles went back respectively to plate and saucer. She colored as she watched these signs of concern. "I know it's too brutish of me," then she cried; "but the fact is there's a most thrilling chance occurred, far, far better than the hat shop, *and*"—she reached across a hand to lay upon the hand still holding the pink cake—"this is the really magnificent point, darling dad, there's not, this time, one single penny piece for you to lay out, as to my dying day I never shall forget how you did then. Mum"—her other hand went upon her mother's—"it's an interior decoration business. It's—"

Succinctly, as all stood planned when in rapid days it was agreed to, the thrilling chance stood within the doors of the recently opened showrooms of Sabrina Smith in Sloane Street. The name Sabrina Smith meant nothing whatever, on first announcement, to the vicarage. In the homes of those regularly to be met in the gossip columns of the popular Press it meant the extreme tip of the then vogue for colored ceilings and scumbled or otherwise decoratively treated walls enclosing appointments similarly unusual. Sabrina Smith could, in short, for a stinging fee, make a room so unusual as to be, to ordinary people, unusable. A middle-aged whirlwind of emotionalism robed always in flowing deshabille, Mrs. Sabrina Smith employed for the execution of her designs young artists who slapped you up frescoes or friezes of startling projection before you had time to realize what you had let yourself in for either in cost or in curiosity. It was from one of these artists, met first at the chummery, then at the A.O., that Ruth learnt of the glowing opportunity which now she prevailed upon the vicarage to let her embrace. Scumbled in temperamentalism on a steely business mind, Sabrina, in addition to her stinging fees, drew commissions from the furnishing and art firms to which she introduced her clients. Certain of these had recently set her up, at no risk to herself, in showrooms in the Sloane Street premises. She was taking on two or three assistants who not only should learn the art of selling antiques but, in her studio, the art also of internal decoration. She took on Ruth.

"And I know of," Ruth had disclosed when announcing the project at the A.O. tea-table, "an absolutely marvelously ideal place where I can live. It's a women's hostel in Bloomsbury. Two most frightful pals of mine are there and about fifty others. You each have a most topping little bed-sitting-room of your own and everything else is in common and all run to be as cheap as possible and yet absolutely top-hole. You collect your own meals on a tray in the dining-hall and there's even a laundry with every conceivable gadget where you can do your washing. It's a sort of university college and service flats and hotel all rolled into one. It's marvelous."

Here for this second start "on her own" she was accommodated. The hat-shop start had taken her eighteen months along the course of life. Interior decoration advanced her six fewer, twelve. For her footing in it no single penny piece, as delightedly she had shown, was desired of the vicar. On the other hand, as further details had adduced, no single penny piece of salary was received during the first, the pupilage, year. At the end of that time salary plus commission was to make Ruth handsomely self-supporting and might indeed have made her so had not, unfortunately, the termination of the period coincided with the abrupt cessation of Mrs. Sabrina Smith's interest alike in showrooms and in pupils. In dramatic obedience to her temperamental impulses she returned to her Chelsea studio. With dramatic suddenness, in no degree crestfallen, on the contrary in highest spirits, Ruth reappeared at the vicarage.

"Matter of fact," after the huggings was her vivid explanation, "the show's gone bust."

"Bust?" echoed the vicar, overjoyed at his daughter's unexpected arrival but startled by the catastrophic motive power which now appeared to have hurtled her.

"Absolutely sky high. Sabby suddenly declared that if she lived in the showrooms another day she'd go round them with an ax, and we three pupes are bunged out on the bleak and inhospitable high and dry. Matter of fact, darlings," gaily she went on, "it's a *jolly* good job it's over, and I'm *jolly* bucked about it, and so will you be when I tell you. I've lost a job that was only costing you money, darling dad, to keep me at it, but I've *got* a job that's going to let me not only pay for my own nosebag, straw and stable, but, after a bit, send down a few bags of oats to you two adorables as well.

"It's a tea shop," sparklingly she revealed to the slightly bewildered adorables, "a ladies' tea shop in Kensington run by two most frightful pals of mine at the hostel. They've been at me to join for months and it's only because I felt it my duty to stick to the thing you'd planned for me that I haven't bunged in with them long ago."

This rendering of the Sabrina Smith episode as a vocation selected for her and pursued only by sense of filial obligation was a sufficiently suitable culmination of the surprises of her listeners during the recital. Realization of the deeper significance of the occasion soon followed. It stood in the fact that Ruth's engagement in the new, in the tea-shop, project, was launched in terms of her emancipation from the vicarage as established fact. A job had fallen through. She showed it as unquestionable that at once she entered another. The hostel not the vicarage was now her home.

10

For three years onwards thus it stood. She stayed now for a five days' rest. They were devoted almost solely to her parents, to the vicar especially, two evenings only at the A.O. Then to the tea shop, to her hostel, to three years of recognized independence she was gone. The tea shop went presently the way of its bubbles precedent. Gaily she fluttered into employment successively in a florist's, in a beauty parlor, as receptionist at a fashionable photographer's. Oxygen from the vicarage purse assisted occasional breathlessness in these flittings. On the whole, joyously always, she kept herself going pretty well. Then something happened, exactly what she was only to hint, never quite to explain, to cloud her ardors. As unexpectedly as after the busting of the decoration enterprise, one day she came home, the trunk accompanying her emphasizing the intention which now, causing a heart to bound, she declared.

"I'm through with all that," this time were the words of her return.

They were somberly spoken. As if twinged by realization of her tone's dissonance from the rapture of her reception, with flash of smile she thrust her hand again into her father's just relinquished.

"I'm home for keeps now, dad," she told him.

Not her own volition was in fact to determine the permanency thus assured. It happened that at this time, too, decisions not of her own contemplation were gathing about the vicar's other daughter.

Three

HE LOOKS very different in mufti."

Mary's husband, at that time her betrothed, was by no means the only holder of a temporary commission in the 1914-18 war of whom, on his demobilization, this was said by somebody who previously had never seen him but in khaki. The noun uniform is exactly described by its adjectival use. It gives all its wearers a uniform appearance. Dressed precisely alike, the most dissimilar figures become alike. Even the faces seem to be in ranges of a pattern. Eight hundred men in civilian clothes are as many individual units, easily distinguishable. Paraded as a battalion they are, in general look, as one. The mold prints deeper yet. Manner and manners drill gradually into a common line. Given some months in uniform, the wearer, man or woman, not only externally but down to the superficies of character is all of a piece with his or her comrades in arms.

Thus was it that when the war uniforms were stripped the individual changes frequently were striking. Not only an outer covering had been shed, an inner also. A caul had invested the personality. It came away with the uniform. The true disposition was revealed.

To Mary, Walter Norman strongly presented such change when, newly out of uniform and out of caul, he met her for that day's shopping in town on the evening of which with slight frown she had made remark on the difference in him to her mother. There was nothing about him, in common fact, at which a next young woman, at which Ruth, for instance, or Philip's fawn, would have frowned. They would

293

have thought him a rather jolly round-faced ass in a rather untidy blue serge suit and pre-war bowler hat, jolly free with his money. They would rather have liked him, though not, as Ruth would have said, for keeps.

Mary, who loved him and who proposed to have him for life, did not, however, care to have a jolly ass about her, round faced or long, not even for an afternoon, certainly not as a husband for keeps. She was constitutionally disturbed by an ass, particularly by a jolly ass. Her instincts protested at an untidy suit, baggy at the knees, shiny at the button-holes. Equally they disliked a pre-war bowler, too high in the crown, faintly greenish where the sunlight caught it. Particularly they protested at freedom with cash, even more at free and easy ways.

Entirely unaware of presenting any points open to criticism Walter sharpened them all by arriving ten minutes late at the arranged meeting place, outside Piccadilly Circus tube station. He came up, far from hurrying, with his head buried in the midday edition of an evening paper, its sheets held wide in either hand. Mary had seen this newspaper reader drifting towards her, bumping into and being bumped by people, and had thought how bad it looked. She was astonished when he lifted his face to see that it was Walter. Beaming delight he loosely crumpled the paper and dropped it in a large ball at his feet. Her tidy mind quivered. "Oh, Walter; litter." He kicked the ball aside and into the way of a passer-by who stumbled over it. "Fell out of my hand," he laughed and made to kiss her in greeting.

"Not here, Walter," she deterred him. There raced through her mind, "How thoughtless to drop that paper like that; how bad to walk reading it like that; how odd he looks in that suit and that hat."

He proposed lunch at "the good old Troc, or, if you prefer, the Cri." When, at her request, he had explained this alternative into the Trocadero or the Criterion she said at once that both were much too elaborate for a simple little shopping lunch; an A.B.C. or a Slater's was the thing.

He made a grimace. "Oh, I say, not one of those tea-shop places. I'm fairly dying for a pint of lager."

It was her turn to "Oh."

"Oh, Walter, not for lunch, surely?"

The rather inane grimace showed itself again. She never had seen it under his military cap. "For lunch, you bet." He tipped back his odd-looking bowler. "What is lunch without a lager?" he histrionically apostrophized.

"Put your hat a little more forward, dear."

They compromised on a Corner House. A waitress was standing by the table of their selection. "You at this table?" Walter genially greeted her. "Right. You look after us and I'll look after you." He handed her his hat. *"Mon chapeau.* Mine's a large lager, very large and very cold, and a large steak, also large, *not* cold." Cheerily he seated himself. "What about you, darling?"

"Please bring me," Mary addressed the waitress, "a cup of tea and a poached egg."

Her voice had something of the chill desired in the lager beer. Walter did not notice it. "Oh, I say, rot," was his noisy observation. "You must do better than that."

To avoid being thus coaxed before the waitress she changed to a chicken patty. When the girl was gone, "Walter, dear," she began. "I wish—"

"Staff of life?"

She took a roll from the basket which, with grin suitable to his facetiousness, he was holding before her. She disliked the type of humor which calls a thing by jocular phrase. His *"Mon chapeau,"* particularly when addressed to a waitress, had been of the same kind. Now, neglectful of her, "I wish—" he was tugging at a jumble of letters in his breast pocket.

"Lot here to show you."

With new disfavor she watched his wrestle to extract the mass and then its higgledy-piggledy flop upon the table. Her eye went up to the odd bowler hanging greenishly beneath a light on its peg. It seemed the symbol of all this change in him from his khaki smartness and seemliness.

"What was in that paper you were so absorbed in?" she inquired. "I've been meaning to ask you. Any conference news?"

"Starting prices," he grinned up from his letter sorting.

"Starting prices?"

"You know—where the dickens has this thing got to?—the betting on the racing."

"Oh, Walter, you don't bet, do you?"

"Oh, once in a blue, if some chap puts me on to a good thing. Ah, here it is. Look, darling, this is from the man I'm taking over from about our house—"

She did not enjoy the meal. Her practical mind had pre-arranged all items of the day's program. A little shopping lunch had been one. The bill, when it was presented, shocked her. When they got up Walter, as he took up the slip to pay it at the cash desk, fumbled in a pocket.

"Here, I've got some coppers," she said.

"That's all right." He put down a shilling, then a sixpence.

"You're not going to tip all that?"

He showed his other coins. "Or half-a-crown," he grinned. He reached for the pre-war bowler. "Come on. I feel fine now."

As he gathered his change from the cash desk and turned to her, "Do you put down," she asked him, "all your spendings when you get home?"

"Put down?"

"As accounts. You keep accounts, don't you?"

"Not I. Not things like that."

With sign familiar to the vicarage she compressed her lips.
He had had, from her point of view, an unchecked run thus
far in this rather disturbing day. Now she put her hand to
the controls.

"Walter," she said firmly, "you must. I'll buy you a book."

2

That "must," that firm setting of her hand upon the controls, went to bed with her that night. As a delicious sigh
transports the tired out to slumber, so concentration upon
the word and the action passed her contentedly from rest-
lessness to sleep. Over the events of the day she had been
wakeful but she had not been worrying. She was too self-
assured ever to worry. When difficulties confronted her she
never fretted at their foot. She searched their cliffs for a way
over them or through them, then impassively took it.

The day had been disturbing. Throughout it, surprising
change, unexpected discovery, in Walter had confronted the
ordered process of her way of life. As encountered, as perplexedly she had moved on from one only to meet the next,
they had continuously puzzled her. Now, got to bed, alone
in quiet darkness, she set them out again and took a calm
look at them. Speedily she saw that they had been no more
than varieties of slackness. The harness of his uniform, the
bridle of discipline, heretofore had stiffened him. He had
slipped out of these healthy restraints and— Mary smiled
to herself. Complacently she as it were glanced about the
harness room of her own nature. Plentifully she saw it hung
with bridles and strappings similar to those of military pattern. They gleamed there ready for the moral welfare of
anybody with whom she happened to be joined. She had

shown them to Walter when he had jibbed at the idea of keeping accounts. They were that "must" of hers, that movement of her hand to the controls.

Recalling her exhibition of them, the smile with which now she saw herself reaching them down for permanent use on him was an affectionate smile. She loved Walter fondly. Heretofore, gently pleasuring herself she now realized, she had loved him with her heart only. Her heart was but a secondary seat of her emotions. She thought that everybody's heart should be. Governance whether of oneself or of another should be from the head. In the courting, the khaki days, Walter had exhibited nothing that required her to put, so to say, her head at his disposal. Today he had revealed himself prone to carelessness, to weakness of character. She could improve him, she could mold him, she could stiffen him, she could bring out for him the best that was in him. By doing all this she would give him happiness in measure such as, without her loving firmness, he could never approach.

Time was to question this.

It chanced that at that moment as, smiling over the upright happiness she was to contrive for him, she fell asleep, Walter was very happy indeed in a fashion much more to his taste than that thus devotedly preparing for him.

He was pleasantly semi-tight at a night club.

3

If Walter Norman was like many other young men in showing himself very different in mufti from what he had appeared to be in uniform, he was in wide company also in that he returned to civil life not quite of the same disposition as that in which he had left it. He had left it entirely content with his work and prospects in a leading insurance company, the Professional, up which he was steadily rising, entirely content also with his outside world as, with that means of support, he created it. He returned to the one and to the other not quite so content. The war took men out of settled existence. It introduced them to new ways and standards of life. When it ended it left many of them unsettled. Some natures, as some medicines, are all the better for being shaken up. Others, as some wines, are best undisturbed. A heap of scorn is poured on those who, as the saying is, live in a rut, but much of the world's essential work is done, as much of its happiness is found, in ruts. A plowed field, for that matter, is all ruts. It is precisely from its ruts that it produces its yield. Where a hunt has galloped across it the crop is to seek.

Walter, before the war galloped across his patch, had always been a cheerful, easygoing young man, fond of what he called a spot of fun, but wearing always a starched collar. His temporary commission taught him to wear a soft collar. When, formerly, he buckled himself into starch of a morning he thought of his daily round with amiable interest. Slipping, now, easy comfort about his neck, he thought of his work with a certain disfavor. In starched linen he had been well content with life at a steady jog. In undressed linen he had a tease to get a kick out of life. In his stiff collar he never would have been seen with his head in a midday special, studying starting prices. It was in a soft collar, similarly, in uniform while on leave, that he first went to a night club. Neither of these particular disportments was or ever became an excess with him. They are mentionable as a part of his disposition only because, like the other manifestations, they were no part of his fancy while in his pre-war rut.

When he left the Professional for the army he stood next on the list for a branch managership. When he was with the Army of Occupation after the Armistice, highly charged with great issues now to be determined he showed Mary a letter from his head office informing him that the manager-ship at Gradington, now vacant, was awaiting him as soon as he could get demobilized. His lover's heart, pounding in his khaki bosom, informed him, by love's magic, that, as she read, she was asking herself, "Why has he shown me this?" When she had finished he told her.

The incidence of the soft collar on his post-war appoint-ment was that when he went with Mary to Gradington it was in a soft collar and with soft-collar outlook that he began his work there. He was going to work jolly hard in his office, but he was not going to kill himself at it. He would justify his directors' confidence in him when at his desk; but he proposed to have a jolly cheery time when away from it.

Thus he thought. One of the first notable things, in point of fact, that happened to him at Gradington was that Mary said he must wear a stiff collar, not a soft one. The soft was quite correct for Saturday afternoons. For his office, as for Sundays, it was, she said, incorrect.

"Really, dear, I insist."

4

When they went up to the Midlands they did not, natu-rally, live in industrial Gradington. They lived in Dursley, its residential suburb. Nice people live in Dursley, nicer, Mary soon was writing to the vicarage, than in Upton Springs. Whether actually the residents of Dursley were pleasanter or more worthy than those of Upton is not for examination. The reason why Mary preferred her new neighbors was because her position in regard to them was very different from her status in her father's parish. At Upton she had been a daughter of a house. In Dursley she was a mistress of a house. There she had been subordinate.

Here she was in command. This exactly suited the nature which first had manifested itself in her administration of her dolls' reformatory. Into her occupation as a married woman, as a housewife, as a hostess, as a helpmate to her husband, as, in due course, a mother to her children, she entered with the same absorbed earnestness, the same masterful air, as had characterized all her pursuit of her intentions from her nursery to her war service. In the pleasant little villa, garden surrounded, which Walter took over from his predecessor at the Professional, Mary set herself to give her husband the best-run house in Dursley. Walter soon knew that he had it, starched.

Gradington was twelve miles from Dursley. At the outset of their married life Walter went daily to and fro in the little car which his parents had given him as a wedding present. Mary drove in with him, bringing back the car for her own use during the day and running out to fetch him at six in the evening. Later on he suddenly began regularly to be delayed at the office without, unfortunately, having known in time to telephone that he would be. This kept Mary waiting, a thing her punctual habits detested. Always as he came, at last, hurrying out she engaged his interest in her entry, in a little memorandum book kept in the car, of the duration of her waste of time. Walter was frightfully apologetic. When to his dismay he was shown that he had thus incommoded her to a total, in ten consecutive working days, of nine hours and twenty-four minutes he suggested, and she agreed, that in future he should come back by train. He showed then that a season ticket was cheaper than a daily single. Adding the cost of petrol for the morning run it was obviously wasteful, he said, to have a season ticket and use it only once daily instead of twice. Much pleased at this rare actuation of her husband by economical principles, Mary consented. She had not a suspicion that in fact he was actuated by, that the whole thing had been elaborately devised on account of, his preference for a noisy smoking carriage, packed with his pals, to a dignified ride on which, Mary disliking smoking in the car, he could not get out his pipe.

The incident was symptomatic alike of the husband's reaction to the seemly conditions of life produced for him by his wife and of the wife's inability to imagine such reaction. Walter was given by Mary, as she had set out to give him, the most perfectly run house in Dursley; and he was not constituted to appreciate a perfectly run house; his nature was towards a make-do, chuck-it-where-you-like-and-leave-it-where-it-falls house. She, for her part, knew that he had, in perfection, everything that a married man should wish to have in his home, and it never occurred to her that he could do other than appreciate it. She would have been, as in time she was to be, stupefied at discovering otherwise.

When they had been married six years the position thus was that there dwelt in this house a perfect wife, two perfectly managed children, Joan aged five and Michael nearly four, two perfectly managed servants, a perfect cook-general and a perfect nurse-house-parlormaid, and one perfectly managed husband. Not a thing in the house, not a piece of furniture, ornament or even book, ever was out of place. Not an item of its routine ever occurred a minute after or a minute before it was appointed to occur. There was not a remotest corner of it in which even a magnifying lens would have discovered a speck of dust. There was not a drawer which if opened (and they all opened with smoothest precision) did not reveal its contents at a glance, meticulously arranged.

Walter's clothes' and writing-table drawers at Dursley were, when he first used them, more like rummage bags or lucky dips than any other form of receptacle. When he had

experienced for a month or two the chilly shock of pulling
into view grim array where he had expected cheery chaos
he could not but himself begin to operate what Mary, kind
but firm at his elbow, impressed upon him as being the ele-
mentary principle of order, namely, that it is just as easy to
put away a thing tidily as to throw it in anyhow. ("Really,
dear, you must. I insist.") It was done for him if ever, in spasmodic hark back to his instincts, he forgot to do it himself.
Everything was done for him. The nurse-house-parlormaid
nightly laid out for him his starched shirt and dinner-jacket;
the cook-general nightly sent up to him a three-, sometimes
a four-course dinner. Morsels, daintily served, a single glass
of Graves, took the place of the gross steak and onions and
the pot of beer, consumed in his day clothes, which in less
perfect circumstances might have been his portion. Mary's
example gave him, furthermore, the refined pleasures of sipping his single glass. Her attention to his well-being rescued
him from his earlier unhealthful heartiness of throwing it
down at a gulp and looking round hopefully, but fruitlessly,
for another. Coffee in a cup of egg-shell capacity followed
the repast. But for her thought of him, topping up the evening with a whisky and soda, brown in hue, might have
been his lot.

He might have had, as is the lot of less-cared-for husbands,
a room of his own disordered with careless use and hoarded
litter. He had instead a little apartment so scrupulously neat
that he never could leave it, even for an hour, without finding on his return that the chair cushions had been shaken
out, the windows opened, the ash-trays emptied, the pipes
and books replaced in rack and shelves. Nothing, to his
knowledge, ever wanted "doing" in the house. If hinges ever
squeaked, if windows ever rattled, if fastenings ever loosed,
workmen, presumably, set them to rights. Never needed he
to feel himself called upon, as are thousands of less fortunate

husbands, to potter about the house with an oil can, with a screwdriver, with a hammer and nails.

Outstandingly of all, perhaps, in the smoothness of his way in his home was the fact that his children were never permitted to be a tax on him. As first Joan, then Michael arrived, Mary impressed upon Walter that she proposed to bring them up, and she did bring them up, on a principle which gave them their every proper need and attended their every genuine discomfort. It followed that anything they might want was not good for them to have, that anything they might profess to suffer was a pretense to engage sympathy or indulgence. Such requests and such protestations were, therefore, Mary said, to be firmly ignored.

Both directly and indirectly Walter was thus saved the cares and the engagements of fatherhood borne by the commonality of fathers. The earlier you began with this system the quicker, Mary said, the invaluable lessons arising out of it would be learnt. When therefore Walter sped to soothe crying proceeding from a perambulator apparently forgotten down the garden Mary sped after him to bring him away. "Really, Walter, you mustn't. I insist." He was never, later on, under the necessity of bringing home an unexpected gift in his pocket. To do so taught children, Mary said, to expect gifts. He never had to pretend to be Father Christmas. As Joan and Michael would have to know in time that there was no such existence as Father Christmas, or as a fairy, it was manifestly wrong, he was told, to deceive them with legends and with the reading of fairy tales and then to let them discover that they had been deceived. When, again, he came home of an evening, he never had to rush upstairs to them to give them some fun before they went to sleep. Visits, much less excitement, were not proper for them, Mary said, before they went to sleep. She ruled also, thereby saving Walter from calls upon his time frequently demanded of

fathers, that it was not good for children while of nursery
age to be too much with their parents. Walter never had to
go into the nursery to romp with them. It was good for
them, Mary said, to be "brought in" to their father, clean
and prettily dressed.

5

With everything, even his children, thus dressed for him,
and himself, as it were, sedulously fashioned to suit the picture, Walter owed so much happiness to his wife as, having
regard to his nature, not altogether to surprise her by being
sometimes almost emotional about it. Oddly moved, "I'm
not sufficiently grateful for all you do for me," he sometimes
would come out with. Herself entirely unemotional, Mary
greatly disliked emotionalism in those about her. Her
wriggle from Laura's caresses in her Mother Bunch days,
her "Mother, you do make a fuss" at demonstrative affection
shown her in her girlhood, were reproduced, once they were
well married, in restraint of any of Walter's manifestations
of fondness, in deprecation also of fondlings and huggings
between him and the children.

For his, as she termed them, absurd expressions of gratitude for what she regarded as mere wifely and self-respecting
duty on her part she made a slight allowance. They arose,
she knew, in part from a streak of sentimentality in him, in
part from a certain intermittent religiosity that he had. The
sentimentalism she strove, for his good, to wither by ignor-
ing it. As to the pious fits, herself consciously good, his own
spasmodic devotionalism was, as she saw it, the miserable
sinner type of religion, aware of need of grace, frequently
beating his breast in despair of it, achieving it for, sometimes, as long as three days together, and during that time
gushing with amends for past misdeeds, usually imaginary.
She made allowances.

More charitably viewed, his religion was, in fact, that of a man of great weakness of character, wistfully hanging about the skirts of regeneration, too infirm of purpose to enter in and embrace it. It was, again, that of a man distressedly aware of his own failings but crying to be ridded of them by a miracle, by a conjuring trick, by, as the Athenians at Mars Hill, some new thing; inherently unable himself to cast them off by faith. Thus seeking, from time to time he would pick up, bring home and earnestly study the latest publication in the vogue for books written to make religion "easy," short-cutting the New Testament for the "plain man," short-circuiting the Church for the "modern mind."

It was after spiritual wrestlings in these fashions that he would come out with his protestations that Mary did more for him than he deserved, with his emotional contrition that he did not fully appreciate all the happiness with which her care for his home surrounded him. She would repress her instinctive deprecation of emotionalism into a laugh having no more than a tincture of chill. "Oh, don't be so silly, Walter. Of course you appreciate it. Of course I know that you do. You don't have to tell me so."

"Mary, you don't understand," he would strangle out, red, unhappy. "I ought to realize all day long all that you do for me, and I don't realize it. I've got everything here with you that I could want, and I'm not properly alive to it. It's there, but I'm not taking it, not letting myself take it."

She would laugh again; the chill, for his good, more pronounced. "You really are too ridiculous. When I think you're unappreciative I'll tell you so. Do drop the absurd subject."

A twinge would cross his face. A muttered, "Oh, well—" would follow it.

Of these signs at their time she thought nothing. Mere

petulancies as she considered them to be, she gave them no more attention than she paid to his groans when he was triflingly out of sorts, with a boil or a stiff neck. It was her practice never to encourage anyone, especially her husband or her children, to make a fuss of himself. When, later, events caused her to review affairs, she stigmatized the twinge of face and the muttered words as sulkiness. She called them sulkiness because that was the hardest word she found it possible to apply to what were the sole instances of any differences between Walter and herself that she could remember.

It was shortly before Joan's seventh birthday that she was made thus unsuccessfully to search the past for explanation of the amazement with which suddenly he confronted her. She could find none. Those sulky signs apart, she could recall no cloud whatever across the bliss she had contrived about him and in which, in her view, they had lived. There never had been a cloud. There never had been between them even a temporary coldness such as sometimes transiently estranges the most affectionate of couples, let alone an open quarrel. How could there have been? She had given him a perfect home. How can fault be found with perfection? At what was broken upon her she was as dumbfounded as should be the reader. The comparison is exact. Mary naturally knew much more of Walter than the looker-on at these pages has seen. As a summary, however, only of what she regarded as significant in their life together the record set down might have been done by her own hand. "Yes," she would have said of it, "that's all there ever was, one long perfection of domestic well-being. That's the amazing thing about it."

6

He had gone up to town to stay a night for his anuual meeting with his directors. On the morrow of his setting out she was expecting a letter from him by the afternoon post. It would say whether he would be returning that evening or, as sometimes had happened, must stay another night. The day brought her a telegram as well as a letter, both shocking her.

The telegram arrived just as she happened to be thinking that the postman would shortly be along. It was smoothly brought in by the cook-general on a gleaming silver salver. The nurse-house-parlormaid was out with the children. In her absence the general, perfectly managed, could do parlor work as featly as on her night out her companion could serve a dinner. At sight of the buff envelope Mary gave a little frown which Walter would have recognized. Why, the frown said, should he have sent a telegram when either he could have written or he had written? If the former it was a lazy extravagance, if the latter it betokened change of plans, want of orderly arrangement of duties.

However, the message, when, lips compressed, she opened it, proved not to be from Walter. It was from the vicarage. She caught her breath as she read it. Her heart seemed momentarily to stop. She screwed up her eyes as they gazed upon the words. Dampness squeezed through the constriction making the typed strip illegible. A tear concentrated out of the dampness and with a loud plop plunged itself into a great splash upon the page. With catching breaths, teeth on lip, handkerchief to mouth, she strove to keep back those which strove to follow it. For ten minutes, quivering, she sat thus before the re-entry of the maid, this time with a letter, disturbed her. In that period pictures, projected by the telegram, streamed across her mental image; thoughts,

memories, poignancies, regrets, across her mind. The last
time she had fought loss of self-control was at the news of
John's death. She fought it now as she had fought it then.

At the entry of the maid she got up, not to let her emotion
be seen, and went across the room. At a gesture from her the
girl put the letter on the table at which she had been sitting
and withdrew. She went back to her chair. The interruption
had checked her tears' assault upon the fortress of her eyes.
She sat gazing desolately before her. Presently automatically
she took up the letter. An unexpected postmark above Walter's familiar handwriting aroused, then dully dropped, her
interest.

"Leamington Spa." That was his parents' home. Why on
earth had he gone there? What did it matter? Indifferently
she broke the sealing. What did anything matter?

The first lines of the letter, a very long one, acquainted
her, with a blow like a crash on the head, with that which
mattered to the exclusion of the news in the telegram and
of all else in the world beside. He was leaving her. He was
never going to see her again. He was going to America. He
would be on board his boat at Liverpool when this, sent for
forwarding to his parents, would reach her. Edna Blackett
was going with him.

She sat stunned.

In her sensory paralysis her mind fumbled out to a subsidiary point as will the fingers of the semi-conscious grope
towards some object shapelessly seen and not required.
Edna? Edna Blackett? She knew no one called Edna.
Blackett? Blackett? *Mrs. Blackett!* He had gone off with a
woman, with a neighbor, with that young American widow
who lived in that appalling pigsty of a house with those two
frightful breeched and booted Bingham girls, breeding cairn
terriers. He had gone off. He had deserted her.

She sat stupefied.

Four

I'M HOME for keeps now, dad."

Two days after those words had been spoken they stood in red ink at the head of Laura's monthly letter to Bishop Hubbard. She exchanged a serial budget with the vicarage's dearest friend. "Oh, such good, such glorious news," this number, under the red ink blazonry, had begun. "You've guessed, of course," it went on, "who spoke those red-lettered words. As Ruth said them she thrust her hand into dear Gordon's with that gay, heartening smile which she keeps specially for him, and I declare that the years visibly fell off him as he heard her and as he received her lovely gesture. It was the day before yesterday that (as you shall hear) she arrived. I declare that he is going about the house now looking as he looked in the decade before last! As soon as ever he could he hastened with his happiness to God. He was an hour on his knees. I know, as you will know, that all that time, not praying as sinners like me pray, he was just thinking 'I'm home for keeps now, dad' in God."

This was ecstatic diction. Not by a note did it over-express the effect upon the vicar of Ruth's homecoming "for keeps." Its significance was that he was susceptible to such effect. Years can visibly fall off only if visibly they are heavily borne. Newcomers of the first breaking-out of Upton Springs from nest to rookery had noticed that their vicar looked older than his age. The influences that they brought with them, the modern outlook of which they were the representatives, were not of a sort to make him younger.

Life was being lived at high speed as the century moved

towards its 'Thirties. A launching ship, its ties knocked away, gains momentum with each foot of the greased slipway. National life in England, its old standards cut adrift by the war, careered with less and less restriction as each year took it further from the stocks Nineteen Fourteen-Eighteen on which it had been reconstructed. The old social ties, their customs and manners, their duties and obligations, were shaken off. They had rooted deep in the English scene. Depth, whether of thought or of activity, was now the last thing anybody wanted. Reaction from the pit of the war had demoded all that. What now was sought was anything and everything that made life easier, surface stuff well greased; flats because they did not tie you down; cars because they rushed you *away* and rushed you *to;* cinemas and radio because they needed only your eyes and your ears not your brain; noise, crowds, because silence, sequestration, threw you, undistracted, upon the exertion of having to think. Cocktail parties were found slicker and livelier of effect than tea parties. Prepared foodstuffs in natty cartons avoided not only the nuisance of cooking but, many of them "predigested," the nuisance even of digestion. Restaurant life showed up and did away with the boredom of family life. Childless marriage saved money and responsibility. Synthetic compositions, cheap to buy, took the place of natural products demanding care in use. Substitution of similar kind became popular in spheres other than the markets; expediency, synthetic religion, for Christian faith; material considerations, synthetic conscience, for spiritual values. All the old ways, the old traditions were, in the new jargon, debunked. Ballast was jettisoned. Everything was speeded up.

These manifestations of the new age arisen out of the ashes of the war were no more confined to the British among the nations than to Upton Springs in the British Isles. In forms even more destructive of the old order they ran through Europe. The vicar of St. Luke's had preached the war as accountable by the unseating of Jesus Christ in the hearts of the nations. There were those who, observing the spirit of Christ now newly rejected rather than newly besought to earthly kingship, predicted humanity's release from the past war to be but a headlong launching, gathering impetus down the greased ways, to the next.

The vicar's visibly increasing undue weight of years was not of being among these gloomy prophets of new and greater holocausts to come. He was too gentle of mind to conjure calamitous effects out of what he took to be, and sought to minister to as, but human thoughtlessness. He had had, indeed, he could have told himself, a fresh fair start with the new elements which, streaming in to make rookery out of nest, rapidly gave him as it were a new parish. The newcomers, speedily overlaying the old residents, ousting them as has the gray squirrel the red, knew nothing of his war troubles; to such of them as they came perfunctorily to hear of they paid no account. The age had set itself to forget the war; on such of its aspects as it chose to glance back it looked with new eyes.

Minna's case was an example. She had been a public scandal. She now was no more than "Some foreign governess or something who used to live at the vicarage—the old vicar had children there then, though it's hard to imagine it—and who committed suicide or something." That she had thrown herself down Giant's Gyll because, being German, her life was made intolerable in the place, was impossible to credit. Had not men of our Army of Occupation brought home German wives?

John's case, again, far from being as before a slur on the vicarage, now gave it luster. This lamented poet chap John Brecque, said newcomers to the parish, this "Paradise Destroyed" man that there was all this talk about, was no other, if you please, than a son of the old vicar here! Because, indeed, the young poet had had his home in Upton Springs the booksellers of the town, long after the first fame of the work, always kept "Paradise Destroyed" in display. In one shop or another it was a common sight to see the vicar standing where the three or four copies lay, bending over them, gently fingering them. People would nudge one another, pointing out his occupation. He had drifted in as he passed and presently he would drift out again. "No, nothing this morning, thank you, Mr. ——" he would smile to the bookseller. "Just looking round, you know, just looking round," and he would smile at any others, known to him or not, in the shop, and take himself forth, bowed, slow of gait, steadying himself with a hand to the doorpost as he passed through the entry.

The frequent incident, rather pathetic as some termed it, gave him a favor of people. Some knew, further, that with the early proceeds of "Paradise Destroyed" he had presented the library of Upton School with the welcomed addition of a fine bay window, seated for comfortable reading, designated on a plaque *"The John Brecque Memorial Window. He spent many happy hours in this room."* Others who had been left alone in the vicarage study when calling to see the vicar told of his boy's portrait on the writing-table and of the quotation written beneath it within the framing: *"He alone cannot lose those whom he loves who loves all in Him whom he cannot lose."*

That the poet had been a pacifist in the war meant nothing whatever except, in many quarters, the entirely understandable fact that that was what a young man of such brilliant intellectual parts well might have been. The principles of pacifism, even though roundly disagreed with, now were tolerated. It was to happen that a leading pacifist who had been in the civil prison with John was to be created a peer.

Contemporaries at Wadham had been lusty among those who had thrown stones at John and at the vicarage because of John. The Oxford Union was to pass a resolution maintaining it as no part of a citizen's bounden duty to take up arms for King and Country. These were no manifestations of a seeping of pacifism into the national spirit. Coming cataclysm was to witness that the meteor flag of England did yet terrific burn. It was to expose, too, forever the tragic delusion that the wild beast in man can be exorcised by methods other than the sword.

Yet the slur of pacifism, as that of harboring an enemy national, thus was sponged from the vicarage into the remoteness of old, unhappy, far-off things remembered only by those who have experienced them. The vicar, in the jargon of the new day now dawned about him, could have made a come-back. As one emigrated to the Colonies because of having tarnished his name at home, in the changed composition of his parish he could have started afresh, made good. That he did not do so, that still and increasingly he found his old perplexities amongst his new faces, was because while his people now lived in a swift today he remained in a thoughtful yesterday. The speeding up of life since the war had run past him. Whereas when he first came to St. Luke's he had been in some ways before his time, he now in all his ways was behind the time.

2

How far behind the times he was his sermons all too frequently showed. Recurrently, they ran counter to popular tendencies. A factious element had arisen in the newly established Parochial Council. Led by one Pettersen, a builder with a grievance, it was the opinion of this captious party that his sermons estranged not only the regular attendants at St. Luke's but those parishioners who, coming rarely or never, were the very ones, it said, which St. Luke's should go out of its way to attract.

If they came never, inquired Colonel Gilling's successor as vicar's warden Mr. Fingest, who had been in his day a noted entomologist, if they came never, how should they be affected by the sermons, antagonistic to them or not?

"Because when a sermon's like what it was Sunday before last it's all over the town, talked of," fired the builder, as always when in debate hotly loose in grammar. "All here's read, I suppose, the column the *Gazette* made out of it, views of cycle and ramblers' clubs and whatnot? Crop of letters there'll be following it, and if there's one supporting the vicar's way of thinking, well, I'll be surprised, that's all."

This arose out of a sermon in which the vicar, speaking of the modern decline in Sunday observance, had touched on the old-fashioned custom of the "Sunday suit."

"Even for church attendance itself," his kindly tones had said, "the old practice of dressing in what used to be called our Sunday best is not now always observed. There was something in that practice, you know. I was in London last week and was in St. James's Park. It was the day of a Buckingham Palace garden party and I stood for a delightful ten minutes watching the gay, smart folk going in at the palace gates. So smartly groomed, so beautifully gowned they were, that you might have guessed, even if you had not known, that they were presenting themselves to pay glad homage and loyalty to their dear king." He paused. "Well, we come to church, don't we, to pay glad homage and loyalty to a King of Kings? You see what I mean, don't you? You see how it was that as I came away there crossed my mind the contrast with the easy indifference to appearance with which many of us accept our Lord's invitation to come into his presence in his house?

"Many churches," he went on, "now have a special Sunday service for open-air young people, for hikers and ramblers and cyclists. I think it delightful that these healthy folk should pause in their happy exercise to give an hour of their time, dressed just as they are, to the house of God. But you can imagine with me, can you not, a picture in the same frame infinitely more delightful? Imagine if a visitor from some other planet descended to find all our nation decked in its best, all with radiantly happy faces passing through the streets to various centers of their towns. Imagine him, on inquiring the reason of it, being told, 'Why, the day is Sunday, King of Kings' Day. Everyone is hastening, dressed for the occasion, to one of our Lord's receptions in one of His palaces, there to pour out the happiness that we have of Him.'

"We can't lift all our dear land to that," the vicar said, "by next Sunday. We can't lift all Upton Springs to it immediately, nor even all this our own parish. But most certainly we can raise ourselves to it at once in our own persons, in our own family circles. Radiantly we could feel as we dressed of a Sunday morning 'I am going today to have audience of my King of Kings in His court. I must look at my best as certainly I shall be at my happiest.' Our example would spread. Our children perhaps would see our English Sunday a Royal Invitation Day indeed, God's Fête Day. . . .''

Across its tea-cups a previous generation of his regular attendants had resented his addresses as always appealing for some stupid thing, over its port wine for some damn thing. Here, in his fresh fair start, was one of many instances in which, now over the cocktails, resentment similarly was aired. To stand there looking down on you and remark on the clothes you had chosen to wear was most impertinent, it was dashed cheek. In the middle of his references two young men and two young women, conspicuously dressed for the countryside, got up and spectacularly clumped out on hob-nailed shoes. Someone during the week following chalked across the churchyard notice board "Hikers barred." The local paper aired the point beneath provocative headlines. At the Parochial Council meeting people's warden Mr. Eldon, head shrewdly to one side, adjudged that there was something in what Mr. Pettersen said, you know. Mr. Fing-est, dashing anew the jungle from his eyes, eagerly hunted to find it among the views which followed. The vicar came home tiredly, weighted, perplexed.

Dispiritedness, perplexity of these orders reached a partic-ular head in a matter which, gathering during the latter years of Ruth's life on her own, throbbed disquietingly at the time of her return for keeps. That was why he had so marked a joy of her arrival.

3

The matter had issue in a confluence in the affairs of St. Luke's of two much different personalities. One was Mr. Pettersen, the other a wealthy newcomer, Mr. Harkness. Mr. Pettersen was short, spare, dark, intensely black along the shaving line, febrile. When he was crossed he was imme-diately all eyes and teeth, aflash in blackness. He was easily crossed. He was one of those people who not only are quick to take offense but who appear to suspect offense in half that is said to them; who, when asked if they had seen something mislaid by the inquirer, sense at once accusation of having stolen it. The type is found more commonly among what are called the half-educated; its simmering sensitiveness similar perhaps to the tenderness of a half-healed wound.

Pettersen was not considered one of the leading builders of Upton Springs. Through his late father and his grand-father one of the oldest established, he thought that he should be thus considered and this was his grievance. It was sharpened by the arrival and the activities of new building firms attracted by the exploitation of Upton Springs. Two occurrences in the parish of St. Luke's caused it to develop a particular animus against the vicar. Both were before the builder became a member of the Parochial Council. They were indeed, to the end that he might get to close quarters with the object of his spite, the reasons for his seeking election to it.

One was the matter of a street widening at a short bottle-neck caused largely by St. Luke's parish hall on the one side and Pettersen's office premises on the other. Convinced that his property must come down and anticipating the handsome compensation which would enable him (in his words) to "do down" his rivals from more impressive and better situated quarters, the builder was in high delight. By an amended scheme, as things turned out, a new way was struck through the parish hall site, leaving the Pettersen side untouched. The builder's "do down" intentions, in so far as exercise of burning grudge could effect them, incontinently were transferred from his business competitors to him who should have been his spiritual consoler.

To this smoldering within three months a lively and a bitter savoring fuel was added. Out of the blue, almost literally out of the blue since it was caused by atmospheric action, came discovery to the vicar and churchwardens of alarming deterioration throughout almost the whole face of the stone of which St. Luke's was built. So gradual the decay had been that, as time's changes in a face of life association, it had never been noticed. It happened that the Diocesan Surveyor spent a week-end with friends in the town. Unable to leave his professional eye at home he had carried it over a church or two of the district. At St. Luke's, startled, he had called for a hammer and a ladder. There followed the bringing in by the vicar and churchwardens of an architect of the surveyor's recommendation. Calamitously thereafter came a report. The Parochial Church Council, the responsible authority for fabric repair, found itself faced with a provisional estimate for reconditioning throughout of some eight hundred pounds.

Building firms who should be invited to tender for the work were suggested by the architect. Pettersen's was not on his list. It was by the vicar's especial wish that he "as member of our own parish" was included. His tender, arriving with the rest, was not the lowest. Not recommending him before, the architect had no reason to do so now. The council, through its chairman, the vicar, awarded the contract to one of his Upton Spring's rivals.

"I knew it," declared Pettersen, dark, eyes and teeth aflash, to his friends. "I'll even with him."

His reference was not to his successful rival. For evening with a vicar there is no more favorable vantage ground than membership of his Parochial Church Council. To secure it may be sufficiently easy. Pettersen beat up his friends in the parish. He entered his name, they entered their names, on that Electoral Roll with which, as giving them a voice in the administration of their church, the vicar, his parishioners said, was "for ever pestering you." He had friends who already were on the roll. At the next Annual Parochial Church Meeting he was elected a member of the council.

Never dreaming that he was being as it were hoist with his own petard, the vicar had spoken to Laura with high pleasure of the sudden little influx on to the roll. He warmly welcomed Pettersen on to the council. Characteristically believing his designs to be suspected and their discovery thus dissembled Pettersen received the congratulations much as a badger might attend the friendly advances of a guileful terrier. He soon showed himself out to give trouble. His criticism of the church dress sermon was an instance in point.

4

Mr. Harkness, the wealthy newcomer whose interest in St. Luke's was to flow into Pettersen's interest, had no grudge against the vicar. Far from it, he had for him, on the contrary, the odd liking, a sort of amused wonder, which sometimes will be aroused in one walk of life by crossing another incomparably different.

On the forest outskirts of the parish of St. Luke's there had been completed, some six months before Ruth's return home, a residence which to the dullest intelligence trumpeted abundance of means and stint of refinement. Turreted here, cupola'd there, approached by massy iron gates in which writhed strange devices picked out in gilt, The Towers, as it called itself, looked like an aberration between a Turkish baths and a pantomime castle. Learning that occupation had been taken, observing for himself indeed the pair of twenty-foot cars, one yellow one green, that now prowled about the entrance, the vicar, first inscribing "Mr. J. Harkness, The Towers," on a file of his card index of parishioners, duly called. The door was opened to him by a manservant conspicuous by an oddly flattened nose, very thick ears and very large hands.

"Mr. Harkness at home?" pleasantly inquired the vicar, extending a visiting card.

The man had appeared a degree more taken aback, presumably at sight of a clergyman, than had been his inquirer at an appearance so unlike that of the conventional footman or butler. He contracted heavy brows above the card, then looked inaccommodatingly upon the visitor.

"What's it for?" he inquired.

"Why, to, to take to your master," explained the vicar, surprised.

"I know," breathed the man heavily, "what to do with cards. What's the business of it, I'm asking?"

Some would have put him sharply in his place. Some would have been disagreeably discouraged. The vicar smiled blandly. "The business? Why, it's a call; just a call, you know. I'm the vicar of the parish."

"If it's subscriptions," announced the other, adding his own corollary to this explanation, "Mr. Harkness don't give 'em, not at the door."

"It's just a call," smiled the vicar.

Fingering the card, the man took a look at the back of it as if for help. Finding none, "Well, I don't know, bothered if I do," he admitted.

"Perhaps if you took in the card," amiably suggested the vicar.

With customary simplicity relating all this afterwards to Laura, "At that," he told, "the poor fellow, for whom really I felt very sorry, very doubtfully admitted me. I was taken into a quite enormous hall, hung all round with stag heads and weapons and things, and with two very tall armored figures standing in it, holding lances, dear, and into a room almost as big as my study but used, I think, as a kind of cloak-room; all pegs, you know, with some coats on them, but with a large table and chairs; in any other house it would have been quite a dining-room, except for the pegs, of course. And then in about five minutes, no, three perhaps, the man reappeared, *much* more obliging, and took me into a positively immense room, the drawing-room as I would have called it except for a large marble-topped sort of arrangement covered with decanters and things, but referred to by Mr. Harkness, and most rightly, as the salon."

It was in this impressive apartment that the creator and

owner of these palatial surroundings presented himself as, surprisingly even to the vicar who prejudged no man, a quiet, kindly faced, bald, gold-rim-spectacled little person in a neat blue suit and sedate brown tie. Suavely greeting his visitor, he apologized for his delay in appearing. He had been in his hot-houses, he explained, when the house telephone had told him of the arrival; and he opened then a turn of speech as odd, having regard to his mild appearance, as was his mild appearance having regard to his style of residence.

"And then to have stood you," he continued his apology, "in that silver ring instead of passing you in here, into Tatts so to say, where he might have seen you'd got the check to, I'm ashamed for that chap of mine, Mr. Vicar, straight I am."

Grasping from this only the fact that the manservant was in reproof, the vicar hastened to excuse him.

"Oh, but he was civility itself, I assure you, Mr. Harkness. He wasn't, I thought, very familiar with clerical dress and didn't quite know—"

"First time in his life," agreed Mr. Harkness, "he's ever spoken to anyone riding in your colors, I'll lay the odds. He's a— But what'll you take, Mr. Vicar, excusing my manners," he broke off, gesturing as he did so towards the console-table described to Laura as a marble-topped sort of arrangement, drink ladened.

"Nothing, nothing indeed," replied the vicar, involuntarily raising a deprecating hand between himself and the species of private bar.

"Smoke?" inquired Mr. Harkness, touching a cedar-wood cabinet beside the table in some secret way so that a shutter moved smoothly up its face revealing trays of cigars one above the other, each tray labeled.

"Indeed no."

A movement of his host's fingers caused the shutter now to move smoothly downwards.

"Neat?" suggested Mr. Harkness, observing the rounded eyes with which these processes had been watched.

"Very," assented the vicar, speaking with the something lost note of one entirely unaccustomed to be offered drinks and cigars at three o'clock in the afternoon.

"T.T. and non-smoker myself," chattily affirmed Mr. Harkness, "outside the betting though that is in my line of country. Sit down, Mr. Vicar, do. What was I telling you when I offered you to have one? Ah, that man of mine; he's new to the course as butler, y'know; he's a pug."

"A pug?" queried the vicar, eyes newly round.

"That's right," nodded Mr. Harkness, and discerning then that his visitor was not perhaps entirely at rights in the matter, "a bruiser," he explained.

"A bruiser?" The vicar's eyes were wide.

"Ah, you're down the course, I see," genially smiled Mr. Harkness, "and natural, no doubt. Why, when I say pug, Mr. Vicar, and bruiser, boxer I mean, fighter, sparring partner, you follow me? I'd a bunch of 'em about me in my business one time; had to, y'know."

"A—a bunch of boxers?" inquired the vicar, enormously mystified. "Might I ask, am I very rude, I do sincerely trust not, what *is* your business, Mr. Harkness?"

It was the other's turn to show round eyes. "Me? Why, I'm Jack Harkness."

"Jack Harkness?" The tone of the echo showed the echoer no wiser.

"You're telling me," inquired Mr. Harkness wonderingly, "that you've never heard of Jack Harkness?" He leant forward as one gazing incredulously upon a defiance of natural law. "You're never going to tell me, Mr. Vicar, that you've never seen in your paper, and I'll lay the field whatever it is you read, bar none, that you've never seen advertisements of Hark Forrard and Co.; 'Jack Harkness And No Limit' down in the corner?"

Profoundly distressed in this apparent committal of a social enormity the vicar clutched anxiously at what defense a dim recollection might offer. "I really must admit—" apologetically he hesitated. "I can say that I do fancy I have seen the name Hark Forrard in advertisements. Yes, I feel sure I have. I have associated it, I am afraid, with hunting —it is, I believe, a hunting term—which is entirely without interest to me, and what may have appeared down, as you say, in the corner of the advertisement, I am afraid that stupidly I have never read. I really—"

Mr. Harkness, sitting back relieved, waved friendliest dismissal of the shortcoming. "Ah, nothing to apologize for, my dear Mr. Vicar," he made assurance. "You're a bit down the course as to its being hunting, though we're ready, of course, to cover the hunt meetings, S.P. What we are as a matter of fact, what Jack Harkness stands for from here to Australia and back again, is the biggest firm of commission agents in the world."

Impressed but uninformed, "Commission agents?" the vicar questioned.

"Bookmakers."

The vicar put hands to the sides of his chair. "Bookmakers? You're a—a betting bookmaker?"

Mr. Harkness laughed comfortably. "I'll say I am."

The vicar stared, speechless.

"I never," he told Laura, "was more completely astonished in all my life." His dumbfoundedness was in no degree due, as conceivably in certain of his cloth it might have been, to finding himself on chatty terms with one of a profession beyond the pale. Every man was to him his brother man. His astonishment was due to his life-long conception of a bookmaker as a cartoonist's bookmaker, a vast crimson-faced man in draught-board checks, banded cigar in one hand, a champagne glass in the other. That this sedately dressed, quiet-voiced, spectacled little teetotaler—"My dear, I was literally astounded. I don't know what he must have thought of me."

What, thus dumbly stared upon, Mr. Harkness thought was evidenced in fact by what most pleasantly he said.

"You'll not hold with that, no doubt," he smiled, "book-making?"

"Well, you won't mind my telling you, I'm sure," said the vicar, recovering himself, "that I cannot but regard betting as one of our greatest, one of our very greatest national evils—"

"Naturally you can't," courteously agreed Mr. Harkness, "naturally, Mr. Vicar."

"Thank you. But that's not the slightest reason, not the slightest, why I shall not always think of you just as of any other of my parishioners; and you, I do hope, always will think of me as your vicar."

"You're on a winning horse I will," declared the book-maker. He extended a hand in genial pledge. The vicar, highly joyed, grasped it warmly, and rising, took with it the opportunity to leave.

"And perhaps," he said, as they toured the wide spaces of The Towers towards the hall door, "I may have the great pleasure of seeing you in my church sometimes?"

Mr. Harkness regretfully posted himself among the non-starters in that event. "I work mighty hard all the week," he explained, "and Sundays I like to rest abed and then take a run in my car and a bit of golf and that. That's what I've put up this little place for. And my good lady and my boy and girl they're the same, I'm afraid. But you're my vicar, all in, run or not; first time ever I've nominated one either;

and any week-end you or your good lady's passing and care
to drop in for one, or any time there's any little subscriptions
you're making a book on—good-by, Mr. Vicar, *good*-by."

The vicar took himself home as happy as ever he had been
after an addition to those over whom his shepherd gaze
benevolently would roam when nightly he thought in God
of his flock. He liked Mr. Harkness. He prospected eagerly
hopes of seeing him in St. Luke's.

It was through the bookmaker, nevertheless, that, not
long afterwards, he was to find himself at loggerheads,
grievously distressing him, with a considerable body of
parish opinion, Pettersen led.

5

The raising of the funds required to wipe out the debt
incurred by the reconditioning of the decayed stone work
was made, not long after Mr. Pettersen's election to the
council, the duty of a sub-committee, the vicar, because of
the importance of the matter, its chairman. Pettersen was
one of the first to offer himself for membership. This much
pleased the vicar. Conscious even by then of the persistence
of the builder's carpings he foresaw here opportunity of
evoking a friendlier spirit. Pettersen no doubt would have
an especial zeal in seeing that a building debt was discharged. They could not but work amicably together.

The first meeting of the sub-committee disabused his
hopes. There would be a Gift Day, of course, the vicar proposed. He felt, too, that, in this first year at all events of the
fund-raising campaign, the proceeds of the annual sale of
work must be allocated to the purpose.

"You won't like that, vicar," suggested a member.

"I shall not indeed," smiled the vicar, and sighed.

Everybody knew why. The sale of work, ever since the

vicar first instituted it, had been held exclusively in aid of his pet enthusiasm, the mission field. Unpretentious, not seeking to attract attendance from outside the parish, the annual function undeniably was what Mr. Pettersen, later in the proceedings, was to stigmatize a one-horse show. Anxious above all that its contribution to mission work should be, as it were, the personal gift of persons actively interested, the vicar discouraged for it the term "Bazaar" together with all the subsidiary features which commonly that term connotes. He felt, he was fond of saying, that the proceeds of time and thought given to handiwork definitely for the sale went to their object with higher blessing than those of extemporized side-shows.

"Well, let's make sure," broke in Mr. Pettersen, "that you don't have to let down your missions by giving up the sale of work to the debt more times than you *will* like."

He came out with this explosively, as if he had been stung; defiantly, as if he had been challenged. The vicar bent towards him invitingly.

"Let us indeed, Mr. Pettersen—if we can. How—?"

Blackness, teeth and eyes in full discharge, "Why, by making of it this time," declared Pettersen, "a proper slap-up bazaar, not just the old ladies' and schoolgirls' collection of crochet and tea-cosies and that like of gimcracks it commonly is. People's got no use for that sort of thing nowadays. Queen Victoria's dead and all that like of 'sales of work' dead with her. What people wants today," vehemently continued the builder, sparking this way and that from face to face about him, "is something with a bit of go in it an' a chance of picking up a shilling where you put down sixpence, fun-fair machines and raffles and that. Wash out this sale of work name for it and these tupp'ny little handbills in people's windows. Poster it all over the town as 'Bazaar and Fun Fair,' lucky programs, raffles and all that, and you'll bring all the town and take all the town's money. That's what I say. Now?"

He glared defiantly upon the vicar. Murmurs of assent on the one side, doubtful shakings of heads on the other (equally augmentive of the builder's heat) now directed themselves also towards the opinion of the chair.

"Well, that's a first suggestion," amiably pronounced the vicar, "to make our sale of work something bigger than it's ever been yet, and with that I'm sure we all cordially agree. Mr. Pettersen"—he smiled towards the builder—"has been perhaps a little hard on our usual little displays; but we've never professed them, Mr. Pettersen, to be more than pleasant little family sort of affairs, and all our regular workers would take your criticisms, as I do, in the friendly spirit in which I know you intend them. I agree, though in a way I should regret it, that bazaar might be the better title for a bigger effort; and if we feel that we have risen to the heights of a really attractive bazaar I agree, too, that we should consider circularizing the whole town instead of the parish only. Those are just the ideas that we are here to discuss and we are all most grateful to Mr. Pettersen for giving us a lead on them. There's just the point of a fun-fair side. You made me for a moment a little anxious there, Mr. Pettersen. You weren't meaning, were you, these spinning wheels and rolling penny boards which—?"

Pettersen's facial batteries, thinly masked during this hearing, sprang into open view. "Certainly I was."

The vicar shook his head pleasantly. "Oh, no, no, no, really."

"Why not?"

The shot was plumb, raspingly discourteous. The vicar's cheeks pinked but he smiled his answer. "Why, because imagine them, Mr. Pettersen, at a church bazaar. They're open gambling."

"Gambling! Have you ever seen 'em?"

"Yes, indeed, quite recently, at the Cottage Hospital bazaar at the Assembly Rooms."

"Ah," Pettersen flashed. "There you are then. What's good for one bazaar's good for another."

The vicar's head renewed its kindly negation. "No, no, Mr. Pettersen; at a lay bazaar those devices are admissible perhaps, though even there, in my opinion, not desirable. But at a church bazaar quite, quite unthinkable." He glanced about the table at which they sat. "All here, I know, will tell you so."

"Tell me so! Naming no names, not what there's the slightest shame to it, there's members here I saw at the hospital fun-fair machines, so now! Will you put it to the vote?"

The vicar knew no answer to wrath but the soft answer which not always turns it away. "Really, it's not a question for a vote," he said suavely. "Believe me, Mr. Pettersen, it's scarcely even a question calling for my decision. It goes without saying that any form of gambling—"

"I agree," "I agree," came voices. "The vicar's perfectly right, Mr. Pettersen."

The builder took defeat in his type's approved manner. "Very well then, I'm put in the wrong," his bared teeth emitted. "I've give up my time to come here help the council wipe out its debt, and the vicar's put me in the wrong, and that's that. I'll be told next, I'd not be surprised, that raffles aren't to taste neither."

"Ah, raffles," voiced a member approvingly, "that's different."

"Yes, now, a good raffle or two," chimed in another.

Pettersen had kept his burning gaze upon the chair. He saw the vicar, his smile gone, blink unhappily. *"If* permitted," he rasped.

"Really I am most sorry." The vicar moved uncomfortably, uncomfortably repeated himself. "Really I am most sorry, Mr. Pettersen, to appear to run counter to your ideas, but raffles are not, I am afraid, permissible. Quite definitely they are disapproved of by the great majority of church opinion. Quite definitely, as a means especially of furthering church work, they—"

"One moment, please," requested Pettersen, aggressively polite. "I've come here tonight with an offer, and my offer I beg leave to make before it's put out of my mouth. Here's my offer, generous or not it's for others to say. I offer to put up for raffle for our bazaar whatever of a choice this committee here assembled may choose. I'll raffle a sewing-machine or a ladies' or gents' super-grade cycle or a portable wireless or for that matter anything to equal cash value. That's what I've come prepared to do and that's what, as clearly heard, I've done."

He flashed his gaze about the company. Nods of commendation, murmurs of approving interest, heightened the glare with which then he carried it to the vicar.

Whether he had come to the meeting gift in hand as he had intimated or, on the spur, had produced it, as the dog in the elegy its madness, to gain some private end, was a question with which a sharper chairman might with self-advantage have met the glare. The vicar sought self-advantage never. His thought here, as always, was solely of the other's feelings. His eyes unhappy, his voice reluctant, "Most appreciatively, Mr. Pettersen," he said, "I hear your most generous offer, most regretfully I cannot but decline it. If, in the same generous spirit, you will give a little thought to the matter, you will see, I am sure, that raffles, however innocently participated in, are nevertheless clearly a form of chance, a lottery just as much as this Irish Sweepstake against which the Post Office is now taking action is a lottery." He glanced about the table. "I am agreed with, I'm sure."

On the whole he was, not warmly however. The general feeling was that raffles were entirely harmless, thorough good fun, highly attractive, but—"Since you put it like that, vicar"—no doubt out of place at a church bazaar. Pettersen took no part in these exchanges. He sat drawn rigidly back in his chair, savagery in chains. When "Since you put it like that" tailed off the matter, the vicar gave kindly lead to a general look towards him for his compliance. His offer had made him the protagonist of the question. It was felt his due that his endorsement should be asked.

He gave it with head still pressed rigidly against the high back of his chair. "Twice I've been put wrong," he delivered, "although well meaning and thinking to do right. Two slaps in the face I've had. Hereinafter I'll best keep my mouth shut."

Shut he kept it for the remainder of the sitting. At following meetings of the sub-committee, whensoever responses to the efforts to raise the funds enabled him to imply "What can you expect?" vindictively he opened it. Opportunity of the kind was not wanting. The parish had grown. Support of the needs of its church had not grown with it. That its church was one of its bounden interests was far from being of general recognition. To a considerable proportion of its homes the notion of contributing to any appeal of St. Luke's except, with perfunctory coin, its offertory bags, was as outside normal thought as was, to a proportion as considerable, the idea of going to church at all. The parish contributed its quota, handsomely and regularly, to the cinemas, garages, creature comfort and luxury shops of Upton Springs; of its church's quota to the diocesan funds half of it had not so much as heard. From pew-rents, affecting the vicar's income, to Sunday collections, affecting his church's activities, a gradual falling off marked the yearly balances. When it came to Gift Days and the like for raising new funds for a new purpose enthusiastic response was to seek. In two years from the day of the inauspicious first meeting of the sub-committee but some four hundred pounds had come to hand.

It was in this position of the efforts to raise the required sum that Pettersen's intention to keep his mouth shut, observed by using it only to bite, was dramatically announced to be foregone. A full meeting of the council was due. Members read in the agenda "Announcement by Mr. Pettersen regarding the fabric reconditioning debt fund." When it came to be made those who were also members of the sub-committee realized that their own first meeting had been precisely a miniature rendering of a major sensation.

6

The builder's sole disclosure as to the terms of his announcement had been a sufficient portentousness in regard to it to persuade the secretary to give it place in the agenda. It stood last on the paper. He opened it with words that caused a lively stir of attention. "I have pleasure in announcing that I have had the good fortune to be the means of obtaining a donation to the fabric reconditioning fund which wipes out the entire debt."

That he had brought with him no bushel under which to hide the light of his own part in this act of munificence he proceeded to show. The "I's" in his story were as prominent as were, during their flashes while he spoke of the unenterprise that had yet been shown, the eyes in his head. A wealthy gentleman, he said, had recently come to reside among them. Better aware of the quality of the speaker's professional work than were perhaps some (flashings towards the vicar) this gentleman had employed him in some outbuilding requirements at his residence. Most friendly relations had arisen between the parties. Mr. Pettersen, as it appeared, "stepped in regular for a glass of wine." Over one such glass the wealthy newcomer had confided to the builder his wish to pay his footing in the place. Did Mr. Pettersen know of any quarters wherein this would be welcomed?

"Did I?" rhetorically inquired Pettersen of his expectant audience. "Many quarters I might have named, having had interests in this town dating back further than perhaps am credited with in certain quarters. One I knew, however, which, though rebuffed more than once in my efforts to help it, I let stand first with me. I mean St. Luke's; and St. Luke's, as being this gentleman's parish church and badly in debt on a fabric outlay, I told him straight."

He cleared his throat impressively. "Ladies and gentlemen, Mr. Harkness, to name the donor, Mr. Jack Harkness of The Towers, has empowered me to inform the vicar that he will have great pleasure in handing him a check in total discharge of the fabric fund debt, five hundred pounds, odd shillings and pence."

The sensation, the congratulations mutual and particular, were yet in full tide when it was noticed that the look upon the vicar's face was astonishingly the reverse of that on every face before him. With his churchwardens and curate, the council secretary and treasurer, he sat a table facing the chairs which accommodated the general members. He did not always rise for the purpose of speaking. He was risen now. Mystified, all saw that his look was gravely troubled. The hubbub of sensation dropped, then ceased abruptly.

"But, Mr. Pettersen," the vicar spoke, his voice a half-toned mingle of concern and doubt, "but, Mr. Pettersen, do you know, are you aware, what Mr. Harkness is?"

Pettersen also had spoken standing. He had remained

standing, figure of acclamation. He had but just seated himself as the vicar spoke. Now he sprung from his seat, as Athene from the head of Zeus, fully armed: "What he *is?*"

"What his profession is, how he makes his money?"

"He's a commission agent."

"He's a bookmaker."

"What of it?"

It could be said that every jaw hung dropped. Of what the vicar was going to make of it an intuition presented itself to every mind. It stood in each as before the eyes suddenly might stand upon the threshold a spectral figure, its purpose prickingly surmised, about to declare itself. Where had been the ozone of jubilation in the air now was the oppression of a bated wonder.

"This has come very suddenly," nervously the vicar spoke. "I somehow sense a feeling, I hope I may be wrong, not entirely in sympathy with what I have to say. My immediate feeling is that St. Luke's cannot benefit itself by this means. My instinctive feeling is that it cannot accept, as would happen, into its very stones, money which, however generously intended, is the direct proceeds of one of the great national evils against which the Church sets its face."

From every breast the suspended wonder discharged itself audibly in a single expiration. It took shape then in that stir, in that murmur, in those movements and in those half-caught tones of disquiet which a past journalistic practice conveniently interpolated in reports as "(sensation)". The vicar had expressed hope of incorrectness in his sensing of the feeling of the assembly. In those disturbed sounds he knew that he had sensed it aright. He dropped his eyes to his churchwardens. People's warden Mr. Brian Eldon's pose showed clearly that he saw something in it, whether in the sensation or in the point which had aroused it was not to be detected. Mr. Fingest, elbow on table, hand feverishly to forehead, was in excited whisper at the secretary who sat beside him.

Pettersen had not sat down. "Will you tell that," stridently his demand came, detonation as it were of the murmurs, "to Mr. Harkness, to his face?"

• "Certainly I will," the vicar answered. "I have already met him. I will explain to him—"

"Ah, and he'll like to be told, I don't think, that his money's dirt." The builder flashed stimulating eyes about the gathering. "If he is so to be told?" he declaimed. "I come here with news I thought would make a nice hum, seems to me there's a nicer going to be made!" Assenting sounds encouraging him he hotly faced again towards the table. "I know, I reckon, what's thought down here amongst fellow members, perhaps—"

A woman member stood up. "We don't all, I think, want Mr. Pettersen to be spokesman for us." Her accents had the suggestion of an intentional refinement. Pettersen took them with a flush. Only momentarily, however, was he discomforted by them. "Personally I was delighted," they continued, "to hear what he had to tell us and taken aback, I am afraid, by the vicar's view. Perhaps we might hear what the churchwardens think."

Not in the vicar's favor, the interposition gave him, however, at least a means towards that authority of chairmanship in which he was lacking.

"Yes, I think, Mr. Pettersen," he was able to say, "if we both sat down and heard, perhaps our wardens first, and then all wishing to speak—"

He set the example. Pettersen, all dark nods and steely glitter, followed it. The vicar found Mr. Fingest's and Mr. Eldon's heads against his own in swift counsel, given and sought. Realization of the seriousness of the issue sobered the characteristics of their temperaments. Mr. Fingest's hand was to his forehead but in concern not in thrill. Mr. Eldon's head was towards his shoulder but what, thus perched, it saw it now did not hide. Whispering with the vicar, both questioned his attitude. Finding him assured in it, both, as each in turn addressed the meeting, gave him, as always, their loyal support. This was a question of principle, they said. Whatever might be the individual view of individual members of the council, matters of principle might safely be left to the vicar, must, they thought, be so left and corporately supported. The secretary contributed, a shade dully, "I agree"; the treasurer, when his turn might have come, presented himself apparently lost in pencil and paper calculations; Mr. Sladd, funereal behind his heavy spectacles, affirmed, as heavily as briefly, that other view than the vicar's was unthinkable.

Then began the offensive. If among the general members there was any agreement with the vicar's attitude it was nowhere so assured of itself as to find expression. It preferred to hear what others had to say and incisively it was told. In summary the arguments ranged themselves under two leads. If this offered gift, said the more moderately voiced of these, had come from Mr. Harkness in, so to say, his professional capacity, much might be urged against its acceptance. A check from Hark Forrard & Co., name notorious, well might be looked at askance in St. Luke's banking account. But it had not thus come. It came from Mr. Harkness in his private capacity as a resident in Upton Springs and as a parishioner. Was the man not to be allowed a private life? Was his vicar, of all people in the world, to deny it to him?

The vicar was sitting with his hands tightly clasped before him. He saw now, though not even yet so clearly as in coming days he was to see, the strength of the feeling he had aroused. His pained eyes showed it. The whiteness beneath the pressure of his finger-tips upon the backs of his hand revealed it.

A man's private monies, gently he made reply, were not disassociable from their public earning. To take from a man's one hand what principle refused to take from his other was, quietly but firmly he declared, an hypocrisy. To accept into the House of God under one name what would not be accepted into it under another surely was worse than an hypocrisy.

As at advancing tide mutteringly the waves draw back to surge again, so opinion in the body of the hall mutteringly discussed this view, then, on its second leading argument, surged anew.

This second lead was Pettersen's. Its supporters heard it, as himself he delivered it, with a "That's got you" air. If Mr. Harkness's big offer was dirt, triumphantly challenged Pettersen, then so of course must be his small offerings. If he attended service one Sunday at St. Luke's, were the sidesmen to be instructed not to pass the offertory bag to him?

As a House of Commons report would have said "(laughter, cheers)".

The vicar, fingers more tightly pressing, eyes more pained, could only weakly shake his head. "I have expressly told Mr. Harkness that I hope to see him at our services. The case then would be entirely different. No impulse bids us ask of each coin in our offertories how it came to be there. They are raised before the altar as one, the widow's mite with the unmissed note, the hardly earned with the easily come by. Here we are offered to be relieved of our privilege of rebuilding to the glory of God by money which we know came to its would-be donor in wide reverse of any thought of God." He bent forward a working face. "Indeed, indeed it is a different thing."

But the whole issue of the matter, together with its implications of the vicar's future relations, not with the council alone but widely in the parish, came with the suggestion and with the reply with which at length the meeting closed.

"Well, I'll beg leave," flashingly enunciated Pettersen, "to bring the point to this. The council's responsible for this debt, not the vicar. We're to foot the bill, not him. Who pays the piper calls the tune, so I've heard. We're offered the money, it's for us, I lay down, to say if we choose to take it."

"Hear, hear," acclaimed many voices. "I agree." "Yes, yes." "That's surely plain."

The vicar said very quietly, "Mr. Pettersen, forgive me, no; it is not the council, I think, to whom the money is offered. You said when announcing it that it was to me that Mr. Harkness was generously ready to hand a check."

Pettersen tossed a hand in scoffing dismissal. "That's all one to him who he makes out his check to. Pay his footing in the place, that was his words to me. Vicar or Parochial Church Council, what's the odds to him?"

The vicar raised his tightly locked hands as though, expressive of his emotions, they moved in their own pain. "But I shall go to him after the meeting," he said, "and explain to him that his check, to whomever made, cannot be accepted."

Again was the expiration of pent emotions in one single sound. Here was deadlock. Ultimatum. The last item on the agenda quite clearly had reached its end. There was a drawing in of feet, a reaching about for coats and hats.

Last word, nevertheless, was with Pettersen. As the meeting dispersed, "Wait to see what the parish says to it," violently he flung out across the heads. "Wait to see what they'll give to the fund when they hear one of theirselves has offered the whole sum and been insulted."

The vicar, all others gone but three, yet sat on in his place, hands yet clasped before him, head bowed above them. The two churchwardens, appreciating presently a wish to be left, went also. The curate put on his coat, looked, hesitated, then spoke.

"Is there anything I can do, vicar?"

The vicar raised eyes that regarded but did not appear to see his questioner.

"I have been so anxious to draw out that man's friendship," he said.

Five

WHAT the parish had to say to it was in full first flood when Ruth, through, as she declared, with all that had drawn her from home, came back to the vicarage. Its reception of the vicar's attitude to Mr. Harkness's offer bore out Pettersen's warning. Mr. Harkness's own reception of it on the other hand did not.

"That's quite all right, Mr. Vicar," immediately and heartily declared the bookmaker when the priest's stammered explanation had made end. "It's your stable and you've the perfect right, same as every owner, not to run your colt for the stakes if you find the weight not to your liking. That's quite all right. Don't you apologize. If you think I'm going to lay an objection before the stewards because you've put a monkey back into my pocket you're thinking me the first man in racing that ever did; and if you fancy I'm going to lash out behind because you don't like the colors in my saddle you've studied the form all wrong. I respect you for it. You've said to me, 'Jack,' you've said, 'I like you as a man—'"

"I do indeed, Mr. Harkness," here declared the vicar, no less moved by these asseverations because their diction was largely unintelligible to him. "I do indeed."

"And me you," agreeably rejoined Mr. Harkness. "'I like you as a man,' you've said, 'but my trade don't like your trade,' same as many a man's stomach," picturesquely illustrated the bookmaker, "can't abide what his appetite is partial to, lobsters with me. 'My trade says your trade is rank poison,' you've said, 'and if I let my church feed oats out of

340

your bin, why, I'm nobbling the colt and selling the stable.'
That's what you've said, Mr. Vicar, and that's straight talk
and I respect it. You're sure you won't have one, not to keep
the night air out? Ah, you're T.T. same's me, I forgot.
Good-night, Mr. Vicar, *good*-night, and remember what I
say, that's quite all right."

With the parish it was as quite all wrong. It was ridiculous, said the parish, preposterous, monstrous. "Well, if
that's the way," said the parish, "the Church treats a good-
hearted chap, no wonder people have no use for it." "Publi-
cans and sinners!" exclaimed the parish, "they got different
treatment in the Bible if my memory serves me right." *"Have*
you heard the latest about the vicar?" inquired the parish.
"Isn't that just him all over? I've *never* heard such nonsense."

The *Gazette* in its brisk feature of local innuendoes arranged under the heading "A Little Bird Tells Me," gave
first place to "—That the vicar of one of our churches, badly
in need of funds, has refused a check to the whole amount
offered him by one of his parishioners. —That the parish
does not feel very proud of itself when meeting that parishioner. —That evidently the vicar doesn't think very much
of him. —That the parish isn't thinking very much of its
vicar."

Some little time earlier the churchwardens had circular-
ized an appeal for the fabric reconditioning fund, a form
for enclosing with donations attached by perforation to their
letter. Consciences in regard to such are frequently solved by
not tearing them up immediately but putting them aside
until, as with correspondence sufficiently long neglected,
response to them has gone by default. Several now were
hunted up. Their perforated attachments came to the vicar
endorsed, some anonymously, "The writer—", some with
open censure, "Mrs.——" or "Mr.——" in various renderings

of "—is glad to be able to understand that the full sum required has been offered and that donations are not, therefore, now required."

2

All this, new upon him, was why his heart kindled to the arrival of his Benjamin with that whelming gladness described by Laura in her letter to Hope Hubbard. Laura shared his troubles, Ruth rejoiced them away. The difference in effect upon him between wife and daughter was something as the difference between the grateful comfort of the fireside and the brisk exhilaration of the open. In Laura he browsed an old book, known and loved in every line; in Ruth he turned the crispness of a new, losing himself in gay and lovely fancies. With his wife he trod a fond familiar path, rosemary hedged; beneath his daughter's feet, the ways she led him, primroses ran. Laura was grafted into him, his life's complement; Ruth was offspring of his life, his heart's issue.

In the first flush of her return he would awake of a morning as a child awakes to realization of a birthday. "Ruth is here!" Before he was dressed actuality of her presence would touch him, quickening him. She would call to him from the garden. There she would be, blowing him a greeting kiss, holding up flowers. "For you!" Or she would tap on his door while he shaved. "Morning, dad. Slept well? Feeling fine? That's jolly good." When he came to breakfast, fresh and lovely as a rose she would greet him; kissing him between the caress of her hands on his cheeks; going out to the kitchen just before he was ready for his toast so that she might make it herself just to his liking; settling him afterwards to his work, seeing that he had all he wanted, helping him if she was able; through the day attending him, slipping her arm in his when they took walks. He could have found her as her companionship ministered to him in his Apocrypha: "She was ruddy through the perfection of her beauty, and her countenance was cheerful and right amiable."

One charm in particular that she threw over him Laura loved to see. However briefly separated from him in the occasions of the day she always greeted him as though for the day's first time. Looking up as he entered a room, seeing him as herself she made entry, encountering him in the street, waiting for him outside the church after a service, "Hullo, *dad!*" always was her greeting. Its message was, "Well, of all the unexpected and delicious delights—!" This is the loveliest message in human intercourse. We know it in perfection in a plane below us, in the inarticulate writhings and fawnings of our welcoming dog. We imagine it in perfection in a plane above, at reunion with loved spirits after death. The vicar knew it in perfection often in a day from his returned nestling. His face then would take Laura behind the years.

Herself Laura would catch sometimes in Ruth's face shades never presented to the vicar. In her father's company the daughter keyed her note as one keys it for an invalid. Worries are put down outside the sickroom door. Ruth saw the evening shadows about her father. Always she brought him the morning. Alone with her mother she would allow what secret thoughts she had to steal about her face. Once she suffered them to stand there while she spoke.

The occasion was one of the vicar's afternoons for his fortnightly round of calls at the council cottages estate. Mother and daughter were taking their tea in what was still called Minna's workroom. Silence had followed light conversation. "It's ever so darling of you, mum," Ruth suddenly broke into it, "never to ask me questions."

The topic of their previous words had been discussed with amusement. They had gone into the silence on a laugh. Her statement's irruption was entirely unheralded. "You can't tell," she went on, "how I've loved it that y u haven't."

"Darling, it's not because I haven't noticed—" Laura said softly.

"I know it isn't. I know you have. That's why I've loved you so for not asking. You've seen me looking a bit out of the party and you've wanted, I know, to give me a fold-up in your arms as you've done many a time on this very sofa after Philip, when we were kids, had hurled me out of one of his games."

The sofa was the battered old nursery relic whose long-suffering springs Philip's wild boundings had finally flattened. Minna had dragged it in here so that she could "sit with the children." Mother and daughter were on it now. The smile their eyes exchanged at memory of those hectic days quickened the bond between them which Ruth now was touching.

"I've had the fold-up, mum, just by sitting with you thinking my thoughts and knowing that your heart was giving it to me. That's the thing about you. One can just let oneself go and, without speaking, *feel* you, like waking chilly in the night and pulling up the eiderdown."

By that very nature which the tribute implied Laura made no actively responsive gesture. She said softly, "Let yourself go this time out loud, darling."

Ruth slightly straightened herself, a quick negative of her head with the motion. "No, mum. That's not done today. Life's different now from what it used to be. Letting yourself go the way you mean we call bleating, being sorry for yourself, sloppy, and asking someone else to slop back. Life's lived in the bone now, mum, all the soft stuff cut away. You can't bleat, make excuses for yourself, ask sympathy. In our code that's *the* offense."

"Do what you can do, darling; what the code lets you do."

Ruth put forward her left hand. "It lets me that," she said. She   cated the third finger. "Have you noticed that, mum?"

Above the knuckle at the place of her pointing was the mark a ring had made.

"Oh, darling, you've been engaged?"

Ruth's face twitched. "It was frightfully tight. We couldn't get it off to have it eased so we let it stay on." She gave a jet of a laugh. "He said it showed how inevitably we were bound. So when it had to come off it left a mark." She put the hand to her breast and met her mother's eyes. "And on my heart, mum."

"Oh, my Ruth."

The code that cut away all soft stuff stood violated in moisture down upon which eyelids squeezed. "Give me just one fold-up, mum."

She must have been three minutes with her face to her mother's breast, arms tenderly about her, five words her only utterance.

"He was rather brutish, mum."

Enfolding closer, the arms invited more but no more came. Disengaging herself she raised her lips, clung while she kissed, then with a quick motion sat up. "Dear mum," she smiled, misty, blinking. She sat back. "There, that's that. How about another cup of tea?"

3

She never again referred to the subject yet there was connection with it, Laura believed, in an announcement touching the use of her time with which, but a day or two later, she came out as suddenly as with that touching the wound in her heart. She had let slip some of the soft stuff. It looked rather as if she would evidence that the mark on her heart, as on her finger, was but skin deep; that she didn't really care.

Mother and daughter again were alone together. Ruth had just come in from some morning shopping. Putting down the provision basket, "Mum," abruptly she smilingly announced, "I'm going to click for a job of work."

"You are, dear?"

"Oh, down here, of course," Ruth reassured the implication of the question's tone. "I'm not leaving old dad again, don't fear. As what they call a dance hostess, mum. How do you think of it? Rather fun, eh?"

"As a dance hostess?" Laura had smiled happily at the daughterly solicitude. In her new question again was the inflection of a secondary meaning.

Ruth took it for unfamiliarity with the term. "That's what they call it, yes," she explained. "All the hotels where there's regular dancing have one now; finding people partners, sort of getting the starch off, you know."

"Oh, I know, yes," Laura said quickly. "That nice Miss Stevens was dance hostess at the Pump Room until she left to get married. Your father and I looked in at the Barnardo's Home Ball last year and thought how delightfully she did things and how pleasant it all was."

This was hurried over as if a preamble. In a different voice "Darling," Laura went on, "if this that you speak of is anything like that—"

Ruth nodded, gleaming. "It's exactly like that. It's what it is; dance hostess at the Pump Room."

"Oh, at the Pump Room."

The Pump Room Hotel, resort of College and Academy

parents, had its foundations, as its brochure told, in the rank and fashion of Upton Springs' first fame. It had a standing not only in the town but through the county. Laura's voice as she pronounced its name said all this so plainly and with so great relief that, "Why, where did you think?" Ruth could not but smile.

"I was afraid," Laura's tone took the note indicative of ground that might be delicate, "you might be meaning the A.O."

Ruth laughed. "Good mum, a dance hostess is a starch remover. If there's one thing you won't find at the A.O. it's starch."

She had not been to the road house since her return. It appeared now that had she wished to do so she would have met disapproval.

"Well, I'm glad anyway, dear," Laura said, "that it's not there." She stepped more boldly on to the ground she had mistrusted. "There's been a lot of talk about that place, Ruth, since you were last here. I've been going to speak to you about it only there's never been occasion. Your father, I know—"

"Oh, it's never," Ruth broke in, "worse than cheery. Goody-goodies have probably got peeved because the croquet lawns have been cut out. Anyway it's not in this picture. No, this is the toney old Pump Room, mum. You do agree it's rather jolly for me, don't you?"

"Darling, I do indeed."

"And dad will? He's rather yesterday about some things, old dad. *I* think he was, as I've told you, about that book-maker's money that's made beastly people so beastly to him."

Laura did not take up a point previously debated. "He won't be," she asserted, "about this, I'm sure. He greatly en-joyed that hour or two at the Barnardo dance. He spoke to

Miss Stevens about how pleasantly these things seemed to him to be done nowadays, and spoke to me afterwards about what a nice occupation it must be for a girl."

"Good old dad. Well, now he'll see Miss Brecque in the occupation."

"I'm sure he'll love to. But do tell me about it, darling; how you got it and—"

"I slid into it," Ruth declared, "off a banana skin, as you might say. The Pump Room has just recently broken out into a new ball-room, you know. I'd heard that a dance hostess was going to be engaged, presumably they've waited till the new room before filling up on this Miss Stevens, and when I was out just now I met old Spiers, the manager. You know him by sight of course; dapper little ass in spats and cuffs but not half bad. Well, I ogled him for the job in that languishing way I've got and that's about all there was to it. He's seen me back along hoofing it at the A.O.; which he did say was getting a bit near the hot part of the stove, by the way, and he leapt at me, if you'll believe it, like a famished tiger on a tethered goat. Two quid a week retaining fee, which includes Fridays and Sats. and general smelling round, and ten bob a night galas and such. It is rather a whiz, isn't it?"

The vicar, without using the term, agreed, when he heard of it, that it was. Laura had been right. She was right too on a ground for her belief in his approval which she had not mentioned to Ruth though she had inferred it. He thought, as did she, that the entertainment provided by the Pump Room appointment would remove wish for that of the A.O., now askance in responsible quarters. It gave him moreover, as it had given Laura, the occasion, not till then arisen, for expressing disapproval of the road house. It was in terms more direct than had been hers that he took it.

"I'm delighted, my dearest child," he concluded his approval of the hotel engagement, "delighted. To see you as happy as this has made you makes me only wish you might have such a satisfaction once a day." His face showed his delight.

"If a stained glass window chap could see you beaming as you are just because I'm beaming," Ruth declared, "he'd long to fit your dear face with a halo." She kissed him. "I certainly do love you, dad."

"Then you can promise me something," he smiled upon her. "Ruth, dear, you used to go a lot to that A.O. place. It's very badly spoken of now. Things go on there now, I'm told, rowdiness and all that, which make it far from being a place I would like to think of you at. I'd like you, dear, to promise not to go again."

"Oh, dad!"

His memory threw up one of those treasures which the subconscious mind will secrete through a lifetime. That exclamation in exactly that quick, low surprise, that startled discomforted pinkness of her face accompanying it, had been hers exactly when, munching her bread at tea as a tot of five, she had suddenly found a shed first tooth in her mouth.

He had laughed, all present at the table had laughed, then. He now had that poignancy of feeling which will twinge a parent when such a vision of a child's years of innocence comes at a crossing of its wishes when adult.

"Why, Ruth, dear, would you mind?"

He remembered her cautiously feeling for the tooth, her eyes charged with concern. Cautiously, as it were feeling her way through the concern which her expression showed, she spoke now.

"Yes, I would, dad. As a matter of fact I'd planned—when I was looking out my dance frocks just now before you came in—I'd planned to ring up someone for an evening there tonight or tomorrow before I start at the Pump Room on Friday."

He was unhappy. "I really would rather you didn't, Ruth."

They were in the study, he in his chair, she standing before him, the table between them. She took up an opened circular wrapping and with slow fingers tore it this way and that, meditating.

"I like the old A.O. I've had good fun there."

"You've done without it all this time, dear."

"I haven't felt like it, that's only why. I've not felt like going out at all since I came back. Now I do."

"You'll have the Pump Room."

The fragments she tore had reached now a thickness difficult of further shredding. "The Pump Room's just happened"—she tugged at the wad, then managed to effect a division—"to come into the scheme."

"The scheme?"

She cupped the pieces in her hands, her eyes upon them. As one looking upon a crystal and reading therefrom, "It's odd," slowly she said, "that last night I made up my mind to chuck lying low as I have been doing and to let myself go again. Of course it was the A.O. I thought of. Now comes this really rather absurd idea of yours, dad, just because of a few old goodies as I've explained to mum. It's the promise you want that gets me. I hate most frightfully not to do anything you ask me but—"

She looked up suddenly, eyes brightly loving. "Look, dad." The paper fragments streamed to the table through her hands. "There goes the A.O.—for now. I won't go there at once as I'd intended. Perhaps I never will. Perhaps the Pump Room will fill the bill and I won't want to. But it shall stay *perhaps*. We won't have a promise in the business. If I *should* want to—"

She had stretched her hands to him as she spoke. He took them, beaming. "Dear child."

The weeks moved on. Over at Dursley they were bearing Mary towards a stupefaction of which they gave her no hint. Here similarly, gliding that new reach into which the river of the vicar's life had turned in his joy in his daughter's company, they were in fact verging towards one of those cataracts over which it is out of still water that life so often plunges.

Six

D<small>AD, I TOLD</small> you that if ever I *should* want to go to the
A.O.—"

This was shortly after an Easter which had brought the
vicar happiness whelmingly greater than that abundance
which spiritually the season always brought him. It was the
first Easter since his refusal of Mr. Harkness's offer to liqui-
date the fabric debt. Ruth's home-coming having been at
the outset of the feeling thereby aroused in council and
parish, it was the first Easter also since her return. A sudden
suggestion of hers, made in Holy week, caused its particular
happiness.

The three were at breakfast. The vicar had received in his
mail the printer's proof of his monthly pastoral in the forth-
coming issue of the parish magazine. He had glanced over
it as it lay beside his plate, then, stopped eating, he had sat
looking before him, his face troubled. He often sat like that.
Mother and daughter exchanged by look their sympathy for
him. Laura drew the proof towards her, then, with another
meaning signal in her eyes, passed it to Ruth. It was the
thoughts arising out of the pastoral's conclusion which, both
knew, were troubling him. It drew attention to the heavy
debt still outstanding on account of the fabric repair. It gave
three sentences of considerate reference to the scant response
to the charge over recent months. It expressed hope in the
opportunity which would be offered by the fund Gift Day
in the following month. An outsider would have detected
a certain restraint in the lines. Those to whom they were
directed, knowing the circumstances of the position, would

read them as the writing of an embarrassed, a faltering pen. He who had written them was hearing in his imagination the comments with which they would be read.

Laura said, "Dearest, we know what you are thinking about. Don't let yourself start the day with it. People already are forgetting all that Harkness business. Soon it will be quite forgotten."

The vicar turned heavy eyes towards her. "If only there was something I could do."

It was then that Ruth turned the breakfast into an occasion of miracle.

"Dad," suddenly her fresh voice cried, "I've *got* an idea." He gave her his fond smile.

High import in her face. "There's a thing," she dazzled back, "it's just this minute come to me, that I do believe would squeeze their beastly sourness right out of them, even out of that cloak-and-dagger fox Pettersen. Dad, if you could afford it, *if* you could, why not announce that, 'for reasons which all will understand,' or some such words, you have decided to give the whole of your Easter offering to the debt fund?"

Laura's exclamation, her start back in her chair, her transfixed gaze at Ruth from that position, were the manifestations of one lost in wondering admiration. The vicar, even more deeply lost therein, gave the performance of one blinking his way out of a cave into sunshine. He was the first to speak. He said on a gasp, "Out of the mouth—!"

"Of babes and sucking-pigs," took up Ruth, immeasurably delighted at her scheme's reception.

The parody caused Laura's transfixion to break in a laugh. In gasp also, "Ruth, it's a wonderful idea," she then said, "wonderful."

"The, the *rightness* of it," declared the vicar. "I have deprived the parish of what was offered them, how utterly right that I should make amends."

Sparkling in her success, "You could afford to do it?" Ruth questioned her parents.

It meant, pew-rents fallen as they had, the loss of almost a quarter of their income. Laura cried, "Oh, we can, we shall, we must. Oh, dearest, the effect it will have on everybody, the change for you that it will make!"

The vicar responded to her, "My dear love, I look upon it as a guidance from above"—he stretched a hand to Ruth—"sent, my darling child, through you. Of course, of course we shall afford it."

"Ah, and don't forget, darlings," Ruth cried, patting the hand she still held, "that there's that two jimmy-o-goblins a week of mine to fill the hole, every brass of it."

Shaken heads, faces moved by her impulsive generosity, greeted her words. "My child, as if—", "Dear Ruth, who would hear—?"

"Oh, but there jolly well is," she persisted. "Who calls the tune pays the piper, didn't you say old cloak-and-dagger said to you? Well, he's right for here. I called this tune and I'm jolly well going to pay my bit for it. Jolly well!"

The vicar, yet shaking his head, got up. "I'd like just to go to my study," he said. He was wiping his eyes. He put his hand on his daughter's shoulder. "When I exclaimed 'Out of the mouth—' just now, I hadn't thought as fully into the significance of the verse as now I have. Dear child, and Laura, *'Out of the mouth of babes and sucklings,'* it goes, *'hast thou ordained strength . . . that thou mightest still the enemy and the avenger.'* Far be it from me ever to think of any of my people as enemies, but I do feel that this must surely still the impatience they quite naturally have had with me over this matter. God bless you, my child." He stooped and kissed her. "I bless God for bringing you back into my life."

2

It magnified the vicar's happiness in the plan, the vicarage's happiness in his, that the offering accruing to him by the services of Easter Day was handsomely above its average. This was not due, well he had reason to know, to esteem for him of his regular worshipers. It was due to the crowded congregations, begun with the very considerable gathering at even the six o'clock Celebration. These were composed of members of that very large body of persons, increasingly observable in England at that time and since, who, rarely if ever attending public worship on ordinary Sundays, make point of doing so at Easter and at Christmas. Their joint contributions enabled his use of his Easter offering to be in the sum of £137.

"For reasons which all will understand." A meeting of the council prior to the Easter Vestry fell in the following week. He used Ruth's very words in making his announcement. Not Ruth herself, not Laura, could have wished better of its reception. In the murmur of surprised appreciation that greeted it elements of self-reproach for hostility, of conscience pricked recognition of magnanimity, of doubt, thus pricked, that he should be allowed to take such step, were detectable. In the convenient generalizations of "Those of us who perhaps may have—", "Some of us, I think, will feel—", these elements were given open expression by supporters of the vote of thanks proposed by Mr. Fingest. Pettersen supported it. Cloak and dagger thrown aside at this disarming gesture by his chosen adversary, flashingly the builder challenged contradiction of his assertion that the vicar had shown himself "a white man." He went further. As the meeting was breaking up he came to the vicar with outstretched hand. "I reckon you've done an A1 thing, vicar, A1. I beg leave to take back all I've said, spoken when hot. Anything I can do now to help on what you've helped handsome you can rely on me to do."

The vicar trod home (to call Ruth to him for his fond embrace) with that grasp warm in his hand, those words tuneful in his ears. This was the man whose friendship he had tried so hard to win. In winning it out of the very pit whence had come Pettersen's bitterest animosity he would have said that his happiness arisen out of Ruth's idea had reached its full. Succeeding days brought more. Up and down the parish, the news becoming known, he sensed a warming of feeling towards himself. Donations to the debt fund came to him through the post. In one form or another, "A little contribution," significantly ran their accompanying letters, "in support of your own most generous action."

The very sermon he had preached on the day of his collection of the means of his action added to his felicity. For that also he had, he declared, Ruth to thank. When he had faced his crowded congregation, chairs necessitated up the aisle to accommodate it, it was because of Ruth's plan that he was able to be glad in the thought of the gift for his act of well-doing that must come to him from so great an assembly. That led him on to welcome in words not in his meditation when he had prepared his sermon the many whose rare occasion of public worship he knew it to be. Smilingly stating his gladness in seeing such numbers attending the greatest festival of the Church's year, he paid tribute to the feelings which caused such gatherings on that day and on Christmas Day.

"But may I suggest," he asked, "to those who are thus moved only on those two occasions how they would think of themselves if they manifested their love similarly, by but two visits a year, to a great earthly friend? If we have a great friend, one to whom we owe everything, and whose house is but a street or two away, do we visit him only on his birthday and on—how shall we make a parallel with Easter?—on the celebration of a supreme triumph of his career? Do we otherwise give him to feel that we 'never go near him' as the saying is . . . ?"

Laura, acutely sensing as always the reaction of those amongst whom she sat, told him at the happy lunch (Lent's passing in celebration) at which the three sat together, "Dearest, that was a most telling illustration. I could feel how it told. As we came away I heard people talking about it. We walked behind a jolly-looking red-faced man who looked as if—well, never mind that—who said to his wife, I suppose it was, 'Yes, that bit about only looking up a pal twice a year got me, I will say. I vote we jolly well have a cut in a bit oftener, what?' Didn't he, Ruth?"

"He did," Ruth affirmed. "Dad, it was a jolly good point. It fairly got people."

"It was your point," the vicar, utterly delighted, beamed. "It was through you, dear child, that the thought came to me."

The *Gazette,* too, thought it a jolly good point. Again, but this time headlined and editorially commented upon in spirit much different, the local paper gave prominence to a sermon by the vicar of St. Luke's. On the first and again on the second Sunday after Easter unmistakably he saw his congregation augmented by new faces. His happiness brimmed. Not in years had such tranquillity, such still water, stood about the vicarage.

"Dad, I told you that if I ever *should* want to go to the A.O.—"

How, his heart asked him, could he deny her? He had been seeking some means, some gift, some treat, in especial expression of the whelming of his love for her, in the happiness her presence, through God, had brought him. He had been looking in the shop windows, studying advertisements, consulting with Laura. Now herself she was presenting, not means of carrying out his intention, but opportunity merely of a negative favor, occasion not to withhold that which would give her pleasure, choice between causing a radiancy or a cloud upon the lovely face he loved so dearly.

How possibly deny her solely on scruples, hearsay founded, that the road house was not a place he would wish her to frequent? Could it harm her, one visit? Nothing could harm a spirit so caparisoned in its own loveliness as hers. Was his objection, indeed, based only in his own prejudices, not in thought of impossible effects on her? She had set her heart on the occasion. It was the A.O.'s annual Anniversary Gala Night. There was going to be, she had said, no end of a glorious show, a cabaret, Tom Turner's Band, spot-light prizes. She would go with the Turners, the two girls, their brother and two friends, the most decorous bunch, she declared the Turners to be, in all Upton Springs. "Dad, I've most faithfully kept the promise I never made. I've not been near the place. I'll not want to again, I don't suppose, in moons. Even now if you think No I'll take it no more hardly than go upstairs and quietly bung myself out of a window. But, oh, I *do* want you to say Yes."

He turned his look to Laura's look. Those thoughts upon his scruples met their counterpart in the eyes he met. And Laura's eyes, having exchanged them, danced.

"This once," she said.

The vicar turned to Ruth. "This once," he smiled.

He was recovering from the hug which exactly recalled to him the paralyzing hugs of her schoolday affections, Laura was undergoing her turn for it, when Ruth, yet hugging her mother, broke into the final ecstasy of her impassioned cries. "And now, before you can wink, I'm off to Lucy Grey's.

She's put aside for me a model frock, only over from Paris yesterday, that— Well, you wait till you see me in it."

"I will pay for it," declared the vicar.

She was speechless.

"Yes," beaming, he nodded. "Ever since Easter I've been trying to think out a present for you. It shall be this marvelous frock."

3

They saw her in it at eight o'clock on the evening of the Gala Night. Laura, a shade momentarily discomforted in her eyebrows but enchanted in the Eve behind her eyes, called its color harlequin blue. The vicar, sheerly dazzled at front view, exclaimed, when the vision of loveliness turned about, "But, my child, good gracious, you've forgotten to put on the back part of it!"

The vision rang with delight. "No, it's there all right, dad, large as life and *just* as natural. We wear our own backs now."

She fronted him again, dazzling him anew. He still was in his adoring ravishment by her when there burst in all the party which was to take her to her fun. One member of it had been sufficient, it could have been supposed, to fetch her out to the waiting cars. The evening was being met with so huge an excitement that to sit still when there was opportunity for movement apparently was beyond contrivance. All five, three young men, two girls, personable, noisy, gleepacked creatures, came crowding in. The vicar, had he not been previously informed, would never have suspected any of them of being members of the demurest family in Upton Springs. All were strangers to him and to Laura. Introductions were rattled off. Bewildered, he shook hands each time with the wrong person, twice with one. He found himself being carried with the throng for the purpose of speeding it off in its conveyances. Then he found his daughter's arm slipped in his and bewilderment went at her touch.

"You like them, dad?" she whispered. "Betty and Ann are pretty, aren't they?"

He accomplished one of his rare bright thoughts. "You make them both look very plain," he said, and loved her happy laugh, the squeeze her fingers gave his arm, as they passed outside.

April had filched the evening from June. Before the gate stood a saloon car in the driving, as it became apparent, of one of the attendant young men, and a long, low to ground, two-seated open sports model. This was the property of the Turner brother. "Oh, wizard! I hoped you would," Ruth cried when he announced that he had kept for her the seat beside him.

"But, darling, your hair," Laura made objection.

"Mum, look, I've brought this tulle for the very purpose."

She was about to step in when the vicar, for reason other than Laura's, joined the dissuasion. He had a nervous distrust of that type of car. However harmlessly he saw its kind standing outside a house or in a dealer's window he associated it always with the high speeds at which he had seen it driven. "Ruth, dear child," he hesitantly spoke, "I really do think that what your mother says— More than that, I really would much rather you didn't go in—"

There was embarrassment in speaking thus before the car's owner. Gratefully he saw that the young man was pleasantly regarding him. "Mr. Turner, to tell you the truth, you'll think me very stupid and all that, but your car, so low to the ground, you know; so dangerous, I stupidly always think—"

"Dad," Ruth broke in, "of course I'll go in the other."

"That's quite all right, sir," heartily accepted the owner. He was an athletically built, good-looking young man; in the Air Force, Ruth had said. "Absolutely all right. I'm jolly sorry not to chauffeur my dance partner but I absolutely understand how you feel. My old governor thinks just the same about the bus as you do. Hi, Bill," he called, "come and hunk your carcass in her, Ruth's going in the ladies' compartment."

Animatedly she stepped into the saloon car. There was a noisy drum of starting up, a chorusing of good-bys. Her bewitching face leaned to them from the window, an arm held out to them. "Darlings, have a snug evening."

The vicar caught her fingers. "Enjoy yourself, dearest child."

The moving car drew her grasp from his. As though he would bring back to him what now, as the road's bend was turned, was taken from his sight, he stood with the hand through which hers had passed still extended.

Laura, who had been waving, took his arm. "How lovely she looked. How excited she was."

4

She was still thus speaking, he something quiet, when they re-entered the hall. A little tremor shook him.

"Dearest, you found it cold?"

"One of those sudden shivers," he explained, "that's all," and immediately stood still, thinking, looking puzzled.

"Yes, dear, what? You've forgotten something?"

His brows were puckered, his look absent. "No, I seem to be remembering, half remembering something."

He was smiled at. "Tell me."

His responsive smile was abstracted as his look. "One of those odd feelings of having done a thing before."

Her eyes questioned interestedly. "Oh, I know the funny sort of thing you mean. But done what? What was it?"

Absorbedly, "Exactly the same thing," he said, "in exactly the same conditions."

"It is odd. But what to do with what—with seeing someone off? With coming in with me arm in arm?" She laughed. "With that shiver?"

He started out of his absorption. "Yes, the shiver." He held up an alert hand. "Yes, all of it—seeing Ruth off—coming in with you." He touched his forehead. "Someone with us," he groped. "Someone—it's coming back—*Minna!*"

She gave a little cry. "Minna, of course! Oh, but I know it now. It's come to me just as to you. It *has* happened before. It was seeing Ruth off her first morning to school. We watched her from sight, skipping along with Mary, turning to wave to us from the corner. Oh, I can see her now, the little angel; the three of us, dear Minna with us, standing at the gate just as now. And we came in just as now. And here, no, it was just at the doorway, I'm sure it was, you had one of those sudden shivers. All over again, the very things! Dear me, it's all so vivid now that I can remember the very words that were said. Dear Minna as we watched from the gate, *'That girl never has walked of herself'*—oh, can't you hear dear Minna's voice?—*'since she was born. That girl would skip to a funeral.'* And your own words, dearest; yours when that shiver came, *'Dear me,'* you said, *'how quiet the house seems without her.'*"

Laura had ejaculated all this; breathless as it were by the flooding up of the memories from within her. He had followed them, she had seen, as clear to him as to herself. On a crest of her animation she drew breath. "It's amazing," she exclaimed, "it's uncanny all to have come back so clearly just from—to me from when you said 'Minna'; to you from what exactly? What began it, I mean? Was it her waving to us from the car? Us standing waving to her? Our coming in together—?"

He had followed her memories but not with her thrill. He had listened to her, she had seen, rather as though it was to a remoteness that he was listening, had regarded her rather as though it was some recondite inwardness that in fact he watched. He said now somberly, "No, it was the shiver that brought it back. . . . Yes, the shiver." He gave her his hand. "Let us sit down together, my love. I feel a little, a little heavy, oppressed somehow."

5

In the night she awoke. Moonlight through the unshaded windows showed her all the room. Across the little space between their beds she saw that he lay on his back, his arms extended on the coverlet, his hands clasped. It was not the pose of slumber.

"Are you awake, dearest?"

"Yes, my love."

"Can't you sleep, dear?"

"I woke up. I'm listening for Ruth."

"For Ruth? Oh, dearest, you'll never drop off if you do that. What's the time, do you know?"

"It's a quarter to three."

Laura was startled. "To *three?* But she's in, surely? She said about one."

"I know she did. She isn't back." He turned towards her. "I'm worrying, Laura. I feel anxious."

Aroused as ever at his smallest concern, at once she raised herself on her elbow. "Oh, my dear, why ever should you be? You know what these things are. It was to be a special night."

"I'm anxious."

"Oh, too foolish, really. Whatever is there to be anxious about?"

"Cars. You hear of these things."

She knew by a twinge that his anxiety sought to communicate itself to her. She would not let it. "You absolutely never," she declared, "hear of them on a lovely night like this. Light as day and no traffic on the roads—this is the absolutely *safe* time for motoring, everyone says."

He was not to be lulled. "I wish I had asked her not to come back in that open car."

Again she felt the twinge. Again, for his sake, resolutely she stifled it. She leant over towards him, smiling. "Dearest, you're *determined* to be anxious. If that open car is all you're worrying about, you as good as did ask her. You asked her not to go in it and she didn't. She'll know you'll not wish her to come back in it and she won't. There!"

She stretched across a hand to him. He pressed it. But he did not speak.

"And how do you know," newly she rallied him, "that she's not in all this time and sound asleep?" She released his hand. "I'll go and look. *What* a laugh at you if—"

"She isn't. I went to see half an hour ago."

"Oh, Gordon!"

The thought of him getting from bed while she slept to visit Ruth's room, returning heavy with anxiety while still she slept, pained her. "Oh, you shouldn't have." Distressed, she was momentarily bereft of her cheery discouragements of his alarms. In the next second a distant sound gave her happy tongue.

"Oh, listen," her cry was. "A car—yes—coming? *What* did I tell you?"

They held their breaths. Rushingly the sound increased, came full towards the house, then changed its note to that of slowing down and braking.

"*What* did I tell you?"

Her bed was the closer to the window. She threw back the clothes.

"No, you stay, dear," she bade him as, sat up, he made to do likewise. "I'll look."

She peered through the pane. "Yes—stopping here—yes. It is the open car as it happens." Her voice dropped a note. "No, open but different, a black one it looks." Her voice bated. "Two men in it."

"Two men?"

She turned head and shoulders, thrusting an arm towards him, the hand's palm upwards, in motion of restraint. "Stay, dearest, stay. I'll tell you." She reverted her gaze. "Chauffeurs, I think; peaked caps. One's getting out. No, it's—"

She snapped her lips together. The car was a police car. The peak-capped man who had alighted was a policeman. His eyes scanned the house. They saw her and he made a saluting gesture and stooped to the gate latch.

She looked around again. "Stay, dearest; please stay. It's just some trouble with their car, I expect. I think they want something. I'll ask them."

She threw up the sash. The policeman was on the lawn beneath the window, looking up. By some dreadful intensity of vision that it seemed to her she had he stood in the moon's light focused as though it was along a search ray that she beheld him. He wore a sergeant's chevrons. He looked very young for a sergeant. Dear Gordon had been unable to see the point of the amusing aphorism that when policemen begin to look young to you it is a sign that you are beginning to grow old. He had a little fair mustache. His chin had a little cleft. A button of his tunic was unfastened. Her eyes pierced these things—for ever—upon her brain while her brain sought speech. She could feel the piercing. She could feel the writhing for words. She articulated, "Yes? Do you want anybody? Is anything—?"

The sergeant gave a little cough behind his hand. He had a white glove. It was turned back at the wrist. "I was wanting just a word, if I might, with—"

She thrust down a hand at him, its fingers wide, its import unmistakable. She called, "With me, yes, I am Mrs. Brecque." She leaned out and down towards him, her fingers, emphasizing their previous message, now urgently upon her lips. She sent a whisper. "Has anything happened?"

Rather absurdly he raised himself on tip-toe. "A bit of an accident, madam. Your daughter—"

She saw his eyes shift from her face. She felt a hand on her shoulder. "Let me come."

"Oh, Gordon." She gave him room.

The vicar spoke down: "An—accident—to—my—daughter?" His voice was from the back of his throat. He seemed to fetch the words up one by one.

The sergeant, rather absurdly again, said, "Good-morning, sir. I'm sorry, yes, bit of a hurt to the young lady in a bit of a car overturn, sir."

Producing the words singly as before, "Is—she—badly—hurt?"

The sergeant put his white-gloved hand to his mouth while he cleared an obstruction in his throat. "A bit badly, yes, sir. Perhaps if you was to come down—"

"We'll come," Laura said.

6

Their dressing-gowns hung behind the door. "Our dressing-gowns," she said and went to them.

While she took down the vicar's he stood motionless, unheedingly, his arms hanging by his sides, his head bent. She got him into it. When she had tied the cord she raised her face to his and kissed him. He just stood there. "Your slippers, dearest." He raised one foot and then the other as she touched them. She put on her own wrap and shoes. "Let me go alone. You stay, dearest."

"No, no."

She took his arm.

The vicarage had never been able to afford itself electric-light installation. On the landing she pulled the chain of the gas by-pass. When they were in the hall she took him to a chair. "You sit down, dearest." She lit the light, then went to the front door and turned the key. The police-sergeant stepped in, cap in hand. She closed the door and went back to the vicar and took his hand. "Tell us, please."

"Perhaps if you was to sit down, madam—"

"No, no, I'd rather stand. Please tell us."

The sergeant ran a tongue tip round his lips. A little jerk of head was decision for automatism as the best means of getting through with it. With one brisk forward step, cap held to breast by both hands, he was at evidence in the witness-box. In high-pitched, unnatural voice, "Was proceeding on car patrol with P. C. Jenkins," he broke out, "through Boscombe quarter of forest when observed headlights descending Hangover Hill—"

"Through Boscombe—Hangover Hill?" Laura interrupted him. "But that couldn't have been— Oh, can you have made a mistake? My daughter was nowhere near there. She was at the A.O. road house on the London road. She—"

The irruption on his routine manner unbalanced the police-sergeant into normality. Letting swing his cap to his side, relaxing his rigidity, "Probably having a bit of a run round, madam, before coming home," he said. "Car was a long way from us, of course," he went on, conversationally now, something soothingly. "Top of the opposite rise, Twist Hill as they call it, we was; but I pulled in to my side, not to give it an encounter on those hairpins, and switched off my heads. I'd not done it twenty seconds when the car was set for the bend for the dip to the valley, if you know that part, madam, and it—well, it didn't quite make the bend."

Stopping, he brought up his cap again, revolving it now in both hands, examining its surface.

Laura looked down. The vicar sat chin drooped on breast. His right hand on his lap had the forlorn suggestion that a hand has when it lies palm upwards, the fingers slightly contracted. She stooped to the hand she held and pressed it to her lips.

The sergeant blew something from his cap. "Bit of a fall down there is there"—his voice came from him reluctantly—"as perhaps you'll know. Young lady she lay bottom of it, car rolled away beyond her. Young gentleman, young Mr. Turner over to Southfields as perhaps you know, he'd been thrown clear or some such, not hurt to speak of. He was bending over her when we got there"—the reluctant tones trailed away—"attending of her as you might say," unwillingly they came again, then desisted.

"Yes?" Laura made whisper. "Yes?"

The sergeant made a double clearance of his throat. "Why, we telephoned the ambulance, of course, from the A.A. box there and, and it came along of course and, and took 'em."

"To the hospital?"

He had been looking towards her rather than at her. He gave her now a full, intent look. "Yes, madam." He spoke abruptly.

"Here? To this hospital, St. Mary's?"

He dropped his eyes to the vicar's bowed head, then turned them full again upon her and now more highly charged. He said steadily, "That's where Mr. Turner is, madam."

"But my daughter?"

Again the lateral, then the direct, the speaking look. "There was no private ward vacant to put her, madam." He coughed. "Knowing the young lady, the night surgeon was very sorry about that."

"Where is she, please?"

The sergeant drew forward a chair which stood against the opposite wall. She made a negation with her head but put her hand to the chair's back.

"Where, please?"

He made a half turn from her towards the front door. "I'll be waiting just outside there," he said. He held a hand slightly towards her in readiness of support. "She lays in the mortuary, madam."

Seven

WITH the hand that had been on the chair back Laura at those most lamentable words fluttered a weak dismissal motion. The sergeant walked from the hall. The vicar's chin still lay on his breast, his head sunk. Immediately the door closed Laura, that she might have his eyes, dropped on her knees. She put her hands on his hands and looked up into his face. "Oh, my dear," she said, "oh, my dear."

He had spoken no word in all this time. He said nothing now.

She gently chafed his hands.

Presently she said, "Come up to bed, dearest."

His eyes though directed upon hers had not seemed to see her. Now a recognition stirred in them. "No, I must go to her," he said.

"Presently, dearest; in an hour or two: in the morning: come now and lie down on your bed for a little."

Tonelessly, "No, now, my love. I will dress." Slowly he made to rise.

She got up. "Wait, dearest, while I speak to the sergeant."

In the mortuary. He did not speak while she helped him to dress. She essayed little observations, purposely not to the subject. "It will soon be light," "Here are your braces; I'll do them," but presently desisted. He was sunk too profoundly in his thoughts, she saw, to hear her. He sat on his bed while she did her own dressing, not looking at her, looking always, head drooped, upon the ground. The police-sergeant had sent up a car from a garage. He was waiting

370

for them at the door of the mortuary and took them in.

The floor was of stone, the walls white tiled. A powerful light burned in a round globe in the ceiling. Above a porcelain sink a tap was dripping. Three low trestles stood in the room. Two were bare. A sheet covered that which lay upon the third. They went to it. The sergeant with a motion of his hands looked at Laura. Her eyes signaled him Yes. He drew back the sheet to the body's breasts, then went away.

One shoulder strap of the Paris model that had bewitched her and which she had bewitched was sundered. Her face on that side and her forehead and her shoulder were darkly mud stained. Her aspect otherwise was not amiss. The grace that she had had in life lay exquisitely upon her in death.

The vicar put out trembling hands to her face. With an infinite solicitude brokenly his voice came: "My child. My child."

He stooped over her, lips to lips. Then he drooped slowly to his knees, his arms across her form, his head between them.

Laura knelt on the other side, holding his hands. She could hear the ceaseless dripping of the tap.

At the meeting. "That man knew," Laura said, "that it was your wish she should not go in his car. He killed her."

That was on the afternoon of the visit to the mortuary. In the morning of the following day the driver of the car was in fact brought before a magistrate and after formal police evidence remanded. Later he attended the again formal proceedings in a coroner's court. He presented himself then at the vicarage. He stood, anguish ridden, in the study while the maid announced his call to those whom he had come to see.

When the girl had left them the vicar and Laura looked

one upon the other in grievous question. Laura's face hardened to the aspect it had worn with her words of the previous afternoon.

"I could not trust myself," she said, "to speak to him."

The vicar had little bettered the profundity of desolation in which he had at first been plunged. He met conditions as they arose but it moved Laura to see how he met all that came from her with the docility of one who, unable to help himself, is concerned not to give trouble.

"I will see him," he said.

"What will you say?"

He sat with no signs of moving. "God will tell me."

When after some minutes, she knew how occupied, he at length got up it grieved her to see that at the door he must lean one hand on the frame while with the other he turned the handle. His tread across the hallway had a shuffling sound. She went then swiftly to follow him. He was in the study entrance as she reached the hall. She heard his voice, infinitely gentle:

"My poor young man; I am so deeply sorry for you."

The message. The caller did not stay beyond the echo of those words. They broke him utterly. He could not. Laura, herself humble in them, went out with him. As he took leave, "Please tell him," he said, "a thing that I came to tell him but could not. I tried to but you saw that I couldn't control my voice to him, not after what he had said to me." He brushed his hand across his eyes. "Ruth spoke just before she died, Mrs. Brecque. I was bending over her before the police came up and I just caught it, one word said twice. I thought the first time that it was 'bad,' that she felt bad, you know. But I bent closer and she said it again. It was 'Dad.'"

The vigil. She was brought in her coffin, unclosed, to the vicarage on the evening before the funeral. It was trestled in the hall, fragrant with the scent of the spring blossoms which Laura had set to receive it, altar candles burning. When the bearers had gone the vicar lifted the cambric slip which lay upon her face. Cushioned and covered there in white velvet and white silk it could have been believed that she no more than slumbered. As he raised the slip Laura saw his face twist with a dreadful emotion. She had seen the same contraction of his features when she told him of Ruth's dying murmur of his name. She thought it due now to recollection of that poignant message come to him as he looked upon the lips whose final utterance it was.

But it had, as she learnt, another cause.

In the last hours of darkness before the morning she persuaded him from his vigil beside the bier. From his bed to hers, suddenly, when she had thought him dropped asleep, "Did you see me," he spoke, "twinge when I lifted that veil from her face when they brought her in?"

"Yes, I did, dearest."

"Yes, you surely must have. Laura, a memory came to me then that twisted my heart around. I had uncovered her beloved face there in that same place in the hall once before. It was that first afternoon when we all first arrived here, Minna, John, all; all so eager, the children so excited. Do you remember how suddenly we missed her, the baby, and rushed about alarmed and found her there bundled in rugs beneath the stairs? Do you remember how I turned back that tartan shawl and showed her baby face crowing at us all? It all came back to me, in a flash, Laura."

She turned her face to the pillow, pressing it down.

At the funeral. She had taken him to the graves behind the wall of the Children's Piece. Room for one other interment stood on each side of those who rested there. He said, "Here, beside John." She agreed, then saw his face and mien, new burdened with years by days, and on a poignant thought said, "Dearest, no, let it be here on Minna's other side; Minna in care of them, do you see, as she used to be across the wall, there?"

In the particular docility that now was his he patted her hand. "Very well, my love."

He would not take the funeral service, he did not think he could control his voice. Hope Hubbard, whom Laura would have asked, was on holiday in France. A fellow vicar of Upton Springs took it. All the churches of the district were represented. The tragic circumstances of the event in parish feeling, the number of Ruth's local friends further afield, caused the church to be filled, the wreaths to be remarkable in number.

Mary could not come. She sent a telegram, "My deepest grief with both yours. Deeply regret great trouble here prevents coming to funeral. Writing." Philip was away on his ship on China station. Prudence came. Philip's fawn, picture of demure affection, said when she arrived, "Dearest father and mother, let me stay with you, will you, a long time? It will be good for you both, won't it, to have someone in the house with you? Please let me be the one."

She sat on the vicar's other side during the service. When at its conclusion the chief mourners should have followed the ministers behind the coffin down the aisle she looked inquiringly at Laura across the bowed figure between them. The vicar had been on his knees throughout, his face in his hands. He made no motion now. Laura touched him and stooped to him, whispering. He raised his head. A weakness was manifest in him. Prudence and Laura gave him help beneath his shoulders. He put out his right hand to give himself the support of the book ledge in rising but, oddly, fumbled for the ledge while his hand was still short of it. They assisted him to seated posture. He seemed to let them have all his weight. Laura was anxious. "Are you all right, dearest? Is anything wrong?"

His lips were apart, the lower hanging a little. His eyes swam in tears; wetness glistened on his cheeks. He fumbled outside the pocket where his handkerchief showed. Prudence put the handkerchief in his hand. It dropped and he fumbled again outside the pocket as though he thought it still was there. Laura took it up from his knee and gave it to him. He slowly wiped his chin with it, not his eyes or his cheeks. He made no attempt to move.

All in the neighboring pews were looking towards them. A man came to the front of their seats. "He's a little overcome, Mrs. Brecque."

"Oh, Doctor Laurence, he is ill."

"It's been a little too much for him." The doctor bent forward. "Vicar, you'd better rest here a little. I shouldn't go on if I were you."

His concluding words appeared to recall the vicar to a consciousness of the occasion temporarily lost.

"We must: go on," he said to Laura. His tone was louder than the conventional church whisper. It was thick as though he had something in his mouth. After his first two words the motions of his jaws were as though he must shift the obstruction before he could effect the second two. He began to get up.

The three about him helped him. "Ought he to?" Laura asked.

"Let him do as he wishes while he finds he can. I think that in a few steps—"

He got along sufficiently well though patently infirm, Laura at one arm, the doctor at the other, to the church door. The procession had halted, awaiting him. A lady walking with a stick had followed them. "My wheeled chair, Mrs. Brecque," she said. Laura nodded gratefully. The tears ever behind her eyes, flowing at the service, were in check again at this new responsibility cast upon her. The doctors said, "The very thing." Prudence brought forward the chair, standing there in the porch.

Laura said, "Dearest, you've been a little faint. I think if we wheel you in this."

He made no demur. He appeared almost to take seating himself in it and then being wheeled along as though that were an expected part of the ritual in which he was engaged. While the lamentable office at the grave-side was recited, the desolating rites—"earth to earth, ashes to ashes, dust to dust"—performed, he sat with tears welling ceaselessly in his eyes, overflowing and running down his cheeks. He made no attempt to dry them. Now Laura, now Prudence, would touch a handkerchief to his face. He evinced no consciousness of the attention.

"Shall I take you close, now, dearest?"

"Yes."

He gazed down upon the coffin a long space.

"We'll go: in now: my love."

They got him to bed, the kindly doctor helping. All that, too, the vicar took without demur, as normal. Laura left Prudence with him while she went downstairs. The doctor essayed to reassure her. "He's had a slight stroke, Mrs. Brecque; nothing very serious, really; a slight hemorrhage on the left side of the brain, affecting his speech a little and his right arm a little. All that will tend, you'll find, to diminish from what you've seen of it today. Keep him in bed, of course. Quite soon you'll have him about again little amiss. Nothing of great consequence, I assure you."

When she went up Prudence, seated by the bed, greeted

her with finger to lip. Lying on his back the vicar appeared
to be dozing. Prudence pointed to his right hand. "He asked
for that." His hand held a ribbon of harlequin blue. It had
lain on Ruth's breast, almost detached from her frock's
corsage, as she lay in the mortuary.

Laura stood at the bed's foot looking down upon her life's
companion. "Quite soon have him about again little amiss?"
God will it so. But she knew, as certainly as if the fingers of
a hand wrote it on the wall above him, that the years of
their life companionship now stood numbered.

Eight

Philip, when a year later he came home, found conditions at the vicarage on which he gave Prudence his opinion in round terms. It was a damn shame of Mary, he said, to have planted herself and her kids on the poor old governor like that. He had thought so, as Prudence knew, when he first heard that she had gone there. He thought it a jolly sight more now that he had been down to the vicarage and seen it for himself, "Bossing old dad, and old mum too, in that off-the-ice way she's always had. You'd think, 'pon my soul you would, that they were pensioners living on her instead of the other way about."

"Yes, but what else could she do?" was Prudence's inquiry. "I mean where else could she have gone when Walter left her?"

"To his parents of course. She's their daughter-in-law. Their precious son had carted her. It was up to them to make her a home."

Prudence grimaced. "You heard all about the perfectly blazing row she had with them. They sided with their son absolutely; told Mary that she had made his life a creeping misery—"

Philip laughed. "'A creeping misery!' Yes, that was a gorgeous phrase; I yelled when I read it, and told chaps, and it became a regular expression in the ward-room." He laughed again. "It was absolutely true, mind you. We saw it for ourselves, didn't we, when we stayed at Dursley with them that time? The poor devil couldn't blow his nose without watching her over the top of his handkerchief to see if

378

he'd pitched the regulation note." He lit his pipe. "I suppose I shall have to wring his neck," he announced between puffs, "if I ever meet him; but I swear I'll tell him while I'm squeezing that if I'd been in his shoes I'd have used 'em to do a bunk in quicker even than he did."

Prudence gave delight in imagination of this moving spectacle.

"All the same," Philip, having joined in it, went on, "it fairly got my goat the way she's taken everything into her own hands down there and the way she's operating it. I gave her a few kind words on the subject."

"You spoke to her about it?"

"You bet I did. I told her that dad had had a damn rough passage ever since John died, and was broke up to nothing now by poor Ruth's death, and all of it on mum's shoulders, and that it was damn bad luck that just when they ought to be in harbor at the end of the old man's days she and her kids should come along and make 'em up anchor and start all over again."

"What did she say?"

"Just what she would say—that on the contrary, tragic, though I didn't seem to realize it, her own position was, for them it was the very best thing to have children in the house to cheer them up and herself to manage for them and look after them. That's her all over, you know. Ever since I can remember her she's never been able to let anybody manage their own lives. She knows what's best for 'em and goes about with a pained smile doing it all day long."

"Of course it has been rather tragic for her."

"It isn't now. She's never so happy as when she's bossing a show. She bossed the bottom out of the creeping misery's and now she's got another with two people to boss instead of one. It's tragic for them, damn tragic, though they're both too much saints to realize it."

"Phil, if only they would come out to South Africa with us."

Philip, leaving China station, had left the navy. Prudence's father, dying shortly after Ruth's death, had bequeathed them jointly his estate, amounting to some £2,000. Philip had had his fill of the sea. He wanted now his fill of companionship with his fawn. Old shipmates had written him glowingly of the man's life they had found in farming in Rhodesia. The pair had put their windfall into this enterprise. Down at the vicarage Philip had been reiterating his begging that the vicar and Laura should come out and make home with them.

"They definitely won't," Philip reminded her. "I told you the old man's final reason. He'd have been, he said, loath in any case to leave what he calls his people while he still had life to give them. But that apart, there was Mary and her children. The vicarage and his means while he kept the incumbency made a home for them. He couldn't give it up. I told him that we'd fork out something a year for Mary if he'd come; but I couldn't deny of course a certain risk in it, that we might conceivably find we'd pulled a bloomer and not be able to remit to her. I couldn't deny, either, that what we could send wouldn't keep her, at all events at first, as comfortably as the vicarage roof keeps her. He's a saint and he's taken up this new cross as a saint would. She planted herself on him and nothing's going to make him think of unplanting her. *That's* the tragedy of it."

2

Mary's planting of herself took place within a fortnight of her desertion. That she should do so she took for granted, not waiting for invitation, asking permission, or even presenting the step as being the sole plan open to her. The letter in which she poured out her tears for Ruth and her deep sense of her parents' grief, told also the story begun with the words, "And now I must tell you the terrible thing that has happened to me." It ended, "I shall, of course, come with the children and live at the vicarage. About that I will write again in a day or two."

The day or two was filled to the exclusion of all else with the blazing row with Walter's parents of which Prudence had reminded Philip. It was the culmination of relations which always had been, in the most frigid sense of the term, "strained." Mr. Norman had acquired in a small textile manufactory in Lancashire the sufficiency on which he had retired. He and his wife described themselves as, and looked to be, and were, a "homey" couple. At their homey villa in Leamington Spa the hour they enjoyed most was that of their homey high tea. "We're homey, you know," they were fond of saying as they passed the cups and the baked ham and the plates of scones. It was almost their first words to Mary on the occasion of their daughter-in-law-to-be's introductory visit to them. "I'm afraid she's not very homey," was their first private comment on her; and, as rapidly they came to realize how far from homey were the conditions into which she had taken from them their adored only child, their bitterness against her was sore. Walter had come to them late in life. They idolized him. She had robbed them of him and was keeping him in a strait-jacket. They burned against her. From the termination of their first visit to the best-run house in Dursley their attitude towards their poor dear (as thenceforward they spoke of him) boy's wife was to "get at" her through him much as sometimes a stepmother will get at her predecessor's child through her own. "This is for *you*," they would underline in sending him presents capable of being shared. On the increasingly rare occasions of general meeting, pointedly they would address themselves to his comfort and his entertainment, as pointedly overlooking hers.

With the crash of Walter's abscondence restraint of getting at Mary in these indirect fashions was removed. In full discharge the parents let her have their pent-up feelings.

"We forwarded you a letter from Walter yesterday," came their communication to her, "the contents of which we know. Naturally we are broken-hearted at what has happened to our poor darling boy, but for *you* we have not the smallest sympathy whatever. It is *you* who are responsible, first and last and all the time. Our boy is a good, dear, loving, Christian boy. Before he met you he would have died rather than do what he has done. It is *you* who have driven him to it and have ruined his good name and his career. Ever since you married him you have made his life a creeping misery."

The acid pen with which Mary answered these forthright opinions joined the blazing row as by spontaneous combustion of chemicals. "Your vulgar abuse" opened her nib's first dip; "Your vulgarity of course you cannot help, but your crassitude—" prefaced its second. In succeeding exchanges the attributes of the creeping misery's wife as seen by his parents and of his parents as viewed by his wife, not to say those of the levanted misery himself, were thrust to and fro between Leamington Spa and Dursley on, as it were, red-hot pitchforks. If either side had ever had any idea of homey support assisting the home uprooted it was impaled and carbonized in the spark-flying clash of prongs. Mary's second letter home designated the bedrooms which she and Joan and Michael would use.

It gave explicit instructions for the arrangement of the rooms. A later writing, giving notice of her arrival, enclosed requirements for the children's meals and time-table of their day. This letter added that Walter had taken with him half of their banked savings. With the half left and with the estimated proceeds of the sale of the furniture she expected to have some £1,500. This she proposed to invest. "It will help towards their schooling."

3

It was in bitter humor that she came into the vicarage life. What had happened to her, first stupefying her, envenoming her next while faithfully she dealt with its protagonist through the feelings of his parents, then turned gangrenous within her. She was mortified. She was humiliated. All her life she had approved of herself. At Dursley, proud of herself, of her home, of the model husband she had trained, she suffered that fall down which are precipitated those only who have stood lofty in their own esteem. Aware of subtle showings-off of her establishment to less accomplished married women, aware indeed of being held up as pattern to neighboring wives, she well knew the bringing together of smirking heads which her desertion would cause. That apart, she well knew, further, the invidiousness that will attach to a woman above whose head is written the words "Her husband left her." General opinion can ascribe but two alternatives to explain that superscription: Either that he preferred another woman to her, the contemplation of which is gall to the abandoned; or that he evidently could not put up with her, which is wormwood.

Mary hastened with all speed from Dursley because there her crash was a public spectacle. She could none other than come to Upton Springs where, in tones of "Her husband left her," it reverberated.

It was darkly that she came. The mold lay fresh upon Ruth's grave. The vicar was but a day or two out of the bed in which the shock of his younger daughter's death had laid him. Mary was in no mood to compassionate the relics of sorrow with which on her arrival the house was hung. She was embittered.

4

"I think, mother, that I'd better take over all the household management."

This was said at the end of the first week. "For me to tell you," it continued, "what the children should have and how I wish it prepared, and then for you to order it and tell Hetty about it, is a very unpractical arrangement, especially when it all goes wrong—like this."

With a knife Mary scraped vigorously at a slice of liver before cutting up for Joan and Michael. It had all gone wrong because Hetty had cooked it with an onion. "*Most* annoying," declared Mary, scraping. "I told you so particularly that I don't allow garnishings of any kind in the children's cooking. Really *most* vexing."

"My dear, they might like it," blandly observed the vicar. "They said how good it smelt." He reached out and squeezed the chubby hand of Michael.

"Father, do please not teach the children to put their hands on the table. I daresay they would like a great many things that are not good for them. Half my object in their dietary is to prevent the greediness that comes from tickling the palate with spices and condiments."

"The mistake, dear, arose," Laura said, "through my asking Hetty to cook one piece with an onion for your father. She's dished it up all together. It was thoughtless of her, but with separate cooking so often to do for the children she gets—"

"Mother, do please let me point out that the separate cooking in this case was for father, not for the children. For that matter, father could very well have gone without his garnishing, I should have thought, and then the trouble would never have arisen. That's how I should have arranged it."

The vicar ate guiltily. Laura, more disturbed at the effect

of this upon his appetite (anxiously watched) than at her own reproof, essayed a bright word to Joan. "Please let her get on with her food, mother," Mary interposed, and the meal proceeded in silence.

In similar repression of talk the meals in general largely were taken. The vicarage table was now again well filled. Where had been only two, then all too briefly three, now were five, two of them of prattle which well might have recalled to the board echoes of the days of its earliest cheer. When the vicar, bettered of the immediate effects of his stroke, first came down to the dining-room, Laura had gladness in the thought that but two days now would show him his grandchildren's shining faces where Ruth's smiles had lit his eyes. Seven days of it, some twenty-one meals, had shown him on the contrary schooled looks whose schooling was carried to correction of himself and of Laura whenever they attempted to enliven them. Mary did not approve of the children talking at their food. They were not there to chatter. They were there, she said, to eat what was put before them, whether they liked it or not and with scrupulous regard to manners throughout the process. The effects, alike of silent commiseration with the unnatural spectacle and of reproof when it was given expression, were damping. Laura found, too, that she could not address herself to her husband with the same intimacy now that a second pair of ears received what was said. With, "What was that? Tell me about it," Mary would take up a remark on some passing local subject; with, "Who is that? Tell me," would catch up mention of a name unfamiliar to her. Very often when she was told, either her comment would kill the topic or by expressive silence she would render it equally difficult to pursue. When herself she enlarged an opinion she showed impatience with the vicar's slowness of perception, greater since his stroke. Laura would catch her, too, looking frowningly upon maladroitness which now sometimes he had with his knife and fork or spoon. Meals were not very happy occasions.

5

Occasions unhappier yet were opened by the liver episode's outcome in Mary's suggestion that she should take over the household management. The vicar now took a rest after lunch. So did the children, a disciplinary silent repose unmitigated by books and continuing until they were summoned from it. Mary closeted her mother for arrangement of the plan. Laura agreed with it. "I think it much wiser, dear, that you should order the meals, and very sweet of you to offer to do it. Of course—"

"That's settled then," said Mary, overriding any reservation that the "of course" might have preceded. "I'll go into the larder tomorrow morning and start forthwith. I'll total you the books each week, and it will be well, mother, for me to go into the whole of your budget for the year—you still make that, I suppose—so that I can know how to administer things.

"Roughly," she went on, "I've already worked it out. Our coming into the house makes the spread-over of father's income much what it was when we were all children; easier actually, as I'll explain. In those days it maintained, additional to your two selves, Minna and us four children. Well, I come in now in Minna's place as it were, and Joan and Michael as, so to speak, myself and John. That leaves free the expenditure that used to go on Ruth and Philip. That's what I meant by the position being easier actually than it then was, and what I propose is that we keep another servant on the strength of it. The work is going to be too much for Hetty alone if the house is to be run as I would like to see it run. With Minna we had, you must remember, practically a second servant. I can't take her place in those respects if only because I shall be effecting a saving in another way by educating my two at home for much longer than we children were taught before we necessitated school fees. Joan and Michael are now seven and six. I'm more than qualified to coach them for at least three years to come and I'm more than willing to do it. The whole position seems perfectly simple to me and I should like to set about getting this second maid at once."

This cut-and-dried scheme, run off without pause and oblivious to all considerations but her own, was so much the characteristic Mary of the dolls' reformatory upwards that Laura could have smiled. Long custom, too, of seeing Mary's affairs entirely in Mary's own hands, equally of being hectored by her daughter, assuaged in her the feelings which might have been aroused in another by the calm assumptions on which the plans were based. She had delighted in Little Mother Bunch. Amusement had tempered both her own and the vicar's increasing awe first of the Academy university degree student, then of the independent war worker and fledged woman. The ascendancy thus amiably given to the daughter over the years was not to be challenged now that the mother was advancing in age. Much less was it to be withstood when asserted while yet were being suffered tears for Ruth, anxieties for her husband.

Misgivings working within her while Mary's views were tabled repressed in her, however, inclination to smile at the manner of them and compelled her to question their matter.

"But, my dear," nervously she opened, "what your father's income could do in those happy days when all of you were children was much beyond, I am afraid, what it can do today. It—"

"Why? It's the same, isn't it?"

"Even in gross amount, dear, it's not actually the same. Pew-rents have fallen off and—"

Mary was annoyed. "I don't see how that can be. The

parish has grown out of all knowledge, they ought to be more. If they're less father must be to blame, no one else can be. Anyway, it can't amount to much and, as I said, with only two children instead of four there'll be a margin."

Laura shook her head. "Dear, indeed I am afraid there won't be. Falling off in gross amount is far, far from being the only thing. You weren't housekeeping before the war so you don't realize, of course, that cost of living is now double, I think it is actually exactly double, what it used to be. Income tax is four times the amount. If we had to bring up you four children now I really don't—"

Mary was more annoyed. "I hadn't thought of that. No, I'd quite overlooked that. It's really very vexing, very." She loured at her mother rather as though holding her responsible. As if then letting her off with a reprimand, "Well, the thing to do," she continued more briskly, "is for me to go into all the figures with you and see for myself exactly how we do stand and how best it can be administered. There's my own forty pounds or so to set off against the reduced means and I haven't the slightest doubt that I can effect quite considerable economies in the household management. Several little things I've noticed already. Father, for instance, appears to be the only one who eats marmalade. There'll now be jam for the children, so why bring marmalade into the house? Then that patent cereal that he has at breakfast while everybody else likes porridge—"

"Oh, but, Mary," Laura broke in, "whatever little trifles your dear father fancies are the very last things—"

"Mother, if the income can't, as you say, do what it did, fads and fancies surely are the very last things it should provide. Anyway, those are just things I happen to have noticed, and I'll see. What I really want to square up the figures to when I go into them is this extra maid. That I do feel we must have. She needn't, now I realize how things stand, be a trained servant; with my supervision just a first situation girl will do perfectly well. I'll go this afternoon to—"

Laura was twisting her hands together. To save herself from the consequences of destroying yet further elaboration of Mary's intentions gave her courage to interrupt them where they stood. "Mary, dear," she hesitated, "for this coming year at all events I am afraid that any idea of extra help in the house is quite out of the question. Even if you and the dear children had not come to us it was not going to be an easy year. Your father has had no Easter offering."

Into Mary's face sprung startled incredulity. "No—Easter —offering?"

The twisting hands constricted. "That is, he's had it but he's, well, he's given it away, dear."

"Given it away? His Easter Offering? A fifth, a quarter of his income? Mother, what *do* you mean?"

Laura told. Through ordinary letter gossip Mary had known of the fabric fund debt. Of Mr. Harkness's offer, of her father's step in amends for his action in regard to it, she knew, till now, nothing. In successive stages of this her usurpation of the vicarage finances she had been first annoyed, then more annoyed. At what she now learnt a bitter wrath possessed her.

"I never—" was both the beginning and the end of the diatribe in which she expressed her feelings. "I never in all my life heard anything so, so monstrous. For father to refuse that offer on those ridiculous grounds was, really I can hardly find words to describe such, such preposterous bigotry, was father at his unbelievably stupidest. For him to throw after it the whole of an established source of his income was the act of, simply, a fool."

She flung from the room. At the door she turned. "Whose precious idea was this, giving away his offering, I mean? His? Yours?"

Laura was wiping her eyes. "It was Ruth's."

"Ruth's!"

Nine

A RAKING together of all the embers of her life-long disapproval of her sister's ways was in the flinging back of that name at her mother. There was much more. In her bitter disgust at this hurt done her and her children by the dead—a year on means straitened to poverty level—Mary in her withering pronounciation of the name cast away also compassion for her father's sorrow. Till then she had suffered pity to moderate the censorious impulses which by this manifestation of his case and by that he aroused in her. Always certain little characteristics of his had vexed her. Enhanced since his visitations by grief and by sickness they irritated her the more. She was naturally quick, he naturally slow. She had returned to his roof in circumstances exacerbative of her impatience; it was in conditions augmentative of his drag alike of motion and of mind that he presented himself to her.

Had his reproof at her hands for what he had done stood only in her expression to him of her feelings on the Easter offering matter, time, overlaying the affair, must have reinstated him in her graces. It was a bitter reproof. "If only I had known," was the piteous burthen of his response. "If only I had known that the money would be required for you, dear."

She gave no pity. "If only you had known! If only you had known what was going to happen to Ruth no doubt you wouldn't have let her go to that night-club, with a frock for the purpose."

His eyes filled with tears. "Yes, yes; I tell myself that."

But the reproof could not be kept kindling forever. The year without the offering was got through. At Mary's behest savings were drawn upon to ease it. A year and then another year spread across its memory. There remained constant her checking of little aggravations which, put up with in the first week, were sharply brought to book immediately sympathy was withdrawn in the monetary disclosure. Vagaries and disabilities resultant on the stroke were outstandingly their cause.

"Father, *must* you go on wiping your nose fifty times after you have blown it?" This was his trick of passing his handkerchief endlessly to and fro after he had used it.

"Was I, my dear? I really had no idea that I was," he would smile. Fumblingly he would put it away.

"Father, *do* you want to eat that piece of meat or don't you?"

This was his poking of a morsel round his plate, endeavoring to fix it. "Well, perhaps I don't really, dear," his smile would come. He would lay down his fork.

Laura anxiously would protest, "Oh, but, dearest, you've eaten nothing."

"Quite sufficient, dear, quite sufficient," would be his assurance.

"Just a little more, dearest," from Laura.

From Mary: "Surely, mother, he knows best."

Unhandiness apart, always a slow eater, his mastication had become distressingly slow. All but himself would finish, even Laura, trying hard to accommodate her pace to his. Mary would sit with hands folded on the table before her, mouth twitching. In many ways of the kind he earned her censure. Her silent regard of them was as painful to Laura as her open rebuke. Remonstrance was brushed aside. "Nonsense. What do I ever do more than expostulate when he irritates me, as sometimes he does, almost beyond endurance? What little correction I do give him is infinitely better for him, let me tell you, than your indulgence. He isn't aware of these things that he does. If he is told of them, gradually he will correct himself out of them. If he isn't they will get worse.

"Apart from anything else," Mary's vindications of herself in this wise often would run on, "correction of his habits and his mannerisms is necessary because they are most harmful for the children to witness. I think constantly, but you never do, of the effects upon their young minds of having to live with an old man in his condition."

Laura had thought much, in point of fact, upon a contrary aspect of this situation. Anxiously watching him, lovingly attending him, in the diminution of his powers and in the sorrow of bereavement whose shock had been its cause, she had much hoped that, benefit out of burden, the grandchildren would give back to him gladnesses he had lived in their own children's nurseryhood and schooldays. He rarely was with them but they involved him, as event proved, in checking by their mother. Unable to disport with them actively, he had a delight in their company about his knee while he told them stories or bantered with them. Mary stopped that. His authors were interdicted. Jack the Giant Killer and such (as she termed them) gross legends, Hans Andersen and similar (as she said) ridiculous fancies were not for Joan and Michael's sanely cultivated minds.

His own inventions were equally at fault. Stories of animals invested with human qualities and leading human lives were his great forte. Pigs that went to school, rabbits that kept house, ducks that kept shops, had delighted all his own, from John to Ruth, Mary herself, and immeasurably himself in the telling of them. In reproducing them again, a child at either hand, he lost himself in relived joys as Laura had hoped he would. Mary would not allow them. Animals

that talked and behaved like human beings were preposterous abnormalities, bad for children.

Old Testament stories came also under her ban. If he
must present the Creation and the Ark as facts, the tyran-
nical and meddling God of the Israelites as the same God as
Him to whom Joan and Michael said their prayers, he had
better not interfere in their religious instruction at all. "I
would much rather, father, that you left *all* that entirely to
me."

That did pain him, Laura knew.

2

But he never, at that or at any other of her reprimands,
complained. Earnest to smooth difficulties, not by suggestion
to magnify them, "Were you hurt at all, dearest," Laura
sometimes would feel her way, "when Mary seemed a little
annoyed with you today?"

"No, no," he would smile. "I was sorry, that's all, that I
had vexed her. She's a little quick perhaps sometimes but
we must always remember, my love, how very sad her case
is. We must make every allowance for her. She means to be
kind, I know, even when she seems hasty. I am rather slow,
I am afraid, and naturally it annoys her."

He gave up his marmalade and his cereal. He was losing
his taste for both he found, he told Mary, and really she
need no longer get them for him. "Well, it will help her, I
know, with her housekeeping," he explained to Laura's remonstrance. "There's so little I can do that pleases her, and
that did, I saw. I am so very glad that I thought of it."

The note in both these references to her, as in all, was of
those newly gentle accents which had become his while
Ruth's body had awaited burial. That yet greater gentleness
in him, persisting, stood now always in his face like, Laura

thought, a silver lamp. No sting, no snub, at Mary's hands diminished it. No parish or parochial council perplexities, full tided again after that lull, clouded its luster. No physical as no mental weariness, heavily impeding him now, dulled its gleam.

His life should now have been lived, for his condition's sake, very quietly. It was unquiet. The presence of an unsympathetic third about them lost him that restfulness which was his when in Laura's company alone. The closeness with which every penny spent must be watched (and by Mary was watched) deprived him of little comforts which might have been his. Parochial Church Council and the general body of his parishioners quickly forgot alike the acclaim they had given him in his amends for the Harkness incident and the sympathy extended to him at Ruth's tragedy and at his illness. Difficulties in the one quarter, apathy in the other, troubled him as much more now than even formerly as his capacity to deal with them was less. His slowness in getting about and in writing increased his labors in his duties. His preparation of his sermons took him greatly longer. There was heavily imposed upon all these taxings of his powers the fact that leisured annual holiday was now not to be had. The children had to have change of air in the summer. It was only by his taking a country duty that they could be given it. So it had been in the old days when also family provision had run his means to their limit. But then he was young, his loved about him. Now he was old, ringed with sad memories. At a time when he should have been setting down active life he was compelled again to assume its obligations.

All this was nothing to the parish. Momentarily he had come out of its captious indifference into the fickle light of its approving and of its sympathetic recognition. Now, more vulnerably in respect of his lackings, more obscurely in re-

spect of his years, he was passed back into its indifference
again. It had but perfunctory association with religion. What
heed should it have of the pains of him to whom it opened
no fuller part in its life than that on Sundays he should offer
it a conventional means for that association?

Through all his heavy way, and through the parish's indifference to it all, he carried his face's silver lamp. *"He
alone cannot lose those whom he loves who loves all in Him
whom he cannot lose."* Ruth's portrait stood now with
John's on his table. His hours given to his thinking in God
were longer now than the protracted periods that always
they had occupied. There loving all, alike those whom he
had lost, those who harried him and those who passed him
by on the other side, when he came out from these associations the lamp in his face showed itself trimmed anew.

3

It was at the end of the November of Mary's fourth year
as administrator of the vicarage that he took a chill which
had him abed for the fondest look he had from her in all
that time; a fonder perhaps, such was at once the happiness
and the melting from which it sprung, than she had given
him since she was a child.

He had taken his chill from a bad wetting on the occasion
of a council cottages' visiting. Rain drove on a bitter wind
when he set out. Laura tried hard to dissuade him. No, no,
he had never missed and on no account would do so now.
The cottages were expecting him. At more than one tea
would be waiting him. He would drink enough tea, he
smiled, to neutralize all the rain that ever fell.

However efficacious that remedy might ordinarily have
been it was discounted by the fact that shoes and clothing
for Michael and Joan caused his own shoes and coats to be

worn for longer than their makers would have cared to
guarantee them. He returned "wet through." In the evening
he was chilly, the next day out of sorts; now abed.

It was Laura who brought him there the news of the
momentous event that had come to Mary.

A very Ruth in her joyously impulsive entry, "Dearest,"
she burst in to him as he sat propped up at his breakfast
tray, "Dearest, a miracle, a miracle has come to Mary; oh, a
miracle. She's heard from Walter. He begs her forgiveness.
He loves her more than he has ever loved her. He wants her
and the children to join him at once, at once before Christmas so that they may all spend it together. He's sent her a
draft for a hundred pounds. He's well off. He's doing splendidly in business out there. He long ago separated from the
woman he went out with. He says that his love for Mary and
his longing for her and his begging for her forgiveness—oh,
begging; you wait till she shows you the letter—is because
he has found God. He was always religiously minded, she's
now just told me, and trying, as she calls it, to get religion.
Now he has come under this Oxford Group and has found
in it, he declares, what he has been looking for all his life,
and can't rest, he says, until he is joined in love to her and
to the children again."

All this breathlessly, a very Ruth in her utterance as in her
entry, Laura poured out into ringing ears. Seated on the side
of the bed, too excited even to remove the tray from his
knees, she held the vicar's hands while she poured out her
transports. His returned pressure, his gleaming face, showed
her raptures to be his own. There was not a thought in either
breast of the lifting from themselves by this wonder which
had happened. This was the lifting from their daughter of
the evil that had fallen upon her. This was her upraising to
pinnacles of joy. They rejoiced in it for her with a thousand-
fold of that same selfless parental rejoicing which had filled

them when she went up for her prizes at Academy Junior. "How is she taking it?" agog, the vicar asked.

Laura gave him the eyes in which parents tell their fond confidences about their children across the children's heads. He gave them back, and happily they laughed. "Why, you know what she is," Laura set the confidence into words. "She wouldn't come out of her reserve, not if the crown of England was handed to her on a velvet cushion; and she hasn't, yet, at this crown of her life being handed back to her in the sheets and sheets which Walter has written her. When she told me of it as soon as the children had left the table, and while she read me bits, her manner, honestly, was that of a schoolmistress announcing that a pupil has confessed at last and debating how he should now be dealt with for his good. When I rushed around and hugged her she gave me almost exactly her Little Mother Bunch 'Oh, mother, you do make such a fuss.' But, oh, dearest, I could see the joy behind her eyes. What wouldn't I give, oh, what wouldn't I, to see her break down, as I know she must, the poor darling, when Walter puts his arms around her when he dashes on board their ship to greet her."

"She is going to him?"

"Oh, of course, of course she is. For the children's sakes, as she says, but— Here she is."

Letter in hand, Mary entered. There certainly was no conspicuous foreshadowing about her of that breaking down in Walter's arms of Laura's prediction. "Oh, dear, that tray," were her first words. "Do catch it, mother, it's almost off the bed." Vexedly she caught it up herself and vexedly looked upon it. "Father, you've scarcely touched your egg. If you feel you don't want what's sent up to you, do please try to remember that if it's not played about with it can be used by someone who will appreciate it."

She set down the tray, collected crumbs from the quilt,

tidied the bedside table, then spoke to the point, restrainedly.

"Well, mother's told you the great news, evidently. It is great, I admit that. It's very, very wonderful. The wonder of it is this change of heart in Walter through the Oxford Group. I hope you'll admit now, father, what you have always refused to when I have spoken to you about this Group movement. Walter had our church at Dursley just as many here, religiously inclined as he always was, have St. Luke's. It didn't give him, and St. Luke's would never have given him, what the Group has. I hope you will think about that. I'll read you his letter."

The vicar, duly chastened but in his joy irrepressible, stretched out his hands to her. "My dear, dear Mary, let me tell you before you begin what boundless, what inexpressible, happiness I have in this miracle of gladness that has come to you. By whatever means God has expressed Himself to Walter, His love and His power—"

She cut this short by accepting, graciously enough for her, the invitation of the extended hands. Taking them she offered him her cheek. "Thank you, father."

"How happy I am for you. How happy I am."

She touched his forehead with her lips, "Thank you, father. I'm happy too, of course I am, if only for the children's sake. Now I'll read."

There were, as Laura had said, sheets and sheets of the letter. Not one of them but, either in whole exposition or in constant reference, was given to the Oxford Group. Mary would remember, Walter said, how he was always seeking a way of grace and never finding it. Even while he was planning "the heinous sin" of deserting her, even while he was openly "living in sin," still, "the Hound of Heaven ever pursuing me, I was torturedly hunting my soul for peace even while I fled it." The Oxford Group gave him, at last, exactly what he had always sought. In one moment he was in his lifelong fetters. In the next he was "Changed." He knew now that all through his life at Dursley and ever since till his changing something had stood between himself and God. It was his refusal to give "Absolute Love." With this letter he was removing that refusal.

All this was pure Walter of the religiosity habit. It unquestionably was a Walter dramatically purified. More materially he told, touching his "companion in sin," of mutual disillusion, agreement to differ, and separation after little more than a year in America. He had found a footing during that period in a real estate business in the western city from which he wrote. Enterprise, energy and certainly luck such as he had never known at home had prospered him amazingly. He was doing splendidly. Here was his draft for Mary's and for the children's passages and for their well doing. They must, must, must, take ship at once and join him before Christmas. He represented himself as unable to eat or sleep until he should receive her cable.

She was going, concluding and getting up Mary announced, to send that now; thence to town to see about passages and passports. If she was characteristically undemonstrative in expression of her change of fortune, characteristically also was she swiftly efficient in her prosecution of the means to encompass it. Last moment cancellations enabled her to procure berths in a boat sailing that day week. The brief days were hourly occupied in outfitting preparations. The vicar, scarcely seeing her, saw the more of Laura. Apparent inability to get better of his cold gave Laura concern. She did not like the look of him and got Doctor Laurence in to see him. He protested much at that and she found comfort in the fact that, though he seemed to tire easily, he took the liveliest interest in the travelers' preparations. He caused Laura to procure four newly minted halfcrowns from the bank, and from the jeweler's two little cardboard boxes and pink cotton-wool. On the day of departure he drew the boxes from beneath his pillow, one each for Michael and for Joan.

4

It was after Mary had taken sufficiently affectionate final leave of him that, returning, she brought to him that fondest look he had had of her since her childhood. Almost at the hall door from his room to join the children in the car, Laura waiting with them, on a sudden impulse she turned and went back to him. He had not heard her footstep. She saw that his gaze as he sat propped up had remained in follow of her just as she had seen it as she left.

"Father, I don't like leaving you in bed like this."

"My dear, I shall be up in a day or two."

"Father, you have been so, so patient with me, so loving—"

She was kissing him.

"You have been a dear, kind, loving daughter."

He was patting her shoulder.

She was crying.

At the door, "Good-by, good-by," she called.

He put out his hand in benediction. The novel illumination of tears in her eyes caused her to see it bloodless, frail. "God go with you, my child."

They were going by car to London. It started and then the front door closed. Laura came in. He was drooped back on his pillows. "Oh, my dearest, you are tired. All these good-bys—"

"Just a little tired, my love. I'll lie down, I think."

She sat beside him, holding his hand. "Rest, dearest, rest. We're alone together now."

He pressed her hand.

5

He weakened. But a mildest disorder had at first entered his blood. A younger man or one of his age of constitution less impaired would have made nothing of it. But he was a traveler who had come a long journey. It had lain through an unkind country in the years of the war. He had carried onwards the hurts therein received, one never susceptible of healing. At Ruth's death he had been as it were set upon along the road and robbed, badly beaten, permanently injured. Thence the way had turned uphill, the load heavy, the footing rough. He had not the vigor to throw off the petty ambush which now, with his chill, had waylaid him.

Rendering his case in terms closer to medical diagnosis, the distemper which at first had no more than lurked about the fringes of his health now began gradually to invest his system. Doctor Laurence when first consulted had been briskly cheery. He would look in again, he had said, in a couple of days unless advised that there was no occasion. Now, coming daily, he began to show a slight concern. "He's not picking up as he should," he told Laura. "We'll have to look after him."

She looked after him, devotedly, anxiously, a further six days.

"He's getting so weak."

"Well, you naturally notice it more with him lying in bed. He hasn't occasion, you see, to exert himself. He wants rest and nature is seeing that he gets it. I'm a little bit, what shall I say, disappointed not to see the energy flowing back quicker, but don't let yourself exaggerate symptoms, Mrs. Brecque."

But the doctor, she saw, was paying now a very close attention to his lungs and his heart. In the early hours of a morning three days after those words were spoken she found herself confronted with that which left room for no exaggeration. She did not awake and then perceive it. As if she had been told in her sleep what was toward, she came from unconsciousness straight into panic. In the same moment that she was soundly asleep she was sprung from her bed.

He was in a most dreadful shivering. His teeth chattered, all his body shook. But he burned, almost to the touch, with fever. She did what she could for him. The shivering gradually abated, then ceased. The fever stood. His breathing seemed to her very quick. A short cough worried him. The vicarage had no telephone. Meditated installation had been set out of thought with the giving up of the Easter offering. With Mary's coming it had there remained. When Laura heard the maid dressing she sent her to bespeak the doctor's first visit. She brought back word that he was coming immediately. By next day the parish had it casually about that the vicar was "down with pneumonia."

6

"You must get some sleep," Doctor Laurence said. "He wants watching all the time. It's all nursing now. You must have help."

This was to Laura's refusal to share her tending of the patient with a nurse. She agreed then, and a nurse came; but save for brief hours of the night and for snatched meals scarcely touched she never left his bedside. He worsened. She saw the track of his temperature on the nurse's chart burning its way along the line 104°, jetting upwards to 105°. A dusky flush suffused his face. His breathing took the pace almost of panting. The short, hard cough shook him intermittently. The spit to be wiped from his lips was viscid, of a rusty tinge. He had much pain in his chest.

He was not always, though restlessly awake, visibly conscious of her presence. But she would sit stroking his arms and she had the feeling that her touch penetrated to him in the dark and remote fastnesses in which his fever held him down. On the day before the onset of this grievous state he had asked her to bring him up the contents of what he called the children's drawer in his writing table. She had brought those which pillowed on the stack of childish early writings and first school exercise books. They lay beside him, dimmed with time, shabby, moldering away; John's first school cap at "Kilbracken," Philip's first "Worcester" cap, one of Mary's improvised dolls, the bead necklace which Ruth had won as Sleeping Beauty at the Assembly Rooms. She would put one or other beneath his fingers on the quilt. "Rest your hand on that, dearest. That's John's Kilbracken cap." "Do you feel how nice and cool that is, dearest? That's Ruth's Sleeping Beauty necklace." His fingers would grope at the article. He would seem to know.

His mind frequently wandered. Always it was among the children in the early days that it traveled, speaking to them by name, generally John. More than once "Next year we'll have a wigwam there," his lips muttered, "a settler's cabin; we must have that next year." He spoke with Minna. "Dear Minna; what should we do without you?" Frequent on his lips was "Laura." For years he had rarely used the name; "My love" had always been his term. Now even when consciously he spoke to her it always was, as aforetime, "Laura." That for some reason touched her breaking heart with an ineffable poignancy.

On the eighth day, five days as it was before Christmas Day, he was sunk, as she could not but see, almost irrevocably low. Now his occasional muttering was each time and only her name.

"Laura."

"I am here, my darling."

"Laura . . . Laura."

"Here I am, my darling, holding your hand."

"Laura. . . ." He sounded to be blinded, groping his way; to be lost in darkness, feeling his steps.

"I am here. I am holding you in my arms. Laura's arms are holding you, my beloved."

Late in the afternoon his mind, some hours speechless, gave sign of other occupation. He was in semi-coma now. Surprisingly he opened his eyes. "Yea, Lord," his voice whispered. His lids fell. "Speak, Lord for thy—"

Guided, she who watched him was assured, by Him with whom he spoke he passed into coma.

7

At three in the morning the shallow breathing made sudden catch, then dreadfully changed its note. Laura had been kneeling. Swiftly she stood, and then bent over him. Those long-drawn, shuddering inspirations which now she witnessed she knew to be his spirit's straining at the last bonds which held it to its earthly lodgement. Agitatedly she motioned the nurse from the room. One flesh a lifetime she had been with him she now supported in her arms. Secret to themselves must be the agony of this dread sundering by bill of death. Poignantly she cried his name to him, entreating, if not stay, a word, a look. He could not hear. He was engaged upon that other summons which with "Yea, Lord," he had answered.

Longer and longer, more labored and more labored yet, the inspirations grew. She would have said that from the pit of the collapse of each in turn ascent could not be made again. She could have thought that at the crest of each the spirit, poised, would wing away before the jealous and reluctant flesh again could drag it back.

"Gordon, Gordon."

There came a longest poise, a collapse then, cataclysmal as though all stability within the frame had shattered in the downfall.

Was the soul foundered in that wreck, pinned in the ruins of its house, dead, entombed?

Nay, on the sound of a tiniest sigh, scarcely to be heard, tenuous as the ecstatic after-moment of the last note of music, rapturous in recognition of the infinite it sprung from earth, away. . . .

Ten

H OPE HUBBARD came to bury his friend. He had been the vicarage's first visitor. He came now as its last.

He said to Laura:

"What shall you do?"

"I shall go to Philip and Prudence in Rhodesia."

"Do you remember the first day I came here?"

"I well remember it."

He stood beside her where she sat by the drawing-room window. He stood in his gaunt height, chin dropped on breast, eyes pensively upon the garden. "I see it as it had been but yesterday," he spoke. "We were on the lawn there, we three. I could point you the very spot. Philip was stuck up in a tree and refused to come down. The children's voices came to us. Then they came running to us to tell us of Philip. Can you hear them, see them?"

She caught her breath. "As yesterday," she said.

"Ruth was in her pram, just there. Gordon showed me where he planned to build a wigwam for the joyous scraps just over there by that wall. You—" He turned towards her. "I see you clearly as I first saw you then. Young you were, vivid, darkly shining. Now we are old, you and I. We are old and I can tell you these things. You were 'black but comely'; that was my thought of you." He laid his hand upon her head. "Gray now, going white, but comely yet. Take up your life again, my dear. It is not in the grave where tomorrow we will lay him, nor will be he, his dear body only. Your life is above with his in God; it is before

406

you also with that good Philip and that gentle fawn of his as you have called her. Take it bravely up, my dear."

2

When he went up into the pulpit at the funeral service to speak an address he stayed but briefly there. The church was crowded. After all, Christmas rush or not, you had to be at the vicar's funeral. All the names would be in the *Gazette*. You had to be there. Look at the holly. That's the bishop. How grim he looks.

He stood several moments staring down upon the crowded pews in silence. For uncomfortably long he thus stood. What is he glowering at like that? Why ever doesn't he begin?

"I come," he suddenly, surprisingly, theatrically, begun, "I come to bury your vicar, also to praise him." He paused, returned to that glowering silence which now was yet more discomfortable to sit beneath. He pointed downwards to the coffin, standing where Ruth's had stood. "This man of God ministered to you and to your predecessors for thirty years; for a lifetime; for a period so long that there might be, there may be, sitting among you now those whom he has christened, has married and whose children have been brought to him for christening." He paused again. He trod down slowly to the coffin and laid his hand upon it. "For thirty years this man of God in his every look and word and action has shown those of you who have eyes to see the spirit of Jesus Christ, his master, dwelling among you." He looked upon the people. "How many of you have had those eyes?" He paused and asked again, "How many?"

He said: "I loved this man—did you? I knew he walked with God—did you?" Again the pause. "This man of God all his life looked for a City, a City which hath foundations whose builder and maker is God. How hard, how heavy, how sometimes piteous—and pitiless—has been his way, those of you who have hearts to know perhaps may something know, something." He lifted up his face and looked high across the heads of his listeners. His voice took resonance. "Well, he has found that City. Its gates have been opened to him. The hand that has guided him all his life has drawn him in. The voice that all his life he has heard has welcomed him, 'Well done, thou good and faithful servant, thou hast been faithful in few things, I will make thee ruler over many things. Enter thou into the joy of . . .' "

However, there were at that moment late-comers hurrying up the church approach: "Just like the vicar, really it is, to have his funeral, of all days of the year, on Christmas Eve. . . . Granting his good points, it really is, one can't help saying, extraordinary, how up to the very last he manages to aggravate one. It really is, one can't help saying, a good thing that at last there will be a change. . . ."